The Pagalan Chronicles

Book 1 Search for Morganuke's Roots

ANDREW HOULSTON

authorHOUSE

AuthorHouse™ UK
1663 Liberty Drive
Bloomington, IN 47403 USA
www.authorhouse.co.uk
Phone: UK TFN: 0800 0148641 (Toll Free inside the UK)
   UK Local: (02) 0369 56322 (+44 20 3695 6322 from outside the UK)

© 2024 Andrew Houlston. All rights reserved.

No part of this book may be reproduced, stored in a retrieval system, or transmitted by any means without the written permission of the author.

Published by AuthorHouse 10/30/2024

ISBN: 979-8-8230-9000-1 (sc)
ISBN: 979-8-8230-9001-8 (hc)
ISBN: 979-8-8230-8999-9 (e)

Library of Congress Control Number: 2024919874

Print information available on the last page.

Any people depicted in stock imagery provided by Getty Images are models, and such images are being used for illustrative purposes only.
Certain stock imagery © Getty Images.

This book is printed on acid-free paper.

Because of the dynamic nature of the Internet, any web addresses or links contained in this book may have changed since publication and may no longer be valid. The views expressed in this work are solely those of the author and do not necessarily reflect the views of the publisher, and the publisher hereby disclaims any responsibility for them.

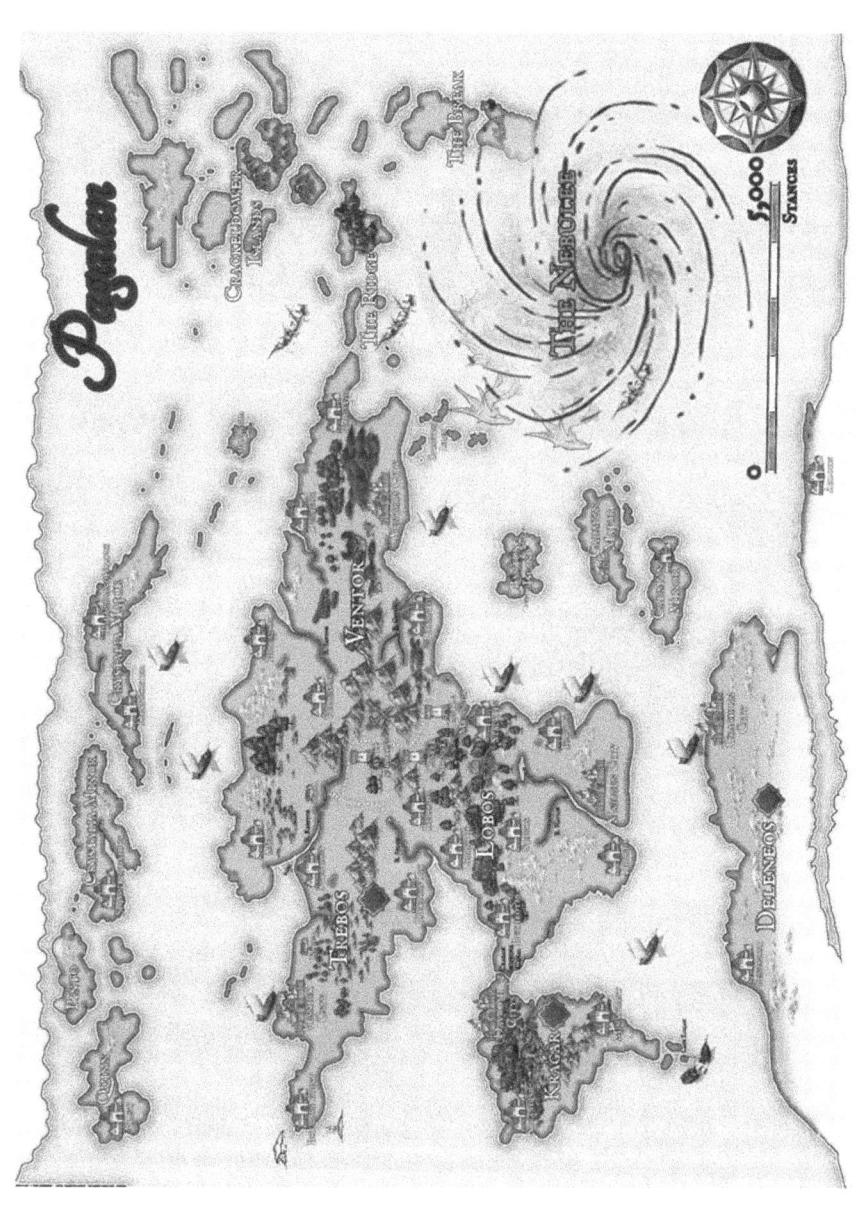

CONTENTS

Chapter 1   The Island 1
Chapter 2   The Growing Menace 11
Chapter 3   The Hunt 21
Chapter 4   The Voyage 28
Chapter 5   Cradport 41
Chapter 6   The Returning Hero 52
Chapter 7   Settling Down 66
Chapter 8   The Militia 80
Chapter 9   The Island War 97
Chapter 10   Leaving the Island 114
Chapter 11   A Captain's Tale 124
Chapter 12   The Mainland 137
Chapter 13   Trial by Fire 146
Chapter 14   The Smuggler 154
Chapter 15   The Captives 165
Chapter 16   Keeping Watch 175
Chapter 17   On the Move 179
Chapter 18   Stacklin 192
Chapter 19   The Front 199
Chapter 20   The Chase 207
Chapter 21   Retracing Steps 215
Chapter 22   The Optoglean 225
Chapter 23   The Aftermath 235
Chapter 24   The Divided Friends 246
Chapter 25   On the Trail 255

Chapter 26 Back at Stacklin 262
Chapter 27 Trial by Religion 269
Chapter 28 The Reunion 276
Chapter 29 Preparations and Goodbyes 286
Chapter 30 Into the East 292
Chapter 31 The Nebulee and the Ridge 302
Chapter 32 Into the West 316
Chapter 33 The Last Leg 324
Chapter 34 The Chace 331
Chapter 35 The Wise One 342

CHAPTER 1

The Island

Morganuke sat on the beach, listening to the waves crashing against the rocks and contemplating his life on the island of Banton. It was midday, and the sun felt warm on his pale young face. Seabirds circled above him, screeching their call.

He looked out over the bay and spotted a group of small fishing boats a little way out to sea. Fishing was important for the island, as it was the main source of food for the people. Most of the coastal homes engaged in fishing in some way. The boats bobbed up and down as the waves washed beneath them. It seemed to Morganuke that they were dancing to a tune of their own making. *What would it be like to sail on the open sea?* Morganuke thought. *There must be so many things to see and strange to visit if I went to sea.*

He watched two children playing beside the sea a little further along the coast. They danced around the waves, laughing whilst they splashed each other with the salty water. He remembered the times when he was a boy doing similar things, although he was usually by himself. He often would hunt for crabs in the rock pools close to where he was sitting now. With a bucket in one hand and a small net in the other, he would look earnestly in each pool, hoping to find a crab or two to take home. He breathed a big sigh and tasted the salty air. Oh, what it was to live beside the sea and enjoy the sights and sounds of the beach life!

Morganuke had lived on the island for nearly eighteen years, after being found abandoned as a baby by Fraytar, his friend and mentor. Not knowing Morganuke's origins or who his parents were, Fraytar had taken Morganuke to a kindly couple on the island. Stovin and Plarem could not have children of their own and so had taken him in gladly. They had loved and cared for him over the years, adopting him as their own son and ensuring that they brought him up as best they could. With the help of a retired Professor, who was an old family friend, Morganuke's adopted parents made sure he had a good education.

Morganuke had found it difficult to fit in with the other island people. With silver hair, pale skin, and red eyes, he looked very different from the other locals and had often felt awkward around them. He had been very miserable through his schooling years, as the other children often taunted him, making fun of his looks. On one occasion, when a group of children were being particularly hostile, the name-calling and poking fun at him had gone on for most of the day. One of the bigger boys seemed to be the ringleader, coaxing the other children to make fun of Morganuke. His rage built up slowly at first, but with the constant ridicule from the other children, Morganuke soon felt that he was going to burst. He focused his thoughts on the ringleader, feeling a warmth growing inside his body, and intensely imagined the boy falling flat on his face. At that moment the big boy suddenly tripped, as if a rope had been tied to his feet. Morganuke thought it very strange and coincidental but laughed along with the other children; relieved at no longer being the centre of attention.

But in many other ways, the island was idyllic; with beautiful, varied countryside and easy access to the beach. But Morganuke had wanted to see more of the world; to visit the different lands that Fraytar had told him about.

Morganuke stood up and clasped a handful of round smooth pebbles in his hand. Walking up to the sea edge where the waves lapped the soft sand, he started throwing the pebbles one by one into the water. Each pebble splashed against the waves with a gentle plop. He often did this as a boy and considered himself a fair shot with the stone. Sometimes he would challenge Fraytar to a competition to see who could throw the furthest. But these competitions never came often enough for Morganuke, as Fraytar would spend many months at sea and only came to visit between voyages. Lately, his visits to the island had become even less frequent as his voyages took him further and further out to sea. Fraytar had promised to take Morganuke out on his ship sometime. As much as he loved the island, Morganuke was very keen to travel and see more of the world.

Morganuke looked at how high the sun was in the sky. It was midday already. He remembered that his father had insisted he collect the scythe that Tomlin, the local blacksmith, had repaired and return it that morning. He also wanted to make sure that the blacksmith's daughter was still at home. He had been sweet on her for some time but had not had the opportunity to get to know her properly. *Oh, sweet Calarel*, he thought as he ran up the path leading from the beach. *She is so beautiful and perfect, but I just know that she wouldn't be interested in someone like me.* He had often tried to introduce himself to her in as confident a manner as he could, but something always went wrong. Either he would get tongue-tied or do something clumsy. It was so frustrating, but he thought her so lovely that he was determined not to give up.

It was about two stances to the village of Peblock, and Morganuke did not relish the fast-paced walk in the midday sun. He foolishly had forgotten to bring any water with him, and he was getting quite thirsty. He hoped old Tomlin would give him a mug of water or, even better, of nice cool ale. The track became quite steep the further he got from the beach, and his mouth felt very dry. Fortunately, it was a well-worn track with no boulders to stumble on, due to the many feet (human and animal) that had trampled over it through the years.

The sounds of the sea and the seabirds calling were now in the distance, replaced with the sounds of songbirds and the occasional bee buzzing around the wild summer flowers that bordered the track. The sandy dunes gradually gave way to green fields, with clumps of trees here and there. The path levelled out, and thoughts of Calarel and how cross his father would be about him being late spurred him to run faster. He was quite out of breath when he reached the village, and sweat dripped down his face.

Now I'm sweaty and stinky. What will Calarel think about that?

All seemed quiet. Very few people were in the streets, and he preferred it that way to avoid their stares. He walked along the dusty road winding through the village, small cob cottages with small well-tended gardens lining each side.

Morganuke came to the crossroad that marked the centre of the village. Tomlin's smithy was a little way down a lane. As he walked into the smithy's shop, the heat from the forge hit him like a wall. Tomlin was pumping large bellows that fed the fire. Sweat dripping from his forehead, he had a determined look as he focused on the forge. His face and balding head were covered in charcoal dust. He was short but made up for it with a stocky, muscular build.

"Hello, Tomlin," Morganuke shouted over the din of the bellows and fire in the forge. Tomlin didn't seem to notice, still intent on pumping the bellows. "Hello, Tomlin! I have come to pick up my father's scythe."

This time Tomlin heard, swinging his head around to see who was shouting but continuing to pump the bellows. His puzzled look quickly changed to a pleasant smile.

"Ah, young masser Morg, what can I do for he?"

"I've come for my father's scythe."

"Yes, your father's scythe, 'tis ready."

Tomlin reluctantly stopped pumping the forge bellows, leaving Morganuke feeling a little guilty for interrupting. The effort to sustain the heat of the forge now would be wasted.

Tomlin was one of the few islanders who made Morganuke feel accepted for who he was, and so he was a frequent visitor to the forge. He liked to watch the smithy work his magic with metal.

"Spec your father will mek good use of this here, as I'm sure he's a lot of hay to get een," said Tomlin as he brought down the scythe from a hook on the wall.

"Yes, there is a lot of hay still to get in, and we need to make the best of this dry weather," answered Morganuke. He took the scythe from Tomlin and propped it against the wall whilst he rummaged in his baggy pockets to find a small purse with the money his father had given him that morning for the repair. Morganuke hoped it was enough.

"That'll be two flants please, as 'tis fur yer father," stated Tomlin.

Morganuke scrabbled in the purse and was relieved to discover he had enough. He then remembered how thirsty he was, and hoping he would get to meet Calarel inside Tomlin's cottage, he asked, "Could I have a drink of water please? It's been so hot today, and I left the house with no drink this morning."

A wry smile came over Tomlin's face. "Is he sure 'tis just water you're wanting, young masser Morg? I've some nice cool ale int cottage if he rather."

Morganuke blushed, hoping that he had not made it too obvious how fond he was of Tomlin's daughter. "Yes, please, that'll be lovely."

They entered the blacksmith's cottage, and Morganuke was delighted to see that Calarel was sitting at the table, eating. He blushed again as she glanced up to see who was with her father. *She is so very pretty*, he thought. Her high cheekbones, olive skin, long dark-brown hair and inviting brown eyes made Morganuke a little dizzy. *She is the most beautiful girl I've ever seen,* he thought.

"H-h-h-hello, Calarel," said Morganuke clumsily in the best voice he could muster. "Er, um … how are you?" The more he tried to sound confident, the more his voice came out squeaky and hesitant.

Calarel just gave a low indistinguishable grunt in answer.

"Now, Calarel, 'tis no way to treat our guest, and he be a paying one at that," said Tomlin.

"It's okay, I'm sure Calarel is very b—" and in mid-sentence Morganuke tripped on the edge of the table leg, toppling head over heels and landing just beside Calarel.

Oh no, why am I such a fool round this girl? Please let the ground open and swallow me, thought Morganuke, looking up to see the amusement on her face.

Calarel got up from her chair and left the room with the words, "I'll leave you men to talk your business in peace."

Morganuke could not have been more devastated at how badly their meeting went, but at least she had spoken more words to him than she had ever uttered in his direction before.

Tomlin placed two freshly poured mugs of ale on the kitchen table. "There you be, me lad. Gatt, take no notice of Calarel, she can be a little frolly sometimes. Now, tell us yer plans. He knows you're welcome to work apprenticeship eer, don't he? I knows ee's ard worker and ave a good eye for working metal."

Morganuke took a long sip from his mug of cool ale. It tasted good and made him feel refreshed. "That's very kind, but I still have commitments on father's farm. Besides, Calarel would hate the thought of me working here, she really dislikes me."

"Steady on, masser Morg, don't take what her ses to heart. I think she's a soft spot for he, but you'll need to keep trying and not be a sissy. Try being more confident and look out fur yer actions, that way you won't stumble and mumble."

"Thank you, Tomlin, I take your advice. I'll think on it for a bit if you please."

Morganuke finished his ale, forgetting for a while how angry his father would be about him being late. Then he quickly got up, said his goodbye to Tomlin, and continued his journey home, remembering to pick up the scythe from the blacksmith's shop on the way.

The walk home from Tomlin's was uneventful and slightly easier now that Morganuke was refreshed with the ale. He kept a fast pace, as he wanted to get home as quickly as possible, and hoped that his father would not be too angry with him. As he got nearer to the farm, the countryside became richer and more diverse. Trees lined the lane, providing shade from the sun, which was still very warm mid-afternoon. The scythe he was carrying made things a little bit awkward. He tried using it as a walking stick, taking care that he didn't cut off his head in the process. The long blade did come close more than once.

As he walked down the final stretch of the lane, Morganuke could see his home, the small farmhouse nestled between two outhouses of fair size, all made of cob with thatched roofs, and a gentle spire of smoke rising from the chimney. A few fields of bright yellows and greens surrounded the farm buildings with crops at different stages of growth.

There were some cows and sheep in other fields, providing a chorus of animal song. The smells and sounds of the farm was a pleasing welcome.

Morganuke walked through the gates and headed to the nearest outhouse. Inside, he placed the scythe against the wall, ready for his father to use later that day. The building was full of dust and crammed with well-worn farm implements. At one end was a partitioned area where hay had been stored ready for the animals' winter feed.

The path leading from the outhouse to the door of the farmhouse was dry and dusty but offered a welcome familiar sight after the long hot run home. Morganuke entered the little farmhouse, cluttered with furniture and kitchen utensils, and saw Plarem busily cooking at the stove. The room was filled with the fragrance of burnt wood and mutton stew.

He walked over to his mother and gently hugged her, "Hello, Mother!"

Although she was not exceptionally short for island people, she came only up to Morganuke's shoulders. Her dark olive skin, dark hair, and brown eyes were typical for the island population. Her face was homely and kindly, with few signs of her true age. She gave Morganuke a wide smile. "Hello, Morg, how's your day been? Did he remember to collect the scythe from Tomlin? You're later than expected, and your father has been asking after he."

"Yes, I remembered. It's in the outhouse. It only cost two Flants and I got a mug of ale from old Tomlin as well."

"That's good because your father wanted to finish cutting rest of grass meadow t'day. Hope you're not too fuddled from that ale as you'll need to help him".

Morganuke looked over at the pot that his mother had been stirring. The rich odour of his favourite mutton stew hit him as he bent over to smell the contents, making him feel very hungry, though dinner was several hours away.

"How was your day, mother? I see you've been cooking something tasty for dinner."

"Yes, I've been busy. This morning I've been tending animals before starting to cook the meal. Sheep'll need shearing soon, and one has an injured leg that'll need seeing to. Cows were a handful milking today, and Popple kept trying to kick milk pail over and swishing me in the face with her tail."

Morganuke gave a deep sigh and sat down at the small table in the kitchen area. "Nothing's ever straightforward. We already lost one sheep from that wild animal attack the other day."

"We've a lot to be thankful for," his mother declared. "At least we can feed ourselves and make something from what's left over. Things be difficult, but we'll get through. The important thing 'tis to support each other."

At that moment Morganuke's father burst into the little farmhouse. "That sheep with injured leg needs ointment!" Stovin blurted out angrily. "It must have done it on a damaged fence. We'll need to fix that. Do we have any ointment left, Plarem?"

"Yes. I kept it from when t'other sheep got injured," she answered.

"Then get it, and I'll tend to sheep now," demanded Stovin. "You can come with me, Morg, I'll need you to hold the sheep whilst I see to it, and I want to finish cutting the meadow t'day. Expected you to be home earlier, why you be so late? I've told he before 'bout your daydreaming, boy. 'Tis not good enough, and you'll have to change your ways if you want to get on in world."

Like Plarem, Stovin had olive skin and dark hair with brown eyes. He stood just a hand above Plarem and so was shorter than Morganuke. However, his stocky build presented as strength, and his deep voice had the sound of authority to it.

"Did you at least remember to get scythe from Tomlin?" Stovin asked Morganuke as they walked out of the farmhouse door.

"Yes, it's in the outhouse."

"Then bring it with the hay fork. We can go straight to the meadow to cut grass after tending sheep and fixing the fence."

The injured sheep was in a field close to the farmhouse, and so it didn't take them long to reach the place where it was bedded in hay at the corner of the field. They walked over to it, quickly counting the other sheep as they went.

"I count all ten sheep," Stovin said. "That's good. At least we've not lost any more." He knelt beside the injured sheep and applied the ointment. "Hopefully that'll do." He placed the bottle of ointment back into his bag. "Thank goodness for Taplin root. I don't know what we'd do without it, hard finding 'tis, but heals well. Now let's see to that fence, can't afford to lose any more sheep so need to make sure wild animals are kept away."

They worked quickly to fix the fence with wooden props cut from a neighbouring hedge. "That'll do for now," Stovin said finally as he got to his feet and looked around the field. "Now, let's go finish off cutting the meadow. Morg, you turn the hay already cut, and I'll cut the remaining grass."

"Father, you seem upset today, is there anything wrong?" Morganuke asked as they walked along the grassy field, taking in the fragrance of the sweet-smelling hay.

"You really must stop y'ur daydreaming, son. These losses ain't good, and you need to pay attention to your farm work. We don't know how much longer we'll stay isolated from the mainland war. I've heard there's been some changes on the mainland, and something funny's going on offshore. I'm worried it may muck up island in some way."

Morganuke looked pensively at his father. "How can the war affect us here on island? The mainland is far away and there is nothing here that could interest the mainland folk."

"Shouldn't be so sure of that, Morg. We can't be careless 'bout protecting what we've got. I 'eard that warring tribes be out to take as much as they can, never mind who it is or who it belongs to."

Morganuke thought about what his father had said but still couldn't imagine the mainland troubles affecting their way of life. Nothing bad had ever happened on the island, not that he knew at least, and the mainland was so far away.

No, he thought, *the island is always staying as it is. Surely, we are safe here.*

They continued to walk along the border between two fields before jumping over the stone wall into a meadow, half cut and half with long grass swaying in the gentle breeze. They worked the field without speaking, although Morganuke couldn't take his mind off what his father had said.

What if the mainland war does spread to the island? What shall we do?

The daylight slowly began to fade, but not before they had finished their work for the day. They walked back to the farmhouse in silence, contemplating what might be. The day's toil and the disappointment with Calarel had taken it out of Morganuke, and once he had eaten his long-anticipated dinner, he went to bed and quickly fell asleep.

CHAPTER 2

The Growing Menace

Morganuke found himself in a dark passage that he did not recognise. A faint light coming from one direction drew him towards it. He stumbled about, trying to get his orientation and balance.

This is a dream! Where am I?

His arms flailed about for something to hold on to. At last, he felt a surface that was hard and cold to his touch, like a metal sword or armour, not what he expected for such a large structure. As he slowly felt along, there seemed to be no end to it. The light was growing brighter, and Morganuke slowly followed the line of whatever he was touching to draw closer. On he went, stepping very carefully so as not to fall, feeling dizzy and slightly nauseous.

His mind was racing with dread. He wanted to stop and sit to recover his senses, but something kept drawing him closer to the ever-brighter light. Now he could hear a low buzzing noise, like a disturbed beehive, coming from the direction of the light. The noise filled his ears, overloading his senses, and his heart pumped hard in his chest.

Please make this stop! If I'm dreaming, then please wake me up!

The light was upon him, and the buzzing became almost deafening. His vision blurred and he screwed up his eyes, but he began to make out an outline of something just ahead of him, an indistinguishable symbol on what looked like a large door that shone with intense light.

Squinting, he thought he made out writing on the door, and more clearly a symbol—an eye with a tear seeping from its corner.

"What does this all mean" he asked aloud.

His head spun, and his legs gave way. He thought he might throw up, and he felt himself slowly falling, as though he was in a bath of treacle.

Morganuke woke with a bump and a loud cry as he fell from his bed and crashed his head onto the hard wooden floor. He lay there for a while until he came to his senses.

Oh my, that was a strange, horrible dream, he thought as he picked himself up from the floor. He still felt a little dizzy, but at least the nausea had passed. Morganuke slowly got to his feet and dressed. The clothes he was wearing yesterday would suffice until he could wash away the memories of the bad dream. He made his way down the stairs but found nobody in the house. *They must be tending to the animals,* he thought.

He made his way out of the farmhouse and down the dusty path to the stream beyond the taplin field. Scrambling down the bank, he reached a pool deep enough to submerge himself fully. He removed his clothes and lowered himself slowly into the water, gasping at the shock of the chilly water.

Aaaah! That's better. Good to wash away those bad dream memories.

He lay there submerged for several minutes, taking in the early morning light and trying to forget the dream. Feeling refreshed, he got up, collected his clothes, and made his way back to the farmhouse, not bothering to dress himself, since nobody was in the house.

But as he drew near to the farmhouse, he saw a saddled horse tethered to the fence and heard voices inside, and so he ducked behind the hedge and quickly dressed his still wet body. As he neared the farmhouse door, he heard the voices of his mother and a man. Hesitantly Morganuke opened the door and at once recognised who the man was.

"Fraytar!" he exclaimed in pleasant surprise. "It's so long since we've seen you. Where have you been these past months. Tell us what you've been up to and what exciting places you've seen."

Fraytar turned and looked at Morganuke, a little bemused to hear so many questions at once. He had the look of a typical Delenese sailor, with baggy chestnut-brown britches, black knee-high boots over stockings, a white lace-up shirt, and a thick brown tunic of fine leather, all set off with a large-buckled belt sporting a short cutlass and dagger. His face was lightly weathered, with a neatly trimmed deep-brown beard going grey, matching his full head of hair. Just a little shorter than Morganuke, Fraytar had a stocky build and an imposing presence.

"Morg, my boy," came Fraytar's answer with a broad toothy smile. "It's good to see you! You have grown into a man."

"I'm not sure about that. I've still not seen much of the world, and there's still a lot to learn before I can call myself a man. But it's good to see you, and he must tell us about your journeys since we last saw you."

"A lot has happened," Fraytar acknowledged. "I have sailed far and wide, indeed further than I have ever travelled before. Some of my experiences have been dangerous, and I'm lucky to still be here."

Morganuke and his mother gasped, wide-eyed.

"'It's been so calm here on the island," Morganuke said. "I can't imagine how other places be like you say. Tell us, Fraytar, about these dangers and your travels," he implored.

Before Fraytar could continue, Stovin walked in. He glanced at Fraytar and nodded. Morganuke knew that Stovin had been grateful to Fraytar for bringing Morganuke into their lives, but now that he had come of age, his father was wary of Fraytar enticing him away to sea.

"How be he, Fraytar?" Stovin asked politely. "What's this I hear 'bout danger at sea?"

"I was just about to explain," Fraytar went on. "Our recent voyages took us close to the mainland, just off Stacklin. We knew it was an Epleon stronghold, so thought it would be safe for us to sail there and trade. Little did we know that the Cordinen war tribes had broken through Castle Medogor, just to the north, and were preparing to attack Stacklin."

"'Tis worrying news," Stovin said. "I've heard tales of the Cordinen tribes and their ruthless savagery. They take slaves from anywhere they can and slaughter anyone not doin' what they wants."

"I don't see how this affects us here on the island," Morganuke said. "All these places and tribes that you talk of are on the mainland. Don't know what this means for us here—"

Fraytar put up his hand to interrupt. "The problem is that the Cordinens now seem to be getting the upper hand. Until now, the Epleons have overcome their attacks, keeping things in balance, and that had been so since the war began. Something has recently changed to give the Cordinen tribes an advantage, and if they do begin to make gains further to the south, then it could ruin our trade and any other reliance we have on the mainland. So, it could well affect this island, and very directly."

"Is the war spreading to the island?" Morganuke asked.

How can that be? It's a frightening thought. He thought.

"I don't think so," Fraytar replied cautiously, "but there is no guarantee that the Cordinens will not raid the island—they are just so unpredictable."

"Tell us more of your own experience on the mainland, Fraytar," Stovin asked, sitting down at the kitchen table with them. "How were he put in danger?"

"As I said, we had sailed to Stacklin port, as we had some goods to sell there in exchange for food and supplies. At first all seemed normal, and we had sailed there many times without any problems. Although the Epleons consider themselves superior to outsiders and treat them badly, they tolerate seagoing traders for their own benefit. As we were unloading the cargo for market, we heard a commotion coming from beyond the port, with people running about and screaming in terror. Then we saw them, a band of about a hundred heavily armed Cordinen tribesmen charging down the street, slashing and killing anyone who got in their way."

"Oh my, that's horrible!" Plarem exclaimed. "Why are people like that? How can they just kill like that?"

Fraytar looked around at their worried faces before continuing. "Half the cargo was already unloaded, but we were not risking reloading any of it. We had to save the ship and crew, and so we cast off as quickly as we could, before picking up the wind and setting sail. We only just made it before the Cordinens reached the quayside."

"Then you sailed directly here? When did all this happen?" Morganuke asked.

"We made good speed on the return journey, as the winds were in our favour, but also had to stop off on the other side of the Banton Island to arrange some business, to compensate for the cargo lost on the mainland. So this all happened twenty days ago. Plenty of time for the Cordinens to have progressed further south by now."

The room was silent. Morganuke noticed the concerned expression on his parents faces. He tried to grasp what Fraytar had told them, but found it difficult to take in.

Fraytar finally broke the silence, turning to Morganuke. "I have a favour to ask you, Morg,"

Morganuke had been deep in thought but snapped to upon hearing his name. "What is it?"

"I know you have been longing to sail on my ship, and an opportunity has come up for you to do so. A short trip to the other side of the island. I mentioned before that we have business there to make up for the cargo we lost on the mainland, and your help would be welcome. You would only be gone for two weeks or so."

Morganuke looked at his father, who had a disapproving look on his face. "Would you mind if I went, Father? I know there is a lot to do with the hay harvest."

Stovin gave a deep frown. "No! Absolutely not!" he bellowed. "Fraytar, what be he thinking? He just told us 'bout dangers he were in, and now he wants to take me son to those same dangers. There's too much work on the farm. 'Tis a stupid idea."

Morganuke felt his face grow red with rage, and he didn't stop to hear any more. He got up and stormed out of the farmhouse, slamming the door behind him. He stopped to listen to the conversation between his parents and Fraytar through the door and was surprised to hear his mother's voice.

"Stovin, we cannot protect Morganuke all his life even though we be wanting to. He's a man now and needs to make his own way in world. 'Tis no good forcing him to do something he doesn't want to do. You know his stubbornness, and he would do what he wants to do anyway. 'Tis better that he does it with our blessing."

"Plarem is right, Stovin, you must know that," Fraytar added. "This voyage is a short one, only to the other side of the island. We don't expect any dangers, and I will make sure that Morganuke is looked after. It will be good experience for him and benefit him in the long run."

Morganuke had to contain himself from cheering when he heard his Father's response, now sounding calmer.

"Very well, he can go, so long as he's back in time to complete hay harvest."

When Fraytar told him of his father's decision, Morganuke gave a broad smile and punched the air with his fist, but Fraytar interrupted him before he could say anything. "The conditions on the ship are far from luxurious, and you may not like it," Fraytar advised. "Before you make your decision, I will show you the ship. If you still want to go, and so long as the captain agrees, you can stay on board. If not, then I'll bring you back, and we'll say no more about it."

"As you say, Fraytar. When will you show me the ship?"

"We plan to set sail at high tide tomorrow, and so I'll show you the ship today. Get what things you need quickly. If you decide to go, you will stay on the ship tonight. You can ride behind me on the horse I have borrowed to get to the harbour quickly.

"There's something else," Fraytar added. Morganuke sensed a more serious tone to his voice. "Just before we cast off, I spotted two men on the quay behind the Cordinen tribesmen, and they had similar features to you, Morg, with silver hair, pale skin, and tall. For all the stances I've travelled, I had not seen someone like you before, me boy. I know you're interested in finding out where you came from, but I hope that these people, whoever they are, are not helping the Cordinens."

Morganuke kept silent for a moment, deep in thought about what

Fraytar had said. *What if I come from a people that are helping to commit such horrible actions? If it is not bad enough already being so different from others around me. Whatever the situation, I must find out the truth of it.*

Morganuke went to his room to gather his things. *What should I take?* He thought as he sat on his bed. His mind was in a daze. For so long he had wanted to go on a sea voyage, but this was so sudden and unexpected. *Do I take warm clothing or something to keep me cool? What if I get seasick? Oh bother it! Just get on with it. I'm sure everything will be alright. I trust Fraytar.*

Once Morganuke had finally decided on what to take and packed his things, he joined his parents in the kitchen to say goodbye. His father was sat at the kitchen table, whilst his mother stirred a pot of something on the stove. Morganuke sat down at the table with his father.

"Father, are you angry with me for wanting to go to sea with Fraytar?"

His father looked at him and kept silent for a few moments before saying, "no, son." His father's expression had now softened to one of resignation. "You must be doing what he thinks is right for he. I'll not stand in your way. Just come back to us."

Morganuke felt relieved by his father's words and gave him a hug.

"Make sure he keeps warm and eat proper food," Plarem added and gave Morganuke a hug as well.

Morganuke then left his parents and joined Fraytar who was already mounted the borrowed horse. This would be an unfamiliar experience for Morganuke, as he had only ridden a horse once before. Fraytar helped him up, and off they cantered towards the harbour, six stances along the coast.

Morganuke felt exhilarated as they galloped along the coastal track, even though it felt a little uncomfortable. The wind against his face and the smell of the salty sea air refreshed him. He was looking forward to seeing the ship but was slightly nervous about the journey; this, too, would be a completely new experience for him.

I hope I don't do something silly and make a fool of myself. What will it be like sailing on the open sea? Will I get sick or fall overboard? Bother it! I must stop worrying so.

Soon the harbour came into sight a little way in the distance. Several ships were anchored in the harbour, and Morganuke wondered which one was Fraytar's. The noise of the bustling docks became louder as they approached the outskirts of the harbour.

"There she is," shouted Fraytar over his shoulder as he guided the horse to a tethering post next to the docks, "the three-masted ship right in front of us."

Morganuke looked up to see the three-masted carrack alongside the docks. At about one hundred and fifty steps long, she was smaller than Morganuke had imagined, but elegant and broad in form. On the forward bow he could see the name *Aurora* standing out in gold lettering. The crew were busy loading wooden barrels onto the deck to be stored in the hold.

"Right then," Fraytar said as he climbed off his horse, "let's go and find the captain."

Morganuke climbed gingerly down from the horse and followed Fraytar onto the ship. They climbed onto the upper deck at the stern and went to the captain's cabin.

They found Captain Amannar sitting at his desk, looking at papers quizzically. He was a large man with a big round tummy, and even though he was seated, he gave off a commanding presence. His large black beard covered the lower half of his face, but his visible features were weathered and tanned. He briefly continued reading before looking up at Fraytar. "You're back, and who's this with you?" he asked.

"This is the lad I was telling you about. He has now grown into a man from the baby I found those eighteen years ago and is very capable. His name is Morganuke, but we call him Morg for short. He works on his father's farm and is a dutiful son and a diligent worker. As we are short on crew for this essential trip, I thought that he would come in handy to help on board during this voyage."

"Well, did you indeed, and without consulting me first?" Captain Amannar asked. "What experience has he had on a sailing ship? Can he handle rigging, does he know how to tie a proper knot? Can he swim?"

"I have never been to sea, sir," Morganuke admitted. "But, as Fraytar said, I'm very capable and a hard worker. I can swim, at least."

Captain Amannar continued to speak to Fraytar without giving Morganuke a second glance. "Taking on a lad of his age and lack of experience would be a serious mistake, especially given the danger and importance of this trip. I cannot allow the lad to sail with us."

"I will vouch for him, Captain," Fraytar replied. "I have known him many years and can guarantee that he is trustworthy and a fast learner. I'm sure he would be an asset."

"I can do many different things, and I am sure I can quickly learn the ropes to be of help on your voyage," Morganuke said earnestly.

Captain Amannar turned back to address him directly. "I cannot allow you to sail with us! No, we are very busy and have a lot to do before we sail on the next tide, so I must ask you to leave the ship and let the crew continue with their work, which of course includes Fraytar. As first mate he must ensure that the work is completed by the rest of the crew on time. Fraytar, please make yourself present on the deck immediately and ensure this young man leaves the ship."

Fratar nodded towards the door to indicate to Morganuke that he should leave. Fratar stayed with the captain whilst Morganuke complied with Fratar's silent request.

Morganuke rested his arms on the rail of the upper decking, watching the activity on the main deck below. Crewmen were busily stacking; some were shouting orders and others doing the lifting. The barrels seemed heavy and Morganuke wondered what they contained. Three huge masts rose from the main deck to what seemed a dizzying height to Morganuke. He looked towards the bow of the ship to see another raised deck, like the one he was on, although narrower.

Well, I suppose I'll have to walk back home now. At least it's e only six stances and so shouldn't take me long. Will I be ever get a chance to go to sea again?

He sighed and was about to descend from the upper deck when something came flashing through the air and embedded itself in one of the barrels on the deck below. It was a flaming arrow, and flames quickly started to spread.

"Fire! Fire! The pitch is on fire!" shouted one of the men on deck.

There was frantic activity on the main deck, with men trying to stamp out the flames.

Without really thinking, Morganuke raced over to a damp sail lying on the deck, that had just been removed from the rigging before the pandemonium started. He gathered up the cloth and raced over to the barrel, now engulfed in flames. With one mighty effort he threw the damp sail over the barrel, covering it. Steam and an angry hissing came from under the sail as he smothered the fire.

The crew who had stayed on board stood open-mouthed around Morganuke, watching him in disbelief.

"You scabby worms!" came a shout from the upper deck. It was Captain Amannar, drawn out of his cabin by the commotion and leaning over the upper deck railing. "You would let my ship burn and leave a boy to save us all! How did the fire start?"

"It was a fire arrow shot from somewhere on the dock, Captain," shouted one of the crew.

The captain looked at Morganuke. "Boy, come back up to my cabin."

Morganuke, still a little breathless, gathered his composure before walking up the steps to the upper deck and into the captain's cabin. The captain had returned to his desk, and Fraytar was standing beside him with a slight smile.

Captain Amannar looked straight at Morganuke; his expression now softened. "That was a very brave thing you did, and you saved the ship with your quick actions. How you managed to lift that wet sail I'll never know. Must have weighed at least fifty fetlons. You do seem to be a very capable lad, so I will allow you to sail with us."

CHAPTER 3

The Hunt

Captain Amannar stood on the upper deck of his ship, looking over the lower decks, as Fraytar and Morganuke stood beside him. "Fraytar, go look for the culprits who attacked my ship and bring them to me."

"Yes, Captain," answered Fraytar. "I'll take Morganuke with me, if you have no objections." Captain Amannar nodded his approval.

"Can you remember which direction the fire arrow came from, Morg?" asked Fraytar.

"It happened so quickly," answered Morganuke, "but I think the arrow came from somewhere on the docks forward of the ship."

"Then that is where we'll start looking."

Fraytar turned to the captain. "Do you know what motive there would be to attack, Captain?"

"It could be a rival trader or someone knowing who we're trading with. As he knows, our customer is not popular on Banton Island cuz of previous dealings with the Cordinens. If someone knew where we were taking the pitch, then they may have wanted to stop us somehow, and firing a flaming arrow directly on the pitch barrels would be a good way to do that," Captain Amannar answered.

"So, who is likely to know that we are selling the pitch to Vorderlan? Maybe we should start with Straplin. He sold us the pitch and could have guessed who we are trading with," Fraytar surmised.

The captain looked glumly around stroking his big black beard. "We must sail at next high tide. Do what you can to find the culprits, Fraytar, but we must sail on high tide."

"I'll start will Straplin to see if he knows anything at all, and I'll take Morg with me," stated Fraytar before turning to leave the cabin, coaxing Morganuke to follow him.

Fraytar and Morganuke walked across the decks, dodging crew members busying themselves preparing the cargo and the ship's rigging. Men were running this way and that with some purpose in mind, following the orders of a robust man with long greasy hair who was shouting commands and expletives on the lower deck.

"Drogar," Fraytar shouted as he walked up to the greasy-haired man, "do what you can to get the ship ready, as we sail on the next high tide."

"Will do," Drogar answered, and then continued to shout his orders at the men on deck.

Fraytar turned and left the ship with Morganuke, walking over to his large horse still hitched close to the harbour's edge. He mounted and helped Morganuke onto the back of the horse before they trotted off down the street towards the trader's office.

It didn't take them long to reach the office. The two men climbed down from the horse and approached the trader's office door.

"Right then, Morg, let's go and have a word with Straplin and see if we can find out what has been going on behind our backs."

Fraytar gave three hard thumps on the office door. There was no answer, and so he gave the door three more thumps, this time a little harder, shouting, "Are you in there, Straplin?"

A faint rustling from behind the door preceded the sound of footsteps and bolts being slid back. The door opened with creak, revealing a skinny, huddled old man with a straggly grey beard and long hair. "What is it you want, Fraytar?" asked the old man.

"Let me in, Straplin, so that I can talk to you. I need some answers about our latest trading deal."

The old man reluctantly stepped aside to let Fraytar and Morganuke into the dingy office. Inside, the only light came from two small dirty windows at the front of the building. There was a single wooden desk with a chair to one side, and a set of large drawers placed behind this. Papers were scattered on the desk, and the whole room gave the impression of a chaotic work style.

Straplin walked over to the chair at the desk and sat down with a deep sigh. Fraytar followed him and sat on the edge of the desk.

"Now, Straplin, maybe you can tell me something about what is going on with the pitch that we bought from you." Fraytar peered directly into Straplin's eyes.

"What? What do you mean? The deal was true and honest, I don't know what you're saying," Straplin retorted.

"I don't want to hear any of your lies! Now tell me what you know before I start getting very angry," Fraytar boomed, bringing his face up close to Straplin's.

"Th-th-they made me tell them—" Straplin stammered.

"Tell them what?" demanded Fraytar.

"Tell them who you were delivering the pitch to," Straplin answered. His eyes were looking wildly around the room, as if he was searching for some way out.

"Who were 'they'?" Fraytar pressed.

"Three of them, there were. I don't know their names, but I have seen them before around Dunbar. The biggest one had a scar down the right side of his face."

Satisfied that Straplin was telling the truth, Fraytar moved away.

"Three of them, you say? And you saw them near Dunbar," Fraytar summarised. "I'll make my way to Dunbar. Morg, you make your way back to the ship and bring some of the crew for backup. Make sure you let the captain know what's going on."

With that, Fraytar left the office, with Morganuke closely following, and jumped on his horse. Morganuke watched him canter off down the street towards Dunbar before making his own way back to the ship to get help.

It was only two stances to Dunbar, and so it didn't take long for Fraytar to reach the outskirts. He dismounted his horse, tethering it to a nearby tree, and began slowly moving, crouched, towards the village. The daylight had faded by now, and he could clearly see the light from oil lamps coming from a nearby inn.

He moved slowly towards one of the windows of the inn and peered in. Two groups of men sat drinking ale at separate tables, and a man on his own stood by the fireplace, smoking a pipe. The smoke from the pipe trailed gently into the air, the man focusing intently on the flames in the hearth. The light from the fire lit up his rugged face, and as he slowly turned towards the window, he revealed a scar down his right cheek.

Fraytar and the man he was looking at both realised immediately that one was hunted, and the other was the hunter. The man dashed towards a door at the back of the inn, whilst Fraytar ran along the outside front wall and crashed through a gate to gain access to the back. He caught a glimpse of the man jumping over a fence into the lane leading out of the village. Fraytar ran back to his horse, mounted, and galloped in the direction the man had gone.

On reaching the lane, Fraytar halted and looked around for signs of the man but saw nothing. He trotted onward. Some way ahead, he caught a glimpse of someone running and dug his heels into his horse to gallop in that direction.

Fraytar hadn't gone far when suddenly he was struck by something across his chest that knocked him backwards out of his saddle. With a crash, he hit the ground, and everything went black.

When he woke, Fraytar found himself tied to a tree with three men standing around him. One was the man with the scar down his right cheek, the man he had been chasing. For a moment Fraytar couldn't remember what had happened, until a pain across his chest and his aching back reminded him that he had been knocked off his horse.

"Ah, you're awake at last, sailor," said the man with the scar. "I know who you be. Maybe we can demand a ransom for he from your captain."

"You'll never get away with this. Captain Amannar's men will catch up with you scum and skin you alive," Fraytar retorted.

The three captors laughed loudly. The man with the scar replied,

"Is that so? We have powerful friends who will make sure that doesn't happen. Maybe we could take you to visit them. They may give us a good price for he to make a good slave, I'm sure."

Fraytar shuddered, for he realised whom the man could be referring to. *It must be the Cordinens*, he thought.

"We should at least get a good price for this shiny cutlass and these fine boots of yours," continued the scarred man, "and your horse'll also fetch a good price. Or maybe we just kill you now and have done with it."

Fraytar squirmed against his bonds, desperate to set himself free and take his revenge on these men. Suddenly from behind the three men, four other men came screaming out of the trees, rushing at Fraytar like wild animals. Fraytar closed his eyes and waited for the blows to land on him from these madmen.

This is surely the end, he thought in desperation. He heard the blows but strangely felt no pain. He felt the warm splash of blood against his face, but still he felt no pain. Slowly he opened his eyes, and in surprise he saw Morganuke and three crewmen standing over his captors, who were now lying on the ground, bruised and bleeding.

"How did you find me so quickly?" Fraytar gasped as he pulled against his bonds.

"Let me untie you first," Morganuke answered as he began to untie the ropes around Fraytar's body and arms. "We heard your horse neighing by the trees and came to investigate. Then we heard the laughter of these pigs and crept up to surprise them. And surprise them we did."

Fraytar threw down the ropes and looked down at the three men on the ground. "We'll have to take these men back to the ship as soon as possible. We must sail on the next high tide, and time is fast running out. They don't look like they can walk very far in the state they are in, and it'll take hours if we walk with them."

Fraytar turned to the biggest of the crew members. "Crouch, make sure they are tied up securely. I'll try to find a horse and cart so that we can take them quickly to the dock."

Fraytar quickly found his horse and galloped off in the direction of Dunbar, soon returning with a horse and cart and his horse in tow. "Right, get the prisoners loaded onto the wagon and we'll make our way back to the ship," Fraytar shouted to the crew as he slid the cart to a halt.

They heaved the wounded men onto the cart, and the three crew members squeezed themselves on, with Crouch driving. Morganuke jumped onto the back of Fraytar's horse and off they sped in the direction of the docks.

The sun was now starting to rise, and the birds sang their early dawn chorus. After all that had happened, it felt strange to Morganuke that other things in the world were just carrying on as normal. He thought how different things had felt only a day earlier. Now he was dashing across the countryside on the back of a horse, trailing a cart full of wounded men who had attacked them earlier, with the threat of war spilling onto the Banton Island upon them. He had not slept in this time, and events were catching up with him and leaving him feeling exhausted.

When they arrived at the ship, all seemed calm and quiet, in contrast to what they had been experiencing. Fraytar jumped off his horse and instructed the men to unload the prisoners. He spotted Captain Amannar on the upper deck of the *Aurora* and shouted up to him. "We have found the attackers and brought them back here for questioning."

Captain Amannar nodded in approval. "Excellent! Bring them on board and secure them in the cargo hold for questioning. We must prepare to set sail."

The crew who had rescued Fraytar carried the prisoners on board and took them to the lower decks. The injured men groaned as they were carried, one cursing under his breath, "You dogs, you won't get away with this! Our friends will get their revenge."

"Quiet, scum! Your friends will never find you again," Fraytar responded.

When the prisoners had been secured in the ship's brig, Captain Amannar came to confront the three captives.

"So, you would dare attack my ship!" he shouted into the faces of the three men. He walked in a circle in front of them, pulling on his big black beard. "Tell me who put you up to this, and I'll ease your suffering."

The three men did not respond except to groan and curse under their breaths.

"Maybe I should start taking your fingers one by one until you tell me what I want to know. Tell me who put you up to attacking my ship?"

"Our friends are stronger than you could imagine," one of the prisoners mumbled loudly, "and they will get their revenge."

Captain Amannar walked over to Fraytar and in a low voice said, "I am sure that the Cordinens are behind this. We have no idea how many are on Banton Island, and we must be extra careful. I want to double the watch through the voyage. We must be extra vigilant. I want guards outside the brig at all times. They'll have to come with us, for we have no more time to spare on this side of the island. Now, let's prepare to set sail."

CHAPTER 4

The Voyage

On the *Aurora*, the crew were preparing to leave the dock. Morganuke was standing on the upper deck, watching what was going on, when the captain shouted to him, "Boy, you can go down and help on the ropes."

Morganuke felt very tired but complied with the captain's orders. He made his way to the back of the line of crewmen who were holding a long rope tethered from the stern all the way to the front of the ship and then out to the dock. Other crewmen were holding ropes bound to the sails that were still rolled up. For a moment all stood by waiting for the captain's command.

"Get ready to haul on the forward spring!" yelled the captain. "Pull!"

With that command the crewmen holding the rope leading to the dock began to pull in unison. A beat from a drum rang out, and the crew sang a rhythmic shanty. Morganuke tried to follow as best he could, initially losing his timing and almost his footing but improving as time went on.

Slowly the ship began to move, creeping slowly first and then increasing speed. Morganuke was amazed at how only a dozen men were able to move such a heavy ship. As the ship moved forward to the end of the dock, the captain shouted, "Release the forward spring."

With that, the rope tethered to the stern of the ship was released, and the men dropped their hold on it, letting it slide away from the ship. The momentum of the ship was such that it continued moving forward out of the dock before the captain gave another order: "Raise sails!" The other crewmen pulled on the ropes holding the sails to release them. Immediately the wind filled the triangular sails on all three masts, and there was a detectable increase in speed as the wind drove the ship onwards out to sea.

Morganuke looked around the ship, taking in the scene and the smell of the fresh sea air. He could feel the spray from the sea as the ship danced over the waves crashing against its bow. The taste of the salty water against his lips was strangely intoxicating, and he felt alive. *I'm at sea at last*, he thought.

The rest of the day went smoothly, and it stayed sunny for most of it. Taking the Southwood route before heading east, they kept the island within visible range on the port side. Morganuke continued helping the crew with all jobs on the deck. There was plenty to do, with rigging to tidy up and the deck to scrub down.

Later in the day, he helped in the galley to prepare the meal for the crew. The ship's cook was a portly man with a jolly face framed with a curly grey beard. His head was almost bald, with only a few grey wisps of hair still growing around the edge.

"Well, laddie, how be he enjoying your first voyage?" the cook asked as he pushed a pile of tamor roots across for him to peel. Morganuke immediately thought of his mother when he saw the roots. He imagined her peeling off the bark-like skins and them frying them in goose fat.

"It's quite an experience and I'd not realised how busy it would be," answered Morganuke as he took the roots and plopped them into a bucket of water in front of him. "How long have you been sailing on ships? Have you always been a cook?"

"I've been sailing since I wuz a bay, so more yurs than you ken imagine, bay. Doing odd jobs when I first started yer on ships, bay. I think 'twas my third ship when I started cookin' If I remember rightly, first job I 'ad was peelin' roots, so you've got a grand job there, bay."

"Have you been on any dangerous voyages? I'm thinking this may be a dangerous voyage," Morganuke said as he continued to peel the tamor.

"Been on a few, but always come out right. If you've got a good cap'n then it makes a difference, and we 'ave a good captain on this ship, bay. So never you mind whether 'tis a dangerous voyage or not."

Morganuke peeled his tamor roots in silence, thinking about what lay ahead on the voyage. His feelings were mixed between excitement and concern about what might happen, given the events that had occurred already.

Later as the sun was going down and the sea breezes grew chillier, Morganuke leant on the railing in the centre of the lower deck, watching the coastline of the island pass by as the white waves crashed over the rocks. The seabirds circled above the ship, calling out in hope of a morsel of food from the men scurrying on the deck below them.

Before the sun had disappeared completely, Morganuke climbed the steps to the aftercastle and watched the sun slowly sink below the horizon, casting a deep red glow across the sky.

He was startled by a loud clatter of metal striking metal. *What's that?* Morganuke thought in worried anticipation. *Is this another attack?* He turned to look in the direction of the noise and was relieved to see the cook striking a pan lid with a metal knife.

"Food's ready," shouted the cook.

The crewmen quickly made their way to the galley area. Morganuke was not only tired almost to the point of exhaustion but also very hungry, as he had not eaten since early that day. He made his way towards the galley behind the rest of the crew. The smell of cooking permeated the air as he got closer, and his stomach started to rumble. He picked up a metal plate from a pile at the galley entrance and followed the line of crewmen inside. There the cook placed a ladle of stew onto his plate and gave a sly wink.

The stew tasted good, along with the ale that he had picked up at the same time, and with his belly full he was now ready for some sleep.

Morganuke made his way to the crew's cramped sleeping quarters on the forward castle. Inside, it was cramped, and the stench of stale sweat filled his nostrils, almost making him gag. There were ten crewmen already asleep lined up on the floor head to toe. Even with the chilly sea breeze, Morganuke decided to sleep outside, propped up against the crew accommodation wall. He managed to find some old sacking to wrap himself in before snuggling down to sleep.

Morganuke found himself in a deep valley next to a swiftly running river. He could hear a low humming noise coming from just ahead and felt drawn to it. Slowly he moved towards the source of the noise, and as he got closer, he saw a dark cave at the base of a cliff wall; its blackness framed by the light grey of the cliffs. He made his way to the entrance but found nothing but blackness inside. Though he felt unnerved, he moved further into the blackness as the humming noise grew louder. He made out a dim glimmer of light ahead and without conscious effort approached it.

This seems strangely familiar. Am I dreaming or be this real?

When he got almost on top of the light source, it was so bright that his head began to ache, and dizziness overcame him. *This must be a dream*, he concluded. Still the noise increased, and the light got even brighter. The dizziness got worse, now making him feel nauseous, and he did not appear to be in control of his actions. Then a familiar sight was presented to him within the light: a bright door with the image of an eye weeping, this time with a red tear.

He was almost at the point of touching the door when his senses became overwhelmed and felt himself falling, slowly falling as if in quicksand. Further down he fell until he was shaken hard.

Morganuke woke with a gasp to find Crouch standing over him, shaking him while shouting in his ear, "Wake up! It's time for you to go on watch."

He came around, reorienting himself to his surroundings. He was still propped up outside the crew's sleeping quarters on the upper deck.

His head ached, and he did not feel rested, troubled by the dream he had had.

"Come with me!" demanded Crouch.

Morganuke slowly got to his feet and followed Crouch to the lower deck, where he was given a mop and bucket and told to scrub down the deck. Still tired, Morganuke nevertheless started to scrub the deck as he was asked. He had been scrubbing for several minutes when Fraytar came over to him.

"How are you enjoying your first voyage, Morg?"

"I'd not realized how hard it would be on a ship," answered Morganuke. "There's so many jobs to do, the conditions are cramped and uncomfortable, and there is the never-ending threat of being attacked."

Fraytar looked down with his hand on his chin and thought for a moment before he continued. "This is only a short voyage, and so conditions are much better than they would be on a long voyage, where the food would be a lot worse and conditions barely tolerable. But the rewards can be considerable and worth the moments of discomfort."

"Where are we going and how long will it take to get there?" Morganuke asked as he continued to mop the deck.

"We are heading for Cradport on the eastern edge of the island. With good prevailing winds, it should take about seven or eight days," Fraytar answered. "Do you regret coming on the voyage?"

"No, I realise it's good experience and it's helping toughen me up. I am determined to stick this out and maybe one day travel to the mainland."

"Good lad! That's what I like to hear. You have already proven yourself to the captain, and I am sure you will turn out to make a good sailor," Fraytar said over his shoulder as he walked away.

Morganuke continued with his duties until he heard the already familiar clang of metal as the cook announced that the early morning meal was ready, bringing him much relief. The nausea had left him but was replaced by a gnawing hunger in the pit of his stomach. As before, he queued outside the galley and waited to be served his morning meal. Most of the other crewmembers either took little notice of him or were quite friendly—a welcome break from the constant gawping he would have been subjected to on the island. A couple of the sailors had seemingly taken a dislike to him, possibly feeling jealous because he had won the captain's favour so quickly. But overall the crew seemed a bit more accepting of his differences, maybe because they'd seen so much in their voyages.

After his meal, Morganuke had another opportunity to rest. He made his way up to the crew sleeping quarters and lay down outside on the deck, wrapped in his make-do sack bedding. He was completely exhausted. He woke up feeling refreshed from a dreamless sleep that had come quickly. It took a few moments for him to realise that he was on the deck of a ship. Several crewmen around him were preparing for their next shift, and he realised that it was his turn as well. He got slowly to his feet, yawned, and stretched, feeling a little bit achy from the hard decking.

Clouds covered the sky, making it difficult to determine the time of day. Further out to sea, Morganuke could see dark clouds on the horizon and heard a faint rumble of thunder. The wind had picked up significantly, and he had trouble keeping a firm footing on the deck, which was now slippery from the rain.

"Reduce sale and lower top mast," came a voice from the other side of the ship. Immediately crewmembers began taking in the sail whilst others started disconnecting and lowering the upper mainmast.

Morganuke could see Fraytar on the lower deck. He was giving orders to some of the crew, and Morganuke moved quickly but carefully down the steps to ask him what was going on.

"There's a storm coming, and we need to prepare the ship to make sure we weather it," Fraytar answered between his swift orders. "Go with those crewmen and take up the ropes. They will show you what to do."

Morganuke made his way to the crewmen and grasped the end of a ropes they were pulling. Morganuke pulled with all his might, not really knowing what the rope was doing.

The daylight grew dimmer as the wind and rain increased in intensity. The ship was lurching violently as it smashed against the massive waves. Suddenly there was a crash as timbers fell against the deck, ropes thrashing about as though they were live snakes. No one was beneath it, and crewmen quickly gathered round to recover what had been part of the mainmast. Morganuke helped as best he could without knowing what to do.

He looked across the lower deck and saw a crew member fiddling with some ropes, securing part of the on-deck cargo. Some of the crates began to slide away from their bindings. He shouted to the crewmember, but he just ran away. Morganuke ran to the crates before they completely detached themselves. As he did, he felt a massive blow against his body that enveloped him in seawater and knocked him off his feet. He slid across the deck towards the side railings at great speed, then smashed against them and somersaulted over the top. He just managed to grasp the rail and found that a rope had wound itself miraculously around one of his feet, preventing him from being swept overboard. With the constant pounding of seawater and the rocking of the ship, Morganuke felt his desperate hold slipping.

Just then strong hands grasped his shoulders, and a force pulled him back onto the ship's deck. It was Crouch. Never had Morganuke been so glad to see a familiar face, even if it was Crouch.

"You don't get away that easily, laddie," Crouch shouted, patting him on the shoulder and smiling.

"Th-thank you, Crouch," Morganuke gasped.

Crouch handed him the end of a rope. "Now tie this around your waist and follow me." Crouch led Morganuke to a hatch towards the stern and beckoned him through the opened door, which led down to the brig. "You can help keep an eye on the prisoners whilst the storm continues."

Morganuke followed Crouch's directions, climbing down the ladder and untying the rope around his waist as he did so. He made his way further down to the brig, where the three prisoners were being held. Two crewmen were keeping watch over them, sitting around a single lantern which was swinging violently from side to side, attached to a hook on one of the crossbeams and kept as far away from the flammable cargo as possible. The three prisoners sat upright when they spotted Morganuke through the locked cell door.

"What's a Pale One doing here on the ship?" said the prisoner with a scar on his face.

"What do you mean by 'Pale One'?" asked Morganuke.

"You look like one of those silver-haired ones we've seen on the mainland, working with—" The scarred prisoner stopped himself.

"Working with who?" Morganuke pressed.

"Never you mind. It just looks like some folk we seen on the mainland, that's all," the prisoner responded in a surly fashion and said no more.

Are these the same people that Fraytar had seen? Morganuke wondered.

With the constant pitching of the ship, it was difficult for Morganuke to stand, and there was little to hold on to. Morganuke found himself a place to sit and made himself as comfortable as he could. He was sure that he would be there for some time as there was no sign of the storm easing up. He had to make sure that he didn't fall asleep, even though he was feeling quite tired.

For several hours, the prisoners and the guarding crew sat in silence, grasping what they could to stop themselves being thrown about as the ship continued to pitch violently. It seemed there would be no end to it, and Morganuke expected them to be smashed against the rocks at any time.

But at last the rocking eased, and the violent pitching was replaced with a rhythmic rise and fall. Eventually the hatch opened, and Morganuke could see Fraytar smiling at the entrance. "You can come up now, Morg. The storm has died down, and I'm sure you would like to get some sleep in your comfy bed."

Morganuke didn't need telling twice and quickly climbed the ladder to the main deck. It was still dark, but he saw signs of the damage caused by the storm.

"Is there much damage to ship?" Morganuke asked. "It was like the storm would never stop, and I saw part of the rigging fall."

"Part of the main mast has been damaged, and we will have to repair that as best we can once we reach the small port of Fettleridge. It should only delay us by a day," Fraytar answered.

Morganuke grimaced at the thought of further delays. "When I was with the prisoners, one of them mentioned that they had seen people who looked like me. Do you think they are the same group that you saw with the Cordinens when they attacked Stacklin?"

Fraytar thought for a moment before answering. "I don't know. To be honest, there's still a lot I don't know about the mainland. For all we know, there may be a lot of people that look like you. Don't worry too much about it. Hopefully we will get more answers when we reach Cradport. Now go and get some sleep while you can."

Morganuke made his way to the upper deck crew quarters and settled himself in his usual spot outside. He took little notice of the continuous babble from crewmembers around him as the watch was changing. Some were making their way to the sleeping quarters, and others prepared themselves for the next shift. Exhausted, Morganuke was oblivious to the goings-on and wrapped himself in his make-do bedding, immediately falling into a dreamless sleep.

For the next two days the journey was uneventful, and regular chores were carried out on a routine shift pattern. Morganuke had another stint in the galley with the cook and enjoyed hearing the old man's stories of his sailing exploits. It was good to get into a routine without being interrupted by some calamitous event.

Arriving at Fettleridge was another new experience for Morganuke. Although he had explored much of the island, as large as it was, he had never made his way to Fettleridge. He was excited about exploring somewhere new. *This be the advantage of a sailor's life*, he thought, *you be getting' to see knew places.*

The town was quite difficult to approach from inland as it lay on one side of mountainous terrain. Morganuke guessed that the town's population largely relied on the sea for food, trade, and travel. Even though the port was quite small compared to Tannisport, many small boats and medium-sized ships were docked there. The surrounding rocks and mountains made an ideal harbour, protected from the open sea, and was an ideal place to complete the repairs to the *Aurora*.

With her sails down, the *Aurora* was manoeuvred gingerly to her docking point in the harbour using rowboats. Once in place, the ship was secured with ropes on the dock. Morganuke was glad to see the gangplank go down and to feel his feet once again on land. He had been given leave to do some exploring whilst the ship was being repaired.

Once off the ship, Morganuke looked around the harbour, watching the many people scurrying by as they busied themselves with their tasks. There were carts loaded with cargo from the ships and men pushing barrows full of goods that the town needed.

This is a very busy place, Morganuke thought. *Now where should start looking around?*

In one corner of the harbour square, Morganuke spotted a street lined on each side with houses and open storefronts. A small crowd had gathered around the stores to do their shopping. *That looks like a likely place to investigate*, he thought and started to walk towards the street.

When he was halfway across the square, he heard a voice call to him from behind, "Hey, Morganuke! We are off to the inn. Do you want to join us?" Morganuke turned to see that it was Crouch with two other crewmembers. He nodded in appreciation and joined the group.

They walked down the street that Morganuke had been heading towards and continued for thirty paces or so before turning down another side street. A few paces further they came to the inn, a small bustling place with music and song coming from inside. Morganuke thought that it looked jolly and an exciting place to visit but was glad that he wasn't alone. Inside several groups of people sat at tables, singing along to the music, which was provided by a man playing the fiddle and a woman singing.

Morganuke then realised that he didn't have any money on him and apologised to Crouch.

"It's okay, lad, the ale is on me," Crouch kindly replied.

Morganuke was surprised at Crouch's response, as he had seemed quite stern and hard on the ship but now seemed very approachable. He had also saved Morganuke from falling overboard during the storm. *You can't judge folk on first encounters*, he thought.

The group found a table in the corner of the inn and sat down. A young woman in an apron soon came over to take their order.

"Four ales, if ee please," Crouch asked.

"Very well, sir," answered the barmaid with a smile. Morganuke thought her quite pretty and was pleased when she smiled at him when she returned with the ales a little later. *There's no odd looks from the folk here so far*, he thought gratefully.

As the four of them sat enjoying their ale, an argument started up between two men at a table on the other side of the inn. The group of four turned to watch the commotion and recognised one of the men as a crew member.

"I wonder what that's all about," Crouch commented as he sipped his ale.

"You cheat!" came a shout from the other table.

Crouch's inquisitiveness and his keenness to protect a crewmember got the better of him, and he walked over to the table to see what was going on. Morganuke followed him. When they got to the table, they saw a man seated with four ceramic pots turned upside down in front of him. The crewmember had left.

"What's going on?" Crouch asked the man seated at the table.

"Bad loser, that's all," answered the man. He fiddled with the ceramic pots in front of him. "We were playing hide-the-shell on a bet. I hid the shell under one of these pots, moved them about, and he had to guess which one the shell was under. Quite simple, really. Except for him, it appears."

"And what would he have won if he did get to guess correctly?" Crouch asked.

"I charge half one flant a go, and you get four times the stake return if you guess correctly," answered the man.

Crouch thought for a moment before tossing a one flant coin onto the table. "Right then, let me have a go. Here's your money."

The conjurer took out a small shell from his pocket and placed it under one of the ceramic pots. He then shuffled the pots over the tabletop whilst Crouch and Morganuke closely watched. When the man stopped moving the pots, he asked them to choose which one the shell was under. Both Crouch and Morganuke seemed confident that they knew which pot to choose, and without hesitation Crouch pointed to one of the pots. The man turned the pot over but there was no shell. Both Crouch and Morganuke gasped in surprise, whilst the man turned over another pot to reveal the shell.

"I gave you one flant and so I'll have another try," Crouch said impatiently.

The conjurer repeated the exercise, and when he had stopped moving the pots, he looked intently at Crouch, waiting for his guess. Crouch paused, thinking carefully, looking at each of the pots.

Morganuke had also been watching carefully and was convinced he knew which pot the shell was under; however, he had thought that the first time. He kept looking at the pots, thinking over and over, *I wish I could see what was under the pots. Just turn over the pots.*

Crouch was just about to point to one of the pots when someone standing close by lost their balance for no apparent reason and fell against the table. All the pots tipped over at once … and no shell was to be seen!

"What!? Where be the shell? I cannot see the shell. So, you were cheating my man!" Crouch, exclaimed, red-faced and very angry.

For a moment the conjurer said nothing—he was too surprised all the pots had been knocked over and his trickery had been exposed. How he had only placed the shell by sleight of hand once the pot had been chosen, was now made clear. "What—what—what—er, how did that happen?" he began to stammer.

"Your cheating has been shown. Now return my money and the money you stole from my man!" demanded Crouch.

The conjurer was so shocked he didn't know what else to do or say, so he threw some coins on the table and then hastily left the inn.

Crouch gathered up the coins. "Well, I think we've had enough 'fun' for today. Let's make our way back to the ship and see how the repairs be going."

But Morganuke was thinking how strange it was that the pots were turned over just as he was wishing for it. *Strange coincidence*, he thought, *or is it?* It was not the first time something similar had happened. He remembered the boy who had been taunting him at school and how he'd fallen flat on his face

---

Morganuke returned to the ship with the others, commenting on how funny the conjurer's face looked when he realised he had been found out. It was a good relaxing break, and Morganuke had appreciated being away from the ship for a while.

On reaching the ship Morganuke was made aware of a lot of commotion on and around the ship. The captain was on deck shouting expletives and ordering the crew to look here and there, but they didn't appear to know what they were looking for.

When Morganuke and the others got close enough, Crouch shouted up, "What has happened, Captain?"

"Those scum prisoners have escaped with the help of a rogue crewmember and injured two of my crew," Captain Amannar shouted back.

"I'll take two men and search the docks, Captain," Fraytar said, who had been standing beside the captain. "They can't have got far."

"Do as you will, Fraytar. We must find them or else they will warn our enemies where we be heading, for they have surely guessed our destination," the captain said. "We must sail as soon as the mast be repaired, whether they be found or not. So do your best to find them as quickly as you can."

Fraytar and the crew returned sometime later but had not found the escaped prisoners. Morganuke looked on helplessly as the captain cursed and ordered the ship to set sail. He then joined Fraytar on the main deck.

"What will happen now?" Morganuke asked

"I hope this doesn't come back to sting us," Fraytar replied, looking despondent. "It's now a race between us reaching the other side of the island, and the prisoners and that rogue crewmember warning our enemies."

CHAPTER 5

Cradport

The first two days of sailing after they left Fettleridge went well, and good progress was made. On the third day the wind dropped, and the ship lay becalmed some way out at sea. There was nothing to do but wait for the wind to return. Fraytar and Morganuke were on the upper aft deck leaning on the rails, watching the crew biding their time on the lower deck. The captain fumed behind them.

"Blast the weather!" exclaimed the captain, glum-faced, pacing up and down the upper deck with his arms behind his back. "At this rate our enemies will be waiting for us by the time we get to Cradport." He looked up at the sky, grimacing, and then went back into his cabin, slamming the door behind him.

"Does this happen often?" Morganuke turned to Fraytar and asked.

"It happens occasionally. When it does, it can last for days," answered Fraytar. "I can understand the captain's concern. I remember once sailing in the south-western seas and being becalmed for almost five days. It was such a relief when the wind did finally return."

"Have you travelled all over the world?" Morganuke asked. "You must have seen so many different places."

"I've travelled most of the seas, except the south-east—and that is a place I would never want to go to," Fraytar said. "There are many tales about the nebula in the south-eastern seas, but no one who has seen it returns alive. Not as far as I know, anyways."

"How do you know this for sure if no one returns from that place?"

Fraytar frowned. "Just that ships are recorded as sailing into the nebula and then are never seen again. 'Tis true nobody can tell of witnessing what's within that place, and so there are no maps of the area."

"What do you think is there to make ships disappear like that?" Morganuke asked.

"I don't know and can't imagine. All I know is that I've no desire to go there myself, nor should anyone else if they be right-minded."

The two stood in silence for a while, watching over the lower decks. It was strangely quiet as the ship stood still in the seawater, which now was as smooth as a millpond.

Morganuke finally broke the silence. "Do you think the captain will do more runs like this to make up for losses? Or will he return to the mainland?"

"It's up to the captain," Fraytar answered. "Given what's happened so far, he must be wary about continuing this trade route after we've delivered this cargo. With the growing war our options are few, and I don't see it getting any better any time soon."

The familiar clanging of metal announced the midday meal. Fraytar and Morganuke made their way along with other members of the crew to the galley.

The meal provided a respite from the tedious waiting in the midday heat. Tempers were being pushed to the limits as crew members quarrelled amongst themselves. There was little to be done until the wind returned so that they could continue their journey, but some of the crew found odd jobs, played dice, or just sang shanties to pass the time and ease the boredom.

The evening bought no respite, and the calm continued through the night. Some crewmembers stayed on watch to keep lookout whilst others slept. Morganuke took his usual spot outside the sleeping quarters and dozed. He didn't need his makeshift blanket, as temperatures were still high with no wind to provide a cooling relief. Eventually, Morganuke managed to fall asleep.

Morganuke found himself on a strange ship with a huge blue eye peering from the upper foredeck. He looked across the water towards a cove set in a mountainous terrain. As the strange ship got closer to the cove, a medium-sized town in the shape of a horseshoe came into view. The town surrounded the harbour and docks. Just beyond were almost vertical grey cliffs. Morganuke felt himself drifting off the deck of that strange ship with its large blue eye focused on the town. He drifted over the water towards the houses and then beyond, towards the cliffs on the other side.

Halfway up the cliffs, immediately above the furthest inland townhouses, but not too far from the harbour's edge, Morganuke observed a glow. He drifted closer to the source of light, ascending without any effort. The glow slowly turned to a red shimmering flame. He seemed to hover there in front of the flame for moments.

Where am I, he thought, *this be another dream but what does it mean?*

Above the red glow he now noticed a bright white light bursting from the cliff. Its source seemed to come from a ledge immediately above the fiery glow. He now felt himself drifting up towards the bright white light, about the height of eight men above the red glow. Closer still he drifted, until he made out a familiar scene, a door and the symbol of an eye with a blue iris and a red tear. Immediately in front of the door was a large boulder on which he focused for a moment.

Suddenly, the boulder rolled forward beyond the ledge and dropped downwards. As the boulder met the fiery glow, there was a flash before it disappeared into nothing.

Now Morganuke felt himself being pulled by some invisible force towards the door. He could hear the familiar hum that had haunted his previous dreams, and his senses began to be overrun with the dizzy nausea that got stronger as he neared the door. Almost at the point of touching the door, he started to fall slowly as he had before into that treacle-like bath.

Morganuke woke to a gentle breeze on his face, propped up against the wall of the crew's quarters and still nauseous. He slowly came to his senses and pondered on what he saw in his dreams. *The door! I be keep seeing the door, and the blue eye in those dreams. What does it all mean?*

Fraytar appeared in front of him. "Morganuke, the wind is picking up, and soon we can continue our journey at last."

Morganuke got slowly to his feet, the dizziness and nausea gone. He looked around and saw that the crew were already hoisting the sails.

It took two more days to reach Cradport. "Destination ahead!" came the call from the mainmast lookout overhead, and in the distance Morganuke could see the outline of a town and docks. The wind was blowing against the sails, and the hull was rising and falling over the waves causing spray to wash over the bow. As the ship drew nearer to the entrance of the harbour, Morganuke could just about see people moving on the dock like little ants scurrying about.

Behind the townhouses, laid out in a horseshoe and framing the harbour, Morganuke could make out steep grey cliffs. Then he realised with horror and astonishment that this was the place he had seen in his dream! *How can this be? This be just like the place I saw in my dream. What does this all mean?*

"Well, Morg, what do you think?"

Morganuke jumped. He hadn't even heard Fraytar come up behind him and couldn't speak for a moment. His mind was still racing.

"It's—it's ... er ... I've seen this place before, Fraytar," he finally managed to get out.

"What do you mean?" Fraytar asked with a puzzled look. "Have you been here before?"

Morganuke turned and looked Fraytar in the eye. "I have no memory of visiting this place before, but I've seen it in a dream. It's as clear as day to me now and it looked just like this place. I can't explain it."

"You've been under a lot of pressure," Fraytar said, now looking a little concerned, "and a lot has happened to you over these past few days. I hope that bringing you on this journey is not bungling you. All the things that have happened so far must be unfamiliar and frightening."

"No! No, I did see it in my dream, and I'm not bungled, whatever that be, or frightened. I'm just a little uncertain about what a dream like that could mean." Morganuke wished to say no more on the subject, and Fraytar made no further attempt to press the issue. They made their way to the lower decks for the docking.

"Right," Captain Amannar said, "let's go have a word with our friend Vorderlan." He strode across the gangplank and onto the dock. Fraytar followed close behind, giving Morganuke the nod to come too.

The townhouses were arranged in a horseshoe shape around the dock with steep cliffs behind, just as Morganuke had seen in his dream. It was about the same size as Tannisport and just as busy. Several ships were docked in the harbour, and workers were bustling amongst these, unloading their cargo. There were occasional shouts from dock workers directing the traffic of carts as people made their way through the narrow streets.

Vorderlan's trading office was across the dock in the middle of a block of shops and townhouses. When Captain Amannar reached the office door, he pushed it open forcefully. The door opened with a whoosh and cracked against some crates stored behind it. Vorderlan dropped the papers he was holding and jumped to standing behind his desk. He was a tallish but skinny man, clean-shaven with long black greasy hair. Morganuke saw that his britches were a little too short for his long legs whilst his shirt and jacket were too big for his thin body. "Amannar! What do you want?" he said indignantly.

"Tell me why my ship is being attacked!" Captain Amannar demanded.

"What do you mean? I know nothing about any attacks on your ship," Vorderlan snapped.

"Since taking on this trading request of yours, my ship and its crew have been subject to attacks. Now tell me why that should be."

"I don't know who is attacking your ship or why. I am only fulfilling an order for the Epleons on the mainland," Vorderlan said, slumping back down in his desk chair.

"The Epleons, you say? Then it must be something to do with the Cordinens," the captain accused.

"I daresay it is. Some Cordinen soldiers have been sighted in the area recently. They are a frightening lot. Look as though they were bred just for fighting." Vorderlan shuddered.

"So the Cordinens are behind these attacks," Fraytar said, "and that the war is spreading."

It's true then, Morganuke thought, *the war really has reached our island.*

"This is becoming too dangerous and costly for me," the captain said. "This will be the last batch of pitch that I deliver to you, Vorderlan." He turned and marched out of the office, Fraytar and Morganuke following.

Morganuke's mind raced as they walked along the winding streets back to the ship. Everything his father had said was coming true. They would no longer be isolated from the mainland war. He looked around at the town and the cliffs behind, remembering his dream. *Am I still dreaming? Will I wake up soon and all this will go away. Maybe I'll wake up in my own bed at home.*

Once back at the ship, Captain Amannar set to urging the crew on. "Quick as you can, men! Unload that cargo so we can get out of this place and back to safety."

Fraytar watched the captain as he turned to ascend the steps to the upper deck. Then there was a loud whoosh, and the captain halted abruptly and fell forward on his face. Blood started to flow across the deck.

"We are under attack! Take cover!" Fraytar shouted, taking

command. He dived across the deck taking shelter behind some cargo. Morganuke quickly followed him.

"Everyone keep down and watch for more where that came from," ordered Fraytar to anyone that could hear.

"Look out! Arrows!" came a shout from Crouch on the other side of the deck. Fraytar looked up to see a hail of arrows heading for the ship. Some plummeted into the water, but others found their way to the ship's deck.

Fraytar called out to the captain and saw him stir. He ran over to where the captain lay.

"Captain, we need to move you to cover," Fraytar desperately shouted in the captain's ear. "Drouger! Get the ship's surgeon now."

Just then another volley of arrows started to rain down. Instinctively, Fraytar threw himself across his captain and felt a tremendous jolt of pain as one of the arrows embedded itself in his arm. Without thinking he pulled the arrow out from his arm, which caused it to start bleeding profusely. The pain was severe, but he kept his senses. Fraytar focused on the captain again and yelled out in despair when he realised that an arrow was now embedded in the captain neck.

For a moment Fraytar forgot the battle and knelt beside his dead captain. *I must lead these men now my captain is dead*. He forced himself to stand and started to encourage his men, disregarding his own safety.

Fraytar noticed that arrows were also being shot from enemies stationed around the houses, picking off some of the crew. Several men now lay dead on the deck. The ship's surgeon darted from one stricken crewman to another. He looked around desperately and realised the only way to overcome the assault was for some of the crew to flank the attackers. They had determined that most of the attackers were positioned in the cliffs behind the town, where they could pick off anyone leaving the ship and moving towards the houses. Fraytar called Crouch over and gave him the plan.

Crouch readied six men to disembark in stealth from the other side. They would then make their way to the dock from the water, hopefully avoiding detection from the group stationed on the cliff and those stationed around the houses. The men lowered themselves into the water with ropes, mindful to keep as quiet as possible. Fraytar watched Crouch and his men swim towards the dock and scramble up to some houses for cover.

With horror, Fraytar then heard a shout come up from one of the houses in the town: "I see them!" Several arrows then made the way towards Crouch's men.

Morganuke joined Fraytar on the main deck, still taking cover behind some of the cargo.

"What going on? Is there anything I can do? Morganuke asked.

"I've just sent Crouch with six men into the town to try and flank the attackers on the cliff but they are now pinned down by other enemies in the town."

Morganuke studies the cliff and the ridge where the main attackers were believed to be. He then remembered his dream and finally realised what it was telling him. The boulder, he thought. The boulder above the ridge. "I know what to do! Don't worry, I can help'!"

Before Fraytar could stop him, Morganuke jumped overboard. The water was very cold as he plunged below the surface and came up gasping. It was as much as he could do to stop himself crying out. He started to swim in the same direction as Crouch's party.

No, he thought, *I need to go in the opposite direction, as the enemy's attention is on them.* He turned and swam in the opposite direction towards the other side of the harbour, where he scrambled up onto the quay. The enemy's attention was on the ship and Crouch's party, and they did not spot him as he crawled towards the first line houses. He made his way through the narrow backstreets until he came to a clearing between the houses and the cliffs. It looked very exposed, and he couldn't see a way of making it to the cliffs without being detected.

Well, that's no good, Morganuke thought, *this is too exposed, and I am just as pinned down as Crouch is. I need to find another way.*

Morganuke rummaged around the houses close by and found some old dusty sacks to use as makeshift camouflage. *I don't know if this will work*, he thought, *but at least I'm only one person and so there's a chance they will miss me.*

Morganuke raced across the open ground and into some bushes at the base of the cliffs. It seemed a good place to stop and plan his next steps as he was to one side and not immediately in their field of view. He thought of his dream again and looked for a way up the cliff. Although steep, it was not sheer and with care should be possible to climb. He began to make his way upwards, stopping every now to plan his next few steps.

Once he had climbed halfway, he could see most of the houses below him. Some of the houses were sheltering the enemy, and he could see arrows being fired from these towards the point where he assumed that Crouch's group were sheltering. He looked across to the point on the cliff where most of the arrows had come from and could just make out some movement. He scanned the cliffs above the movement and spotted an outline of what appeared to be a ledge. *That where I need to go*, thought Morganuke, *that is where the boulder will be ready to roll down on the enemy.*

It was a very precarious climb, up and across to the ledge, and Morganuke nearly lost his footing more than once. At last, he reached the ledge, expecting to see the boulder that he'd seen in his dream, but there was none. Now what? He looked around the empty ledge he had risked his life to climb, apparently for no reason. He crawled to the edge of the ledge and looked down. From there he could see another ledge immediately below where their enemies were positioned, with bows drawn, arrows waiting to be unleashed. As he peered below, with half his body extending from the ledge so that he could see clearly. He watched as the enemy continued to shoot their lethal arrows towards the *Aurora*. He felt helpless and started to feel his anger increase, a warmth started to flow through his body. He wanted so much for the rocks to fall on the hated enemy. Then he felt a rumble. Faint at first, the rumble turned into a roar of sliding rock as he felt the ground slipping under him. He quickly rolled to one side grasping a craggy piece of rock just as the ground from under him slipped away.

Morganuke clung on desperately as he watched the ledge he had been standing on disappear. He looked down to where the enemy had been stationed on the ledge below only to see a pile of rocks. He then heard a commotion from the houses where he'd seen the other enemies. He watched as Crouch and his men got their revenge on the remaining attackers.

The aftermath of the battle was a very sad scene. Morganuke watched from the deck of the *Aurora* as the enemy bodies that were retrievable were stacked up in the harbour and burnt by some of the crew. The bodies of Captain Amannar and ten *Aurora* crew lay on the deck. The *Aurora* survivors had sewn their dead comrades in sailcloth and added weights in readiness for committing to the sea.

Morganuke was only too glad to see the cargo unloaded after all the trouble it had caused. Fraytar hadn't bothered to question Vorderlan's involvement in the attacks and seemed only too glad to receive the payment. Once repairs and preparations for sailing had been completed, the crew got ready to set sail. With only half the crew, Morganuke knew that would be difficult. There was an uncanny silence as the ship left the harbour, with just the sound of the sea breeze and the waves against the ship. Morganuke thought of it as a lament for the fallen crew members, dropping his gaze to hide the tears in his eyes.

Once they were out at sea, Fraytar called the crew onto the deck where the wrapped bodies lay. He then cleared his throat to begin his speech, and nervously rubbed his injured arm, which had been bandaged.

"These men fought bravely and died so that we could prevail. Let us not forget them. Our captain lies here after bringing us safely through many dangers. His sacrifice will never be forgotten. Let us now lay these men to rest in the deep and ensure that we make the remainder of our lives worthy of their sacrifice."

With that, the bodies were gently carried to the edge of the ship and dropped into the ocean, one at a time. Once done, the men returned glum-faced to their duties.

Fraytar and Morganuke stood against the ship's rails looking down at the sea for several moments in silence.

"So, what now?" Morganuke asked solemnly.

"We return to Tannisport," Fraytar answered, without taking his eyes off the sea. "You have more than proved yourself, Morg my lad, but we now need to get you home, and I need to find replacements for the crewmembers that have been lost."

"Mordock, make for Tanisport," Fraytar called out to the helmsman.

Morganuke watched as Fraytar turned and walked towards the captain's cabin, his shoulders drooped and his head bowed. He went over all the events that had taken place over the past days. It was supposed to be a straightforward voyage to the other side of the island and yet so much had happened. More than once Morganuke's life had been put at risk. He'd discovered that he had some powers he knew nothing about, his strange portent dreams. It felt like a story from an action book, and he was one of the main characters. But it all felt so different from what he was used to. He'd been settled in his quiet island life for years. Did he really want to lead a life that was so unpredictable and dangerous. Part of him wanted to go out exploring on other exciting voyages with Fraytar, but then he also wanted to live the live he'd been used to. Did he really want to find out where he had come from that much/ It would mean leaving his parents and he knew that would upset them. It was a very difficult choice that he would have to make.

CHAPTER 6

The Returning Hero

It had been twenty days since the *Aurora* left Tannisport, and the surviving crew were glad to see its outline as they approached from the sea. The return journey from Cradport had been uneventful, although with only half a crew the work on board was heavy. Morganuke helped as the ship approached the harbour and go through the usual docking procedures, this time with more help from harbour workers.

Onlookers lined the harbour walls as the ship docked. The *Aurora* and its crew, especially captain Amannar, had been popular in Tannisport, and the townspeople were pleased to see them return. They were still unaware of the events at Cradport and the loss of the captain and half the crew. Morganuke followed with Crouch and other crewmen as Fraytar disembarked and with some hesitation went to meet the gathered townsfolk.

"Thank you all for coming to greet us," said Fraytar, a little reticent as he stood before them. "I'm afraid I have some bad news. Captain Amannar has been killed along with half the crew following an attack by Cordinen followers in Cradport." The crowd gasped. "If it had not been for this brave young man," Fraytar pushed Morganuke forward as he said the words, "we would have all been lost. This man is a hero and deserves to be recognised for that."

Morganuke was surprised by Fraytar's actions and took no joy in being the centre of attention. The crowd of onlookers had grown by now and began to clap and cheer. Some of the *Aurora* crew then picked Morganuke up and put him on their shoulders as they made their way through the streets towards the nearest inn.

"Morganuke! Morganuke! Morganuke!" chanted the crowd. Morganuke's face flushed, and he felt a little uncomfortable, he was not used to such attention from so many people. Previously most of the townspeople had shunned him, and now they were cheering him on the streets.

The doors of the Nibbling Fish Inn burst open as the crewmembers came in, still carrying Morganuke on their shoulders. He had to duck low to avoid hitting his head on the doorframe. They carried him to a table near the corner and demanded the innkeeper bring them ales all round.

Many of the townsfolk who had been at the harbour now started to enter the inn, and soon the place was a thronging hub of chatter. Although there was sadness over the loss of Captain Amannar and so many crew, the townsfolk had thought the *Aurora* completely lost. They had expected them to return days ago, and with every passing day, the people assumed the worst. So with the *Aurora*'s return the townsfolk were happy to show their appreciation.

Word rapidly spread across the town and to neighbouring villages about the *Aurora*'s return. More people came to see the crew and especially to see Morganuke, who had suddenly become the local hero. Even the town mayor put in an appearance to say a few words and to loan Morganuke a horse as an honour.

As day turned into evening and the crowds slowly melted away, Morganuke was left sitting at a table with Fraytar.

"I should be going home now to see my parents," Morganuke said, looking down into his mug of half-drunk ale. "My father is sure to be angry at me being away for so long after I said it would only be two weeks."

"I'm sure your mother and father will be delighted to see you," Fraytar said, slapping him on the back. "At least it shouldn't take long to get home on the horse the mayor has lent you. You just must remember what I told you about riding, and not fall off!"

The two men hugged each other. Morganuke left the inn to find his borrowed horse, and after two attempts mounting, he seated himself in the saddle and took up the reins. He had to think for a moment which direction he needed to go but was soon on his way. The moonlight between the odd clouds gave him just enough light to see where he was going, and the horse seemed an easy enough ride, once Morganuke had become accustomed to the saddle. It was a lot more comfortable than riding two up on Fraytar's horse.

At the farm Morganuke took the horse into one of the outhouses, removed the saddle, then watered and fed the horse. Turning to the farmhouse, he walked up the well-trodden path with no haste. He felt some reluctance to see his parents, even though he had missed them. He knew he had been away too long and was certain that they would be horrified to know the dangers he had been through.

But before he even got to the farmhouse, the door opened, and there stood his father. The two looked at each other in silence for moments, and then his father walked up to him and wrapped his arms around him.

"It's good to see thee, son," said his father breathlessly as he hugged him tight. "We thought we'd lost you."

"I'm sorry I was away for so long," answered Morganuke. "We had some delays on the journey."

"Come into the house, your mother is waiting to see you," said Stovin, wrapping an arm around Morganuke's shoulder and guided him into the farmhouse. His mother stood at the kitchen table with tears in her eyes. She took a hanky from her pocket, wiped her face, and then hugged her son. "It's so good to see you, son," she said. She sat him down at the kitchen table. "Do you want something to eat? You must be hungry."

With so much going on at the inn, Morganuke had forgotten to eat and so gladly accepted his mother's offer. After the meal, the three sat at the table, Stovin and Plarem looking on in expectation to hear what Morganuke had been up to. He told them everything that had happened: the attacks on the ship, the storm, the becalming, the conditions on board, and finally the battle at Cradport.

"So much for being a safe voyage as Fraytar had promised," Stovin concluded.

"It's not his fault. No one knew what was going to happen and that the Cordinens already had folk on the island. It was a complete surprise to everyone," Morganuke said.

Stovin sighed and scratched his chin thoughtfully for a moment. "So what now? Will the great Captain Fraytar be expecting you to sail away with him for more of his mad adventures?"

Morganuke kept silent for a moment before answering. "He needs to find new crewmembers to replace those lost, but I will not be going with him. I'll work on the farm with you, Father. I also want to work with Tomlin; a blacksmith will be useful on the farm."

Stovin looked relieved and gave a deep sigh. "As long as you are sure, son. That'll please me."

The next day, Morganuke got up early and helped his father with the daily chores. He felt that the routine farming activities was a pleasant return to normality. His experiences on the *Aurora* over the last few weeks seemed a distant memory now, almost like a dream.

Later that day, Morganuke decided to pay a visit to Tomlin to discuss plans for apprenticing as a smithy. The odd day in the smithy would still allow time for him to work on the farm, and his learnt skills would become useful for his father. So as soon as he returned to the farmhouse, he went to ready the horse lent to him by the mayor. He was still a little bit unsure about riding, but the horse had a good temperament, which gave Morganuke the confidence to ride him alone.

The ride to Tomlin's was pleasant enough, with the warmth of the afternoon sun and a slight cooling breeze wafting the sweet smell of freshly cut hay from the neighbouring fields. Morganuke thought guiltily about the hay he had promised to help his father harvest before he was away at sea. Still, he was back now and would make up for lost time as best he could. The rhythmic plodding of the horse had a soothing effect on Morganuke, making him feel surprisingly at ease. Even the prospect of seeing Calarel did not unnerve him, as he was determined not to make a fool of himself this time.

Outside Tomlin's workshop, Morganuke slid clumsily from the saddle, almost stumbling when he reached the ground. *I hope Calarel isn't watching*, he thought as he tied the horse to the railing. He heard the familiar and pleasing clang, clang, clang of Tomlin's hammer coming from the forge. Inside the workshop, he was greeted with the familiar site of Tomlin bent over the anvil with hammer in hand and face as black as soot. Tomlin carefully studied the metal he was shaping, oblivious of Morganuke's presence.

"Hello, Tomlin!" Morganuke finally shouted loud enough for Tomlin to hear him.

Tomlin turned around, and a look of delight appeared on his sooty face when he recognised who it was. "Morg! It's good to see he, and be a hero now I hear." Tomlin put down his hammer and the metal he was working on, and gave Morganuke a solid hug, leaving sooty stains down his already discoloured shirt. "Come in, come into the cottage, and tell us all about your adventures. I'm sure Calarel would love to hear bout 'em too."

The two made their way into the little cottage, and to Morganuke's delight, Calarel already stood at the kitchen table preparing vegetables. Her long brown hair pulled across one of her shoulders. Her eyes looked up briefly at Morganuke, and he felt his stomach go light as she did so. Although Morganuke did blush slightly, he acted as dignified as he could, and with a confident stride he walked across the kitchen and sat opposite Calarel at the table. Then he remembered that he had not changed his clothes since leaving the ship and thought that Calarel would probably think he smelt. *Smell or not, I'm determined not to make a fool of myself in front of her*, he thought. *I'm the local hero when all said and done.*

"Hello, Calarel," Morganuke said. "How are you?"

To Morganuke's surprise, Calarel gave him a smile and answered,

"I'm well thank you, Morg, and how are you? I hear you've been up to lots."

"Yes, he has," Tomlin put in, "and he's goin' to tell us all about it."

Tomlin and Calarel sat wide-eyed, listening intently as Morganuke told them about the voyage to Cradport. They both oohed and aahed at the dangerous and exciting bits of the story. It was difficult for Morganuke when he got to the last battle in Cradport, and he found his voice trembling at times when he told of how Captain Amannar and his crew were cut down by their attackers. But overall Morganuke told the story clearly and confidently, which made an impression on Tomlin and especially Calarel.

Calarel leant forward and took Morganuke's hand. "You were very brave, and I'm sure the crew will be ever grateful to you."

Morganuke felt himself blushing at this and instinctively withdrew his hand, then immediately regretted doing so. He made himself not look down but look into her eyes, which were wide and looking directly at him. "Thank you, Calarel, that is very sweet of you."

"Now then, me lovelies, those stories deserve an ale or two," interjected Tomlin. He went to a nearby cupboard, took out three mugs, poured ale into each, and then set them on the table. "Let's drink to Morganuke and the crew of the *Aurora*," he toasted. They all drank then sat in silence for several moments to remember the lost.

Morganuke finished off the last drops of ale from his tankard before getting to the real reason for his visit. "I've come here to ask he about helping in your workshop, Tomlin."

"Course, me boy," answered Tomlin with a broad smile on his still sooty face. "He knows you're always welcome to start working yeer soon's you like."

"Well, all that ale and talking 'as made me want a swim in the sea. It'll cool me down lovely," Calarel announced, getting up from the table. "So if he'll excuse me, I'll go to the beach."

"I can take you if you like," Morganuke offered quickly.

"Take me? How can you take me? Give me a piggyback you mean?" Calarel answered with a laugh.

Morganuke blushed again. "No, I have a horse, so I can give you a ride to the beach."

Calarel looked surprised, her eyes widening and her mouth gaping open. "A horse, you say? Well, I never! Who would have believed it? Morganuke with a horse. Right then, I'll get me things and meet you outside."

As Calarel disappeared, Tomlin gave Morganuke an awkward smile and said, "Mind you be careful on that 'orse. They can be cantankerous so-'n'-sos. I knows, I've been kicked a few times while shooing 'em. When can I expect you for your first day's work?"

"Don't worry, Tomlin. I'll be careful, and the horse has a good nature," Morganuke assured him before turning the subject back to his apprenticeship. "How does in two days' time sound?"

"That'll do nicely."

When Morganuke got outside, he was surprised to see Calarel already mounted on the horse with reins in hand. "Jump on the back then," she said, looking at Morganuke as if to challenge him.

With a frustrated sigh, Morganuke scrambled up on the back of the horse, with some help from Calarel. As soon as he was seated behind her, she dug her heels into the side of the horse and shouted, "Let's go!"

Morganuke desperately clung on to Calarel as they cantered down the lane and out of the town. He could feel the warmth of her body in his arms and her long hair tickling him as it blew in his face, making it difficult for him to see where they were going. It didn't take them long to reach the beach, and Morganuke was a little disappointed when they arrived. He released his grip from Calarel and awkwardly slid off the horse. She jumped off with ease and tethered the reins to a nearby small bush.

"Come on then, slow pants. I'll race you to the sea!" Calarel began running down the beach. Morganuke stood and watched her as she ran. She wore very modest clothes, which she began to take off as she ran—shoes, big baggy britches and a jerkin, which were discarded onto the sand. She was left wearing just a loosely fitting shirt. Her long brown hair blew wildly in the sea breeze as she ran. To Morganuke's surprise, she jumped straight into the sea.

"What are you doing about your clothes?" Morganuke called out as he ran to the edge of the sea.

"If you think I'm going to swim with no clothes, then you can think again," Calarel snapped.

Morganuke's face turned bright pink as he realised how his words had sounded. "I only meant …" He trailed off mid-sentence as Calarel laughed and splashed in the sea and he realised she was just teasing. Picking up the discarded clothes, he hung them on the bushes next to the horse. He watched Calarel splash in the water as he made his way back to the sea's edge, then lay back in the sand, listening to her giggles of delight and the waves washing up on the beach.

He was starting to doze when he felt a splash of water on his face. "Come on, lazybones, why don't you come in too? It's not too cold—if you leave your clothes on. that is," she teased as she splashed seawater at him again. Morganuke got to his feet, chased her into the water, and started splashing her back until with a giggle she ran to deeper water and started swimming in the opposite direction.

As Morganuke turned to go back to his spot on the beach, he caught sight of a dark shape moving in the bushes on the bank. He looked closely but could see nothing there. *Strange*, he thought, *must be an animal or something*.

After a while Calarel came back to the beach and sat down beside Morganuke. She was wringing wet from the seawater, and her shirt clung to her skin, almost see through. Morganuke could see the outline of her shapely body. He blushed and turned to look out at the sea.

"You should put some dry clothes on, or you'll get cold," Morganuke said as he lay back down on the sand.

"You trying to get me to take my clothes off again?" Calarel joked.

"Of course not, I'm just worried you'll get cold, that's all," replied Morganuke, closing his eyes and resting his head into the warm sand.

"Then what have you done with my clothes?" She bent her head forward and shook water from her long hair, which fell down so it covered her chest and the top of her thighs.

"I'll get them for you," Morganuke said, jumping to his feet. "They're hung up next to the horse."

As he reached the horse, he again thought he saw a shadowy object moving in the bushes just beyond. This time he heard a faint rustling as well. He walked over to the source of the noise to investigate but found nothing.

When he returned, Calarel was lying on her back in the sand, on the verge of sleep. Her chest rose and fell with her deep breathing. Morganuke draped her jerkin and bridges over her, causing her to jump. She sat up, pulled the jerkin over her head, and wiggled into the britches whilst Morganuke took a seat next to her. The two sat there looking out to sea for some time as the sun sank lower in the sky.

By the time Morganuke and Calarel had returned to Tomlin's, it was completely dark. Morganuke was feeling a little dejected, thinking he had missed another opportunity to impress her. They got down from the horse, which this time was a lot easier for Morganuke as he had now given up trying to impress.

"I'll say good night, Calarel," Morganuke said as he turned towards the horse. But something pulled him back; it was Calarel's hand in his. She gently pulled him towards her and softly kissed him on the cheek.

"Good night, Morg. Thank you for today. I have enjoyed your company." With that, she turned and went into the farmhouse, closing the door quietly behind her.

Morganuke stood watching the cottage for a few moments before mounting his horse and trotting out of the town towards his home. Clouds had gathered in the sky, and so there was no moonlight to show the way. Morganuke had to go carefully. His horse continued at a walk, and Morganuke knew it would follow the track.

Halfway home, he thought he heard horses coming up behind him. He stopped his horse and looked around to see who might be following, but the sound of horses now stopped. Convinced he was being followed, he pressed forward, digging his heels into his horse, which promptly galloped down the lane. Morganuke desperately held onto the reins, hoping his horse wouldn't crash into something.

He was relieved when he reached the farmhouse with no further signs of anyone following him. *Did I imagine that?* he thought, *but I was sure someone has been following me today.*

The summer days passed by peacefully. Morganuke continued to work on his father's farm and occasionally in Tomlin's smithy. By late summer, Morganuke was more proficient at blacksmithing and enjoyed applying the new skills he had learnt. On the farm the harvesting had been completed, and the daily tasks were back to a routine steady pace. Morganuke had made a name for himself with the local townsfolk, and they welcomed him whenever they saw him. His relationship with Calarel was getting stronger, and they regularly went on walks or to the beach for a swim. Morganuke hadn't experienced any more feelings that he was being followed and felt less threatened by the war still raging on the mainland.

Maybe things are all right after all, and I can be planning my life settled on the island with Calarel, he thought as he made his way to Tomlin's for a day of work in the smithy. *My differences are less important now that the islanders are more accepting, so I should be happy with living this life. Finding my origins seems less important somehow.*

When he reached Tomlin's smithy, he saw a huge workhorse tethered outside, a magnificent specimen, black with a white stripe down its nose and white on all four legs from the knees down to the feathered hooves. Its withers were a good hand taller than Morganuke, and feeling a little intimidated as he walked past the animal to get into Tomlin's workshop, he gave it plenty of space. The massive horse snorted loudly and nodded its head up and down as Morganuke entered the workshop.

As usual, Tomlin was there to greet him and gave Morganuke a broad sooty smile. "Ah, just in time, Morg. I've an important job for he today. I'm shoeing that big 'orse outside and need you to lift his foot for me. It'll be good experience for he."

Morganuke gaped in disbelief. "How am I going to lift the foot of a great beast like that?"

"Never he mind, 'tis easy really. I'll show he," answered Tomlin as he guided Morganuke out of the workshop and towards the horse. "Now watch me." Tomlin slowly walked up to the horse and rested his hand on its rump before gently patting it. He then went to the nearest foreleg, ran his hand gently downwards until he got just above the ankle, and gave a gentle squeeze. The massive horse visibly shifted its weight from that leg, allowing Tomlin to lift the hoof and tuck its hock against his thigh. To Morganuke's amazement, the horse just stood there, still as can be on three legs, with Tomlin holding the fourth. He then invited Morganuke to do the same. At first Morganuke was a little apprehensive, but after he patted the horse and did the same thing to lift the horse's leg, he felt quite comfortable.

With Morganuke holding each leg in turn and Tomlin removing the old shoe and replacing it with a new one, the horse was shod in quick time. Morganuke felt pleased that he had overcome his fear of the great beast, but it had been as quiet and soft as anything.

With the horse shod, it was time to return it to its owner. Tomlin suggested that Morganuke ride it bareback, whilst he would ride in front and lead it. Tomlin suggested that the experience would do him good and help him get used to being around large animals. Morganuke thought that was easier said than done. He had trouble mounting a normal-sized horse and had never been entirely comfortable with the horse the mayor had lent him earlier in the summer. He was none too sorry when the horse had to go back.

"That be all the more reason why he should ride the beast, me boy."

"How do I get on his back?" Morganuke asked.

"Now, don't show him you're afraid! Climb onto that wall. I'll lead him up to you," Tomlin said.

Morganuke climbed onto the wall, and when Tomlin brought the horse alongside, Morganuke stretched across and clumsily hung over the horse's back like a sack of turnips. Amazingly, the horse just stood there, patiently waiting for Morganuke to correct his seating. It seemed odd without any saddle or stirrups, but the horse's girth was so big that Morganuke still felt comfortable enough. Holding on to its mane, he waited for Tomlin to mount and start leading the way.

With Tomlin riding his horse and leading the workhorse carrying

Morganuke, they made their way down a dusty sidetrack that bordered Morganuke's home farm. Although Morganuke recognised where he was, he wasn't sure what direction they were going in. "Where are we heading?"

"Brackish Manor estate," Tomlin answered as he puffed on a long clay pipe, leaving wisps of smoke trails as they went. "The beast you be sitting on's one of Lord Brackish's main workhorses, and so he's keen to get it back. It should take the rest of the day to get there and back, so I hope you haven't got other plans for today."

Morganuke nodded and resigned himself to the journey ahead. He had been hoping to see Calarel today, but that would have to wait. He was happy enough to help Tomlin where he could, and it didn't seem so bad riding on the big horse. To make up time where the main track was level, Tomlin started a slow trot. The big horse jogged gently along, and Morganuke tightly clenched his legs around its girth whilst he held on to the mane. The late summer had brought shorter days, and Tomlin said he wanted to get back before darkness set in.

At the halfway point, they reached Crowsfeet Hills. They rested there a short time to eat the packed lunch that Tomlin brought with him. Getting off the big horse had been a little bit of a struggle, and getting back on was even more difficult. They found a ledge on the hillside to use as a platform to launch Morganuke onto the massive beast before setting off again.

It was midway through the afternoon by the time they'd reached Brackish Woods, which marked the southern boundary of the Brackish manor estate. The sunlight shone through the leaves like shards of bright spindles as they trotted on the leaf-covered track. A dampness in the air hinted of the oncoming autumn.

Once through the wood, they came to the manor house gates, which Tomlin jumped down to open before leading the two horses onward. The track to the manor house was lined with tall trees and wound its way around well-tended gardens. As they approached the house, Morganuke could see a man standing on the veranda, sipping a glass of something. Lord Brackish, he assumed it was. He looked like the typical wealthy estate owner, dressed in a brightly coloured tunic and surcoat with fine leather britches and riding boots. As soon as he saw them, he made his way down, looking delighted at the sight of the big horse.

"General!" Lord Brackish greeted the big horse, patted its neck and rubbing its nose. "It's good to see you back, and with new shoes." After welcoming Tomlin, he looked at Morganuke, who'd just managed to slide off the horses back by himself before a stable hand appeared and led the big animal away. "Hello, young man. By the look of it, you must be the local hero I've been hearing so much about. I can't think of anyone else in our district that have such distinctive features?"

Before Morganuke could say anything, Tomlin answered, "The very same, Me Lord. He is the toast of Tannisport. This is Morganuke, Me Lord. He is working as my apprentice,"

"It's good to meet you, Morganuke," Lord Brackish said. "I've heard a lot about your exploits and bravery. We shall need men like you as soldiers in the militia."

Morganuke hadn't really thought about the war and the impact on the island since getting back to normal life. Things had been very normal and routine in his life for some time now, and he had lost track of what was going on in the bigger world.

"Militia? Has it really come to that, My Lord?" Morganuke asked.

"Yes, I'm afraid it has. We must protect ourselves from mainland raiding parties. I hear more and more about Cordinen spies every day. I intend to organise a militia in association with other parts of the island communities in the east as soon as possible so that we can protect ourselves. I hope you are with me on this, Morganuke."

"I don't know about the militia, but I will do whatever is necessary to protect my family and my home," Morganuke answered.

Lord Brackish smiled. "I think we want the same thing and doing it together would be the best approach. You seem well spoken. What education have you had?"

"In addition to my normal schooling, I was tutored by Professor Westmund," Morganuke replied. "He took a particular interest in me due to my unusual features and unknown lineage. He wanted me to become a gentleman but that was never possible."

"Ah, yes Obledier Westmund," Lord Brenadere acknowledged. "I knew him well and was very sorry when he died last year. You must miss his guidance. It seems he has taught you well."

"Yes, My Lord, I will miss him."

Anyway, please think on what I have said, and hopefully you will agree to join when we start to assemble the militia. You could make a good officer candidate." Then he turned to Tomlin. "Tomlin, will you stay for a meal?"

"Begging your pardon, Me Lord, but we need to get back home before darkness falls," answered Tomlin.

"Then I will get your payment and let you be on your way."

The business quickly concluded, Tomlin and Morganuke started their return journey on Tomlin's horse. Tomlin kept as fast a pace as he could, cantering the horse where possible. By the time they had returned to Peblock, the sun was just setting on the horizon.

"Well, there it be, Morg. A good day's work done, and a good bit of business with His Lordship. He's an important man round these parts, so 'tis best to keep in with him, me boy," Tomlin said, climbing down from the horse and then helping Morganuke down too.

"He does seem nice, but I'm not sure about what he said about the militia," Morganuk answered cautiously. "Seems a bit extreme to me and will probably stir up trouble, but I'll think some more about it." He set off towards his home, still feeling a little disappointed at not getting to see Calarel that day.

CHAPTER 7

Settling Down

With the first days of autumn arriving, it was time to prepare for the harvest fair. There would be competitions, dancing and music, a time for the locals to get together and enjoy themselves. It was a chance not only to celebrate the successful harvest but to distract from the recent troubles that the mainland war had brought. Morganuke hoped that this year would be different for him, as in previous years he had been shunned by the townsfolk. Now he was considered a local hero, so things should be different. It was also an opportunity for Morganuke to get together with Fraytar and the *Aurora* crew again.

In the days leading up to the fair, the townsfolk had been busy setting up tents and show areas in a large field next to the town. Folk had been preparing their exhibits for the competitions, ranging from cakes to vegetables. Animals, too, were prepared for competition as the local farmers took pride in their stock and wanted to show them off, hoping to win a prize as well.

On the day of the fair, Morganuke and his father led their show animals to the fairground on foot. The prize of Stovin's animal stock was a calf and a sheep that had come second at last year's fair in the best-of category. He was hoping for better this year and had spent considerable time tending to the animal to make sure. Plarem followed the men to the showground, wheeling her freshly baked cakes and preserves in a wooden cart, hoping that her hard work would not go to waste from being knocked about on the uneven tracks that led to the fairground.

It was still early morning when they arrived, but a lot of people had already started assembling their own entries for the various competitions. Flags lined the track leading up to the fairgrounds, with big, coloured banners marking the entrance. There were signs of keen anticipation among the folk gathering there, for this was one of the biggest events of the year.

Once the animals had been taken to their holding area, there was a lot of waiting about until the competition started in each category. The first to go was the calf. It was Morganuke's task to lead the animal around the show ring. At first the calf refused to go anywhere. It took some coaxing from Stovin and Morganuke before it would even move. But in the show ring, it seemed that the animal had a natural talent for showing itself off, walking faultlessly around the ring. When it was Stovin's prize sheep's turn, it allowed itself to be led into the show ring with no difficulty at all. The results brought third place for the calf and another second place for the sheep—not too bad, but Stovin was still a little disappointed for not getting first place. Morganuke on the other hand, was very pleased with the result, considering the difficulty he had had with the calf to start with. The men showed a playful annoyance, when they learnt that Plarem managed to get one of her cakes in first place and a pot of preserve in second. This was an achievement indeed, and she didn't let her husband or son forget it.

With the competitions over, the festivities were about to begin, but not before Mayor Dorian Fellmen gave his annual speech. He stood on a box in front of the crowd, wearing a brightly coloured waistcoat which stretched at the seams from his large pot belly. Mayor Fellmen shuffled his numerous pages of written speech and cleared his throat.

"We are gathered on this happy occasion to give thanks for this year's harvest and all the good things that we have in our community. The many years that I have been mayor I have always … ."

As Morganuke thought about all the things that had really happened this past year, the mayor's voice drifted off into the background noise. The mayor's speeches were boring at the best of times. Morganuke was about to move away from the crowd when he noticed Calarel crouched behind the mayor's box. He couldn't see what she was doing but thought it was something that she shouldn't. He caught her eye, and she quickly put a finger to her lips and smiled before creeping away.

Mayor Fellmen's speech seemed to go on forever, although Morganuke wasn't listening to what he was saying. *The pompous little man is taking these opportunities to build himself up in the eyes of the people*, thought Morganuke. The mayor became more animated towards the end; he flung his arms about, pointed his finger, and punched his fist into his other hand. When he finished there was feeble applause from the people closest to him, and he gave an overly grandiose bow. Suddenly, as he turned to walk down the makeshift steps from the box he was standing on, there was a loud crash, and he went tumbling face first into the muddy ground below. Not being able to contend with himself, Morganuke gave out a loud raucous laugh, which drew a dark look from his parents. Luckily for Morganuke, others were laughing as well, and so he got away with it. He knew that Calarel must've been the cause of the mayor's mishap, which made him think even more highly of her.

After the mayor had picked himself up and scuttled off in embarrassment, the music and fun began. A group of four men in the corner of the main tent struck up the music and singing, which attracted a crowd of revellers to start dancing inside and outside the tent.

Calarel suddenly appeared in front of Morganuke. "Will you dance with me?" she asked, holding out her arms.

"Well, er, I can't dance," Morganuke answered clumsily.

"Don't worry, just jig along to the beat and do what I do," Calarel insisted as she dragged him into the dance area.

At first it was all Morganuke could do to avoid stepping on Calarel's toes. He watched her feet closely as he tried to keep to the beat. Calarel gracefully moved rhythmically to the music. Eventually Morganuke managed to imitate Calarel and keep good time. As his dancing and timing improved, they moved closer together, ending up arm in arm, moving across the dance floor as one.

When the music stopped, Calarel giggled in delight. "That was fun. You're not a bad dancer, Morg."

Morganuke felt his face colour but kept looking at Calarel. "Thank you, I enjoyed that. I'll go and get us some drinks."

As Morganuke headed towards the ale corner, he heard a couple of familiar voices. Turning, he saw Fraytar and Crouch at the side of the tent talking to each other.

"Hello, Fraytar, Crouch. good see you again," said Morganuke as he walked over to shake their hands.

"Hello, Morg. How are you? Looks like you're having fun with the blacksmith's daughter. She's a pretty girl. I'm glad for you," Fraytar answered with a toothy grin.

Morganuke blushed. "We're just dancing, that's all."

"Well, I'm glad I caught you, because we're leaving in the morning. We've finally been able to replace the crew and will be setting sail for the south of the mainland. Hopefully the war hasn't reached those parts yet, and we desperately need to make some money."

"It's a long time to be doing nothing. Have you not been sailing at all since returning from Cradport?" Morganuke asked.

"Just short trade trips, two days at the most, but doesn't pay enough. So further afield we must go and try our luck on the mainland again. You're always welcome to join us, you know that, don't you? But I understand if you can't."

"I wish I'd spent more time with you whilst you were here. I've been wrapped up in my own things and now the opportunity has gone. I can't leave the farm now. My life is settled here. But I wish you all the luck." Still, Morganuke felt a bit glum. "I'll be sure to watch you leave in the morning to say goodbye."

"Well, that be that. Now let's get some more ale," Crouch joined in, putting his arms around Fraytar's and Morganuke's shoulders before leading them to the ale corner.

On the way to the ale corner, Morganuke caught up with Calarel and invited her along. Other members of the crew eventually joined them, and many ales were drunk by all that night. Some of the crew took turns to try and impress Calarel, who took it in good order.

"This crew is a good bunch," Calarel whispered in Morganuke's ear.

Morganuke just smiled at her with a slight nod, thinking, *You haven't been sailing with them.*

The next day, Morganuke was feeling a little delicate after the previous night's ales. Nevertheless, he was determined to get to Tannisport to say farewell to the *Aurora* crew. When he arrived at the docks, the crew had already boarded the ship and were making final preparations to set sail. The gangplank was still down, and Morganuke quickly made his way on board and found Fraytar directing activities on the lower deck.

"So, this is it then," Morganuke said. "You really are finally leaving Tannisport."

"Sure I can't talk you into coming with us?" Fraytar asked.

"I'm sure. My days of expeditions and voyages are done, at least for now," Morganuke answered.

"I have something for you." Fraytar turned to make his way to the upper foredeck and gestured for Morganuke to come.

Morganuke followed Fraytar to the captain's cabin, which was now his. Fraytar rummaged around in one of the cupboards. Finally he brought out a sword and placed it on the desk in front of Morganuke. "This sword was placed in the container I found you in as a baby. I've kept all this time intending to give it to you when you became a man. I don't know its significance but can only guess that such a valuable item such as this is of some importance from where you came from. Look after it and make sure you learn to use it well."

Morganuke took the sword out of its intricate leather scabbard and studied it, open-mouthed, for several moments. The blade shone, and emeralds were embedded in the hilt. "This is a magnificent sword. Must be worth a lot. Why would such an item be left with me?" He ran his finger over the blade and jumped when he felt a stinging pain, where he cut his finger. Blood dripped onto the cabin floor. "It's still very sharp. You've been sharpening it well, Fraytar."

"No I haven't. It's as it was when I found it. I can't guess what metal it's made from. I've never seen a sword like it before. As for its significance, that's something that you will need to discover."

"Maybe you should keep this Fraytar," Morganuke suggested. "Maybe it was left as a gift for anyone who found and helped me."

"You do deserve it, Morg. The sword is yours. It's part of your heritage. No arguments, it's yours." Fraytar replied with a dismissive wave of his hand. "Now, I've got a ship to sail, so let's say our farewell and get you off board."

Fraytar walked Morganuke back to the gangplank, where they embraced before Morganuke left the ship. The gangplank was removed, and then a cheer went up from the crew. "Three cheers for Morganuke! Hurrah! Hurrah! Hurrah!"

Morganuke stood on the dock holding the sword that Fraytar had given him in his hand. He watched the *Aurora* set sail out to sea, not knowing when or if he would see the crew again.

For the next few days Morganuke settled into his routines on the farm and at Tomlin's workshop. The autumn weather was setting in, and the leaves were turning into a rich tapestry of reds and browns. On occasion his thoughts went out to the *Aurora* crew, wondering what they were up to and hoping that they were still safe. Little more had been said about the mainland war in the local community and what this could mean for the island. Morganuke knew that this situation couldn't last forever, as he remembered what Lord Brackish had said about setting up a militia on the island.

On one particularly cold rainy day, Tomlin told Morganuke that he had another delivery to Brackish Manor, this time a consignment of farm tools that Lord Brackish had commissioned. They would need to be delivered by horse and cart. Tomlin asked if Morganuke could make the delivery on his own.

Morganuke had driven Tomlin's horse and cart before, but only on short runs in the village, certainly not one as long as the trip to Brackish Manor. He felt anxious about going all that way on his own.

"Just be sure that he keeps to the main track, and take it steady," Tomlin urged Morganuke as they loaded the last of the tools on the cart. "Don't be tempted to take shortcuts, as the way can be dangerous off the main track."

Morganuke nodded in compliance before jumping up onto the cart. He bid Tomlin farewell and set off down the familiar track towards Brackish Manor, the load of tools rattling loudly in the cart. It was still early in the day, and few people were about in the village. Morganuke was nearing the edge of town when his heart stopped and he felt himself going to a cold sweat. Disappearing behind one of the houses ahead was a man with a large scar on his face. He was sure it was the same man they had taken prisoner on the *Aurora*, the one who had escaped in Fettleridge. He spurred his horse on to a fast trot, which made the tools in the cart jangle harder as the wheels struck ruts in the track. As he drove past the house where he had seen the scar-faced man, Morganuke craned his head to look but saw no sign of him.

As Morganuke reached the main Tannisport road, he slowed the pace of the horse slightly, still wary about his surroundings and whether anyone was following him. He continued the gentle trot. This road was more even and a little wider, making for a more comfortable and less noisy ride. A cool breeze and drizzle left him cold and damp. He drove on for another hour, the plod, plod, plod of the horse's hooves and the gentle rattling of the tools making him quite drowsy. He pulled his cape tightly around himself, trying to keep warm and alert.

As he was nearing the branch to Lost Man's Caves, he heard hooves galloping on the banks above him. Although he couldn't see anybody, he feared the hidden riders were readying for an ambush ahead. He had been nervous about being followed ever since Fraytar had told him about the silver haired people with the Cordinens. The thought of the war reaching the island had also made him anxious.

He stopped the cart for a moment, wondering what to do. *Shall I take a shortcut through Lost Man's Caves? Tomlin said to keep on the main track.* Making his decision, he shook the reins and urged the horse into a canter. When he got to the fork in the road, he took the Lost Man's Caves track, not knowing what was ahead but convincing himself that the shortcut would be the best route.

The track became more and more uneven the further he went. The tools in the cart were rattling and bouncing so hard that they were almost falling out, but Morganuke didn't slow down. He was tossed about on the hard bench seat, almost falling out more than once, but still, he didn't slow down, too fearful of what might be following him. Then, as he came around a sharp bend in the track, there was a loud crack as one of the wheels was thrown off. Morganuke went flying sideways off the cart, landing hard on the ground. Everything went black.

When Morganuke came to, he was lying in a pool of water. His head was throbbing and felt tight down his forehead. He put his hand up to feel and winced as his fingers discovered a cut on his forehead. The light was fading in the sky and not just due to the clouds. Although the rain had stopped, the night was drawing on. He gradually sat up and looked around. The cart was a little way down the track, with one wheel missing and all the tools scattered. The horse was still harnessed to the cart and whinnied when it saw Morganuke moving. Feeling cold to the bone and with his teeth chattering, Morganuke slowly got to his feet and stumbled towards the horse, crawling for the last few paces. Wet, cold, and suffering from a bang on the head, he knew that he had to find shelter and warmth or perish.

Once he had disentangled the horse from the cart, Morganuke climbed gingerly onto its back and rode in a direction he hoped would take him to shelter. He had gone about a five hundred paces when he arrived at some caves. *This must be Lost Man's Caves*, he thought. *I'll shelter here.* There were caves on either side of the narrow track and so he dismounted to investigate the closest. The first two were flooded and not suitable for shelter. By the time he got to the third cave, he felt dizzy and found it difficult to keep his feet. He stumbled into the cave entrance and thankfully found it to be dry inside, and large enough to bring the horse in.

Morganuke struggled to tether the horse inside the cave on some exposed roots and looked around for some suitable material to make a fire. Everything outside was soaked from the earlier rain, and so his search was limited to inside the cave. The light was becoming dim, making it difficult to see anything. He stumbled on some old crates that looked as though they had been there for years. The wood was very dry.

"Now to start a fire," Morganuke said out loud. He broke down the crates and piled the wood. "Father showed me how once but have never tried it on my own. Now how did he do it? Hm. I need to make small bow to help turn a piece of dry wood against some dry kindling."

It was almost dark and Morganuke froze in terror when he heard a wolve howl from somewhere outside. Morganuke scrabbled desperately around outside and within the cave to find the materials he needed as quickly as possible. His heart pounded in his chest as he heard more wolves howling. Driven now by fear, he ignored his pain.

He managed to find a supple branch for the bow outside. It was wet, but that didn't matter. To this he attached the two ends of a leather lace from his tunic to make a small makeshift bow, then fastened a dry piece of crate wood to the middle of the leather bowstring. For the kindling he used the dry moss and lichen he had found. Morganuke placed one end of the dry wood against the kindling and the other against his palm to hold it in place. Moving the bow from side to side, he was able to make the dry wood turn quickly. By now his hands were freezing, and his teeth chattered uncontrollably, making it difficult to keep everything in place and the wood turning. Again and again he tried, getting colder and more tired. His hands grew sore, and he could hardly feel anything.

"It's no good," Morganuke despaired, as the wolves continued to howl.

He flopped down onto the cold ground of the cave. Desperate to get warm and safe, he closed his eyes and tried to imagine being in front of a fire. He tried so hard that he thought he smelled smoke, and opening his eyes, he saw an ember in the kindling. He quickly blew on it. The small flame grew larger until all the kindling was burning. Then he began adding small pieces of wood from the crates, gradually increasing the size of the pieces as the fire took hold. At last, with the comforting flames flickering. he huddled close to the fire.

When the fire began to die down, Morganuke added more wood. He was warming up now, and his teeth stopped chattering. He took off his sodden clothes and spread them beside the fire, but kept the cape wrapped closely around him. He knew he couldn't fall asleep. He had to keep the fire going, not only for warmth but to keep the wild animals away. He had heard wolves howling from outside as he was building up the fire. He stood no chance without it.

Morganuke kept the fire going all night. He started to drift off on the odd occasion, but quickly jerked awake as he felt himself falling forward. By shear willpower he had managed to stay awake on the whole.

At last, the first signs of daybreak appeared across the cave wall opposite the entrance several steps from where Morganuke was sitting. Morganuke struggled to get up. His legs were feeling wobbly, and he felt very exhausted. The horse gave a whinny as Morganuke approached it, before patting its neck and learning against its warm body for support.

Without the cart, Morganuke made good time and was soon riding up the winding path towards the manor house. He was exhausted and his head throbbed. The plod, plod, plod of the horse's hooves was mesmerizing, and he caught himself falling asleep again. He slapped his face several times to keep awake.

At last he reached the manor house and clambered off the horse. He stumbled up the steps to bang on the main door of the house. A footman dressed in a white wig and a red tunic opened the door.

"Is the lord of the house in?" Morganuke asked, bending down to keep his balance.

"Lord Brackish is sleeping. Who may I say is calling?" the footman asked.

"Please tell him that Morganuke is calling. It's important. I have news about his new tools," Morganuke said urgently.

"You really should use the service entrance," the footman said loftily. "I cannot disturb Lord Brackish this early in the day. Please wait out back." The door was hastily closed.

Morganuke resigned himself to having to wait. He walked wearily across the lawns to a garden gazebo beside the manor's hedge. He lay on a fixed bench inside the shelter and immediately fell asleep.

"What are you doing here, you layabout!" a well-dressed young man was shouting as one of the servants shook Morganuke hard.

Morganuke woke with a jump, squinting up at the man who'd spoken, and replied, "What? Er, I'm here to deliver tools to Lord Brackish. Who are you?"

"How dare you. Get off my father's estate immediately! Tavish, escort this man off the estate."

Morganuke looked the young man up and down. He looked a little older than Morganuke's and did bear some resemblance to Lord Brackish. He wore a black fur hat bejewelled and red-feathered, a bright blue satin tunic, and embroidered knee-high boots with metal buckles. Around his neck was a heavy gold chain and pendant, and the rings on most of his fingers each had a single but large jewel. Despite his lack of sleep and hurting head, Morganuke felt an irresistible urge to hit the pompous young man. He refrained and instead asked politely in an official-sounding voice, "Please inform your father that there as been an accident and I need help to recover his tools."

The young man stepped forward and sneered, "How dare you give me orders? Now do as I say and get off this land now. Tavish, get this man off the estate!"

Neither of them noticed that Lord Brackish had appeared. "What's all this about?" he asked.

"This impudent fool has lost your tools," his son snapped.

"Morganuke—it's Morganuke, isn't it?—tell me what has happened," Lord Brackish asked.

Visibly surprised that his father knew Morganuke, the young man nevertheless persisted. "I told you, Father, he's lost your tools—"

Lord Brackish held up his hand to interrupt. "Silence, Justin. Let Morganuke answer, and please give him some respect. Sometimes you are more like the Epleons than I care to like."

"There was an accident on the way here, My Lord. A wheel came off the cart and I was thrown to the ground and knocked unconscious. I had to shelter in the caves before coming here. The tools are scattered and need to be recovered and … begging your pardon, My Lord, but the cart also needs repairs," Morganuke blurted, relieved to get it all out at last.

"You have blood on your head," Lord Brackish observed. "Come into the house and we'll see to your wounds whilst I get someone to recover the tools and your cart." He beckoned Morganuke towards the house.

Inside the lavish manor house, Lord Brackish sent some of his men to recover the cart and the tools, and Morganuke was taken to the servants' quarters. One of the maids washed and bandaged his wounded head, and once his wounds had been attended to, he was taken to a bedroom to recover. The room was small and plain with a single bed to one side. A basin and a jug of water were placed on a table next to the bed. Morganuke, exhausted, took little notice of his surroundings, flopping down on top of the bedcovers and immediately falling asleep.

A couple of hours later, Morganuke awoke to knocking at his door. The door slowly opened, and one of servants appeared in the doorway. "How are you feeling?" the servant asked.

"I'm much better, thank you," answered Morganuke, sitting up in the bed.

"If you're well enough, his Lordship would like to see you in his study." Morganuke nodded and followed the servant to Lord Brackish's study.

Moments later Lord Brackish entered the study. Morganuke was still standing and gave a little bow, making Lord Brackish smile. "No need to bow, Morganuke, I'm not the King. Please take a seat." Morganuke sat in one of the many chairs placed in the study and Lord Brackish took a seat opposite. "My men have recovered the tools and fixed your cart. Now, tell me what happened. You don't seem the impetuous sort, and something must have caused you to dash through treacherous terrain. Why didn't you stay on the main path?"

Morganuke hesitated before answering. "I felt I was being followed on the main track so I took a shortcut through Lost Man's Caves. Thought I recognised one of the men, too—he was the one that escaped the *Aurora* in Fettleridge."

"Yes, I heard about that. I have my sources. Lookouts who keep me aware of what's going on around the island. If you are right about this man, then the time for action has come. I must bring forward my plans to mobilise the militia in this part of the island. Have you thought any more about joining?"

"No, My Lord." Morganuke fidgeted in his seat. "But how much danger do you think we're in?"

"I get many reports about Cordinen followers on the island, and these have become more frequent recently. I fear that an all-out attack may be imminent, and I will not stand by and let that happen. We also have many contacts from the Cadmun Islands to the south. The Cadmunese have been very wary of the Cordinens for some time and have been looking for allies to join them in raising an army."

Morganuke eased back in his seat. "Then if it's really coming to that, I'll do whatever is needed, My Lord."

"How conversant are you with a weapon?" Lord Brackish asked.

"I've been given a sword but need to learn how to use it." Morganuke thought of the emerald-studded sword he had hidden at home.

"Leave that to me. I'll arrange tutelage for you. Now if you are well enough, your horse and cart should be ready for you to return home. I'm sure your family will be worrying about you."

The journey back to Tomlin's was straightforward, for which Morganuke was thankful. This time, he made sure to keep to the main track and didn't detect anyone following him.

Tomlin was waiting outside his workshop, looking perturbed, when Morganuke arrived. "I was worried sick about he. What happened to he?"

"It's a long story. Let's go in, and I'll tell you all about it," Morganuke answered as he climbed down from the cart.

Once settled inside, Morganuke explained everything that had happened: being followed, taking the shortcut, the wheel coming off the cart, and having to shelter the night in Lost Man's Caves. Tomlin started pacing up and down the kitchen.

"Followed, he says?" he worried. "And by those nasties that took Fraytar prisoner! Be he sure about that, me boy?"

"I'm as sure as can be," answered Morganuke. "Wouldn't have taken that shortcut otherwise."

Tomlin stood still, looked at Morganuke, and sighed. "All right me lad, no harm done and you're back now. Better get he home. I'm sure your parents'll be worried too."

CHAPTER 8

The Militia

The day came for the town council to discuss setting up the island militia. The Nibbling Fish Inn was barely large enough to hold all the people who came to the meeting. Everyone knew how important it was and that the outcome would affect everyone on the island. The common room was crammed with people standing shoulder to shoulder and not wanting to miss anything.

The town council members were sitting at a large table at the front of the common room, facing the eager townspeople. Lord Brackish, being the town council chairman, sat in the centre. He was dressed in his fine clothes and wearing a wide-brimmed felt hat topped with a white plume. On his left sat Dorian Fellmen, the town mayor and secretary of the council. Never content with taking second place to Lord Brackish, the mayor sat sternly upright in his seat. To Lord Brackish's right sat Mendor Strant, the town's banker, dressed in his finest clothes like a peacock showing himself off. He was the town's banker and well off, and though he had never reached the higher levels of society, he had always been self-important and liked to project an air of importance. Next to him sat Ladrick Emold, a righteous but humble man who was also part of the middle class in the town. He too had done well for himself, owning a clothing trading business in Tannisport. The final two members of the council were Tomlin and Stovin, who sat on the other end of the town council line. These last three were dressed modestly and acted in a humble manner.

The loud babble from the assembled people was abruptly brought to silence by Lord Brackish giving three loud knocks with a large wooden gavel on the table. "I formally open this town council meeting," he announced. "The top item on our agenda is the creation of a western island militia, to respond to the current threats made to the island population from the mainland, mainly the Cordinen invaders, and to follow the initiatives taken by towns in other parts of the island. The proposal for discussion is for the immediate recruitment of all males on western provinces of the island between the ages of sixteen to forty-five years. The militia will be a standard recognised organisation, commanded by myself. The western militia will in time be amalgamated with militia groups from other parts of the island to form an island army."

The common room remained silent for a few moments. Then from near the back of the crowd, Calarel added her own views. "What about the women?" she demanded furiously. "Why are the women excluded? Why are the women always excluded? Why are there no women on the town council? I propose that women should be allowed into the militia."

Tomlin sat up, visibly shocked, and embarrassed at what his daughter had just said. He looked sideways at Lord Brackish and smiled nervously holding his hands up as if to say, *I apologise for my daughter.*

Morganuke, who was standing near the front of the crowd, turned in the direction of Calarel. Without really thinking, he shouted back in Calarel's direction, "Women should not fight. War is a man's duty and not for a woman. It's the men who need to protect the family, whilst the women look after the family at home."

"That's foolish man's talk, and I will never accept what you say," Calarel retorted, sticking her tongue out.

Lord Brackish held up his hand to command silence. "Young lady, it is out of the question for the women to join the western militia. What they decide in the other parts of the island who can say, but I will not condone women joining the militia here. As Morganuke has pointed out, they should stay at home and tend to the home. There are many duties that the woman can do to help the cause, but fighting should not be one of them. I'm sorry, but this topic is not for debate. Only men will join the western militia."

At that, Calarel forced her way out of the room, followed by a small group of like-minded women. Morganuke tried to follow, but by the time he got outside there was no sign of her. Desperate not to miss the rest of the meeting, he went back inside. *I'll need to talk to her later. I hope she doesn't do anything rash and silly. I would hate to see her hurt in any way.*

Back in the common room, Morganuke discovered that some of the men had raised their concerns about the proposal whilst he was out of the room. "If every man has to join the militia full-time, then how will we continue with the daily life of the town?" one man asked.

Both Tomlin and Stovin nodded in agreement to the man's concern. "He's right," added Stovin. "If there be no exceptions, and all men do join the militia full-time, then it will be impossible to run our businesses." Many in the crowd showed their agreement.

"Who's going to pay for this soldiering?" another man asked.

"Additional taxation will be needed to pay for the militia," replied Lord Brackish. A mass groan went up in the room, and many were starting to look angry. Lord Brackish tried to persuade them.

"I have heard what you all have to say and am willing to compromise to some degree. But war is upon us, and we must respond accordingly or suffer the consequences. If the Cordinens overrun the island, then everything will be taken away from us. At best, we will end up as slaves," he pleaded.

The room was quiet for a while. Morganuke understood their concerns, but he understood first-hand what the threat was. Without thinking how many eyes were on him, he stepped up and started speaking more words that he had ever put together before. "I've seen with my own eyes what the invaders are capable of," he said, "and I can tell you that Lord Brackish is right. If we do nothing, then we will lose everything we hold dear. We'll either be dead or end up as slaves. We must stand up to our enemies and protect our freedom." He launched into tales from his own experience of the Cordinens.

There was no more dissent from the people in the common room, and the look of resignation to the facts was on their faces. The only thing that had not been resolved was the group of women who had demanded that they be allowed in the militia. With the common room settled except for some muttering here and there, Morganuke thought more about what Calarel had said.

What will Calarel do I wander? Was it just an idle threat or will she do something stupid? I am worried about her and must see that she is alright. I at least need to apologise for the way I spoke to her.

Once the proposal to set up the militia had been finalised, the common room began to clear. Morganuke was about to leave when Lord Brackish came over and put his hand on his shoulder. "Thank you for your support, lad. I'm sure you will make a good soldier, but you will need to be trained first. I have the ideal man who can train you in the art of sword fighting. He will come to call on you first thing tomorrow."

Morganuke nodded hesitantly and left the common room in search of Calarel. It was some time before Morganuke eventually found her. She and a group of women were sitting and talking on some crates near the harbour. Morganuke approached warily, and Calarel looked at him coldly. "What do you want?" she barked, grimacing at him. "This is a woman's meeting and not for men to hear."

Morganuke stopped in his tracks, taken back by Calarel's vicious look. He had never seen her look this way before. "I am sorry for the way I spoke to you, Cal. I Only want to protect you and not see you hurt."

"Pah! What rubbish you talk! You're just like all the other men. I don't care what you say or think. We women will do what we need to do regardless of what the silly men think. Now go away and leave us," she dismissed him before turning to continue her discussion with the other women.

Morganuke just sighed and turned around to make his way back home. *What have I done*, he thought. *I never wanted to upset or hurt her. If the women feel so strongly, then maybe they should be given a chance to fight.*

The next day, Morganuke was woken early by banging on the farmhouse door. His parents were already up tending the animals and so he dragged himself out of bed to see who was knocking. After his argument with Calarel yesterday he was not feeling himself and had not slept well. He groaned as he struggled to get out of his bed.

Opening the front door, he was greeted by a sight he had not seen before. Standing at the door was a man slightly taller than himself, with a shock of red hair tied back in a ponytail. He was well built and dressed in light leather armour, with a sheathed sword by his side and a round shield hanging on his back. He had a commanding presence, and it took a little while for Morganuke to say anything.

"Hello, can I help you?" he said nervously.

"Are you Morganuke?" the tall red-headed man asked in a booming voice.

"Yes, I am. Who is asking?" replied Morganuke, still nervous.

"I am Section Leader Seedon Blackhall, Lord Brackish should have warned you I was coming to train you in the art of swordsmanship."

"Yes, I remember now. I just wasn't expecting you this early."

Seedon leant against the doorframe, his bulk almost filling the doorway. "Well, there's a lot to teach you, laddie. The sooner we start the better. Have you got a weapon?"

"I have a sword," Morganuke answered. He went to a cabinet close by and retrieved the sword that Fraytar had given him.

On seeing the sword in Morganuke's hand, Seedon raised his eyebrows. "That's a fine-looking long sword. Where might you have gotten that?"

"It was presented to me by a good friend," replied Morganuke.

"A good friend he must've been, for it is a very fine sword," Seedon commented, beckoning Morganuke to follow him.

When they reached the farm courtyard, Seedon readied himself, sword in hand and asked Morganuke to do the same. Morganuke unsheathed his sword and threw the scabbard to the ground before readying himself in front of Seedon.

"What do you call that, laddie? Your stance is all wrong. Stand like this, and hold your sword like this," Seedon stood slightly sideways to

Morganuke with legs apart, holding the pommel of his sword to one side just below his waste with the blade pointing upwards at forty-five degrees "Now attack me," Seedon instructed.

Morganuke did as he was bid, but with one sidestep from Seedon, Morganuke completely missed, tripped over, and fell to the ground with a crash. Morganuke lay in the dust feeling very undignified with Seedon looking down at him.

"Get up, laddie!" Seedon shouted, positioning himself again with his sword.

Morganuke scrambled up on his feet and attacked again, with similar results.

"I see we have a lot of work to do," Seedon sighed.

The training continued for another hour, with Seedon providing plenty of instruction. Morganuke gradually started to improve, managing to stay on his feet and avoiding being slapped on the bottom with the flat side of Seedon's blade too many times. At last, with Morganuke panting, bruised and a little bloody, Seedon brought a halt to the day's training. "That will do for today, laddie. You have a lot to learn, and I want you to continue what I taught you on your own before our lesson the same time tomorrow morning." Seedon sheathed his sword.

Morganuke leant on his sword as if it were a crutch, breathing heavily and recovering from the exertion. "Phew, that was hard. I thought I would be better than that," Morganuke commented.

"Why should that be," Seedon said dispassionately. "You have not fought with a sword before, that is evident. You will need lots of practice before you can call yourself a fighter. It will get harder before it gets better, and you will find yourself barely able to walk after some of the training. But persist you must be to get to a level where you can fight in my section. Now I bid thee good day, till the morrow." With that, Seedon turned and walked out of the courtyard and out of Morganuke's sight.

Morganuke pondered on his situation. *What have I let myself in for? All that silliness about being a hero, and I'm not able to use a sword properly. Maybe Calarel is right. I'm sure the women could fight better than I can.*

The next day's training started no better for Morganuke, although he had been determined to improve from the previous day. Time and again he attacked Seedon as instructed but always fell short. Soon he felt tired, and the sword felt heavier.

"You're thinking too much about the consequences of being struck by my sword and almost waiting for it to happen. Try to anticipate your moves as well as mine," Seedon advised.

Morganuke, one knee on the ground after his last fall, leant on his sword and thought, *He's right, I be waiting for his sword to strike me? I need to anticipate more move quicker.*

Determined that he had nothing to lose, Morganuke took his stance, readying for an attack. *Anticipate and move. Watch closely what my opponent is doing and counter or get my move in first.* He began his attack. To his amazement, this seemed to work a little better. His movements were swift and without hesitation, seemingly pre-empting Seedon's next move. He stayed on his feet at least.

"Well, that's more like it, laddie. Let's have more of that, and you may end up being able to fight," said Seedon.

The rest of the training session went reasonably well, and Morganuke felt that at last he was making some progress, at least slowly. At the end of the session Morganuke stood upright, poised, not showing the signs of exhaustion he had on the previous days.

"You have done better today, Morganuke. Continue your training, and if you show further improvement, then I may accept you in my section. But there is still a lot you need to learn" Seedon patted Morganuke on the back.

Over the next few weeks of training, Morganuke did demonstrate continued improvement. After ten weeks, Seedon was happy with the progress made and formally accepted Morganuke into his section.

"So, what happens now?" Morganuke asked.

"We continue training until we receive our mobilisation orders or until we need to respond to a particular threat. I intend to assemble the section tomorrow for group training. This will be your opportunity to prove yourself to me and the others in the section."

The next day at the induction, Seedon assembled his section of twelve men in the militia training grounds just outside of Tannisport. Morganuke was thankful that he didn't know any of the other eleven men in his section, as he didn't want the stories of being a local hero to set the men against him. Most were Cadmunese or Delenese mercenaries. The few who came from the island were not local men. They all wore a variation of clothing, some with light armour and others in just normal clothes, as Morganuke was. There was also a variety of weapons, with the outsiders having either pikes or swords with a few bowmen. The islanders, except for Morganuke, were armed with hayforks or clubs. To Morganuke, this seemed a poor array for defending against the likes of the Cordinen soldiers he had seen.

Seedon paired the men up, trying to match them in weaponry and expected competency. He instructed the men to spar and to try not injuring each other. For some pairs, this was achievable, but the less experienced did suffer some minor cuts and wounds as the sparring continued.

Morganuke was paired with a man about the same size who also had a sword. He looked Delenese to Morganuke, but he didn't get an opportunity to ask. At first his opponent got the better of him, but remembering his training with Seedon, Morganuke eventually got the better of him. It came easier with each attack, until he felt his moves flowing without indecision.

At the end of the training session, with everyone feeling tired from the rigour of hours of training with few rests, Seedon called his section together.

"Men, you have done well today for the first training session. Some of you will need improved weapons, and I will see to this. I will not have my section going into battle improperly equipped. Trust and support for one another will do thee well in my section."

The next day, Seedon honoured his promise and presented swords to those without them and light armour to those unprotected. Morganuke squeezed into his new leather armour and admired himself. He now felt more like a soldier, and his previous doubts about his fighting abilities were less of a worry.

For the next few weeks, Seedon's section continued their training.

Camaraderie grew amongst them, and their abilities improved with each session, largely thanks to the overseeing and continued encouragement from Seedon. Morganuke grew to respect Seedon for the soldier and leader he proved to be.

During a routine training exercise, an alarm had been raised in Tannisport and Morganuke had heard shouts and screams coming from the harbour. Seedon ordered his men into a loose formation and to proceed cautiously towards the commotion.

Before entering the town proper, Seedon told the men to stay where they were and ordered Morganuke to scout ahead. He crept low between houses, moving towards the shouts and screams. Before he got to the harbour, he saw about ten Cordinen soldiers dispersed across the docks attacking anyone close by. Morganuke made his way back to Seedon and reported what he had seen.

"Morg, stay back with six men and position yourself either side of that alleyway," Seedon instructed as he pointed towards an alleyway leading to the harbour. "I'll position archers on the roofs nearby and take three men to draw the enemy towards the alleyway so that we can take them by surprise. I'm sure they're not expecting any organised force to attack them and so we can use surprise to our advantage."

Morganuke did what he was asked, taking six men down the alley that Seedon had pointed to. They positioned themselves waiting to pounce on the Cordinen soldiers when Seedon had drawn them close. For moments that seemed like hours, Morganuke waited with his men, thinking about the fight that was soon to begin. In the distance he heard a shout from Seedon, followed by a fearsome cry from the Cordinen soldiers. There were faint sounds of arrows being shot from the roofs above, shot from archers that Seedon must have stationed there with a corresponding thud when the arrow met its target. Morganuke guessed that some of the Cordinen soldiers must've been taken down by the arrows, increasing the odds in their favour.

The shouts from the Cordinen soldiers grew louder, and Morganuke heard running footsteps coming from the end of the alley. It was Seedon, followed by his three men, and following them were six burly Cordinen soldiers. Morganuke gasped at the sight of the Cordinens with their eyes wide and lips parted to show yellow gritted teeth. They carried a huge sword in one hand and a round shield in the other. Their armour was studded leather, and they wore domed metal helmets.

Once Seedon had passed Morganuke and the six men hiding in the alley with the Cordinen soldiers in pursuit, Seedon screamed the order to attack. Morganuke pounced forward towards the nearest Cordinen soldier. He caught a glimpse of the soldier's surprised face as his sword slashed into his flesh. He drove his sword into the Cordinen's torso up to the hilt and then withdrew it in readiness for the next attack. Two other Cordinen soldiers had been hacked down by Seedon's other men, and now three remained surrounded.

"Lay down your swords!" Seedon ordered the three Cordinen soldiers. They ignored his words, launching themselves into the attack with wild eyes and yelling unrecognisable words. Morganuke was taken by surprise, and one of the Cordinen soldiers lashed at him with his sword. He dodged instinctively and buried his own sword into the Cordinen's side. The remaining two Cordinens were soon finished off by the other men.

"Morg, take five men to the other side of the harbour and make sure there are no other Cordinens. I'll search this side with the remaining men. Report back to me in the dock area once you are sure everything is clear," Seedon ordered.

Once they had searched the docks and ensured no more Cordinens remained, the men gathered around Seedon on the docks. "You have all done well in your first fight. I'm sure this will be the first of many. Take pride in your achievements today," Seedon assured his men as he looked around the harbour.

As Seedon's men were finishing gathering the bodies of the Cordinen soldiers and piling them on the dockside, there was a sound of hooves and marching feet from one of the alleyways. As the men turned to see what was happening, Justin Brackish appeared on his horse, followed by about thirty well-armed men in pristine leather armour.

Justin halted his men and trotted up to Seedon, his large brimmed hat with its large white plume bobbing up and down comically. "What is the meaning of this! Why have you chosen to attack without my orders? You should be flogged for this!"

Seedon raised his eyebrows at Justin's outburst but gave no other clue to his feelings. "The town was under attack, and we had to do something quickly to avoid townspeople being hurt or worse."

"Insolent dog!" retorted Justin furiously. "You will address me as sir. You should be punished for this. Wait until I see my father. I'll have you and your men put in chains."

"If we had waited for you, the town would have been completely purged. I did what I thought was best," Seedon answered defiantly.

"Silence, dog! I will have you whipped if you continue to defy me. Now get your rabble of men at the back of the column. There are reports of more Cordinens to the north of here."

Without saying a word, Seedon ordered his men to join the back of Justin's column. With a command of "Onward march!" from Justin, the militia column began to move to the north of Tannisport.

The column marched the rest of the day, and as the sun began to set, Justin ordered camp to be set up for the night. The men busied themselves erecting makeshift tents and building campfires, whilst guards were posted around the camp. Seedon's men were just finishing preparing their part of the camp when Justin came striding up to Seedon with his burly officer at his shoulder.

"Arrange members from your section to form a patrol and search the area north of the camp. We can't be far from the Cordinens, and I want to know where they are." Justin didn't wait for an answer and strode towards the other side of the camp with his aide following close behind.

Seedon chose four men closest to him before turning to Morganuke. "Morg, I'll leave you in command of the section while I take these men out on patrol to see how far the Cordinens are from us. I may be gone all night."

Morganuke nodded his head in abeyance, whilst Seedon gathered his patrol and moved out of camp. Morganuke sat by the campfire, looking into the flames contemplating the situation he was in.

Why have I been given this responsibility? Surely there are other more experienced than I am to act as deputy for the Section Leader. It seems that the war really has arrived on the island now.

Morganuke's thoughts were interrupted by the arrival of one of the other soldiers from the section. "So, Seedon has put you in charge." Morganuke looked up at the man. He was Cadmunese like Seedon, tall with red hair.

"It seems so," answered Morganuke, "although I don't know why."

"I think he sees something in you, and from what I've seen you've already proven yourself to the men. I've known and fought with Seedon during our mercenary time. My name is Lengrond Smidrich, and I grew up in the same town as Seedon. Like many of the other men, I'm happy to fight and not be encumbered with command."

"I am happy to know you, Lengrond. My name is Morganuke Beldere, and I've lived on this island almost all my life. I'm just a farmer's son, and until recently lived a peaceful life, never knowing what fighting is. Now here I am in an army waiting to attack a powerful enemy. How did it ever come to this?" Morganuke turned back to stare into the flames.

"You sound well spoken for just a farmer's son, and that's a very fine sword you carry for one apparently so lowly," Lengrond noted

"I was tutored by a professor as I grew up. He had intended for me to be a gentleman, but nothing ever came of that," Morganuke replied. "The sword was a gift from an old friend. I don't even know where it originated from. Why do you fight, Lengrond?"

"I know not why troubles begin and usually find myself in the thick of things without much thought. Why do I fight, you ask? Well, I tell you, I fight to protect my comrades and of course for the money. Don't worry, Morganuke my friend—I daresay you have great things ahead of you, especially with a sword like that."

The two sat in silence, both looking at the campfire for a while. There was a rustling in the thickets just outside the camp, and a voice went up. "Who approaches the camp? Identify yourself."

"It's Section Leader Blackhall reporting back from patrol." Seedon and his men emerged from the undergrowth, breathless and wide-eyed. "I have to see the band commander now."

"Come with me," answered one of the guards. Seedon beckoned to Morganuke to follow.

Justin was standing outside his tent, talking to his burly aide, Bartok, when Seedon and Morganuke approached him to report. "Commander, I have found where the enemy is. They are barely three stances from here." Seedon pointed to some moonlit hills just beyond. "They are camped on the other side of those hills, at the base. From the high ground we could attack and surprise them."

"What is their strength?" Justin asked trying to sound stern.

"I judged their numbers to be between eighty and one hundred, but if we attack them now, we will gain the element of surprise and overcome the odds," Seedon answered.

"How dare you be so insolent, dog? I will decide when to attack. They outnumber us two to one. We must get more men," Justin sneered.

"But, Commander, if we wait it will be too late, and we will lose the element of surprise. It will take a full day to get reinforcements," Seedon advised.

"Silence, you Cadmunese mercenary dog! Why my father allowed your sort into the militia I don't know. We must make an orderly retreat and get more men."

Morganuke felt even more contempt for Justin than he had when he first met him at Lord Brackish's estate. He found himself fidgeting with the hilt of his sword and immediately lowered his hand when he realized. Seedon gave him a quick glance as he did so.

Bartock gently tapped Justin on the shoulder and whispered into his ear. "Very well," Justin said. "We will approach tonight with full force. But we will not attack until I have reviewed the situation," he concluded, dismissing Seedon and Morganuke.

As Morganuke was leaving, Justin called him back. "I know you from somewhere," Justin sneered. "I wouldn't forget a freak like you, with your silver hair and red eyes. Yes, I remember now. You were that incompetent fool who lost my father's tools. I should have you thrown out of the army. I've got my eye on you, boy. Now get back to your duties."

As soon as Morganuke had returned to the section the call went up to break camp and move out. The force moved quietly through the undergrowth towards the reported location of the Cordinen camp. Seedon's section led the way, as he knew the exact position of the enemy, into higher ground covered with trees to mask their approach. When they reached a point overlooking the Cordinen camp, Justin halted the column and then joined Seedon's section to reconnoitre.

Justin gazed at the camp below with fear in his eyes. "There are too many!" he panted in a squeaky voice. "We must retreat and get more men."

"We are here now, Commander. We must attack or risk being detected and losing the advantage. Do you have any pitch barrels? If so, we could make pitch rotunds and roll them down the hill into the camp," Seedon suggested. "It will cause chaos amongst the Cordinens, easing our attack."

"Yes, I have some in the supply carts, but I'm not using them here. It's too dangerous. We must retreat! Quickly, Bartok, get the men back," Justin called to his aide. His voice sounded even squeakier, and his eyes darted around in sheer panic.

"Commander, you're putting all the men at risk with your indecisiveness!" Seedon drew his sword. "I hereby take command for their sake. Bartok, are you with me or not?"

Morganuke stood next to Seedon, and drew his sword too, ready and only too happy to provide support for his section leader.

"Bartock! Arrest these mutinous dogs!" Justin squealed.

"I'm sorry, Sir, I cannot do that." Bartok said to Justin and turn to Seedon and nodded.

Justin released a squeal but was soon silenced by a gag that Morganuke stuffed in his mouth before tying him up. "Apologies, Sir, but all that squealing will alert the enemy," Morganuke said as he tightened Justin's bindings.

"Bartok, prepare the pitch barrels, then get the men lined up on this hill." Seedon ordered.

The rotunds were quickly prepared, and the men drew up their line. They positioned the barrels, set the pitch alight, and when the order came from Seedon, rolled the rotunds with all their might down the hill towards the camp. Militia archers stood in line with arrows nocked.

A shout came from one of the Cordinen lookouts, but it was too late. The flaming rotunds rolled quickly down the hill, leaving a fiery track behind them, before crashing into the tents with the sleeping Cordinen soldiers inside. Tents began bursting into flames. The screams of men filled the air, some running outside as a ball of flaming flesh. The smell of burning flesh was sickening.

Militia archers then let loose their deadly arrows, bringing down several Cordinens in the middle of the ensuing chaos. Seedon ordered his line of soldiers to charge. Some of the Cordinens had recovered their senses and armed themselves, and others were still trying to escape the flaming tents when Morganuke and the other swordsmen arrived in a shouting, seething horde. The heat and smell was suffocating and Morganuke struggled to keep on his feet. The noise was deafening, with the screams of men burning and the shouts from the attackers. Morganuke sliced his sword this way and that in a frenzy. All the training he'd been through seemed not to be of any use in the chaos he found himself in. Suddenly through the flames came a charging Cordinen, his eyes blazing with hate. Just as the Cordinen was about to bring his sword down onto Morganuke, his head disappeared from his shoulders to reveal Lengrond sweeping his sword through the Cordinen's neck. The two men briefly acknowledged each other before returning their focus to the mayhem of battle.

At the end of the battle there were no Cordinen survivors and a quarter of the militia forces had been lost. In the aftermath, there was no cheering as the militia piled up the bodies of their enemies on the cremation pyres of their burning tents. The militia section prepared to move out, loading the tied-up Justin onto one of the supply carts with his horse in tow.

Morganuke returned home and slept well that night after the exertion of battle. He didn't tell his parents about what had happened and how many men they had lost because he knew they would worry. Stovin had been exempt from full-time service in the militia to tend the farm, but he was still expected to participate in training and wasn't completely isolated from what was going on. As for Morganuke's mother, she had little knowledge of the true horrors that were occurring on the island.

The next day, whilst Morganuke and his parents were having their breakfast, there was a hard knock at the farmhouse door. Morganuke opened it and saw half a dozen militiamen led by an officer Morganuke didn't recognise.

"Morganuke Beldere, I'm placing you under arrest for mutiny and encouraging insurrection in the militia. You must come with us now," The officer sternly commanded.

Morganuke didn't argue and was not surprised at this outcome, given Justin's character. He got himself ready and followed the men, leaving his parents alone in the farmhouse looking worried and baffled.

When they reached Tannisport, Morganuke was taken to an old warehouse where a dark and dingy room with no windows had been adapted into a makeshift cell. He was pushed in and the doors locked behind him.

He heard Seedon's voice in the next room. "Is that you, Morganuke?"

"Yes, it's me. How are you faring, Seedon?" Morganuke said.

"I'm sorry, that I got you into this, but I couldn't stand by and let Justin run away leaving an opportunity to beat the enemy. I know we lost men, but we would have lost a lot more had we not attacked when we did. I would do the same again."

"It's okay. I know you did what you had to do. Justin isn't fit to command."

The two of them sat in their isolated rooms in silence for what seemed like an age. Eventually the doors were unlocked, and the two men led down a hallway to another room that was brightly lit with many windows. There was a large table in the room. Lord Brackish sat at the centre, with his son one side and the mayor at the other. Morganuke and Seedon were made to stand in front of the table.

"You men are being brought here charged with mutiny and insurrection. I have heard evidence from my son, and now you have an opportunity to provide your side of the story," Lord Brackish said sternly, looking at each of them in turn.

Seedon explained everything that had happened and why he had taken the action he took, followed by Morganuke, who backed up Seedon's explanation.

Lord Brackish turned to Bartok. "Bartok, you were Commander Brenadere's aid and present at the time. Please tell us what you saw."

"Me Lord, it is true that Seedon took command of the militia band and tied up your son. However, it is my view that this was justified. Had he not taken the action that he did, your son would have likely alarmed the enemy with his squealing or at best lost an opportunity to surprise the enemy. Through the leadership of these two men, we managed to defeat an enemy almost twice our number."

When Bartok had finished his explanation, Justin began to squeak that this was all a lie, but his father raised his hand to silence him.

Lord Brackish paused for a moment, before giving his decision. "Given the fine characters of the three defence witnesses, I am led to believe that the actions taken were justified and indeed resulted in heroic victory against the odds. I find no grounds to convict these two men, and so my only recourse is to acquit them."

With that, red-faced and bobbing up and down on his chair, Justin began to squeak again on an even higher pitch. Again he was interrupted by his father. "As for you, Commander Justin Brackish, it is evident to me that you are not suited to command in the field of battle. Therefore, I will transfer you to support duties more fitted to your make-up. This hearing is adjourned."

CHAPTER 9

The Island War

Morganuke was glad to get back to normal life for a few days after the recent activities in the militia. It was now the end of autumn, and the nights were drawing in, making the daylight hours precious to get all the farm work done. Morganuke helped his father on the farm as well as spending the odd few hours in Tomlin's workshop. For a brief time, the war seemed a long way away, but Morganuke knew that would not last.

Morganuke was reminded of the rigours of the militia when Seedon called to visit him a few days later. They made their way to the farm kitchen and sat themselves at the kitchen table.

"Can I get you anything, Seedon?" Morganuke asked as he cleared some of the pots from the table.

"Ale, if you have it, please," replied Seedon with a polite smile.

Morganuke poured them both a mug of ale from a leather jack and joined Seedon at the table. "What can I do for you, Seedon?"

"I've been promoted to band commander," Seedon announced

"Congratulations. Who will take your place as section leader? Looks like I'll have to get used to a new leader then."

"Not necessarily. I want you to take my place as section leader. I really appreciated you standing beside me when I stood up against Lord Brackish's son. It showed courage and good judgment."

Morganuke kept silent for a while, taking in what Seedon had said. *Do I really deserve promotion?* He thought. *I was on the verge of panic during the battle at times and it all was so confusing, bloody and the smell - But I suppose I did stand my ground in the end. Fighting isn't as glorifying as some make out.*

"I'm honoured that you think me worthy of promotion, Seedon. I'll gladly be one of your section leaders."

"Excellent! I received word from Lord Brackish that he wants to assemble the whole commune, all four companies of the militia in Tannisport, the day after tomorrow. Our band will be part of the fifth company," Seedon said between sips of ale.

"Forgive me, Seedon, but I'm not yet familiar with all the militia structure. If I am to be leading soldiers, then I at least need to know how our forces are organized. Please would you remind me."

"Of course. A section is the smallest organization consisting of fifteen to twenty troops. A band is the next largest, usually consisting of four sections. Then it's a company, consisting of four bands. Then a commune, made up of four companies. Next is an array, consisting of three to four communes. Then an assembly, made up from three or four arrays. A contingent would be made up of two or three assemblies. The final grouping would be the army, made up of at least two contingents. Currently, the western forces only consist of one commune, but with forces from other parts of the island, it's hoped that a whole army could be created later. Eventually it may be possible to go on and have army groups, but that would be a long way off."

Morganuke glumly stared into his ale. "Thank you for that. It helps me picture where I stand in the scheme of things, still near the bottom. I can't believe how quickly things have changed. It seems that we have a very long road ahead of us when you talk of creating armies and such like. Do you ever get tired? Of the fighting, I mean."

"Sometimes, but there's always something that keeps driving me on. It would be a loss to me without the comradery or the excitement of battle," Seedon answered, taking another sip.

"Are only men destined to fight in wars, or should women be allowed to fight too? There's a girl I like very much, and we argued about women fighting. She took offence and we've not talked since. She feels very strongly about women's right to fight."

"What was her name, and where is she now?" Seedon asked.

"Her name is Calarel, the local blacksmith's daughter. I'm not sure where she is now. I think she went north of the island somewhere." Morganuke answered.

"She may have joined the independent women's militia who are being established in that area. I understand it's being led by Lady Chanterly Bowderlong. Apparently, she's a very formidable wealthy woman, who's financing the group herself.

"Regarding whether women should fight, I firmly believe that they should. Indeed, women are permitted to join the army in my homeland, although none have yet joined the island forces." Seedon said, finishing off his ale.

"That's what I am now realising. I fear it may be too late for me to get back with Calarel, but I will always think fondly of her, nevertheless."

Seedon got up and prepared to take his leave. "Never give up hope, Morg. The day after tomorrow it is then. It should be an impressive turnout to have a thousand men on parade."

The day of the Tannisport Militia First Commune parade came, and all four companies arrived early to prepare. The parade was to take place in the show fields just outside Tannisport. It was a cold day but at least bright and sunny. The men had arrived from all around the western part of the island, arriving on foot or by horse and cart. With over a thousand men assembling, it was a sight to behold and raised the spirits of the local folk. New company banners had been created for the occasion, a green background with crossed swords above an anchor embroidered in gold, and the company number embroidered in red below. Carried by each company's standard bearer, the standards made an impressive addition to the assembly.

The four commune companies lined up in formation at one end of the show fields, each company parade officer shouting their orders individually. At times it looked a little disorganised, and some men had difficulty keeping step or following the orders from their own company officer. This was somewhat to be expected, as it had been the first time the whole commune had assembled in one place. When all the companies had formed up, the parade commander took over direction of the proceedings. As the order was given to march forward in formation to the centre of the showground, where Lord Brackish and other dignitaries were waiting on a raised makeshift stage, drums beat to the rhythm of the marching. The whole commune marched across the field with only a few men occasionally missing a step.

Morganuke, marching at the head of his section in Seedon's band of the third company, was mindful of keeping his men in line, as were all the other section leaders. He was impressed at how things had come together and felt proud marching in what had now become an impressive looking force.

The commune was ordered to halt about ten paces in front of the stage. Lord Brackish then addressed his men. "Men, I am proud to lead such a fine-looking fighting force. No longer will we need to fear the incursions from our enemy. We will resist and prevail to ensure that what we hold dear here on the island is maintained and our freedom is left intact. There is still much to do before we meet the enemy on the field of battle as a combined fighting force. As a militia commune, we must train together to improve fighting abilities as a single force. Outland riders have informed me that similar mobilisations of militia forces are taking place across the island. Soon we can band together to create not just a single militia commune but a whole army. This is the start of something great, and so let us now be proud."

Once Lord Brackish had finished addressing the men, he stepped down from the stage and with the parade commander began to walk down the line of each militia formation for a formal inspection. This took some time, but the men held up well, demonstrating their discipline with pride.

Once the inspection was over, the men were dismissed but not released back to their homes. There would be a series of training exercises over the next few days, and so the commune was to march off to the nearby camp area. Once they arrived, tents were erected to hold all the men. By the end of the day, the camp was ready, and guards were placed outside. Campfires had been set up throughout the camp, shared by several sections.

Morganuke gathered with his men around one of the fires. Provisions had been provided and stew pots placed over the fires to prepare for the evening meal. With the smell of the cooking food and the comfort of the fires fending off the cold night, the men discussed the recent activities and what was likely to happen over the next few days.

"Wonder what we be going to do next?" asked one of the men who sat near to Morganuke.

"We are training as a group, which is something we haven't done yet. We need to learn to fight as a united force if we stand any chance against the enemy," Morganuke answered, looking around at the men sat beside him huddled around the fire.

"Why so many militia? I thought there are only a few of these mainlanders," the man asked.

"Not so. I've heard that there be more and more coming from the mainland each day," answered another man from the other side of Morganuke.

Morganuke shuffled his position to get closer to the fire. "I used to think the same, but from what I've heard recently the Cordinens are taking hold on the mainland and are wanting to extend their control to the island. I'm sure the enemy are building up for some major attacks. It's important that we are ready to meet them when they come in large numbers."

The men around him nodded and gave sighs of reluctant acceptance.

For the next few days, the militia companies were put through their paces, training throughout the daylight hours and sometimes into the night. Companies were set against companies to simulate real battle conditions. At first the results were poor, with the men not able to function well as a single body. However, as the days went on with more training, the efficiency of the simulated battles improved, and the men grew more confident in their abilities.

When the exercises ended, the men were sent home for a short furlough before resuming training. Morganuke took the opportunity to see his parents and Tomlin. Back at the farm things had been progressing reasonably well in Morganuke's absence. Heading into the winter months, the quietest time on the farm, the animals still had to be tended, but as the work slowed, Stovin managed with help from Plarem.

Once Morganuke was sure that his parents were settled and no immediate jobs needed to be done, he made his way to Tomlin's. He was pleased to see the blacksmith's workshop there as usual with the familiar clang, clang, clang of Tomlin's hammer. Tomlin's face brightened when he saw Morganuke, and he beckoned him into the cottage.

Inside, Morganuke was a little surprised and embarrassed to see Calarel there.

"Hello, Calarel. How are you?" Morganuke asked.

"I'm well as can be, thank you," Calarel answered politely with no expression on her face.

Tomlin beckoned Morganuke to a seat at the table and placed a mug of ale in front of him, which he eagerly picked up. "We parted on bad terms last time we met at the town council meeting," Morganuke said to Calarel. "I'm sorry if I upset you, but I just wanted you to be safe. What have you been doing since we last spoke?"

"I've joined the independent women's militia led by Lady Bowderlong," Calarel answered. "She's a very inspirational leader and the women love her. We have been busy training with our group, which is steadily increasing in size."

"I am glad for you, Cal. I do wish you and the other women in the militia the very best. I was wrong to go against your wishes."

"Thank you for your gracious words, Morg. Yes, I'm well, and the women militia are doing a fine job," Calarel replied. There were a few moments of uneasy silence in the room, then Calarel added, "I don't hold any grudges and understand why you said what you said. Best we go our separate ways and forget all about it."

Morganuke's mouth opened, and he sat there not knowing what to say. Glumly he picked up his mug of ale and continued to drink in silence.

Morganuke left Tomlin's soon afterwards feeling deflated. He knew that Calarel had made her mind up that they should go their separate ways. *With the war coming, maybe it's for the best*, he told himself unconvincingly.

The day before the militia commune was due to reassemble for more training, Morganuke received word to report immediately with his men at the assembly fields. He quickly went to round up the men who were staying in the Tannisport area and found them where they said they would be. When they reached the assembly fields, they found men running here and there, seemingly not knowing what to do. Only half the men had assembled, and many were still to be summoned. This chaotic behaviour was very unlike the formal assembly which had taken place just days before.

Morganuke could see Lord Brackish watching his men running around like headless chickens. He looked very unhappy and frequently bellowed to the officers trying to get their troops assembled.

Morganuke continued to assemble his men where he'd been told to. Most of Seedon's band were already in position, but many from the other bands of the company were still missing.

Seedon approached Morganuke, looking pensive. "Glad to see you here with all your men. Well done. As you can see, many other men are still missing. Some search parties have been sent out to round up the remaining men, but I fear this delay will put us at a disadvantage with the enemy. We've had vague reports of a build-up to the north, but their exact location is unknown."

"Where have these reports come from? Do we know how many of the enemy we are facing?" Morganuke asked.

"The outriders who have been sent out across the island to scout for signs of the enemy have reported sightings. They are on the move, so by the time we get the reports, it's difficult to locate their current position.

Could be six hundred or as many as a thousand well-armed Cordinens. This will be a severe test for the commune."

It took most of the day for the men to be gathered and assembled, many having to be recovered by the cavalry. Lord Brackish had showed his frustration over the length of time it had taken to assemble the men. When at last most of the militia commune was finally in place, he ordered his men to remain in camp for the night. With the short winter days now upon them, there would be no time to move camp until the next day.

"Lord Brackish doesn't look please," Morganuke noted to Lengrond who had joined him by the campfire. "We've lost a whole day just assembling our forces."

"This is not a good start for our first real engagement," Lengrond added. "That would not be tolerated back home on Cadmun."

"It's early days and the men still have a lot to learn," Morganuke added.

"There is no time. War is already upon us," Lengrond stated. Morganuke looked at his friend worriedly. "Take no heed of me. I know you will lead us well."

As the sun started to set, campfires were lit, and cooking was started to feed the hungry troops. Morganuke, Lengrond and Seedon sat around the fire. Seedon crouched close to the fire to keep warm, throwing twigs into the flames. "Should be one thing to our advantage, and that is that the Cordinens are strategically weak. They rely on brute force alone. Like a herd of bulls, clearing everything in their path. It should be possible to herd those bulls into a defensive trap, and I'm sure that is what Lord Brackish is planning. He is a seasoned strategist and a good soldier." Seedon threw more twigs into the fire.

"What if the Cordinens take us by surprise here in the camp?" Morganuke asked, getting closer to the fire.

"That shouldn't happen, if the scouts do their job and warn us," Seedon replied. "Commander Yacob Dovadeer is an excellent cavalry commander and the scouts he has in his troop are of the highest quality. He is an islander but has fought many battles as a mercenary commander abroad. I have fought under his command on several occasions. But we do need to come up with a plan beforehand."

No reports of enemy sightings arrived, and Morganuke managed to get some sleep, which was not easy given the tension in the camp.

At first light, Lord Brackish gave orders to break camp and continue northward. Scouts had returned with reports of suitable defensive ground several stances north of their current position, and to there they now headed to set their trap. With no time to spare, Lord Brackish ordered a forced march towards the proposed defensive position, and by midday they had reached the site. The ground chosen was ideal, with tree-covered hills on either side of a valley.

There were still no enemy positional reports, and so Lord Brackish decided to gamble and set up the positions of his foot soldiers immediately. He placed two militia companies on one hill and one company on the hill on the other side of the valley.

Soon after the positioning his three companies, an outrider came galloping up. "My Lord, the enemy has been sighted five stances directly north of here," he reported breathlessly.

It seems my gamble has paid off, Lord Brackish thought.

He called company commander Wansley Forbitton, who commanded the remaining company not assigned to the hills, and Commander Yacob Dovadeer to his tent to finalize his plans with them now that the enemy had been sighted. They were his most senior and experienced commanders and had a lot of battle experience in foreign wars as mercenaries.

Lord Brackish welcomed his two commanders warmly when they arrived and the three then gathered in front of a map of the terrain laid out on a table. "I intend to draw the enemy into a trap I have set in this valley," Lord Brackish explained pointing to the map. "Commander Forbitton, you will position your men in line close to the valley entrance, here. Once the enemy is close you will then draw them into the valley."

"Will they not expect a trap, sir? The valley looks an obvious trap." Forbitton asked.

"I am banking on the Cordinens recklessness in front of the enemy, especially one out in the open as you will be," Lord Brackish replied. "Commander Dovadeer, you will probe the enemy at their current position and lead them towards Commander Forbitton's position. We don't believe that they have any cavalry and so you should easily be able to control your pace to entice them towards you. Again, I'm relying on the Cordinen's recklessness once they see the enemy. Reports from the Epleons on the mainland indicate that the Cordinen strategy tactics leave a lot to be desired and so I am counting on easily outwitting them."

The two commanders acknowledged the plan and left to position their men.

What are we in for now? Morganuke thought as he and his men marched along in Commander Forbitton's company. *I hope Seedon is right about the supposed Cordinen's poor strategy.*

The company continued to march northwards until they reached the head of a valley. Morganuke looked around the terrain that surrounded the company. *This looks too exposed*, he thought. *Why aren't we up in those hills? If the enemy attack us from there, we'll have no chance.* The company continued to wait and some of the men began to mutter amongst themselves. *This seems madness,* Morganuke continued to think. *Why are we just standing here like this?* He looked around the terrain again, trying not to show any concern to his men. He smiled and started patting his men on the back, encouraging them as much as he could.

It then dawned on Morganuke. He remembered what Seedon had said about laying a trap and realized that this must be part of a plan to trap the Cordinens. He smiled to himself for a moment, until he realized that they were the bait for the trap.

Another hour went by, and the men were now getting more restless.

"Stand ready, men!" came a shouted order from Commander

Forbitton, who galloped his horse in front of his line of men. "Stand ready to meet the enemy. Listen for my commands and act on them immediately."

Morganuke craned his neck to see over the soldiers heads standing in front of him. He saw a line of cavalry moving slowly towards them in the distance. *Why are those cavalry troops moving so slowly*? He continued to watch as the line of cavalry came closer. Then they started to gallop towards Forbitton's line, wheeling to the left as they closed in before riding behind the line of men still waiting. Morganuke realized that it was Yacob's troop of cavalry.

Morganuke continued to look ahead, this time he saw several lines of what looked like Cordinen infantry moving towards them. He guessed about one thousand Cordinens were heading straight for them. There was no sign of the other three militia companies and Morganuke just hoped that Lord Brackish had them tucked away somewhere, ready to pounce.

"Wait for my command!" Commander Forbitton shouted to his men. Morganuke and the other men stood ready, watching the Cordinens continue their advance. The lines of militia fidgeted and muttered, waiting for the next command, which surely must come as they were hopelessly outnumbered. Now closer still, the Cordinens began to run towards the militia lines.

"About turn and quick time!" Commander Forbitton shouted. It was an order that was repeated by the individual Band Commanders and the men quickly responded. Turning to face the opposite direction and then running but keeping their formation. They had practiced it many times during their training sessions.

The Cordinens were quick on their feet. Fortunately, they lacked cavalry and so were limited to how fast they could run, but their pace was faster than the militia's infantry. Agonisingly, the chase seemed to go on forever, with the Cordinens drawing closer. Morganuke looked behind him, realizing that the Cordinens were getting closer. *Where are the other companies*, he desperately thought. At last, the valley came into view, which spurred the men on, giving them a second wind, but the lines started to spread out. The Cordinens were almost at their heels when they entered the valley. The Cordinens caught up with some of the tail-enders, quickly finishing them off. Yacob's cavalry had ridden ahead and then suddenly stopped and about turned, forming a thin line some way down the valley. Dovadeer gave a loud order, and men came running out of the trees on either side of the valley.

As the other militia companies fell onto the surprised Cordinens, Commander Dovadeer commanded his men to turn about and join in the attack. Encouraged at the band and section level leadership, the fleeing militia infantry turned to face the fight. Commander Dovadeer's cavalry had formed up into two arrowhead formations and swept past the militia infantry to attack each of the Cordinen flanks. Morganuke and his men found themselves in the centre of the battle. This time Morganuke shouted encouragement at his men as he slashed his sword at the enemy. His emerald studded sword was a blur as he slashed and cut his enemies.

The Cordinens had been taken by surprise as Lord Brackish had hoped, but they were strong and capable fighters. The cavalry, skilfully commanded by Yacob, kept up the pressure and helped swing the balance. They rode around the Cordinen formation, carrying out lightning attacks from behind, before retreating and repeating the attacks. The battle was bloody and horrible, with men's limbs sliced from bodies. Heads rolled along the ground, and the earth became awash with blood.

Morganuke and Seedon's men had been in the thick of it. Morganuke swung his sword and sliced into countless Cordinen bodies. Covered in blood and at the point of exhaustion, Morganuke knelt to take some breaths. His left shoulder hurt and he realized that it had been badly gashed. Blood ran down his left side. Suddenly from behind him he heard a yell, and quickly wheeled around to see a Cordinen about to bring down a giant axe on his head. He tried to lift his sword, but his arm lay limp.

Suddenly the sword left his hand at great speed and dug itself deep into the Cordinen's head. Morganuke watched open mouthed as the Cordinen fell on his face at his feet. Morganuke clambered to his feet and retrieved his sword, the emerald studded handle covered in blood.

He looked at the sword for a moment whilst the madness raged on around him. *What in Crasdredon's name is this sword?*

The battle was now waning, and the remaining Cordinens were quickly finished off. The militia had won their first battle, but at what cost? Only one third of the militia now remained standing, bloodied, and exhausted.

Lord Brackish lay dead on the field. He never knew of his commune's triumph, if triumph it really was.

The militia had lost so many men that they had to reassemble in new units under the remaining few commanders. Seedon was promoted to Yacob's second-in-command.

Seedon gathered the surviving militia into the hills around the battleground, whilst Yacob took the cavalry to scout for more Cordinens. A makeshift camp was hastily erected and campfires lit. Guards were posted at strategic points around the camp. The men were exhausted and many bore wounds of varying severity. Seedon estimated that, excluding the more severely wounded, less than one quarter of the original commune remained fit to fight.

The campsite took on an air of despair, with wounded men lying here and there. The fit and walking wounded also lay on the ground through exhaustion, covered with a mixture of blood and mud splatters. Morganuke glumly looked around his men and thought, *I hope there will be no more battles for some time for these men*. He sat next to his tent; his arm had just been bandaged by one of the medics. He tried holding his sword with both hands. It still hurt but he was able to use his sword.

Morganuke's attention was taken with the sound of horses' hooves and a shout, "Commander Dovadeer's cavalry group returning!"

Seedon and Morganuke quickly moved towards the sound of the hooves to see Yacob ride up ahead of his troop.

"How are the men?" Yacob asked as he climbed off his horse.

Seedon looked at him glumly. "They are in poor shape. Less than a quarter of the men are fit enough to fight. The commune organisation is fragmented with each company sparsely manned and not enough commanders."

"We must move further north towards Tannisport," Yacob said. "There has been an even bigger Cordinen attack in Tannisport, and evacuees are making their way from there to Muskcove to board ships to take them to other parts of the island and hopefully to safety. Reports are that the east of the island is yet to be invaded, and there are more militia groups being formed there. We must help the women's militia to act as a rearguard protecting the evacuees and the ships."

Morganuke froze when he heard Yacob's words. *Tannisport attacked*, he thought. *So close to my parent's farm. I hope they are safe.*

"Where will we go? Surely the whole island is overrun," Morganuke said, kicking the muddy earth below his foot.

"An outrider reports that the main Cordinen offensive is in the west, with little activity so far in the east," Yacob added. "More militia groups are being formed in the east of the island to organise a committed defence, but they can't help now. We are on our own. Now let's go about reorganising ourselves and preparing for what is to come. Seedon, organize the remaining men into two companies and assign commanders to each. Do it quickly, time is running out."

By nightfall the militia had been reorganised into two companies. Morganuke was assigned to lead one and Lengrond the other. Morganuke along with the rest of the militia moved towards Tannisport. *At least with fewer men, there was less chance of being seen by the enemy*, Morganuke thought. *Protect the evacuees the commander had said. We will be lucky to protect ourselves. But I must keep the men going. As the commander said, we are now on our own.*

It was early dawn by the time they had reached the outskirts of Tannisport. They had seen many enemy patrols but so far managed to keep themselves undetected. They had yet to see any evacuees in the area.

Morganuke approached Seedon as they lay low in the surrounding undergrowth, monitoring enemy troop movements. "I must check on my parent's farm whilst here. I cannot leave this area until I know their fate," he pleaded.

"You have a company to command," Seedon answered, turning to look at Morganuke, "and you cannot abandon your men."

"I'll be takin' one of the pack horses and be back as soon as I can," Morganuke said.

Seedon kept silent for a while, frowning heavily. "Very well. I'll give you leave, but make sure you are back within two hours."

Morganuke left one of the band commanders in charge and then began to make his way quietly towards his parents' farm. He came across various Cordinen patrols and kept still as they went by. Keeping to the woods, he tried to take as direct route as possible, but it was difficult and he couldn't risk being detected. As he got close to the farm, his heart sank. Thick black smoke was rising from the farm buildings.

Almost forgetting about needing to keep himself hidden, he encouraged his horse to go faster. He was sickened by what he saw: dead animals lay everywhere, and signs of wanton destruction. *Why*, he asked himself, *such senseless destruction?* He got to the farmhouse itself, which was badly damaged, then peered inside through the windowless openings. He made his way inside and searched every room, but there was no sign of his parents. *Maybe they have been taken or ran away with the other evacuees*, he hoped. *One last look around.* He moved through the farm buildings and into the fields. As he entered the first field at the back of the farm, for a moment he couldn't really comprehend what he was seeing. He sank to his knees and put his head in his hands. He was kneeling before the burnt-out bodies of his parents.

Morganuke stayed there, sobbing for a while, unable to make himself move and almost wishing for the Cordinens to find him. Eventually he made himself get up.

I can't leave my parents like this, he thought desperately. He went back to the farm to find a spade and buried them in the corner of the field where they lay. He felt numb and his limbs moved automatically. He thought about finding the Cordinens, taking his revenge, knowing that this would end his life. As inconsolable as he felt, he knew he still had a duty to the men he was leading, and so reluctantly he made his way back to find Seedon and his men.

"Morganuke, you're back," Seedon said, looking relieved

"My parents are dead," Morganuke answered sombrely. "There is nothing left for me here now."

"I'm sorry to hear about your parents, son," Seedon said.

Morganuke steeled himself for what was to come. "I will do my duty, for whatever good it will do."

"There are no evacuees here," Seedon said. "We should push on north to Muskcove. Return to your men, Morganuke, and look after them. They need you now."

About halfway to Muskcove, the militia came across a group of Cordinen soldiers, about three to four hundred in number. Yacob took his cavalry around the Cordinens to scout ahead, ordering the two companies of footmen to stay where they were and remain hidden.

When Yacob returned he reported that about one hundred women militia were ahead holding up the Cordinens whilst evacuees were making their way to the ships at Muskcove. "If we attack now from behind, we can trap the Cordinens between ourselves and the women's militia. Seedon, take your two companies and attack the Cordinens directly from behind," ordered Yacob. "I will go to the left and attack their left flank."

The militiamen, now revived from their rest, made themselves ready and charged into the back of the Cordinens whilst Yacob and his cavalry attacked from the left. The Cordinens were taken completely by surprise and being attacked from three sides were easily routed, making their escape through their right flank. Yacob ordered the men to stand their ground and not chase down the fleeing Cordinens, as he knew that there would be other Cordinen attacks coming soon.

When Morganuke met up with the militia women, his spirits were lifted when he saw that Calarel was with them, covered in blood from the enemies she had struck down.

Just then Yacob rode up on his horse and dismounted. An older woman dressed in full armour approached Yacob. "Thank you for your assistance. I am Lady Chanterly Bowderlong, commanding the women's militia in these parts. I don't know how much longer we would have lasted. There are many evacuees ahead of us making for the ships, and so we must leave this place and make sure they arrive safely," said the older woman as she sheathed her bloody sword. "Will you stand with us?"

Yacob nodded his head before turning to his men ordering them to reform their lines. Morganuke gathered what remained of his company and formed up with the women. The militia soldiers, now a mixture of men and women, moved towards Muskcove. The frantic evacuees ran before them, desperate to reach the ships before the pursuing Cordinens caught up with them. Morganuke looked back across the ground they had just covered and saw in the distance a mass of dark shapes moving quickly towards them. It was the main body of the Cordinen army.

They reached a series of hills, and the militia encouraged the evacuees onwards. Panic had started to break out amongst the evacuees, who had also spotted the Cordinens chasing them. The Cordinens got ever closer to the fleeing group, formed now from both evacuees and militia. Eventually they got to the top of the hills and over the other side. Below them they saw Muskcove and the ships in the harbour. As if given a second wind, the evacuees ran down the hill towards the rowboats waiting in the cove.

Yacob had ordered the militia to form a horseshoe shape to protect the remaining evacuees onshore. Morganuke could hear the panic behind him and the people running into the water to swim to the big ships. He turned and saw that the ships were now raising their sails and realised that not everyone would be leaving Muskcove. On the hilltop above the militia the horde of Cordinen soldiers appeared like a black tide moving rapidly down the hill onto the waiting militia.

Morganuke stood his ground, his sword in hand and ready to receive the oncoming horde. He ignored the pain in his shoulder.

"Stand fast, soldiers, and hold your ground for as long as you can," Yacob yelled just before an arrow struck him and he fell from his horse.

Morganuke swung his sword at the nearest Cordinen, then again at another and another. Covered in blood, he continued swinging his sword like a man possessed, taking no notice of the fellow soldiers, men, and women cut down beside him. The last he saw before everything went black was Seedon falling to the ground, two arrows embedded in his chest.

CHAPTER 10

Leaving the Island

Morganuke came to with his head hurting and not aware of where he was. He tried opening his eyes but immediately closed them when he felt dizzy and nauseous from his pounding head. He noticed a strange stuffiness in the air and felt the floor rocking slightly, but paid no heed to it as he thought it was due to his head. He tried to recall what had happened before losing consciousness and remembered that he had been on the battlefield with the Cordinens, surrounded by his fellow men and women in arms.

After a while lying there remembering the horrors of battle, Morganuke strained to open his eyes and looked around at his surroundings. Although his head hurt and his eyesight was still blurry, he recognised Lengrond and Chanterly close beside him. It seemed that he was on a ship and thought with relief that he must have been saved by one of the ships at Muskcove. He lay back down with a big sigh and closed his eyes, again intending to rest and hoping that the pain in his head would soon ease.

Morganuke was alerted by Lengrond's voice. "How do you feel?" Lengrond asked. "We've been captured by the Cordinens and bundled on one of their ships to take us who-knows-where."

Morganuke's heart sank. "So we're not on a friendly ship? I was hoping one of our ships at Muskcove would pick us up."

"Sadly not," replied Lengrond as he placed a damp cloth on Morganuke's forehead. "Most of the militia were slain by the Cordinens on the battlefield. They took a few of us prisoner, no doubt to make slaves of us. I thought they would leave you lying there on the battlefield, but some of the Cordinens took particular interest in you and decided to take you with us. You took a heavy blow to the head which really needs treating. You best rest for a while and try to recover."

Morganuke lay back down again, feeling weary from the pain and the realisation that they had been captured. He wondered about all the people who died at the hands of the Cordinens. Most of all he thought of his parents on the farm, which had now all been taken away. So much changed in such a short time. Although weary he couldn't sleep with everything on his mind. He turned to Lengrond, who was talking to Chanterly.

"What happened to Calarel, the blacksmith's daughter?" Morganuke asked.

Chanterly looked up and smiled sweetly at Morganuke. "She's on the ship but wounded. Thankfully, not seriously and should recover."

"I would like to see her when I'm able," Morganuke replied wistfully.

"Soon enough. You should rest now," added Chanterly.

Morganuke lay back down again, now feeling a little relieved at the hint of some good news about Calarel. Soon sleep took him into a dreamless slumber.

Morganuke rested for two days, tended to by Lengrond and Chanterly. He had seen Chanterly only briefly just before the battle at Cradport, and she had then appeared to be someone of cold authority leading the women's militia. Morganuke's opinion of her changed after her tender care for him. True, she was a strong warrior woman, but there was tenderness which Morganuke appreciated.

It seemed strange to Morganuke that they had been left to roam the lower decks freely without being bound. *Maybe this gives us an opportunity for escape*, he thought. *But then where do we go? For all I know we are in the middle of the ocean many stances from land.*

"Why are the Cordinens letting us move about freely and not tying us up?" Morganuke asked Lengrond.

"I assume it's because we have nowhere to run, and we are kept below decks," Lengrond replied.

"Have you seen much of the Cordinens?" Morganuke asked.

"Briefly, when they pass the food and water through the hatches from the upper decks," answered Lengrond.

"It seems mostly women that have been taken prisoner. Why have they taken you and me?" Morganuke asked as he looked around the cabin.

"Can't answer that. You and I have different features from most of the other men, so maybe that has something to do with it," Lengrond replied.

"Rumour has it that you are of particular interest to the Cordinens," interjected Chanterly, causing Morganuke and Lengrond to turn and face her questioningly. "It's also rumoured that folk looking like you, Morganuke, have been helping the Cordinens. So maybe this has something to do with their interest in you. As for you, Lengrond, I cannot guess, but maybe it has something to do with you being Cadmunese like Seedon."

Morganuke and Lengrond looked at each other and shrugged. "No doubt we will soon find out," added Morganuke.

Morganuke put his hand to his waste. "My sword! My sword has gone."

"Well of course it's gone. The Cordinens aren't going to leave us armed are they," Lengrond said with a frown.

"No, course not. It's just that it's special and I think it has some power somehow." Morganuke replied sadly.

"Is it possible for me to see Calarel now, Chanterly?" asked Morganuke as he stood up with some difficulty, still sore from his injuries.

"Yes, that should be all right. She is much improved in health now, although her mind has taken a toll with all that has happened. But she is strong, and I'm sure she will survive it all. Go through that partition, and you will find her there."

Morganuke made his way uneasily between the captive militia women, many still recovering from the battle. He pushed through the partition made of cloth sacking and found himself in a similar area for captive women. With so many confined in a small space, the air was stifling and the smell unpleasant. He spotted Calarel sitting in the opposite corner, looking dishevelled but still beautiful. He made his way over to her and knelt beside her.

"Hello, Calarel. How are you?" Morganuke asked.

Calarel looked up at Morganuke with no expression on her face. Her eyes lacked the sparkle Morganuke had remembered, and she looked at him blankly. "I wish I had died on the battlefield. It would have been a better fate than cooped up on this prison ship. For all I know my family are dead, and I will never see the island again."

"It's not like you to give up, Cal. You fought bravely. Yes it's true we all fought bravely and have nothing to be ashamed of. My parents are dead, and the farm is gone, but I'll not give in. How I wanted to give up when I found my parents dead! But realised it's important to hold on to whatever and whoever remains in our lives," Morganuke added softly as he reached for Calarel's hand.

"You always did talk silly gibberish," retorted Calarel. She moved away and quickly withdrew her hand.

They both sat in silence for moments until Calarel said with slow intent, "your parents are dead? I'm sorry about that. We have both lost much."

Morganuke sighed and leant back against a wooden crate. "Just because we've lost so much doesn't mean that we just give up. I still believe there is a purpose in our lives and in this war. It makes me want to find my origins even more than I did before. I do really want to find out where I came from. Why was I left abandoned as a baby with a great sword at my side?"

There was some commotion as the cabin door opened and two heavily armed Cordinen soldiers walked in. They came straight for Morganuke, grasped him by both arms, and forcefully lifted him to his feet.

"Come with us!" one of the soldiers demanded in a deep voice.

Morganuke was marched out of the prison area and up some steps to the upper decks. It was daylight outside, and Morganuke squinted at the bright sunlight. He hadn't seen the daylight in days, and his eyes were not used to it. As they made their way towards the stern, Morganuke saw many Cordinen soldiers standing or sitting on deck. It was the first time he had seen the Cordinens up close outside the heat of battle. They looked fearsome with thick leather armour over muscular stocky bodies, and they bristled with lethal-looking weapons.

Once they reached the stern, they went up steps to a tower deck from which some cabins could be accessed. Morganuke assumed this to be accommodations for more senior Cordinen soldiers or sailors, maybe even the captain's quarters. Morganuke was forced through the door of a cabin centred between two others of similar size.

Inside, the cabin was sparsely furnished, with a smell of mustiness and leather armour. A Cordinen stood before Morganuke in the centre, rugged in appearance even by Cordinen standard, with black hair greying at the temples. His uniform bore gold stripes along the sleeves and on his shoulders, giving Morganuke the impression that he was someone of importance in the command chain.

"Greetings, Pale One. I am Commander Brelack of the Cordinen expeditionary forces," announced the gold braided Cordinen military man in an authoritative tone. "Please sit." He beckoned Morganuke to a chair in front of him. Morganuke was surprised at how calm the man seemed, even welcoming. Morganuke slowly approached the chair and sat down, then watched intently to see what he would do next.

Commander Brelack slowly walked behind a desk and sat in the chair. "I hope you have not been treated too badly," he said, still calm. His deep voice vibrated in the small cabin. "It's unfortunate that you were taken with the other prisoners, but I am sure you can appreciate that in the heat of battle it is difficult to distinguish … individuals. I will ensure that from now on you get accommodation befitting your status."

Morganuke was now very confused. Why was Brelack treating him with such good intent? "Status? What do you mean? I am your prisoner. That is my status. Why treat me any differently to the other prisoners?"

"Surely you must understand your potential to our cause," Brelack said. "You are in an ideal position to help us, as others of your kind have done and still do."

"Why should I help when you've attacked my people on the island so?"

"Your people? Why do you call them that when it is evident that you are so very different. The island people set themselves against us to no avail. Your people look like you and have been helping us. You must do the same," the commander insisted. His voice did not now sound as calm.

Morganuke sat and thought about what the commander had said. He had known deep down that his origins were not from the island but didn't like to think that he was not one of the island folk. All his experience, all he knew, came from the island and the folk who lived on it. He had lived there all his life and had no memories of anything else. Yet he had a desire to know his true origins. Was this an opportunity to do that? But he would not help the Cordinens' cause. *Just maybe go along for now with what is being offered*, he thought, *and find out more.*

"I need to think about this. Much has changed over the past days in my life, and I can't think straight. Give me time," said Morganuke thoughtfully. He sat back in his chair and folded his arms across his chest.

"As you wish. But I need an answer soon," Commander Brelack beckoned to one of the guards. "Take this man to the cabin we have prepared for him and ensure he gets fed."

With that, Morganuke was led away by the guard to one of the cabins on the upper deck. The guard stood by the open door and waved Morganuke inside, closing and locking the door behind him.

Morganuke looked around the small cabin, which had the same musty smell as in the commander's cabin, though no strong smell of leather armour. There was a bed in one corner, and a bedside table with a jug and basin. In the centre, a meal and drink were laid out on a table that had a chair. It was a lot more comfortable than the accommodation he had shared with the other prisoners, but he would have preferred not to be alone. It was comforting to be with the others, and this cabin now made him feel very isolated.

I must be strong and go along with the Cordinen demands for now until I learn more, Morganuke thought. He suddenly felt very weary and lay down on the small bed. It creaked as he rested his head on the lumpy pillow. He tried to comprehend the magnitude of the changes that had taken place in his life over the recent weeks. He thought back to a time before the war, when life on the island seemed idyllic and the outside world had not touched his little farming life with his parents. Soon he had drifted into a deep sleep.

Morganuke found himself on a grassy plain on a bright sunny day. He didn't recognise the place but felt a foreboding about it. In the distance he saw shapes slowly moving across the plain. He moved towards the shapes without any effort, floating without needing any control over his movements. He could make out the figures of four individuals carrying what looked to be a black oblong object the size of a single bed. The figures held a long pole attached to the object at each corner. They moved in unison towards Morganuke.

As he got closer, Morganuke heard a faint humming sound coming from the object, and markings on its sides became visible. In the centre on each side was the image of an all-seeing lidless eye with a blue iris. He could see the four figures carrying the object clearly now. The figures had silver hair, red eyes and pale skin, like Morganuke.

The humming from the object became louder as Morganuke drew closer, sickening him and making him feel dizzy. His head pounded with the constant drone. Suddenly the four figures stopped and turned their heads towards Morganuke, each looking directly at him as they placed the object on the ground. They turned to face inward over it, holding out their hands and speaking several phrases that Morganuke could not understand. Then a flash of bright white light emanated from the object, and Morganuke could see the top opening like a door. A black sphere arose and drew him towards it. The blackness from the sphere seemed to consume him until there was no light—just complete and utter blackness.

Morganuke woke with his neck hurting from the lumpy pillow. *Are my dreams telling me something again?* he wondered. He thought about the others that had been so vivid he had recognised the cliffs of Cradport without ever having been there before. What about the eye he kept seeing in his dreams? *What is the Cordinen request for me to help* them as others like me are already doing? Are the dreams connected in some way? I must go along with the Cordinen plan for now and find out more.*

He slowly got himself out of bed and went over to the table where the meal had been laid out for him. There was some bread, cheese, and a mug of water. He hadn't eaten for some time and so sat down to enjoy his frugal meal, clearing every crumb on his plate and draining the last drop of water from the mug. Then he went to the porthole overlooking the stern and watched the white foam of the wake. He remembered similar views he'd had on the *Auora* and wondered what Fraytar was doing or whether he was still alive. *Every day we sail I'm leaving the island further behind. What is happening there now? My homeland is gone, and I'll probably never see it again.*

Morganuke tried the handle of the cabin door, but it was locked. *I would much rather be back below decks than stuck in the cabin on my own. There is so much I want to do and find out. But I must be patient and wait for an opportunity to arise to escape; if not from the ship, then from wherever the Cordinens are taking me.*

For two more days the Cordinen ship continued to sail in the same direction. *We've been traveling north*, Morganuke thought. *We must be making for the mainland, but where on the mainland I cannot guess. It will be somewhere in the Cordinen domain. How much of the mainland now lies in the Cordinen's hands?*

Morganuke had been well fed by the Cordinens over the past two days, but he desperately wanted to get out of the cabin. He wanted to see his friends again.

There was a rattling of keys at Morganuke's cabin door, which was flung open to reveal two Cordinen guards. "You're to come with us!" one demanded.

Morganuke was taken to Commander Brelack's cabin and offered a chair as before. The commander stood staring down at him for several moments. He cleared his throat and then went to sit in his chair behind a desk. "Have you come to a decision?" Brelack asked. "Will you work with the others of your kind for our cause?"

Morganuke stayed silent for some moments before asking, "What exactly is it you want me to do?"

"To use your powers along with the others, of course."

So, it's true. My dream is telling me this, Morganuke thought. He pondered for a moment. "There is a condition, if you want me to help you. Those taken prisoner with me should be treated well, and I want to see them. I don't want to be locked in any cabin. I want my sword back too."

The commander frowned and thought for a moment. "Very well. But any trouble they or you cause will immediately mean their death and possibly yours. And if you prove not to be useful to us, then you will all be put to death."

Commander Brelack fetched Morganuke's sword and stood looking at it for a moment. "This is a very fine sword indeed," Brelack said, rubbing his fingers over the bejewelled handle. "I don't think I've ever seen one as fine. The metal is not known to me. This must signify status somehow." Brelack then handed the sword to Morganuke, who gave a stern nod and took the sword. Commander Brelack gave a sign for a guard to open the cabin door.

"I'll allow you free access," Brelack said as Morganuke stood, "but any deception on your part will have immediate consequences." Morganuke left the cabin with sword in hand, this time without an escort.

Morganuke was given some looks from the Cordinens as he walked across the open deck, but he was not stopped. He felt exposed walking about freely and expected to be accosted at any moment by a Cordinen ignorant of Commander Brelack's approval. But when he reached the entrance to the lower decks and asked a guard to let him in, he was allowed in without question.

Inside he was hit by the smell of too many individuals in too small an area. He thought of his own cabin and its relative luxury, feeling guilty, but he had a purpose and had to carry it out no matter how he disliked it. He looked around at the militia women strewn around the lower decks. He counted twenty, and many were injured, with their wounds being attended to. One or two of the women briefly looked up at him with no expression and the others paid him little attention at all.

He made his way to a cordoned-off part in one corner of the lower deck storage, where he found Lengrond, Chanterly, and Calarel huddled together, discussing something. They looked Morganuke up and down, paying particular attention to the sword he was holding.

"Where have you been? What did the Cordinens want with you? Why have you got your sword back?" asked Chanterly.

"They asked me to help them by working with the others like me. They mentioned using some power, but I don't know yet what they meant. I'm going to make it look as though I'll do what they want, because it'll keep you and me alive," Morganuke answered awkwardly, rubbing his free hand on his shirt.

"Pah! You just want fancy clothes, swords and quarters. That's why you agreed to work with them," scoffed Calarel. "Look at you! Scrubbed up cleaner than a new pan."

"That's not fair!" retorted Morganuke. "This gives us a chance to find out what they are doing and keeps you safe. I don't want to help them any more than you do."

Chanterly got up and put her hands on her hips, sighing loudly. "All right! All right! Maybe Morganuke's got a point. We have no clue what the Cordinens will do with us, and maybe this is a way of finding out—and even, hopefully, a way out. We can't give up hope and must grasp at anything that will give us a chance to be free again."

CHAPTER 11

A Captain's Tale

On the *Aurora* Fraytar was keeping watch. Looking over the bow towards Tannisport, to his horror he saw a fleet of Cordinen warships anchored there. He immediately ordered the coxswain to change course and sail northwards further up the coast. Then he turned to Crouch, who was standing on the upper deck beside him. "It looks like Tannisport has been overrun. Where is the militia I've heard so much about?"

"All may not be lost. The militia may be taking a defensive stance further north," Crouch surmised.

Fraytar nodded. "The next nearest anchorage point with access to the coast is Muskcove, and so we'll head there."

Keeping as close to the coast as they dared, the *Aurora* continued sailing northward, hoping not to be spotted by the Cordinens. Fraytar was about to return to his cabin when a shout came from the lookout on the mainmast. "Cordinen ships ahead!"

Fraytar quickly went forward on the bow and took out his spyglass to see for himself. There were two Cordinen ships ahead of them. He turned to Crouch, who had followed him onto the bow. "We cannot go back and risk being run down by the Cordinen fleet in Tannisport. We'll have to head out to sea to outrun the ships ahead. Make ready full sail, Crouch. Let's see how fast these Cordinen ships are."

The *Aurora* changed course, heading further out to sea. They were now sailing against the wind, but their triangular sails tacked well into the wind. The two Cordinen ships ahead of them had seen them and began to give chase. But their square-sailed ships were no match for the *Aurora*, which was soon out of sight.

As the *Aurora* drew close to Muskcove later that afternoon, several ships were anchored around the cove. Fraytar took a deep sigh, hoping that they were not more Cordinen ships. Looking through his spyglass, he could see with relief that they were island ships. "Those are friendly ships. Steer towards the cove, and let's see what help we can give."

A crowd of islanders were lined up on the natural harbour, waiting to board the ships. Rowboats were ferrying others from the shore to the ships anchored in the cove. There was movement everywhere, with people streaming onto the shoreline from the hills inland. On top of the hills that surrounded the cove, Fraytar could see what looked like soldiers. He took out his spyglass realised that they were women dressed in light leather armour and brandishing swords.

The *Aurora* anchored in the cove alongside the other ships and began taking islanders on board from the rowboats. Fraytar watched from the upper deck as the frantic activity took place. "Quick as you can, men. The Cordinens will be on us soon," he shouted to his crew.

Fraytar looked over the decks of the *Aurora* at the growing numbers of evacuees. There were still many onshore yet to be ferried onto the big ships waiting in Muskcove.

"Take as many as you can to the lower decks, Crouch. There won't be any more ships for some time and so we need to get as many on board as we can," ordered Fraytar as he looked over at the other ships still being loaded with evacuees.

"We'll sink before we get out of the cove if we take on many more," answered Crouch, as he beckoned more evacuees on board.

"The ship will hold," Fraytar confidently answered.

Fraytar took out his spyglass and looked towards the hills beyond the cove and saw groups of more evacuees appearing over the brow, followed closely by men and women in armour. He continued to watch as more evacuees and soldiers appeared, this time accompanied by a small band of cavalry. He watched as the soldiers and cavalry formed up halfway down the hill in loose order, making a horseshoe formation between the fleeing evacuees and the top of the hills. Soon after the militia had formed up, a mass of Cordinens came crashing over the top of the hills towards the island militia.

Fraytar braced himself. "Prepare to set sail. We must leave before the enemy can capture the ships. Continue to take on as many evacuees as you can whilst we prepare." Fraytar looked over at the other ships and saw that they were doing the same.

Fraytar surveyed the folk he had rescued from Muskcove, now gathered on the *Aurora*'s deck. They had been close to being caught themselves when the Cordinen ships arrived just outside of Muskcove. They had to make a break for it and were fortunate the wind was in their favour, as the triangular sails of the *Aurora* gave them an advantage over the Cordinen ships pursuing them. They were tracked for the first two days, but eventually Fraytar managed to escape, heading east towards Cradport.

After six more days of sailing, the *Aurora* arrived at the Cradport harbour and gingerly made its way to the docks. It was the first time Fraytar had returned to Cradport since the battle with the Cordinens when Captain Amannar was killed. Fraytar looked around nervously as they entered the harbour, fearing a repeat of that experience. Seeing the many islander ships in the harbour and militia lined along the shore, Fraytar raised a sigh of relief. Cradport was now a militia stronghold.

"So we be 'ere at last." Fraytar turned to see Tomlin watching over his shoulder as the crew readied the ship for docking. "I hopes Calarel be rescued by one of the t'other ships," he added.

Fraytar could see the concern in Tomlin's face but didn't want to raise his hopes. "It's unlikely, I'm afraid. Calarel was almost certainly amid the battle with the Cordinens as we left Muskcove. I've heard that the Cordinens do take prisoners, especially women, so maybe there's hope that she is still alive at least."

Tomlin screwed up his face and looked down at the floor. "That be no life for a yung'un," he added. "If she do be taken prisoner as a slave, do he thinks she can be rescued?"

"At present if she has been taken into the midst of the Cordinen stronghold then it would be an impossible task," Fraytar answered truthfully.

Tomlin stood silent for a moment. "I'll never give up hope. I be sure to do whatever it takes to find my girl. So, what he going to do now, lad?"

"I'll get these islanders onshore and then report to the militia commander to see what they want me to do next." Fraytar beckoned to Crouch, who was on the lower deck instructing the crew to prepare the gangplanks ready for debarkation.

The islander refugees massed on deck nervously shuffled as the boarding planks were laid across to the harbour shore. They seemed eager to get off the ship as quickly as possible and into what they assumed to be safety. The sight of so many militia on the shore was comforting to many, including the crew of the *Aurora*. But it was unlikely that the *Aurora* would stay for long, as there was much to do preparing for the ongoing war with the Cordinens. Fraytar was sure that the militia would have plenty for his crew to do. He longed for the days when he could sail freely without being hunted by an enemy as ruthless as the Cordinens, but his sense of duty had compelled him to do what he thought was right.

Once the gangplanks had been secured, the rescued islanders began filing off the *Aurora* and onto the docks. Some of the militia were waiting to receive them for registration and to direct them to their holding area. The younger ones would no doubt be "encouraged" to join the militia. Groups of refugees brought in by other ships already were being received by the militia. It seemed that the whole of the western island was gathering in Cradport. The streets now teamed with people, many not sure what they were doing or where they were going.

Crouch appeared at Fraytar's side. "What are your orders, Captain?"

"While we're getting the islanders off the ship, round up eight crewmen and go ashore to get supplies. I doubt we will be staying here long. I'll find the militia commander and get orders for our next mission."

Crouch gave a brief nod and turned to follow his captain's orders. Turning to Tomlin, Fraytar asked, "Do you want to come with me to find the commander, or will you stay on board?"

"Nothing fur me to do ye'er, so I'll come with he. Maybe they knows something about the prisoners taken at Muskcove," Tomlin answered.

Fraytar and Tomlin made their way through the streets of Cradport, pushing through the crowds as best they could. There were so many locals and refugees from the west milling about in the streets that it was hard for Fraytar and Tomlin to see where they were going. They headed towards what looked like an official building on the other side of the harbour. It had a large banner hanging above the door, and so Fraytar thought that it may be a militia command point. After much pushing and shoving, they reached the door of the building, where guards were posted outside. Fraytar approached one. "I'm Captain Fraytar DeLance of the sailing ship *Aurora*, and I need to see the militia commander."

"The commander is very busy. Is he expecting you, Captain?" The guard asked.

"Please tell the commander that I need to see him urgently to receive new orders for my ship," Fraytar insisted impatiently. "I have just sailed all the way from the other side of the island, escaping by the skin of my teeth from the Cordinens, and I have no patience dillydallying with you, so please do as I ask."

"Wait here!" the guard snapped at Fraytar before entering the building.

Moments later the guard reappeared at the door and beckoned Fraytar in. Inside, Fraytar found himself in a corridor with several doors opening from it. He followed the guard to a door at the end of the corridor. On opening the door, the guard announced Fraytar's arrival to a middle-aged Cadmunese man in uniform sat behind a big desk. Typical of the Cadmunese, he had green eyes with red hair, spiked here and there with grey. His uniform was an impressive black leather with gold braiding along the shoulders and collar. The commander's cool green eyes studied Fraytar for a moment.

"I am Commander Falcar Tradish. It is good to see you, Captain DeLance. I've heard a lot of good things about you and your ship, and we have a lot to discuss. Please sit, and we'll talk about where you could fit into the scheme of things."

Fraytar pulled out a chair on his side of the desk and then realised that Tomlin was not with him. *I hope he hasn't got himself lost*, he thought. *I don't have time to look for him now.*

Once Fraytar was comfortably seated, the commander began to explain the situation on the island and his view of the Cordinen attacks. It was all a bit political and military minded, and Fraytar only half listened to what the commander was going on about. Suddenly he sat up and took notice at a familiar name.

"I understand that you know a man from the island named Morganuke Beldere. In fact, I've been led to believe that it was you who first found him washed up on a beach as a babe." The commander intently leant forward to hear Fraytar's answer.

Fraytar frowned, puzzling why the commander should be asking about Morganuke. "Yes. Why do you ask? For all I know Morganuke is dead now, killed with the other militia during the west island battles."

"That may not be the case," Commander Tradish said. "We have received information that a race of people having similar features to Morganuke are helping the Cordinens, some call them the pale ones. Our spies within the Cordinen network report that these people have a mighty weapon that only they are capable of handling. They are using it to the Cordinens' advantage over the Epleons. We don't know where they come from, but the number of these people that the Cordinens have access to seems limited. It is our belief that Morganuke has been captured by the Cordinens to add to their number."

Fraytar kept silent for a moment, thinking carefully about what he should say next. "I had heard that these other people were helping the Cordinens, but I'm sure that Morganuke has had nothing to do with that. He has fought bravely against the Cordinens on my ship and in the militia."

"You misunderstand me." Tradish added. "I'm not saying that Morganuke has helped the Cordinens. But if he has been captured, the Cordinens may have the means to force him into helping them, in which case he could become a great threat to us and the Epleons. Getting access to this weapon, whatever it may be, may be a way to rebalance the war. I plan to send more spies into the Cordinen network to gather facts and find a way to get access to the weapon. The Cordinens' current strongpoint may turn out to be a weak link that we can exploit." He paused, watching for Fraytar's reaction. "It may also be a way to rescue Morganuke, if he is still alive."

"If Morganuke is still alive, then I'll do everything I can to help." Fraytar said.

"I want you to sail my spies into the Cordinen homeland of Ventor. Your seamanship capabilities are well known, and your ship is fast enough to outrun any Cordinen pursuers. You will be well paid for your efforts. Do you not want an opportunity to rescue Morganuke?" Tradish asked.

Fraytar did care very much about Morganuke, and if there was a chance that he was still alive and could be rescued, then he would do anything to make that happen. Maybe, just maybe, he could find Calarel for Tomlin as well. "Very well. I'll do what I can to help."

Commander Tradish sat back in his chair; his intent look now replaced with a calm smile. "That is good news indeed," he said. "I'll draw up plans and get my men ready. Please return tomorrow, and we'll go through the details before you set sail. Your willingness to help is much appreciated, Captain DeLance."

Once Fraytar left the commander's office, he remembered that he needed to search for Tomlin. He just hoped that Tomlin had stayed near the front door. As he exited, however, he saw no sign of the blacksmith. Fraytar asked the guards if they had seen the man who had been with him, but they had not even noticed him. *Maybe he went back to the ship*, Fraytar thought.

Fraytar searched the crowded streets in vain for any sign of the blacksmith. He assumed that Tomlin could make his way back to the ship if needed. It took some time for Fraytar to make his own way back to the ship through the mayhem, forcing himself through in some places. When he arrived at the ship, he called up to Crouch, who was supervising the crew preparing the rigging. "Crouch, have you seen Tomlin?"

Crouch leant over the side with a concerned look. "No, Captain. Ain't seen Tomlin, but there were some odd-looking characters asking for he earlier on. Not sure who they be, but I didn't like the look of 'em. They refused to say who they were."

Fraytar puzzled as to who that could be. He then remembered what Tradish had said about sending some of his spies over to see him and thought that's who it may have been. At least he hoped so. "I'm expecting some men representing Commander Tradish and so it may have been them. If they return, please get them to confirm what they want."

First things first, he thought. *I must find Tomlin. Where would Tomlin likely be in times of trouble?* Then he realized that Tomlin would probably go to an inn or anywhere where they served ale.

Making his way back through the crowds, Fraytar stopped a man who was carrying a crate of freshly caught fish. He looked to be local. "Can you tell me where the nearest inn is, please?" Fraytar asked.

"The Jumping Fish, across the courtyard yonder," answered the man, barely looking at Fraytar as he continued his struggle through the crowd.

Fraytar made his way to the place through the dense crowds as directed. Finally he caught sight of a sign painted with a fish jumping out of the sea. The sign swung with a loud high pitch squeak in the wind, audible even over the bustling crowd.

Inside the inn was a mass of people shoulder to shoulder. Fraytar's heart sank as he peered through the dimly lit, smoke-filled room at faces he didn't recognise. He shouted Tomlin's name as loud as he could, but it would be difficult for anyone to hear across the noisy, bustling room. Frustrated, he forced his way across the room until he got to the bar with several drunken men leant across it. He scrambled onto the bar, snatching a large metal container as he did, and then drew out his sword and bashed the container as hard as he could. "Tomlin Francite! Are You Here?" he shouted at the top of his voice.

From the brief lull amidst the drone of gossip and noise came a loud groan from the other end of the bar. "Wha's ... gooin' ... oonnn—*hic!*"

Fraytar tracked the direction of the sound of the groan to a cluster of drunks, amongst which a very unsteady Tomlin emerged, swaying on his feet.

Fraytar jumped down from the bar and grabbed Tomlin just as he was about to fall. "Let's get you back on board," he said. He put his shoulder under Tomlin's arm and helped him make his way unsteadily across the inn, pushing past several folk as he did. Outside the inn, the streets were filled with locals and refugees, some having a purpose and others not seeming to know where they were going.

When at last Fraytar reached the *Aurora*, he helped Tomlin to his cabin and laid him on the bed, leaving to return to his work. Several hours later, Morganuke returned. The blacksmith was awake, mumbling and grumbling and holding his head. "Aaaah, where am I?" he groaned.

"You are back on the *Aurora*," Fraytar answered. "I rescued you from the inn where you'd been drinking heavily. No doubt drowning your sorrows."

"I don't think she be yeer," Tomlin groaned, holding his head and sitting up. "I can't find me daughter, but refuse to give up."

"What can I do with you?" Fraytar sighed, looking up at the ceiling of his cabin. "You'll just have to come with me. I'm going back to the mainland, and we can look for your daughter there. I also need to find Morganuke, who, it seems, has been taken prisoner by the Cordinens. Maybe your daughter has too. I'm led to believe that the Cordinens like to take young and pretty women as slaves."

"Oh, yes. Thank 'ee, Fraytar. You're a good friend."

First thing the next morning, Fraytar made his way to Commander Tradish's office. This time the guards didn't ask any questions, and he was led straight in.

"Ah, there you are. Good. We have a lot to go through before you set off for the mainland," Tradish said briskly as Fraytar sat himself down opposite. "My men paid a visit to your ship yesterday but were sent away. I hope you have now had time to brief your crew. It's vital that these men travel with you to Ventor so that they can liaise with the spies already stationed there. But we need to be careful so as not to raise suspicions with the Cordinens."

"Yes, I hadn't had a chance to talk to my crew before your men arrived. They are fully aware of the situation now, and we are ready for your men to come on board. Of course, you still need to tell me where we are heading," Fraytar said.

"Yes, of course." Tradish rustled through some maps and papers on his desk.

Fraytar shifted in his chair, building up courage to ask his next question. "Commander, I hope you don't think me rude for asking, but I have been wondering why Cadmunese like yourself have got involved in Banton Island troubles. Your lands are far away, and it seems strange that you would come all this way to help the islanders. Mercenaries you may be, but I can't believe that money is your only objective."

"You're a perceptive man, Captain. I like that, and you are right to ask the question. Cadmun Major, my homeland, lies some way south of the Cordinen homeland, Ventor. But it is only a matter of time before the Cordinens set their eyes on our lands. We will not wait for that to happen. Our people have been working surreptitiously with the Epleons for some time to pre-empt Cordinen ambitions of conquest. I'm now happy to work with the Banton Islanders for the same purpose. I hope that answers your question and that you do not doubt my motives."

"Thank you, commander, for your candour. It does answer that question, but I have another. You stated that you have spies on the mainland. It takes weeks for any ship to travel from the mainland, but you have information received recently. We sailed directly from Muskcove following the battle between the militia and the Cordinens, yet you already have information about Morganuke that seems very new. How can this be?"

Tradish raised his eyebrows, studying Fraytar intently for a moment. "The information I'm about to give you must be held with the utmost secrecy. You cannot tell anyone." He paused, still reckoning. "We have come into possession of some devices from the same race of people as Morganuke and those helping the Cordinens. These devices allow us to talk to our contacts even though they are many stances away. Whoever these people are, they possess things that we have never seen or even heard of. Nobody knows where they come from, but their existence will very likely change everything. We stand on a precipice, and with one wrong move we will all fall into oblivion."

Fraytar remained silent for some time, taking in the information that Commander Tradish had just shared with him. This whole episode was much bigger than he had imagined.

"I know this is a lot to take in just now," Tradish continued, "but time is not on our side. We must get down to planning your trip."

Fraytar continued to think about the implications of the strange things he'd learnt. He thought of Morganuke captured by the Cordinens and what they might do to him. His attention returned to Commander Tradish.

"Your destination on the mainland is the Cordinen city of Cryantor in Ventor. This is where the Cordinens take their captives and keep the most of their strange helpers—the Morganuke types, I mean or Pale Ones as they call them. We believe that this is also where they may be taking Morganuke and where we can learn more about this strange artefact that they use as a weapon. There is a secret cove nearby that my men can direct you to under cover of darkness. Once you are landed safely, our contacts will be waiting to guide you in. You will have access to one of the devices we call the talking box, which will allow us to keep in touch. This will give us a massive advantage."

"Talking box or no talking box," Fraytar finally said with great deliberation, "this seems a very risky plan. Take my ship straight into the Cordinen homeland with the massive navy they have in that area? It seems an impossible task. Yes, my ship is fast and nimble, but I will be severely outnumbered and sure to be detected at some stage. Would it not be best to land somewhere in the Epleon homeland of Lobos, which is next to Ventor, and have your men make the way from there?"

"Whilst landing in Lobos may be low risk, getting my men across the front line, which now stretches between Castle Drobin to Castle Medogor and Stacklin, is a much greater risk—and likely to fail."

"But those are strongholds for the Epleons in Lobos," Fraytar said.

"They have fallen under Cordinen control," Commander Tradish informed him. Fraytar was shocked to hear this news. Things had apparently got a lot worse for the Epleon cause since he was last there.

"My spies can tell you where the Cordinen ships are and how to manoeuvre around them," Tradish continued. "The 'talking boxes' will give you the latest information on the enemy's movements by land and by sea. But the Cordinens may well have similar boxes provided to them by their pale friends. We need to find out whether they have this advantage. Our aim must be to shift the advantage to the Epleons, so that the Cordinens must focus only on that war and not expand their territories outside of the mainland."

Fraytar was still doubtful. "Assuming I do get your men to Cryantor, what then? Return here for more ferry trips?"

"For the time being, you will need to stay near the mainland, at least until you hear otherwise. You could take temporary refuge somewhere in Lobos until we know what the next steps should be. We do have other ships in the area, but not in the same class as your vessel and crew—and, I might add, the *Aurora*'s fine captain."

"Very well. I'll go along with your plan," Fraytar said.

"I should point out that any information about the talking boxes and the fact that we are in possession of them must be kept from the Epleons at all costs, Captain," Tradish stressed.

"Why should that be, Commander?" Fraytar asked

"This is due to the influence from the Casdredon religious sect in Lobos," Tradish continued. "They are very influential in Lobos as they are one of the three ruling sections of the Epleon society: the other two being the King's court and the military. The Casdredon priests are very sceptical about anything that cannot be explained by common or proven knowledge. The talking boxes would be an example of that, and they would likely put it down to being some sort of demonic influence or witchcraft. Anyone who is found to be associated with such things could be accused of heresy by the Casdredon priests, which could be punishable by death."

"I understand, Commander," Fraytar replied. "I shall make sure that our talking box remain secret from the Epleons."

CHAPTER 12

The Mainland

In the bowels of the Cordinen ship, Calarel sat with Chanterly and Lengrond. They had spent most of their time together on the voyage, trying to keep each other's spirits up. Calarel couldn't understand how the other two seemed to remain optimistic. She had struggled to accept the situation and felt very depressed. *Things always seem so bleak*, Calarel thought. *I always look at things pessimistically at the best of times. Now I have a real reason to complain and feel bad, but I just haven't got the energy to even do that. I feel like just giving up. If I could get on deck, then I would jump overboard. Anything must be better than this.*

Calarel heard voices from above deck declaring that Cryantor was in view.

"We must be nearing our destination," Chanterly said. She got up to go and check on the other militia women.

"So what becomes of us now?" Calarel asked despondently.

Chanterly turned back, the glow of a nearby oil lamp outlining her handsome womanly face. "For now, we'll have to learn how to be slaves. At least until we come up with a plan. Hopefully, what Morganuke told us will come to something. Do you trust him?" she asked Calarel pointedly.

"He may say silly boorish things at times, but I think I trust him.

At least I trust his intentions. As to whether his plans are realistic, well, that's a different question," Calarel replied, screwing up her nose.

Lengrond looked at the two women in turn and spoke sternly. "Morganuke is true to his word, and he has proven to be a very capable soldier. I trust and believe in him. I'm sure he will deliver a good plan."

The lower deck access door rattled loudly and was flung open. Two Cordinen soldiers poked their heads inside. "All out on the upper deck!" ordered one.

The prisoners slowly got to their feet. After their weeks of being cooped up on the lower decks, muscles were stiff, making their movements laborious. They shuffled out in file onto the upper deck. Calarel squinted in the daylight, her eyes not used to so much brightness, to make out the bleak buildings of Cryantor. "What a glum-looking place this is," she said as she lined up next to Lengrond and Chanterly.

"Put the Cadmun man and the two women with him onto the wagon waiting on the dock," an officer shouted to the Cordinen guards standing close to Calarel, Chanterly, and Lengrond. The three of them were immediately bundled off the ship and onto the waiting wagon and driven off at speed through the city.

"Where can they be taking us?" Lengrond asked, his voice broken by the jolts of the wagon.

"It must be something to do with Morganuke," Chanterly answered, desperately holding on to the side to try to keep from being thrown about.

"Whatever the reason," Calarel said amidst the jostling, "and wherever we are going, I'm sure this is not gonna be a good experience."

The wagon eventually came to a stop, pulling up outside the tall iron gates of a military compound. Once papers had been checked by guards, the wagon continued its progress inside.

"This is a bleak place indeed," Chanterly commented, catching her breath from the bumpy ride. The wagon was now travelling more slowly, giving the three prisoners time to recover and survey the bleak surroundings. They observed guards and slaves milling about the complex and looked at one another with growing dread.

The wagon came to a halt in front of a building, and they were bundled off and inside, where they were marched along a corridor until they got to some stairs. Dark and uninviting, the stairs led them down to the lower floor and into one of the rooms leading off the lower corridor. They were confronted with a room full of young women, all wearing plain grey dresses and a leather collar. In one corner, Calarel noticed a young woman who was cradling a sobbing girl. *Children as slaves*, she shuddered. *What is this depraved place we have been brought to?*

Morganuke was glad to finally reach the mainland, even though it was the enemy's homeland. After weeks of sailing, he had had quite enough of ships for the time being and wanted to get his feet on firm land again. As soon as they had disembarked at Cryantor, Morganuke was taken straight to a military complex in the city. Although he was being shown a bit more respect from the Cordinens, now that he had agreed to help them, the trip from the ship to the complex was not comfortable. He had been loaded onto an open wagon with some of the Cordinen soldiers and driven through the bumpy streets at some speed. Every bump the wagon encountered rattled his bones to the core.

To Morganuke, the city was like nothing he had seen before. There was no grandeur or delicacy. No flower gardens or ornate decoration, and only a few untended withered trees. The buildings themselves were plain and uninviting, mostly built of dark mud and stone, with crude thatched or slated roofs. Here and there Cordinen people glumly set about their business. The few children Morganuke saw seemed quiet and glum; there was no laughter or joy on their faces.

The complex appeared foreboding to Morganuke as they drew up to its massive dark walls, tall as five men, with jagged spikes atop. The only access was through the black iron gates guarded by a host of Cordinen soldiers. The wagon stopped outside the gates, and two guards approached to check the access papers of the soldiers on the wagon.

"We're bringing in a new Pale One. Here the orders are. Let us in now!" said one of the guards on the wagon brusquely. The gate guard briefly checked the papers and then quickly nodded as he handed the papers back. The large gates were opened by other guards, with a crunching sound that jarred Morganuke. He shuddered, wandering if he'd ever leave this place he was about to enter.

Inside the complex were several dark buildings, with a road in the middle leading up to the largest building in the complex. As the wagon headed for the main building, Morganuke surveyed the complex. Patrols of Cordinen soldiers were making their way from one building to another. Some of the soldiers were leading along several other people, unlike the Cordinens in appearance, wearing plain grey clothing and with a heavy leather collar around their neck, with a locking mechanism. *Slaves!* Morganuke thought. It's true then, the Cordinens are contemptable slave owners.

The wagon reached the building at the end of the road, where Morganuke was manhandled off the wagon and his sword removed from the belt around his waste. He was then escorted inside the building, which was even less welcoming than it was on the outside. A long corridor stretched down the length of the building with a large door at the end. On each side of the corridor were other closed rooms. Morganuke was taken to the door at the end.

One of the guards knocked loudly and waited for a response.

"Enter!" came a booming reply.

"Commander General Miliaton," the guard announced, "here he is." He beckoned Morganuke to enter the dark room, very dark and featureless in its decoration and furniture, as all the other Cordinen buildings had been. The man sitting behind the desk looked large and powerful even by Cordinen standards. His skin was darker than that of most Cordinens, his hair black with flecks of grey, and his eyes black like pits of tar. His lips parted to show a set of jagged teeth, and from his mouth came a booming voice.

"So, you are the new Pale One that is here to help our cause. You will have an opportunity to prove your worth soon enough. Rewards you will get if you prove obedient and worthy. Death will be your punishment otherwise." The man in the chair sat back in contemplation. "I'm told that you have friends taken from the island. Death will be their punishment too, if you prove to be unworthy."

"I have already said that I'll help you. I don't care what you do to me but will never help you if my friends are harmed," Morganuke answered as convincingly as he could, considering the overbearing nature of the giant Cordinen before him. "You say that I need to prove myself. How am I to do this?"

"You will be told when and where you need to prove yourself in good time. One chance you will get to do that. Failure will be death for your friends. For now, you will be kept here until an opportunity arises for you to work with your kin and prove yourself," the man in the chair boomed on, leaning forward intently.

"My kin? Who is that? All my family are dead, thanks to the Cordinens," Morganuke answered, then fearing that he may have been too assertive, added quickly, "but that is war, and now I'm here."

"Your kin are your race of people. Those that are helping us in our cause with their powers," the man in the chair replied, unmoved by this response.

Morganuke knew what the Commander General meant but just wanted to hear him say it. "Where are my friends now? I would like to see them. Let me see Calarel, Chanterly, and Lengrond."

"When you prove yourself, you can see your friends. Not before then." Commander General Miliaton beckoned to one of the guards. "Take this one to the Pale Ones' holding quarters."

"Can I have my sword back at least?" Morganuke asked

"You'll get your sword when you prove yourself," Miliaton answered.

Morganuke was escorted from the building and then inside one of the other smaller buildings along the same road through the complex. Rooms ran off a central corridor. Stairs led downwards halfway along. Morganuke looked down the stairs as they walked past them, and he wandered what was down there. It looked even more dark and uninviting than the level he was on. He was then led into one of the rooms running off the corridor. and the door was closed behind him but not locked.

As Morganuke expected, the room was sparsely furnished. A bed in one corner, a table in the middle with a chair. An oil lamp flickered on the bedside table, and the room was poorly lit by the daylight from one small window.

Morganuke felt tiredness overcome him and went to lie down on the bed, immediately falling asleep. His sleep was light and dreamless. He was awoken easily by a faint knock on the door. He thought it strange that someone would knock—he expected a Cordinen to barge in without any announcement.

"Come in," Morganuke said in an uncertain voice.

The door slowly opened to reveal a young woman carrying a tray of food. She gingerly walked into the room and placed the tray on the table in the centre of the room.

Morganuke's breath was taken away at the woman's beauty. She had long silky black hair that hung to her waist. When she turned to look at him, her face was soft and delicate. Her chin narrowed to a dainty fine line, and her large brown eyes drew Morganuke in. She wore a slave's collar over a plain grey dress, which took away nothing from her beauty.

For a moment Morganuke could say nothing. He thought Calarel beautiful, but this young woman was beyond anything he had seen before. She stood in front of him, seemingly waiting to be dismissed.

"Hello, what is your name?" Morganuke managed to ask.

"Melinor," the woman nervously replied. "Melinor Skoln, master. I have been commanded to serve you."

The thought of her having to serve him, or anyone else for that matter, horrified him. "Please don't call me your master. I'm not your master. I am a captive like you. Where are you from before you became a slave?"

"I come from Vesnick City in Trebos, master. My sister and I were captured there during a Cordinen raid many moons ago." Melinor was still nervous but looked a little more at ease.

"You have a sister here too?" Morganuke asked, sitting up in bed.

"Yes, master. She is of the age eight years, and her name is Alorie," Melinor replied, smiling nervously to show the dimples in her cheeks.

"When you say you're to serve me, what does that mean?" Morganuke asked.

"Anything you ask, I must do. If you want food or drink, I must provide for you." She added shyly, "Even my body."

Morganuke was shocked that any person could be used in such a way. "I will not ask you to do anything you wouldn't want to," he replied gently.

Melinor frowned. "I don't really understand. What are you saying, master? You don't like me? You want another to serve you?"

"Forgive me." Morganuke said. "I really like you and am happy to meet you. I want you as a friend rather than a slave. Please continue to visit me, I would like that very much."

Melinor smiled sweetly. *She has such a lovely smile,* Morganuke thought. He looked at her dainty hands and noticed a small plain ring with tiny letters inscribed on it on her thumb.

"Does your ring signify anything? It seems unusual to see a slave wearing such an item." Morganuke asked,

"It has no value other than to me sentimentally," Melinor answered. "The Cordinens take no notice of it as it's worthless to them. I treasure it though, as it was given to me by my father on my sixteenth birthday."

"You must miss your family very much."

"Yes, I do. Thank you, master. If there is nothing else, I shall leave you now." With that, Melinor gave a quick curtsy and turned to leave the room.

"Please come to visit me again soon," Morganuke called after her. Melinor turned to smile at him before closing the door after her.

Melinor walked down the dark corridor, thinking of what Morganuke had said. He didn't seem like the other Pale Ones, who treated her with contempt at best and usually like she wasn't there. Morganuke had been kind and tender to her, but was this just a ploy? She had never trusted the Pale Ones since she learnt that they were helping the Cordinens, and surely Morganuke was no different.

The dark stairway leading down from the corridor took Melinor into the serving slave quarters she shared with several other women.

These were even less inviting than the upper floor of the building, dimly lit with the odd candle or oil lamp, and no windows to provide daylight. Melinor reached her room and went inside.

Melinor looked across at her sister sitting on the bed. She felt very protective towards Alorie, who had been deeply traumatised by the kidnap experience. Although only eight years old, physically small, and a little immature for her age, Alorie was made to work every bit as hard as the other slaves. Her features were strikingly like Melinor's, but her face was grubby from the work she had been doing that day. Melinor would need to address that to avoid punishment from the guards. The Cordinens were very particular about the cleanliness of their female slaves as some were required to work inside the Cordinen officer's houses. For this reason, there were plenty of washing facilities available to the slaves despite the sparse accommodation. Melinor went over to the bed she shared with her sister.

"Hello, Mel," Alorie said. "I'm hungry. Will we eat soon?"

Melinor looked intently at her and wished she could do more for her. They had not eaten yet that day, as they were both being punished for disobeying one of the guards the previous day. "I'm afraid that we shall not eat until tomorrow," answered Melinor sympathetically. "You must be strong. Make sure you drink plenty of water. At least we still have that."

Her sister screwed up her face and threw herself down on the bed, weeping gently. Melinor lay down beside her and put an arm around her, soothing her.

Things were so different when they were free in Vesnick City, in their homeland of Trebos. Until a year ago, Melinor had been working hard in the local laundry, but late in the afternoon she would pick up her sister from classes and they would go swimming together in the sea, laughing and giggling in the water. Melinor was nine years older than her sister, but she had always looked after her. Their parents were kind and did what they could for their daughters, even though they were poor. Melinor's beauty attracted many admirers amongst the locals, but she never had time to bother with boys. She thought them silly and immature and had better things to do with her time. Those days of freedom were long past.

Her thoughts drifted, and Melinor caught herself thinking of Morganuke. *Strange*, she thought, *why am I thinking of him? Boys bore me, and I don't like the Pale Ones.*

The door opened, and three newcomers were pushed inside. One of them was a man she recognised as Cadmunese, an older woman with an authoritative air about her, and a young woman about her age who looked very forlorn. *Why is a man sharing our accommodation?* she thought uncomfortably.

CHAPTER 13

Trial by Fire

A week had passed since Morganuke had been brought to the Cordinen military complex in Cryantor. Although his door had not been locked, his movements were limited by the number of soldiers guarding the complex. He had still not seen his friends and feared for their safety. The only friendly face he had seen was Melinor, who came regularly to bring his food and take his laundry. Though he felt guilty that she had to serve him so but was thankful for the friendly face. He felt that she was becoming more at ease with him as each day went by, and she had stopped calling him master.

It was morning and time for his breakfast. He was looking forward to his visit from Melinor. He sat on his bed waiting, and soon came a gentle knock on the door.

"Come in," he said, trying to hide the excitement in his voice. The door opened gently, and in walked Melinor carrying the usual tray of food, looking as graceful as ever. "How are you today, Melinor? It's good to see you, the only bright thing that I see in this dismal place."

"I'm well enough, thank you," she answered softly. "Is there anything I can do for you today?" she added with a gentle smile.

Morganuke shuddered to think of her being used by men and hastily shook his head. "How are they treating you here? I hope they're not hurting you or are unkind to you."

Melinor's cheeks coloured. "I'm treated well enough. My main tasks are to serve you, and you seem kind enough to me."

"What is your accommodation like? Are you getting enough to eat? If not, then please take some of my food."

Melinor's cheeks went a deeper shade of red. "My quarters are sufficiently comfortable, thank you. I share with a number of other women … " Melinor hesitated before adding, "although there is a man who recently joined us, which seems strange as the Cordinens don't usually keep male slaves."

"There's a man, you say?" Morganuke asked with surprise. "That doesn't seem right. It must make you very uncomfortable."

"It does seem wrong, having a man in the same room as so many women, but I guess they don't have anywhere else to keep him. I think he was a soldier in an army fighting the Cordinens."

"What be this man lookin' like?" Morganuke scarcely dared hope it was his friend.

"Very different from others I've seen. He has red hair and green eyes and is very tall."

"Lengrond! I believe that is Lengrond," Morganuke exclaimed. "I was fighting with him in the same army. Please tell him that Morganuke is well and is looking out for him. Did any other prisoners arrive at the same time?"

"Two women," Melinor answered, "one young and pretty, and the other older but still good-looking."

"That must be Calarel and Chanterly, who I also was fighting with. I knew Calarel from my hometown. Please tell them that I'm making sure they are kept safe too. Don't tell anyone else about this."

"I will speak to them, and I will not tell anyone else," Melinor answered softly. "Now, if there's nothing else, I shall leave you." Melinor smiled and left the room.

So Calarel, Chanterly and Lengrond are safe, Morganuke thought as he ate his breakfast with greater relish. *It seems that the Cordinens are keeping their word, so far at least.*

No sooner had Morganuke finished than there was another knock at the door, this time harder. The door opened, and in came a man with fair skin, red eyes, and silver hair. Morganuke had heard many times about people who looked like him helping the Cordinens, but it was still a shock to see one. Now he knew why so many islanders had treated him like an outsider. He was so used to seeing the olive-skinned, brown-eyed, dark-haired islanders that his own features stood out to him as strange.

"Morganuke Beldere, I have come to take you to your trials," announced the silver-haired man standing in the doorway.

So, this is it, Morganuke thought. *It's time to prove myself.*

Morganuke was led outside the building, where two guards were waiting with a cart. He and the other pale man climbed in.

"Where are we going?" Morganuke asked the other man.

"To a place where you need to prove yourself. It will be a long ride, so make yourself comfortable. If you prove able, then you will be rewarded. If not, then punishment or death will be your lot," the silver-haired man answered coldly before giving the order for the wagon to move off. Morganuke noticed that the man was held in high regard by the Cordinens. *If I am able to earn the same level of trust*, he thought, *then that will give me a good opportunity to do something about our escape.*

They travelled for several hours, with no sign of reaching their destination any time soon. Morganuke decided to strike up conversation with the other silver-haired man.

"What is your name?" Morganuke asked

"My name is Karorkin, of the house Staniplion."

"What is the house Staniplion?" asked Morganuke.

"It is my family's name. Surely you understand about Patronese family houses and their importance?"

"Patronese? Is that what your race is called?"

Karorkin looked at Morganuke with a puzzled look. "Yes, of course it's the name of our race," Karorkin said frowning. "Why is it that you ask these questions when you come from Denesthear yourself?"

"Come from where?" Morganuke pressed.

The other man gave no response and just focused his gaze ahead.

"So you come from Denesthear?" Morganuke tried again, but still the man gave no response.

Morganuke reckoned that it was mid-afternoon, and the sun was roughly behind them so they must be heading west. He tried to remember what he had seen on the maps aboard the *Aurora* those many months ago. Travelling west, he thought, would take them closer to the front line of the war with the Epleons.

At last they stopped and dismounted from the wagon. They had stopped at the foot of a hill that led up to a rocky mount. The land around them was hilly and dry. The ground was dusty, dotted with the odd clump of brown grass here and there. A few cedar trees gave some relief from the monotonous brown hilly landscape.

Cordinen guards began unpacking provisions from the wagon and preparing a camp for the night. "We camp here tonight," Karorkin stated to Morganuke as he pulled a wooden crate- from the wagon, containing bedding and provisions. "We continue our journey tomorrow. I have some blankets you can use for bedding. Sleep well once you've eaten. Tomorrow will be a long day, and you will need your strength."

The next morning Morganuke was still tired and stiff from his night's restless sleep on hard ground with the few blankets he had. Nights could be cold in this land, even though it was so dry and hot during the day. They packed up camp and loaded the wagon to leave before first light. Continuing to travel westward through the day, they stopped briefly at midday to eat. By early evening, they had reached their destination.

They arrived at a campsite on the edge of a large expanse of open ground surrounded by the brown featureless hills. Waiting for them at the campsite were Cordinen soldiers and two more Patronese with features the same as Morganuke, who had arrived a day earlier. An evening meal was provided to everyone by a cook attached with the Cordinen troops. Morganuke tried to make conversation with the other two Patronese but to no avail. As with the other Patronese, these two men were reluctant to say anything to him.

Later that evening, Morganuke wondered around the campsite, closely watched by the Cordinen soldiers. He had noticed a small single tent pitched in the middle of the camp with Cordinen guards posted all around it. *Why is this so important to the Cordinens, and why are there so many guards?* He sat on the ground a little way from the guarded tent but close enough to see the entrance, hoping that someone would come in or out and reveal what was so closely guarded. He watched until late into the night, but no one entered or left the tent. His tiredness caught up with him, and he decided to call it a night.

Early the next morning the camp was roused by shouts from the Cordinen guards. "They're here!" one of the Cordinen officers shouted. "Get the men ready." Morganuke left his tent to see Cordinens quickly moving towards the open ground. He followed until he came to the edge of the camp and could see the clear ground ahead.

In the centre of the clearing stood a large wooden structure, with steps leading up the side to a large platform at the top. Around the base of the structure stood a crowd of men. They were unlike the Cordinens and wore metal armour, some wearing blue surcoats over the top. All had their hands bound behind them and shackles on their ankles. They were being herded up the wooden steps onto the platform. As each reached the top of the platform, Cordinen guards chained them to a post, still shackled.

Alerted by footsteps, Morganuke turned to see the three Patronese approaching him. "The time has come for you to prove yourself," said Karorkin, "and see if you really are one of us, prepared to fight the Epleon enemies in this war." Morganuke realised that the men in chains must be Epleon prisoners and feared for what was about to happen to them. "Come with us," Karorkin demanded.

Morganuke followed the three Patronese to the small tent that he'd been watching the night before. The entrance was now open, and inside Morganuke saw something he recognised with horror.

It was a large oblong box, and as they drew closer, he saw that the centre of the side was decorated with the image of a large lidless eye with a blue iris. On each corner was a wooden handle, and the three Patronese each went and grasped one.

It was the box he had seen four men lift in his dream aboard the Cordinen ship.

"Take up the remaining handle," said Karorkin. Morganuke slowly walked over to the handle and grasped it in his hand. Immediately he felt a force running through his body, like a hot flame, which made him release the handle with a jump.

"Take the handle!" demanded Karorkin again.

Morganuke slowly grasped the handle, feeling the force running through his body but this time he was ready for it.

The four lifted the artefact together and began walking out of the tent and towards the open ground. Morganuke seemed to know where they were heading without being told. The force he felt flowing through him was like hot flowing water, but not so hot as to burn—it almost felt pleasant, even relaxing. The box began to vibrate with a low humming sound coming from it.

At the edge of the clearing, the four men stopped, still holding the humming box by the handles. The humming and vibration from the box became stronger. Morganuke could feel the force flowing through him increase, warming and strengthening him. He could feel the presence of the other three and sensed what needed to be done without questioning or thinking.

The Epleon prisoners on the wooden stage stood looking on with terror, as if they knew what was coming. The Cordinen guards had now climbed down and moved far away from the wooden structure. The Epleons began to tug and pull at their tethers. Some of the men on the wooden stage began shouting for mercy, tugging even more desperately at their bindings.

Morganuke felt himself focusing intently on the wooden structure with the desperate Epleons on top. He continued to hold onto the box, looking at the three Patronese who were expressionless. He seemed to know what was going to happen but was unable to stop himself. A loud rumbling began to come up from deep within the ground, and the wooden box vibrated even more, the humming now drowning out the screams of the men on the wooden structure.

Suddenly, there was a bright flash in front of Morganuke, so bright that for moments Morganuke couldn't see. He felt an immediate release of the pressure that had built up inside him. Closely following the flash was a huge crashing sound, and then a blasting wind pulling Morganuke towards the flash. When Morganuke's eyesight had recovered from the bright flash, he looked around to see that the Patronese and the Cordinens were lying on the ground. Only Morganuke remained standing, still holding the box aloft by the one handle. The vibration and humming from the box slowly died down, and when Morganuke released the handle, the box slowly dropped to the ground. He sank to his knees looking at the place where the Epleon prisoners had been. There was nothing there now but a large crater. Morganuke felt as though he was going to throw up. His head swam as he thought about what he had just done.

After several moments, the three Patronese slowly stood up and looked, open-mouthed at Morganuke. He remained kneeling.

Morganuke felt a hand on his shoulder. "You must be Sharman. No one else has that amount of power."

Morganuke looked up to see Karorkin standing over him with a broad smile.

"You have more than proven yourself," he continued, "and the Cordinens will be very pleased." Morganuke must have looked as uncomprehending as he felt, because the Pale One explained, "You were only supposed to set the wooden structure on fire, not completely obliterate it and everything around it. Only Sharman-level Patronese can do this."

It took some time for the Cordinen soldiers to clear up the wreckage. The force had been so strong that all the tents had been blown down across several stances of ground. Some of the Cordinen soldiers were injured by the blast, and many of the horses had bolted and had to be rounded up. It was mid-afternoon before the party was ready to start the two-day journey back to Cryantor.

Morganuke felt a change in attitude from both the Cordinens and the three Patronese, as he was now able to call them. Finally, he knew the name of the people from whom he came. After seeing the demonstration of Morganuke's powers, they all showed much more respect.

When they reached the city, Morganuke was taken again to see Commander General Miliaton. This time, he got up and stood in front of his desk to greet him in a much less booming voice.

"Welcome, Lord Morganuke, for a lord you must be to have such powers. From now on, you will be known as Sharman Morganuke Beldere and will be granted all the privileges of such a rank. We are very honoured to have you with us, Sharman Morganuke." Miliaton finished his sentence with a slight bow and then retrieved Morganuke's sword and presented it to him. "This is yours I think." Morganuke gladly took the sword from Miliaton.

Morganuke, though disturbed at possessing such powers he did not know the extent of, couldn't believe his good fortune. At last hopeful that if he was careful, he could devise a plan to free his friends and himself.

CHAPTER 14

The Smuggler

The *Aurora* had made good time during the first week of sail after leaving Cradport. The prevailing north-west winds allowed Fraytar's ship to maintain a good speed. Fraytar had spoken only briefly with the spies Tradish had sent when they came on board. He had been surprised by their appearance. He was expecting well-dressed military sorts, but the four scruffy men he was presented with were unshaven, had long straggly hair, and wore tattered clothes, nor were they Cadmunese like Tradish. Upon closer inspection, he realised that the men must have been chosen for their appearance—they had features very similar to the Cordinens' and so wouldn't look out of place in Cryantor.

Fraytar also remained sceptical of the talking boxes and their usefulness. *How can something communicate with someone so far away?* he had asked himself many times. He wanted to see one for himself.

To get to know more of the spies' plans and the talking boxes, Fraytar asked Tradish's men to a meeting in his cabin. Almen Pratage was their leader. He was slightly older than the other three, a veteran mercenary who had fought in many battles. The others were Jovish Partins, Sebrin Jackers, and Albrin Drouger, all seasoned mercenaries and experienced in behind-the-line tactics. On paper, it was an impressive team, despite appearances. When the four muscular men joined Fraytar in his cabin, the room suddenly seemed a lot smaller. Fraytar handed the men a tumbler of rum each.

"I would hear more of the plan to smuggle you into Cryantor. It's a big risk I'm taking with my ship and crew, so want to be well prepared," Fraytar said.

"You have nothing to fear," Almen answered calmly. "We have contacts on and around the secret cove where you will take us, and they can warn you of any Cordinens in the area using the talking boxes."

"I'm to rely solely on these so-called talking boxes, then? What magic is this that allows men to talk to each other, separated by such a distance?" Fraytar asked.

"I can't tell you how these boxes work, but I can assure you that they do," Almen said. "The Patronese have machines that we know little about, these boxes amongst them. They do have some limitations, but we have managed to get around those by stationing ships or hidden ground positions between points of contact. The boxes only work if they have been exposed to daylight for a time and have limited distance, but having additional positions between the points of contact to resend the messages overcomes these limitations."

Fraytar got up from his chair and shuffled from one foot to the other like a bear trapped in a cage. His mind was racing, and he still wasn't at all sure about the plan or whether it was worth taking such a big risk with his ship and crew. "How did you come by these talking boxes?" he asked when he had calmed himself enough to sit back down.

"The actual source of the boxes is a closely guarded secret, but I can assure you they originate from the Patronese." Fraytar was glad to see Almen helping himself to more of the rum. Maybe he'd get more out of him. "We managed to obtain several some months ago and have used them extensively since then to aid our operations spying on the Cordinens. I can demonstrate the boxes to you, if you wish."

Fraytar did wish, but just then Crouch burst into the cabin. "Captain, Cordinen ships have been sighted off the port bow," he blurted in alarm.

Fraytar jumped to his feet and looked at the four men sat in front of him. "You'll have to explain to me how your magic boxes let this happen." He didn't wait to hear Almen's reply and rushed out of the cabin, the four men following him onto the upper deck.

Fraytar looked port side through his spyglass, searching for the Cordinen ships, and located three of them in the distance. "Make full sail, and head north-east!" Fraytar yelled out to the crew. He turned to the four spies. "I don't think the ships have seen us, but we'll outrun them anyway."

Crewmen immediately started raising additional sails, and the ship turned to starboard. Fraytar watched through his spyglass until he was relieved to see the Cordinen ships moving further away. Before long, they were out of sight. Everything returned to normal, and the *Aurora* resumed its original heading.

Fraytar turned his attention back to Almen. "Why didn't your talking boxes warn us of these Cordinen ships?" he demanded.

Almen shrugged. "Captain, our observers are stationed closer to the mainland and around Cryantor. They cannot detect ships this far out at sea unless one of the relay ships happens to see the Cordinens," he replied calmly.

"Very well," Fraytar said warily, "but I want a demonstration of this talking box of yours."

"As you wish, Captain. We'll prepare the box for you. It will need to be out in daylight for at least half a day. We'll let you know when the demonstration is ready for you." Almen and his men dismissed themselves and left Fraytar wondering what he had got himself into.

Later that day, Fraytar was informed that the talking box demonstration was ready. He made his way to the lower deck bow, where Almen and his three men were standing around a large box. The box was as high as Fraytar's waist. He examined it closely, but it was made from a material he didn't recognise. It looks smooth and shiny, like porcelain.

"This looks very strange. What's inside it to make it work so?" Fraytar asked. Almen just shrugged.

"Right then, Almen, let's see how your magic box works," Fraytar said.

Almen touched one of the sides and something seemed to briefly light up from inside the box. He then bent over to speak into it slowly and clearly. "Hello, station one, this is wandering coot. Can you hear me?"

A crackling sound came from the box, like small dry sticks burning on a fire. After a moment, a voice came from the box, "hello, wandering coot, station one can hear you clearly."

Fraytar jumped with surprise when he heard the voice from the box. He walked over to it and closely inspected it again. "That's amazing. Where is the voice coming from?" Fraytar asked.

"That voice comes from one of our relay ships, which is about three hundred stances north of us. I've done what I've said, Captain. I've demonstrated that the box works. Now will you believe us and take us to the mainland as you said you would?"

"How do I know that really is coming from so far away?" Fraytar argued. "You might have one of your men throwing their voice like a ventriloquist or something,"

"Why would I try and deceive you, Captain. I don't want to get caught by the Cordinens any more than you do. Trust me, these boxes do work."

Fraytar stood looking at the box with his chin in his hand for some time. *If it's true then this is magic indeed*, he thought, *but it looks like I will have to place my trust in these boxes and the men I am to smuggle to the mainland.*

"Very well," Fraytar agreed reluctantly, "but I'll have your hide if we get caught by the Cordinens."

When Fraytar went back to his cabin, Tomlin was waiting. "Hello, Tomlin," he said, beckoning Tomlin to follow him in. "How are you keeping?"

"Can't say I take too much to this sailing lark, but I be okay other than that. Keeping meself busy I be, helping cook and some of the other crew." Tomlin flopped into a chair, looking tired. "Has there been any more news about Calarel?"

"No more news, yet. We're still two weeks sail from the mainland and probably won't hear more until we get closer. There's still hope, Tomlin, so don't give up." Fraytar poured them both a tot of rum and handed one tumbler to Tomlin.

"I be not giving up. Just eager to get to the mainland and do something, is all," Tomlin said then took a sip of his rum.

"It won't be like that. I'm only smuggling the four spies before moving further south to wait for more orders. We will need to find out more from the contacts in Cryantor before making any move." Fraytar rested his hand on Tomlin's shoulder.

"I knows it. Just wanna find me daughter," Tomlin answered, glumly looking into his tumbler of rum. "Wish I had forge and hammer to keep me mind off things. I miss the metal."

Fraytar smiled, keeping his hand on Tomlin's shoulder. "Well, I'm afraid forges and wooden ships don't really mix."

Tomlin huffed and took another sip of his rum. "What you think of these 'ere men that come with us from Cradport?"

"Well, they seem capable enough to me and I'm sure they will be an asset behind enemy lines. But will need to get near Cryantor to get them to their destination and that worries me. We are sailing into very dangerous waters and will need every bit of good fortune. But I can't keep running away from this war and so must do my part where I can. When or if we get to Stacklin, I'll talk to the Epleons about helping them. It may pay well too and, as a privateer I need to find funds to pay the crew. Maybe I can do something to help rescue Morganuke."

"I hear Morganuke be like one of 'em strange folk that are helping the Cordinens, but he can't 'ave been helping the Cordinens, can he?" Tomlin asked.

"Morganuke knew nothing about where he came from and I'm sure he wasn't helping the Cordinens. He knew nothing about them until recently. Now he's been thrown into the regime against his will. We must keep our hopes on finding him ... and Calarel of course," concluded Morganuke as he walked to the cabin door and looked out over the decks. His crew were busying themselves with their activities on the decks below. The weather had been kind to them so far, and the sky was a clear blue with the sun still high in the sky.

"Well, guess I better be getting back to me work 'els cook'll wonder where I be," Tomlin said as he raised himself from the chair and walked to the cabin door. "Thank he for listening to an old fool, Fraytar. You're a good friend."

"You're welcome, Tomlin. Any time," answered Fraytar, leaning against the cabin door frame as he watched Tomlin make his way back to the galley.

The *Aurora* sailed on for two more weeks without incident. The weather remained good and everyone on board seemed to be in fine spirits as they closed in on the mainland.

About a day's sailing from the mainland, Fraytar met Almen on the lower deck for an update on the Cordinen whereabouts.

"I can't tell you where they are," Almen said, "but I should be able to tell you where they aren't. I'll be checking with our contacts in the area using the talking boxes. Once we've been given the all-clear, we'll wait for cover of darkness to anchor in the hidden cove we discussed. Our contacts are keeping watch on the route directly south of the cove."

"Just make sure that you warn me if the Cordinen ships are approaching on our position," Fraytar said.

"Then may I suggest, Captain, that you sail immediately to the first point south of the cove. Once there, our contacts can keep us informed of the Cordinen naval movements around the area," Almen answered

Fraytar nodded his head in acknowledgement. "Show me the position on the map, and we'll head there immediately." Fraytar motioned for Crouch. "Crouch, make sure there is a double watch on duty at all times, and tell the men to keep a keen lookout for any ships."

Fraytar and Almen made their way to Fraytar's cabin, where Almen pointed out the holding point and the route to the hidden cove on the map. Fraytar gave orders to the crew to sail. It was some hours before they reached the holding point, and by then it was early evening.

Fraytar stood with the four spies on the bow of the ship in front of the talking box, which had been left in place since the demonstration.

"Will the box work?" Fraytar asked. "The light is failing, and I thought the box only worked in daylight."

"The box will still work in darkness so long as it has been exposed to enough daylight," Almen explained. He touched the side of the box as before, and there was a brief luminous glow beneath its surface where Almen had touched the box before it gave off a crackling sound. He crouched and started speaking into it. "Hello, Station Four, this is Wandering Coot. Can you hear me?"

After a brief pause, the reply came. "Hello, we can hear you. Where are you now?"

"We have reached south point one. Is the coast clear?" Almen asked.

"Patrols along the coast. Way is not clear. Hold your position," came the answer from the box.

"Understood. Message out," Almen spoke into the box.

"The box is showing its worth after all, that's good," Fraytar said. "But we are exposed if we stay here. We must move on."

"Captain, if we move from this position, then our contacts will not be able to warn us. I suggest we hold our position, keep watch, and rely on our remote contacts to warn us should any Cordinen ships come close. We shall keep in contact through the night and can move on when the way is clear." Almen touched the side of the talking box again. It gave a series of crackles before falling silent. Fraytar gave a brisk nod of assent, telling Crouch once more to keep the crew assigned on double watch and then marching back to his cabin.

The night passed into morning. Almen and the other spies checked in regularly with their contacts on land to track Cordinen movements. Indications were that the Cordinens were maintaining their regular patrols and not venturing away from the coast. It was safe for the *Aurora* to stay put throughout the day. As the evening drew in, the land and offshore contacts still indicated that the Cordinens were carrying out regular patrols. Everyone was getting tired by this time as few managed to get much sleep over the past day and night.

Fraytar walked around the decks of the *Aurora* to check on his crew and try to keep their spirits up. He carried with him a small barrel of rum and gave each crew member a small noggin. He laughed and joked with them as much as he could, but inside he was worried.

Once he completed his rounds, Fraytar went to the bow to get the latest report from the talking box. Almen was standing by, puffing on a long thin pipe. Wisps of smoke rose in the air above his head.

"What's the latest, Almen?" Fraytar asked as he approached.

"Just about to check with them now for an update, Captain. The last message indicated that the Cordinens hadn't run a patrol for the last hour. If it's still clear, then we should be able to approach the hidden cove." Almen walked over to the box and touched the side to activate it. It gave off the usual crackles, and Almen gave his usual call sign. Several moments went by with the odd crackle, but no voice responded. Almen waited patiently.

Finally, an echoey voice came from the box. "All clear. No patrols. Proceed to rendezvous point."

Almen and Fraytar looked at each other and smiled.

"Set sail, due north," Fraytar ordered. "Crouch, get the depth rope team ready—we're heading towards the coast. The last thing we want is to bottom out on the sand."

The crew sprang into action, and the *Aurora* slowly made its way towards the coast. They steadily made their way northward for the next three hours, keeping a close watch out for any Cordinen ships. Fraytar knew that they would be trapped if any appeared now.

"Captain, there seems to be a signal due north," came a shout from one of the crew standing on the bow tower deck. Fraytar quickly made his way to where the call had come from and looked through his spyglass to where the crewman was pointing. He could clearly see a light swinging in a small arc.

"That appears to be the signal," said Fraytar, with obvious relief. "Get a rowboat ready for the landing party."

The rowboat was quickly made ready and put over the side. Two crew members climbed in, followed by three of the spies. Almen handed Fraytar a piece of paper. "Here, I've written down instructions for the talking box. Good luck! Thank you for your help, Captain." He climbed down into the rowboat bobbing up and down by the waves.

When the two crew members returned the rowboat to the *Aurora* after depositing the spies, orders were given to make about and head due south as quickly as possible. So far, they had been lucky with no sightings of the Cordinens. Fraytar was now feeling pleased at how things had gone and had been impressed by the talking boxes. *Maybe these boxes will give us the advantage we need*, he thought. The *Aurora* made its way southwards, this time into the wind, requiring the ship to tack at a much slower speed. They made their way back towards the original starting point that Almen had indicated, and the coast remained clear. Once they reached Almen's point, Fraytar ordered the crew to take a heading due south-west, making their way to what he hoped would be the sanctuary of Epleon-held lands.

A few hours later, as Fraytar was standing on the bow tower deck, Crouch approached. The wind was still blowing in from the south, and their progress was still slower than Fraytar would have liked but was still pleased with the way things had gone.

"Where we be heading, Captain?" Crouch asked. "Stacklin was under attack when we be last there. If we go much further south, we be too far from Cryantor."

"Stacklin may not have succumbed, and so we head there first. We can check with contacts on the mainland using the talking box to be sure before committing anchorage," Fraytar answered. Crouch acknowledged the instructions, leaving Fraytar looking out to sea.

Despite the prevailing northerly winds that slowed the *Aurora* painfully, they eventually neared the Stacklin coastal area. Keeping a close watch out for any Cordinen activity, Fraytar surveyed the outline of the Stacklin port. To his relief he spotted several Epleon ships—a good sign. But to make sure, he would need to check with the contacts onshore to find out where the Cordinen strongholds were and if Stacklin remained in Epleon hands.

Fraytar hadn't been looking forward to using the talking box. Although he knew now that it was a good asset to have, it still seemed very strange. Fraytar took out the piece of paper that Almen had handed him to remind himself what to do. He had studied it earlier and carefully went over the neatly written list of contact call points and instructions on how to maintain and use the talking box. He nervously put his hand against the right side of the box and waited for a response. He felt a brief vibration followed by a few sharp crackles, then silence.

Fraytar bent over the box and spoke carefully into it. "Hello, call point seven. This is Wandering Coot. Can you hear me?"

After a slight pause, a voice came from the box in reply. "Yes, we can hear you."

"Who holds Stacklin?" Fraytar asked.

"Epleon holds Stacklin."

"Thankyou. Message out." Fraytar signed off and touched the box again.

Fraytar was relieved but still wanted to be cautious about approaching Stacklin. He covered up the talking box so it wouldn't raise questions if they were boarded. As they sailed into Stacklin harbour, he expected any moment to be surprised by the Cordinens. However, he saw no Cordinens, and several Epleon ships were anchored in the harbour. The *Aurora* was soon docked, and Fraytar readied himself to go onshore to meet the Epleons.

As he disembarked, Fraytar saw several Epleon soldiers accompanying an official-looking individual waiting for him on the dock. They didn't look like a welcome delegation, and Fraytar was wary of their intentions. He approached them, nonetheless. The official was dressed in a neatly tailored and embroidered black uniform with a large floppy-brimmed hat and carried a leather shoulder bag.

"Hello, I am Captain Fraytar Delance of the ship *Aurora*, and I come on behalf of the Banton Island militia on trading business," Fraytar announced in his most confident voice.

"I am the customs officer here in Stacklin, Captain," The official said. He took out a large book from his shoulder bag and scanned through the pages. "I see an entry here for the *Aurora* delivering cargo several months ago, but under the command of Captain Amannar. I see no reference to your name." He looked at Fraytar sternly.

"Captain Amannar was killed by the Cordinens in our homeport on Banton Island a few weeks after our last visit," Fraytar replied. "I took ownership of the ship after his death. We had been partners and the ship bequeathed to me in his will. There must have been an issue in transferring information to you from our homeport registry."

"I see. I'm sorry to hear that," The official answered. "It's clear from our records that the *Aurora* has traded with the Epleons before, and we welcome that. I'm sure you'll understand that in time of war, we will need to search your vessel before we can allow you to come ashore."

"By all means," Fraytar answered. He beckoned the party onto the *Aurora* with his arm and gave a slight bow.

The customs officer made his way onto the *Aurora*, followed by the group of soldiers. Fraytar followed and watched as the soldiers searched all parts of the ship thoroughly. Fraytar's felt his hands go sweaty when they came to the covered talking box.

The customs officer lifted the cover that had been hastily placed over the box earlier. "What is this contraption? A weapon?"

Fraytar managed a chuckle that wasn't too obviously forced. "It's for washing clothes. The smooth surface acts as an ideal platform for getting stubborn stains out." He held his breath, thinking there was no way he would be believed.

The official raised his eyebrows and tapped the top of the box before dropping the cover.

"How goes the war?" Fraytar asked energetically, hoping he didn't look too relieved. "The last time I was here, the city was under attack by the Cordinens. We only just managed to escape."

"We managed to hold back the Cordinens from the city, although Stacklin now stands on the front line, which extends to Castle Drobin in the north," the customs officer said, now sounding more at ease. "You are welcome to stay, but I cannot guarantee your safety, as the Cordinens could attack again at any time."

When the Epleons left, Crouch approached Fraytar, who was making sure the talking box was well covered up. "What do we do now, Captain?" Crouch asked.

"We shall need to restock provisions, and then wait for instructions from our contacts on the mainland," answered Fraytar. "We may be waiting for some time."

CHAPTER 15

The Captives

Lengrond relaxed on his bed in his new quarters. He was glad to have some privacy and not have to share the room with several women, as that had made him and them uncomfortable. He liked his own company and felt awkward around women. He wasn't sure why he had been moved but hoped it was something to do with Morganuke. The Cordinen guards were also not as harsh towards him as they had been. He knew that Calarel and Chanterly also had been moved into their own quarters. Although they were made to work hard, the lifestyle was bearable, and they were not treated as slaves. Still, he wasn't a free man and could not go freely where he wanted. He felt penned up and desperately wanted his freedom.

Lengrond had come from a moderately high-ranking family living on Cadmun Major. His father owned a successful trading company and wanted Lengrond to follow in his footsteps. "One day this will all be yours, my son," his father had often said to him. But Lengrond's heart was not in the business. Ever since he was at school, he had enjoyed watching Cadmun army manoeuvres and listening to the stories that his uncle told him about the army. When Lengrond left school seven years ago, the war between the Cordinens and Epleons on the mainland had already been going on for some time. He knew how much the

Cadmunese feared an invasion by the Cordinens, and he desperately wanted to join the army to help prepare for any war that might come.

His father, however, wouldn't hear of it, insisting that he joined the family business instead. Lengrond remembered how his father's eyes had burned with rage as he screamed, "I'll make sure you never join the army!" He kept his promise by using his influence to persuade recruiting officers not to accept Lengrond into the army.

But with the Cordinen threat growing and the stories of their victories against the Epleons, Lengrond was undeterred, even if it meant going against his father. He had been persuaded to join the fighting as a mercenary by another friend of his, who had trod a similar path to him. He then heard from his friend Seedon about the opportunity to join the Banton militia and help the Cadmunese cause against the Cordinens. So Lengrond had followed Seedon to Banton, where he joined the island militia. Whilst he was now a Cordinen captive because of that, he did not regret his decision. He would not give up, and he was determined to regain his freedom somehow.

A gentle knock on the door interrupted these thoughts. It was Morganuke, dressed in plain leather Cordinen armour with his sword sheathed in its leather scabbard attached to a belt around his waist. Lengrond had not seen Morganuke since he had visited the three of them soon after they reached the mainland. He had obviously been well treated by the Cordinens.

"Hello, Lengrond," Morganuke said, coming to the edge of the bed where Lengrond still lay looking up at him. "How are you?" Morganuke asked.

"I'm better now that I have my own space," Lengrond said smiling. "Do I have you to thanks for that?"

"Possibly. I did say that I would look out for you. It's one of my conditions I set with the Cordinens to offer to help them. Not that I have any intention to help them, but at least if I get their trust, it may give us a chance to escape somehow."

"I know you have our interests at heart, Morg. I just hope we can escape soon and get back to fighting the Cordinens. How do you expect to escape from this place? With its high walls and number of Cordinen guards, it seems an impossible task."

"I'll discuss it with you and the others later. My quarters are best, as I'm sure there are no Cordinen guards or spies close by to overhear us. I did check closely before coming here today but would still prefer to discuss it in my quarters and with Chanterly and Calarel present." With that, Morganuke left Lengrond on his bed to contemplate what had been said.

Chanterly and Calarel had taken solace in each other's company since they had been captured. There was a natural bond between them, with both having the same passions and keenness to fight for their right to be free. Chanterly had become a mother figure as well as a mentor to Calarel, whose mother had died when she was young. They were thankful for being moved from the common slaves' room into a room they shared together.

"What do you think Morganuke will do or can do for us?" asked Calarel as she lay back in the chair running her fingers through her hair.

"I can't tell for sure, but if Morganuke does have some influence over the Cordinens and their helpers, as he claims, then there is a good chance that he can help us," Chanterly replied.

"Anything to get out of this place and to be free again, free to fight this evil regime," Calarel said.

Chanterly nodded. She had been used to a good life, coming from a privileged rich family originating from Lobos. Her parents made sure she had a good education at the best academies, and she had excelled at academics. Her family moved to Banton Island when she was in her early twenties, and their estate on Banton Island had been impressive. She was always looked after by several servants. In her middle years she had established a few trading businesses that were very successful.

But when the threat of war came to the island, Chanterly had not hesitated to get involved. She helped set up women's militias in the western provinces, and with her wealth, she was able to fund her own militia, encouraging local women to join the cause. Calarel didn't need much persuading, with her passion for women's equality and a desire to fight for her family home and freedom.

Chanterly smiled. "I remember the first time I saw you in training, Calarel. You always were a natural-born fighter. It took you no time at all to become as proficient with the sword as more seasoned militia members."

There was a knock at the door. Lengrond had come to visit them. Chanterly invited him in.

"Hello, you two. I've come with a message from Morganuke. He wants us to meet him in his quarters."

"So he didn't come to deliver the message himself." Calarel snapped as she got up from her seat.

"What have you got against Morganuke? He's only trying to help us and putting himself at risk to do so," Lengrond said.

Chanterly gave a deep sigh. "Please don't argue, you two. Let's go and hear what Morganuke has to say. If he hasn't come up with a plan for our escape yet, then I promise you I'll scream, and you can say anything about him."

She got up wearily, and the three of them made their way out of the building and along the common path between the other buildings of the compound. They were allowed to move freely, providing they stayed within the compound. There was no way of leaving anyway, as the walls and gates were closely guarded. They headed towards the large building at the end of the central road, passing by guards and slave gangs carrying digging tools. The Cordinen guards had come to recognise them and so let them go on their way without stopping them. They were permitted to wear normal clothes and not the slave collar, as they were not regarded as slaves. To the Cordinens, this was a big privilege, but the three friends knew they were still prisoners.

When they reached the large building, Lengrond led the way inside and down the main corridor. On the large wooden door of Morganuke's apartment, the name SHARMAN MORGANUKE BELDERE was etched in black writing. Lengrond knocked and waited.

"Do we have to curtsy when we go in?" Calarel asked mockingly.

The door opened to reveal Melinor looking questioningly at the three of them. "Yes?" she asked politely. "Who can I say is calling on Morganuke?"

Calarel gave a startled grunt. "Oh my! He's got women running around after him now," she blurted out peevishly.

Melinor blushed but waited for the three to announce themselves.

"Please tell Sharman Morganuke Beldere," said Chanterly imperiously, "that Lady Chanterly, Calarel, and Lengrond have come in response as bidden."

"Please wait one moment," Melinor answered in a quiet voice before closing the door again, triggering Calarel into giving another grunt of disapproval. A few moments later, the door opened again, but this time it was Morganuke who stood before them, smiling broadly.

"It's good to see you all. You are all lookin' well. Please, come in, you are most welcome," Morganuke said excitedly as he beckoned them into his quarters.

"If there is nothing else, then I will take my leave," said Melinor, giving a quick curtsy to Morganuke, which prompted a guffaw and a mock curtsy from Calarel.

"That's uncalled for, Calarel," Morganuke said sternly as Melinor left the room with her dignity intact. "Melinor is very kind to me and is only doing what she has been told to do by the Cordinens. It's all part of the ruse that I'm maintaining for yours and my own benefit. Trust me, your lives could be forfeit at any time, and I am doing my best to keep you alive."

Calarel felt her cheeks colour and looked down at the floor.

"Anyway, please all sit down. Can I get you any food or drink?"

The three visitors sat in the chairs that had been arranged for them, shaking their heads to decline Morganuke's offer of refreshments. "Tell me, how are the Cordinens treating you?"

After a short silence, Chanterly finally responded. "We have been treated well enough, no doubt thanks to you," she said politely. "Our concerns are about any plans you may have for our escape. You say our lives could be forfeited at any time, and so the longer we stay here as captives, the more risk it is for us."

Morganuke picked up a goblet of wine from the table and took the host's seat in front of them. "I know you are worried about your welfare and are keen to be free again, but we must be careful. If the Cordinens suspect me, then we are all done for." Morganuke took a long sip of wine and then looked at the three of them intently. "I am demonstrating to the Cordinens powers that I didn't know I had. There is a chance that I can get all of you out of this place."

"How?" Chanterly demanded. "How do your powers help us to get free?"

Calarel remained quiet for once—she wasn't sure if she believed anything Morganuke was saying.

"It seems that I have some high-level powers, and they tell me I come from a high order or something. That is why the Cordinens treat me with high regard. They want me to use their artefact, the mighty weapon they have against the Epleons," explained Morganuke, then paused to drink down his wine.

"I think you've had too much of that wine," Calarel mocked. "All this silliness about powers—it's just nonsense."

"It's not nonsense," Lengrond finally interjected after his long silence. "The Cadmunese have known about the Patronese for some time, and their powers and strange artefacts. That's what is giving the Cordinens their advantage."

Calarel thought it suspicious that the Cadmunese had not shared their knowledge about the Patronese with the Banton Islanders before. *Why are we only learning about this now?* She thought. *These box things and the Patronese all seem a bit odd to me.*

"That's right, as I've been saying, the Cordinens want me to work with the Patronese to use those powers," Morganuke added. "Until I came here and saw what I was able to do, I didn't believe it myself."

If Morg is so powerful, then why can't he just send us somewhere else in a puff of smoke? Calarel thought, fidgeting frustratedly in her seat.

"I am expecting," continued Morganuke, getting up to pace around the room, beating the knuckles of one hand into the other, "to be called to the front at any time by the Cordinens, to use their artefact again in a real battle against the Epleons. I believe that will be our chance to escape into the Epleon homeland."

"But if we are still held captive here," Chanterly enquired, "how does it help us for you to go to the Epleon front line?"

"I'm going to ensure that you come with me as a condition for me helping the Cordinens. I hope to create such confusion amongst the Cordinens on the front line that it will give you an opportunity to escape without being detected," Morganuke said.

Calarel was struggling to take this all seriously but bit her lip and kept her silence.

"You said something about using their 'artefact'. What do you mean by that? What is it? Have you used it already?" Chanterly finally asked.

Morganuke stopped his pacing and just stared out the window of his room for a moment. "I had to destroy something … some people. Epleon prisoners that were shackled to a wooden structure. I really didn't want to but had no choice." His head dropped, and he did not look at his three friends.

"But that's awful," cried Calarel, getting up from her chair and feeling her eyes grow big as saucers. "The Epleons are our allies."

Morganuke composed himself. "They would have died anyway. At least I gave them a quick death. The Cordinens were going to burn them alive. It was the only way that I could make them believe I'm on their side," he pleaded. "If I hadn't, we would probably all be dead."

Another silence fell over the room. Eventually Chanterly got up from her chair. "Very well. I haven't known you that long, Morganuke, but by all accounts, you are true to your word. It seems that we have little choice other than to put our lives in your hands." And with that she left Morganuke's room, leaving the door open behind her.

"I'm with you, Morg," Lengrond said before following Chanterly out the door.

Calarel stood looking at Morganuke for a few moments., "Morg, to be honest with you, I'm not sure to believe everything you've told us. However, I'm out of options and so will go along with your mad plan for now." *Am I doing the right thing?* Calarel thought as she followed the other two out of Morganuke's room.

Morganuke stood alone in his room for some time, his door still wide open. His thoughts were racing, and his emotions torn. He tried to convince himself that he was doing the right thing, but he had more doubts than ever. *I need to do more than just ensure our escape*, he thought. *I need to stop the Cordinens bringing such misery on others. But how do I do that?*

Just then he heard footsteps running down the corridor toward his room, getting louder until Melinor appeared at his doorway, out of breath and upset.

"Oh, Morganuke, please help me! It's my sister," she sobbed. "She's fallen down a pit, and I can't reach her. Nobody else will help me." Melinor fell to her knees. "I must get my sister to safety! I fear she has been badly hurt." She began crying uncontrollably.

Morganuke knelt in front of her and gently took her in his arms and comforted her. "You take it easy and breathe slowly, Melinor. Tell me where she is, and I'll come to help rescue your sister," Morganuke said softly.

Melinor stopped her crying and looked thankful to have someone who could help. "Come, follow me."

Melinor led Morganuke out of the building and down the central road leading towards the gate of the complex. Halfway along, she turned down an alley that led to several work buildings laid out in a square. She took Morganuke to a pit, boarded with a low wall and situated in an open space between the buildings.

"She's down here," said Melinor urgently. "Please help her."

Morganuke peered down the pit but could see only blackness. "Alorie!" he called, but there was no answer. "Did you see her fall?" Morganuke asked, turning to Melinor.

"She was pushed by one of the Cordinen guards. She was sitting on the edge of the pit resting after her work, and the guards didn't like it, so one pushed her in as punishment and then just left her. I was standing close by when it happened and ran to the edge of the pit shouting her name, but there was no answer," Melinor said, covering her face with her hands.

"It's all right. We'll get your sister out," Morganuke assured her. He shouted to some Cordinen guards standing close by. "You there! Get me some rope at once."

The group of guards stopped what they were doing and looked round at him. One of the guards walked over to him, looking very unhappy. "We don't take orders from you. Get your own rope," the surly guard challenged him.

Morganuke was filled with rage. He felt a hot trickle rising through his body signalling his inner power starting to build, but quickly suppressed it. "Do as I say, or I'll have you flogged. Do you know who I am? I am Sharman, and you will do as I say."

The guard looked shocked to realise who Morganuke was, then slightly bowed his head in acknowledgement. Soon the guards returned with a length of rope.

Morganuke tied one end to a sturdy fence post set against one of the work buildings and threw the other end down the pit. He grasped the rope, climbed over the lip of the pit, and started to shimmy down the shaft. Some way down, he realised that he had brought no torch to light the way. He cursed his oversight but continued down. Eventually he felt something against his feet—twigs and vines. Morganuke's hopes were raised that Alorie had fallen into the vegetation rather than onto hard ground.

On reaching the bottom of the pit, he began to grope around, the twigs and thorns scratching his skin. His eyes had become accustomed to the darkness, and the light from the opening above was enough for Morganuke to make out his surroundings. He spotted a small body in the vegetation. Morganuke scrambled to where Alorie lay, and with relief discovered that she was still breathing.

Morganuke checked Alorie's limbs to make sure nothing was broken. He then looped the end of the rope under Alorie's arms, securing her by tying the end of the rope back on itself and over her arms. Propping Alorie carefully against the side of the pit shaft, so that her back was resting against it in a seated position, Morganuke tested the rope harness. Pulling the rope until it became taut, Morganuke then started to climb up the shaft, using the rope to haul himself up with his hands and feet. It was a tricky task, and his feet slipped off the side of the shaft several times, but eventually he reached the top and climbed out.

"Did you find her?" Melinor asked desperately.

Morganuke nodded as he caught his breath. "Now comes the tricky bit." He began to pull the rope carefully until he felt Alorie's weight, hoping that she wouldn't slip out of her harness. When the top of Alorie's head appeared, Melinor gasped and reached out to help Morganuke haul up her sister. Together, they gently lifted Alorie from the pit and laid her on the ground.

"Is she all right? Oh, please let her be all right!" Melinor pleaded.

"The pit floor is covered in undergrowth, so her landing was softened," Morganuke said. "I'll take her back to my quarters and ask my friends to tend her. They have some experience in looking after people."

Morganuke gently lifted Alorie into his arms and made his way back to his quarters, with Melinor following closely behind.

CHAPTER 16

Keeping Watch

Melinor sat on the edge of Morganuke's bed, mopping her sister's brow with a damp cloth. Alorie lay on the bed breathing deeply but still not conscious. She had scratches on her face and arms from the vegetation and being hauled up the pit but no other signs of external injury. Melinor tended to her as best she could but felt helpless, not knowing why her sister wouldn't wake up. Morganuke had left to bring Chanterly and Calarel. He had said they had some experience with treating the injured. Melinor wasn't sure about Calarel helping as she had been very unkind to her when they first met.

Alorie began to stir, moaning quietly under her breath and slowly opening her eyes. She began to panic upon seeing the unfamiliar surroundings until she saw Melinor beside her. "What happened? Where am I?" Alorie asked.

"You fell into a pit," Melinor explained softly. "How do you feel? Are you in pain?"

"My back is sore and my head aches," her sister answered as she lay back onto the pillow, putting her arm over her eyes.

"Morganuke has gone to get some help." Melinor said, gently mopping Alorie's forehead again. "He will be back soon. He's the one who got you out of the pit."

"Morganuke? Isn't he the one that you are always going on about? You look all sloppy and silly when you mention him." Alorie said.

"Morganuke is very kind," replied Melinor with a slight smile. "He is kind and gentle that is all. I'm sure I didn't go all sloppy when I mentioned him to you."

Just then the door opened, and Morganuke walked in, followed by Chanterly and Calarel. "Here she is," said Morganuke. "Please see what you can do for her."

Calarel and Chanterly walked over to the bed to check on the girl. "How long she been awake?" Chanterly asked.

"She has just woken saying her back is sore and her head aches," answered Melinor.

Chanterly checked the girl over, making sure she had no broken bones. Alorie watched her nervously, not uttering a word. Whilst Chanterly carried out her examination, Calarel gently smoothed her forehead to calm her.

When she had completed her examination, Chanterly stood up and turned to Morganuke. "She seems to be all right. Here, I still have this essence of taplin root that you can give her. It will ease the pain and help her to sleep. Sleep is her best recovery now," Chanterly said, whilst Calarel continued to comfort Alorie by making funny faces to make her giggle.

Melinor looked on at how Calarel was being very sweet with her sister. *Maybe this girl isn't all bad after all*, she thought.

Morganuke walked with Chanterly and Calarel out and into the corridor. "Thank you, Chanterly, and to you, Calarel, for coming to help," Morganuke said.

"Why are you helping the slaves?" Chanterly asked after Morganuke had closed his door. "Are you not in danger of exposing yourself with this tenderness towards the slaves? It is unlike the behaviour from the other Patronese."

"I'm not one to ignore someone in need," Morganuke answered.

"These sisters have been treated cruelly. You have no need to worry; I will help you escape and not expose myself needlessly."

"Are you sure it's not because you have feelings for the elder sister?" Calarel asked.

"What of it? Maybe I do have feelings for Melinor," Morganuke answered, turning to re-enter his room.

Chanterly stopped him with a hand on his arm. "The longer we are here, the more danger we are in. If you have the powers you claim, can you not just force your way out of this complex and take us with you?"

"It doesn't work like that," Morganuke replied, without looking back at Chanterly and Calarel. "I'm not always able to control the power. The artefact makes it easier and stronger." Morganuke left them in the corridor and closed the door behind him.

Melinor still sat on the edge of the bed, gently mopping her sister's brow with a damp cloth. Alorie lay on the bed with her eyes open, looking up at the ceiling.

"How is Alorie?" Morganuke asked as he walked over and stood next to Melinor. Morganuke caught a hint of her sweet fragrance.

"I think she's a little better," Melinor answered, looking up at Morganuke and smiling sweetly.

"I'll make up some taplin root mixture that Alorie can drink." He walked over to the water jug and poured some water into a tumbler, then mixed in some of the powder that Calarel had given him. "This should ease the pain and help her to sleep."

Melinor took the cup from Morganuke and gave him another smile. Morganuke noticed how bright her eyes were, like jewels radiating affection. She held the concoction to Alorie's lips to drink.

"It's bitter," Alorie said between sips, screwing up her face.

"Drink it, my love," Melinor coaxed, nudging the cup against her little sister's lips. "It will make you better and help you to sleep."

Alorie finished the concoction and soon was falling asleep, breathing deeply, on Morganuke's bed.

Morganuke watched Melinor sitting by her sister, attentive to her breathing until she fell asleep. When Alorie was fast asleep, Melinor turned to sit on the edge of the bed and started to sob. It was the sobbing of someone who had kept her strength for so long and now just let go.

Morganuke's heart went out to Melinor. If he hadn't been in love before, he knew he was now. He slowly walked over and knelt in front of her, taking her hands in his. "I promised you; I'm going to look after you," he whispered softly in her ear. "I'll never let any harm come to you or your sister."

Melinor stopped her sobbing and looked fondly into Morganuke's red eyes. "You are so kind," Melinor whispered. "Why do you want to help us so?"

"Because I love you," answered Morganuke simply.

"The other Patronese that we have seen helping the Cordinens seem cold and ruthless. Even the Patronese that we knew in our homeland were not as kind and thoughtful as you."

"You know of people like me from where you came from?" Morganuke asked, feeling very surprised by this revelation. "How is that? I thought the ones helping the Cordinens were the only Patronese."

"The people in my homeland looking like you were not helping the Cordinens," added Melinor. "They lived independently in a small group close to my home city. They said they had left their own homeland many years ago, but never said where that was."

Morganuke felt excited about the news that Melinor had shared. He had been disappointed after the Patronese he'd worked with refused to say where they came from. Now here was another possible means of finding out more about where he came from and where his people lived. He had to get to see the people that Melinor had mentioned.

CHAPTER 17

On the Move

Back in Cradport Commander Falcar Tradish sat at his desk, going through Banton Island Militia reports from his subordinates. The militia continued to build up in the eastern provinces on Banton Island. With continued help from the Cadmunese mercenaries and the native islanders, the militia force had now grown into an army. With men and women fighting together, the island presented a more formidable force to contend with the continuing Cordinen invasions.

Whilst Tradish was more than satisfied with the situation on the island, his main worry now lay with the mainland. Recent reports had indicated that the Cordinen army was massing on the borders of Stacklin. The previous attack on Stacklin had failed owing to insufficient Cordinen forces and the effective counteroffensive from the Epleons. However, the Epleons had suffered many losses, and their forces in the area had weakened. Another consolidated attack from the Cordinens would almost certainly see Stacklin fall and allow the Cordinen army to rampage into the heart of Lobos.

"Spandor!" Tradish shouted. A Cadmunese soldier opened the door to the office and presented himself. Strandar Spandor was Tradish's second-in-command, about ten years younger. His features were typically Cadmunese, and he wore fine leather armour as Tradish did.

Spandor had travelled to the island with his commander after serving with him in the Cadmunese army for several years.

"Commander?" Spandor asked, standing straight.

"What is the latest report from the spies recently sent into Cryantor?"

"We have a confirmed sighting of Morganuke Beldere, but he is held in a highly secure complex in Cryantor," Spandor reported.

"With the build-up of the Cordinen army outside of Stacklin, I am certain they will attack soon," Tradish surmised, rubbing his chin. "They may decide to use Morganuke in that attack, and so we must continue to keep a close watch on him. It may be our chance to rescue him and disable their artefact at the same time. We must prevent the Cordinen army breaking through at Stacklin at all costs." Tradish absentmindedly waved his hand in dismissal, but before Strandar got to the door, his commander had a second thought. "Spandor!"

"Yes, commander?" Spandor returned.

"It occurs to me that the Cordinens keep the artefact some way behind the front line until it is needed," Tradish said. "Have our contacts ask the Epleon forces in Stacklin to arrange a raiding party to go behind the enemy lines as soon as the artefact is located. That should be where they take Morganuke if he is to use the artefact. It would be our best chance to destroy the artefact and rescue Morganuke before he is forced to turn the war further in favour of the Cordinens."

Spandor nodded in acknowledgement and left Tradish to continue looking through his reports.

The *Aurora* had been anchored in Stacklin harbour for three days. It was becoming more difficult for Fraytar to explain his presence there, and he didn't want to share with them his true reason for being there. Although they were on the same side, the operation to smuggle spies into Cryantor was needed to be kept secret from the Cordinens and Fraytar wasn't sure how secure the Epleon intelligence network was. Fraytar had not received any orders yet and couldn't leave until he had. The ship had already been restocked, and the crew milled about on the decks, doing what jobs they could find but becoming more restless by the day. Fraytar was desperate to be doing something for the war effort but had his orders to stay on standby for the Cryantor operation.

It was a daily procedure for Fraytar to check the talking box to see if there were any updates. As a ruse, some of the crew had hung their washing around the box. Hopefully this would reenforce the notion that Fraytar had given to the customs officer that the box was used as a washing platform. It also obscured any real activity with the box.

On the morning of the third day, whilst Fraytar was moving between crewmembers to keep up moral, Epleon officers asked to board the *Aurora*. Fraytar met the officers on the dock, not really wanting them to come on board unnecessarily.

"Are you Captain Fraytar Delance?" the officer asked.

"I am," answered Fraytar warily. "May I ask who you are?"

"I am Commander Besnit of the Epleon First Group Defence Force," the officer said in an official tone. "You've been anchored here for three days. Do you know when you will conclude your business here?"

"I'm not sure," replied Fraytar uneasily. "We are still waiting to hear from our business contacts, and it could be days yet."

"We've had reports of a Cordinen build-up outside of Stacklin and are expecting them to attack any day," Commander Besnit said. "We need your help to sail some of our men behind enemy lines as a pre-emptive measure. You will be well rewarded. Will you help us, Captain?"

Fraytar couldn't hide the surprise on his face. He had been expecting the Epleons to enquire why he was still in Stacklin—not to ask for his help. *Now at last I can do something to help in this war*, Fraytar thought. "I would like to help you but my ship is a commercial cargo ship, Commander, not a war ship. I don't have any weapons. Don't you have naval ships?" Fraytar asked.

"We do, but not enough that are suitable for an operation of this size. We've heard that your ship and crew are well versed in smuggling people ashore, and we need a speedy ship for escape. You will not have to fight." He paused. "There is an important islander we are hoping to rescue."

Could this be Morganuke? Fraytar wondered. "Then yes, Commander, I'll gladly help you," Fraytar answered. "I'll help you get your men behind the Cordinen lines."

"Thank you, Captain. You will be paid well," Besnit replied with a smile. "I'll give you notice as to when it needs to take place. It could be today, and if not in the next few days, so please be prepared to move at short notice."

This should work well, Fraytar thought. *I'll still be able to respond to any action needed for the Cryantor operation and be doing some good in the meantime.*

Morganuke sat on the ground outside the building where his accommodation was located, his back propped against the wall, watching Cordinen soldiers and the slaves heading to the fields outside of the city for their day's work of digging and weeding. The sun shone brightly in the cloudless sky, providing a contrast to the bleak surroundings of the military complex.

Life in the Cordinen military compound had become tedious for Morganuke and his friends. They were thankful not to be treated as slaves but knew that time was not on their side. Morganuke watched as several Cordinen soldiers harassed some slave women as they were moved from one building to another. The slaves were carrying large wooden crates filled with something that must have been quite heavy. They struggled to carry the crates, and when one of the slaves fell over, she was lashed cruelly by one of the soldiers. He thought of Melinor and her sister and shuddered to think that they must have been treated in a similar way. *I promised Melinor that she and her sister would not come to any harm,* thought Morganuke, *and I will stand by that promise no matter what it takes.*

Melinor and Alorie had stayed in Morganuke's room for the past week, sleeping in his bed whilst Morganuke slept on a makeshift bed on the floor. Melinor had protested, saying they should return to the slave quarters, but Morganuke would hear none of it. After what had happened with Alorie in the pit and Morganuke's observation of how the slaves were treated, he was reluctant to let them out of his sight.

Just as Morganuke started to doze off in the sunshine, he was approached by one of the Cordinen officers. Morganuke recognised him as being one of the Cordinen complex commander's adjutants.

He halted in front of Morganuke. "Sharman Beldere, I am Troop Leader Dronigard. Commander General Miliaton wants to see you."

Morganuke slowly got to his feet. "Lead the way then, please," he said, bowing his head slightly.

When they reached General Miliaton's office, there was the usual knock from the officer and the booming reply from within. General Miliaton stood up and beckoned Morganuke to a chair.

"Sharman Beldere," the general said, smiling broadly showing his uneven teeth. "It's good to see you again. I hope you have been keeping well and that the accommodation we provided you is suitable."

"Yes, thank you, Commander General," Morganuke replied, sitting in the chair offered him. "What can I do for you?"

The Commander General sat back in his chair, looking pleased with himself and with a broad smile still on his face. "The time has come at last," he boomed. "You now have an opportunity to demonstrate your powers against our enemies and finish this war for good. You are to be transported to the front line outside Stacklin, where the final assault will take place."

"If I am to do what you ask, then there are some conditions," said Morganuke with slow deliberation.

"What is it you want now?" Commander General Miliaton sighed. "We have given you what you asked for and have treated you well. What more can you want?"

"If I am to go to the front line, then my friends and personal slaves must come with me," Morganuke demanded, keeping his gaze firm.

"That's not possible," Miliaton responded with some annoyance. "What 'personal slaves' are you referring to?"

"The slaves are Melinor and her sister. They are used to my needs for cleanliness. I have an obsession about needing everything around me in my own sleeping quarters to be spotless or else I can't sleep. They have got used to this and tend to my needs this way well and so that is why I want to take them. I can't even relieve myself unless everything around me before and afterwards is perfectly clean. For example -"

"Yes, I see." The Commander interrupted. "Very well, they can travel with you."

"And my friends Lengrond, Chanterly, and Calarel?"

"Yes, yes. But know this: any dissent or trickery will result in their immediate death." With that, he raised his arm to dismiss Morganuke.

Back in his room, Morganuke explained the situation to Melinor. She was surprised and relieved that she and her sister would not be left alone in the hands of the Cordinens, saying she felt sure they would take their revenge at the first opportunity.

"What will we do when we get to the front line?" she asked.

"You can tend to me as you do now, and I can keep you safe," Morganuke replied. "We will be looking for an opportunity to make our escape. I intend to use my powers to help. These powers are still strange to me, but I'll find a way. Once we escape, then the people like me, the ones you mentioned that live in your homeland—I want to find them, and I hope you will help me."

Melinor nodded her head affectionately and smiled.

For two days Morganuke waited pensively for notification to move out to the front line. He didn't know what might await him there. The thought of killing more Epleons as he had done in his trial horrified him. To keep his friends safe, especially Melinor, he had to comply with the Cordinen wishes—at least until an opportunity to escape arose.

On the day they were due to move out, Morganuke was provided with his own horse, with twenty or so other Cordinen soldiers on horseback. His friends were loaded into a guarded wagon. The small detachment was commanded by Dronigard, who had brought Morganuke to see the Commander General two days before. The detachment gathered on the road running through the complex, and with a clatter of horses' hooves on the stony road, it set off on the twenty-five-day trip to the front line.

The first two weeks of the journey were tedious but went without incident. The ten hours they travelled each day were tiring. The landscape they passed through was mundane and featureless. The dry hills and sparse trees provided little visual stimulation. Comfort breaks along the way were few and very short.

As they crossed the border between Ventor and Lobos, the terrain began to change. Green fields became more prevalent, and the number of trees increased as they travelled further south. Morganuke saw plenty of evidence of recent battles as they travelled through Lobos towards Castle Medogor. The many small villages and towns they passed through were desolate and burnt out. Although many were in ruins, it was still evident that the Epleon towns had been more welcoming places to live than the Cordinen counterparts. There was a delicacy to the buildings, and traces of well-tended gardens. Alarmingly, there was an absence of the Epleon people.

After the third week of travel, the detachment reached Castle Medogor. Once an Epleon bastion, it now lay in ruins. The horses and the wagon trundled into the courtyard of the castle, its walls blackened from the battle which had taken place there weeks before. Several Cordinen tents were already pitched there, and soldiers were moving about the place.

"Unpack and prepare camp," ordered Dronigard. We shall be here for two days."

The camp was quickly erected, and a basic meal prepared. Morganuke had noticed the days getting a little shorter and the temperature cooler as they travelled further south. He and his friends gathered around a campfire that Lengrond had built for them. When it was remarked that Lengrond seemed very adept at utilising whatever was available to create a reasonable camp, he said he had been used to the outdoor travelling life during his exploits with Seedon. He missed Seedon greatly, he said pensively, as they had spent a lot of time together and were good friends.

"I ache all over," Calarel groaned as she tried to make herself comfortable on the ground. "Hours of travelling each day in that bumpy wagon is a nightmare, I'm sure this is some form of torture that the Cordinens have devised for us."

"It could be worse," Chanterly said, gazing into the fire, the flickering light creating shadows that danced across her handsome face. "At least we are still alive and being fed, even though the food is barely edible."

Melinor and her sister sat beside the campfire, cuddling each other. They had been very quiet, and the thin slave's clothes they were wearing did not keep out the cold.

Morganuke kept quiet too, but surreptitiously was using a piece of charcoal to write on a piece of parchment. He looked around, making sure none of the guards were looking, and passed it around the group for them to read.

Don't speak of plans
Cordinens watching and listening
At front line I create confusion
Watch for chance to escape
Keep together and look after one another
If separated head for the Epleon city Protor

As soon as the group all had read Morganuke's message, he threw the parchment onto the campfire and watched it burn.

"'It's getting colder I think," Morganuke said calmly. "This is a bit more like seasonal weather on the island. The further south we go, the colder it will get."

"Just hope they provide us with warmer clothing," Calarel said, moving closer to the fire looking sympathetically at Melinor and her sister. "Or maybe that's another form of their torture—freeze us to death."

Lengrond gave a little chuckle at Calarel's comment and moved closer to the fire too. "Might be worth looking around the castle for anything the Epleons left behind," Lengrond proposed.

"I'll have a look around later," said Morganuke. "The guards are wary of you moving about but should let me go freely."

"Melinor, how are you and your sister?" Morganuke leaned in to ask softly as he got up.

Melinor looked up at Morganuke nodding her head and smiling. It was a strained smile, and Morganuke could see that they were suffering from the cold. He hoped he could find some warmer coverings for everyone.

But his search around the ruined castle site turned up nothing—rusty weapons and broken wooden battlements, but no clothes. He ventured into one of the castle towers, his feet slipping on the stony steps leading upwards. It was dark, with only a faint glow from the campfires outside. He felt his way further up the steps until he came to an open doorway. Feeling his way Morganuke carefully made it through the doorway. It was pitch dark, but Morganuke felt his way through what seemed to be a room. He stopped to listen, sensing a presence in the room, then felt around in all directions to see if there was anything worth taking. Again, he stopped, sensing that presence once more, although this time stronger.

"Hello, is there anyone here?" Morganuke called out. "I know there is someone here. Make yourself known."

There was a brief pause. "Morganuke Beldere?" came a voice from where Morganuke had sensed a presence. "Is that you, Morganuke?"

"Yes, it's me, Morganuke. Who are you?" Morganuke's hand went to the handle of his sword.

"Thought so," a reply was whispered from the darkness. "My name is Almen Pratage, and I've been sent by the island militia."

"For what reason?" Morganuke said, sitting back on his heels in relief and removing his hand from his sword.

"I am part of a network monitoring the Cordinen activities," Almen explained. "We have been looking for you."

"Why are you lookin' for me?" Morganuke asked, half knowing what the answer would be.

"We know that you've become important to the Cordinens in their war against the Epleons and will be engaged in the forthcoming attack on Stacklin. We can't allow that to happen. If Stacklin falls, then the whole of the Epleon homeland is likely to succumb to the Cordinens."

"It's risky the way you are following us like this. How would you stop the attack on Stacklin?"

"I'm glad that we've managed to meet up. It gives me the opportunity to ask for your help. We need to destroy the Patronese artefact that the Cordinens are using. At the same time, we can rescue you."

"I'm not leaving without my friends," Morganuke said curtly. "There are five others that need to come with me."

"My orders are only to rescue you," replied Almen. "Who are these others that you want rescued?"

"Lengrond, Chanterly, and Calarel from the island militia. Then there are two slave girls."

"That's not possible. You are the only one to be rescued."

"Then I'll not allow myself to be rescued," Morganuke said angrily. "We all get rescued, or nobody gets rescued. I insist they come with me."

"Oh, as you wish," Almond said exasperatingly.

"There is something else," added Morganuke. "My friends are not clothed for the colder weather down south. Please get some warm garments, skins of some sort will avoid suspicion. Get them over the next day and hide them here so I can collect them. I'll say I found them."

"You ask a lot," Almen said wearily. "I'll do what I can. Now go back to your friends before the Cordinens get suspicious."

The next night Morganuke returned to the room in the ruined tower. He wasn't really expecting to find anything, as Almen seemed unsure about being able to deliver any garments. After groping around the dark room for a while, he stumbled on a pile of sheepskin mantles bound together. He took the package back to where his friends sat, trying not to be noticed by the Cordinens. They gladly received the garments, and each took a mantle, fastening it around their neck and shoulders.

The next day, the detachment continued their journey towards Stacklin. Morganuke's friends felt rested and warmer with the additional covering, and the Cordinens seemed to take little notice of the new attire. They continued travelling for the next three days, thankful for the additional clothing as the temperature became even colder the further south they went. The landscape became greener and richer as they closed in on Stacklin.

On the third day, they entered a makeshift camp for a detachment of Cordinen soldiers. Morganuke also recognised the three Patronese he had seen during the trial. He looked around for a likely place to be housing the artefact but saw nothing like the small tent that he had seen before. Thinking of what Almen had said to him, he thought it important to find the location of the artefact as soon as possible. He decided to look for the artifact after dark.

When evening came and the soldiers settled down in their tents, except for those on guard duty, Morganuke started to look around the small camp. But after searching for some time, he was close to giving up. The artefact must be closer to the front line, he thought. *That's not good. How are the Epleon insurgents getting to the artefact if it's so close to the main Cordinen force? I need to find the other Patronese and ask them what the plans are, then contact the militia spy.*

Morganuke casually approached one of the Cordinen guards. "Can you tell me where the other Patronese are? I need to speak to them," he asked.

The guard looked him up and down warily. Morganuke had been sensing heightened tension amongst the Cordinens since they had left Castle Medogor. But the guard pointed to one of the tents on the other side of the camp.

Morganuke went to the tent and cautiously looked inside. The three Patronese were sitting together and seemingly meditating. Morganuke cleared his throat to make his presence known. It was Karorkin who opened his eyes first and looked at him, steely red eyes fixed on his.

"I need to discuss the plans for the attack on Stacklin with you," Morganuke stated.

Karorkin's eyes remained fixed on Morganuke. "We are not here to discuss plans with you now," said Karorkin, face expressionless and eyes still fixed on Morganuke. "You will know what to do when the time comes."

"If you want me to help you, then I need to know your plans now." Morganuke did not care to hide his irritation. "I am the most powerful amongst you. It is I that'll ensure success, and so you'll tell me your plans now."

By now all three Patronese were looking intently at Morganuke. One of them got to his feet and walked out of the tent, whilst the other two remained sitting, looking at him.

"Very well. Sit, and we'll tell you our plans," said Karorkin.

Morganuke sat down cross-legged in front of the two Patronese expectantly.

"We shall make our way to Stacklin tomorrow morning," Karorkin explained. "With the level of power that we expect you to provide, it should be straightforward to overcome the Epleon defence and push through their lines at Stacklin. The procedure will be much like it was during your trial, using the optoglean to focus our power on a particular target."

"The opto—what?" Morganuke enquired. "Is that the box-shaped thing that we were carrying during the trial? I don't see it here today."

"Yes, that was the optoglean," Karorkin replied. "It is kept close to the front to ensure its protection. We will collect it tomorrow when we move to the front ourselves."

Morganuke nodded thoughtfully. "I see," he said, getting up to leave. "Thank you for explaining the plans. I'll see you tomorrow." Morganuke then left the tent trying not to show his concern.

Blast it! he thought in frustration. *That is really messing up the plans. I must try to contact the island spy somehow to make sure they don't attack here.*

Morganuke made his way back to his friend's tent, thinking hard about how to contact Almen. He knew he must be following the detachment from Castle Medogor. *If I try to leave the camp to look for clues, then the Cordinens will get suspicious.*

As Morganuke reached his friends' tent, he became aware of how quiet it was. *They must be sleeping already,* he thought. Pulling back the tent flap, he gasped in horror.

His friends were not there.

Stumbling around outside the tent in a panic, he searched for his friends in vain. *They have double-crossed me. The Cordinens must have them.* Rage welled up inside him, and he felt a warmth flowing through his body, getting hotter. He realised that this was his inner power building up and so quickly suppressed the feelings of rage.

Unable to resist his urge to confront a Cordinen, any Cordinen, Morganuke marched over to Dronigard's tent. He was about to barge his way in when one of the guards posted outside grabbed him by the arm.

"State your purpose," demanded the guard. "The commander's not to be disturbed."

"If you want me to help you in the attack tomorrow. you will let me see the commander," Morganuke insisted.

The tent entrance opened, and the commander stood there. "It's all right," the commander said. "Let him in."

Morganuke pushed off the guard's arm. "Where are my friends?" he demanded furiously once inside the tent. "I told your general that I am not bothered what happens to me and will not help you if my friends are harmed. Blast it! You can kill me for all I care. I will not help you."

The commander raised his hands to try to calm Morganuke. "Your friends are safe," he said. "They will remain safe so long as you help us. If you refuse, then if necessary they will be killed, one by one, until you help us."

Morganuke stood silently looking at the commander. He looked down at the ground, realising that he had no alternative. Resignedly, he gave a brief nod to the commander and then returned alone to the tent he had shared with his friends.

CHAPTER 18

Stacklin

The *Aurora* was heavily loaded with men and equipment. Two other Epleon ships were sailing with them to take the Epleon attack force behind enemy lines. The three ships were heading north of Stacklin, where the Epleon soldiers would disembark onto the mainland. The journey was risky, given the likelihood of them being spotted by the Cordinen Navy at any time, but getting the men ashore would also be a huge challenge. Time was not on their side; they had been travelling for just over a day and were still only halfway there.

Fraytar looked across at the decks crammed with men, equipment, and rowboats. The *Aurora* crew had to squeeze through the packed deck as they moved about on their tasks. The Epleon soldiers were not used to sailing, and many were seasick, adding to the already chaotic situation on deck.

"This will be risky," Fraytar said to Crouch standing next to him. "But it's good to be doing something worthwhile rather than just sitting about in Stacklin harbour."

"This does seem a bit desperate," added Crouch. "Not sure we'll be able to outrun the Cordinen ships if they spot us, we are so weighed down. Even if we do, the Epleon ships are unlikely to, as they are slower."

"If we get through this, it will be a story to tell your grandchildren," Fraytar said, half persuading himself.

Tomlin came on the deck and approached. "What be going on now?" Tomlin asked worriedly. "Be us going to rescue me daughter?"

"Not exactly," Fraytar answered, "We are dropping these soldiers off behind the enemy lines so that they can retrieve the artefact. If Morganuke and your daughter are there too, then they can rescue them at the same time. The primary objective must be the artefact, though."

"So this artefact is more important than human lives," Tomlin stated objectively.

"That's not so," Fraytar countered. "Taking the artefact from the Cordinens could save many lives and bring the war to an end."

"Just want me daughter back, she's all I have left in this world," Tomlin said. "I just be holding on to the hope that she's still alive. Do you care about Morganuke and whether he's still alive?"

"Yes, of course I do," Fraytar said hastily. "I know he's not my own son, but he feels like one. Ever since I found him abandoned on the beach nearly twenty years ago, I've felt a close bond with him."

"Strange that he was just left like that as a baby," Tomlin mused. "Little did any of us know that he would turn out to be what he is now."

Fraytar frowned. "I believe that Morganuke has a purpose in this world. What that is I know not, but his destiny is wrapped up in him finding out where he came from. All we can do is help him on his way where we can. I'm sure that his involvement with the artefact is part of that journey."

A call came from the lookout located on the main mast. "Ships ahead of us, Captain!"

Fraytar quickly moved towards the bow of the ship, squeezing his way through soldiers and crew members on the lower deck. He grasped his spyglass from his ample trouser pocket and searched the horizon. To his dismay, he identified four Cordinen warships heading straight for them. Each ship had a ballista fitted to its bow and was at full sail.

"What are your orders, Captain?" Crouch asked.

"We'll have to turn about and try our best to keep our distance until we reach our home waters," Fraytar replied, still observing the ships through his spyglass. "Signal the other two ships of our intent. We must keep our distance from the enemy ships. They are armed with giant ballistas, which will tear us apart if they get within range."

"Giant Ballistas!" Crouch exclaimed. "By the time we have turned about, they will be much closer. I doubt the Epleon ships will outrun them. With the weight our ships are carrying, they are low in the water and so will be slower."

"I know it all too well, but we have no choice," Fraytar said as he moved towards the lower deck, Crouch following. Now on the rear deck, Fraytar looked again through his spyglass.

"They are gaining quickly," he said desperately. "They will be within range before long. We will have to separate our ships. That may give one of us a chance at least. Signal one of the Epleon ships to head due west and the other due east. That may throw the Cordinens briefly and give us some breathing space."

Crouch did as his captain asked, and the Epleon ships complied with the *Aurora*'s signal flags. The three ships began to diverge. The four Cordinen ships maintained their heading for a time then split up, with one chasing each of the Epleon ships and two remaining on the *Aurora*.

The *Aurora* continued its original heading, with the two Cordinen ships rapidly closing the gap. The other ships were now some way off in the distance. Fraytar knew that the Cordinen ships would soon be within range. Normally they would have easily outrun them, but with the *Aurora* so heavily laden, it was not possible.

"Turnabout! Turn the ship about now!" he shouted to the coxswain. The ship began to turn, taking some time to do so. The Cordinen ships continued to home in, changing their direction towards the *Aurora* as she took a wide turn. Two giant ballista bolts came whizzing towards the *Aurora* but fell short of their mark.

"Ram the nearest ship and be ready to board with weapons at the ready," Fraytar shouted to his crew and the Epleon soldiers, now lying flat on the deck. "Get the pitch barrels ready. If needs be we'll take the Cordinen ships down with us."

The *Aurora* completed the turn and headed straight for the nearest Cordinen ship. Two more bolts from the ballista headed towards the

Aurora, one missing and the other smashing into the hull. The bolt was unusually large, but the hull held.

The leading Cordinen ship unexplainedly began turning to starboard away from the *Aurora* and into the path of the other Cordinen ship. It seemed like poor seamanship on the Cordinen's part but was a stroke of luck for the *Aurora*. Soon after, there was a loud crash and the sound of splintering wood as the two Cordinen ships crashed into each other, closely followed by the crashing of the *Aurora*'s bow as it smashed into the port side of the leading Cordinen ship. Fraytar felt himself thrown forward onto the *Aurora* deck.

With all three ships now locked together, the Epleon soldiers quickly got themselves up and jumped onto the first Cordinen ship, shouting their war cry with swords in hand. The Cordinen crew were still sorting themselves out from the chaos of the collision and were not ready to defend themselves. The Epleons tore into them, quickly making their way across the deck of the leading ship and then onto the other Cordinen ship.

The crew on the second ship had more time to prepare themselves. The sound of angry shouts and the clashing of steel on steel rang out as the remaining Cordinens desperately fort to save their ship. The men slipped and slid as they fort on the deck of the Cordinen ship swamp with blood. Eventually all the Cordinens succumbed, and the ships fell silent, with bodies strewn across the bloody decks.

"Quickly, gather any resources you can from the Cordinen ships and set them afire before regrouping on the *Aurora*," Fraytar shouted to the Epleon soldiers and his crew. "The other two Cordinen ships are likely to arrive at any time."

"What about our ships?" asked one of the Epleon officers, making his way back to the *Aurora*.

"I fear they have been lost," Fraytar replied. "The damage to our ship is severe, and we will not survive another attack. We can barely sail as it is."

"Where be our heading, Captain?" asked Crouch as he found his way back to Fraytar.

"We shall have to return to Stacklin," Fraytar answered. "There's no point going on now with so many men lost."

The *Aurora* crew and the Epleon soldiers despondently readied themselves for the return journey, knowing that they had failed at their task. The *Aurora*, though badly damaged, began to sail slowly back the way she had come. The two Cordinen ships blazed behind them, sending a bright red glow across the sea. Fraytar watched the ships burn as they sailed away, the flickering light and shadows from the flames dancing across his face.

His attention was drawn to Crouch, who approached him looking very concerned.

"Captain, the lower decks are leaking water at the bow," Crouch reported. "We can patch some of it, but I doubt it will last the rest of our journey back to Stacklin."

"Set a course closer to the coast," Fraytar answered with a frown. "We'll need to look out for a cove we can use to stop and make proper repairs. I just hope that those other two Cordinen ships are not following us and are discouraged from pursuit once they see the other ships burning. They may believe that the damage was caused by another Epleon patrol, as they are further south than they normally come. I'll come down and look at the damage for myself."

Fraytar and Crouch made their way to the lower decks. The crew and soldiers were busy clearing the wreckage from the upper deck as they moved their way through. Some of the rigging had been hastily repaired to ensure enough sail was available, but progress through the water was still painfully slow.

Once Fraytar and Crouch had reached the lower deck they could see for themselves that the damaged ship's hull would not hold for long. The ship's carpenter was busy patching the splintered wooden planking where he could, but the water was still seeping in at an ever-increasing rate.

"How long will she hold?" Fraytar asked the carpenter as he chopping away at the replacement planks.

"If the weather holds, maybe half a day, Captain," the carpenter replied. "The planks will give way if we get any bad weather."

Fraytar screwed up his face, putting his hand against the leaking planks as if to confirm the seriousness of their situation. "How long would you need to complete enough repairs to get us back to Stacklin, which at the rate we are sailing may be another two days?" Fraytar asked.

"A good full day with the bow out of the water, Captain," answered the carpenter, stopping what he was doing for a moment. Crouch peered closely at the ship's planking.

"Crouch, we shall need to go even closer to shore and find the first safe cove we come across," Fraytar said. Crouch nodded in acknowledgement and made his way to the upper deck to convey the captain's orders.

"Do what you can for now," Fraytar said to the carpenter, "and we'll try and find a suitable place to temporarily dry dock the bow so that you can complete repairs." He placed his hand on the carpenter's shoulder encouragingly.

Fraytar made his way to the upper deck and looked over the damaged bow of the *Aurora* as it made its way closer to land. He surveyed the way ahead and caught a glimpse of the coast. "Keep a check on the sounding weights as we draw closer to the coast," Fraytar shouted to the two crewmen who were responsible for checking the sea depth. "It's high tide, and we shall need to adjust for at least ten stances difference at low tide."

The *Aurora* steadily made its way on a diagonal path towards the coast, with the two crew members regularly calling out depth soundings. Fraytar and Crouch looked out for a suitable cove. It was still too deep to make repairs at low tide, and Fraytar's hopes of finding a suitable anchorage were dwindling as another hour passed. Then he spotted an indent in the coastline.

"Head for that cove, just ahead," Fraytar shouted with relief to his crew.

As they approached the cove, Fraytar asked again for regular depth check updates. To his relief, an eight-step depth below the bottom of the *Aurora*'s hull was found. Once the ship was anchored, the crew waited for low tide, which raised the bow out of the water enough for the carpenter to continue his repairs.

"You have eight hours to complete your repairs," Fraytar said to the carpenter when he reached the lower deck.

"That's tight, Captain," the carpenter answered. "I'll do what I can."

Hours later the sea began to rise, slowly creeping up the *Aurora*'s hull whilst the carpenter desperately continued his work, helped by several crew members. At last the work was finished, and the carpenter stood back to view his work.

"Maybe not my best," he said, sighing with relief, "but it should get us back," the carpenter said to himself.

With the hull repaired and the *Aurora* now floating on the high tide, they set about readying the ship for its journey back to Stacklin.

CHAPTER 19

The Front

Morganuke was woken by shouting as the Cordinen officers barked their orders to their soldiers. He slowly came to his senses and sat up on his makeshift bed, realising again that he was alone. To Morganuke's relief, the Epleons had not attacked in the night as they had said they would, and so hopefully his friends were still safe.

One of the Patronese stuck his head through the opening of the tent. "Rouse yourself, we leave for the front within the hour." Morganuke looked at him nonchalantly and nodded.

Outside the tent, the camp was a hive of activity. More Cordinen soldiers had arrived and were forming up into columns preparing to make their way to the front line. Officers continued to bark orders as the men formed up. Morganuke mounted his horse and made his way alongside the other three Patronese. They looked at him blankly, with their red eyes.

The column moved out of the camp, leaving a dusty trail in their wake. As they moved through the countryside, now less foreboding and even greener than it had been, Morganuke wondered what had become of the Epleon insurgents and the spy he had been in contact with. Would they attack even now, not knowing that the artefact was not close by? If they did attack, how would they fare when the number of Cordinen soldiers had increased threefold?

The sun shone lower in the sky, and there was a cold sting in the air. On they travelled through the morning, and still no attack came. At last, Morganuke spotted the buildings of Stacklin in the distance rising above the city walls. Their ornate shaped roofs pleasing to the eye and very different from the dull, rigid Cordinen architecture. Ahead at the outskirts of the city, Morganuke saw that the lines of Cordinen soldiers were in position and waiting for the attack to begin. His stomach churned as he thought of his friends and the forthcoming devastation he would be forced to inflict on the Epleon defenders.

The party of Patronese rode up to a group of tents situated just behind the Cordinen lines. One of the tents was larger than the other, and Morganuke guessed this to be the command tent. Nestled in the middle of the tents was a smaller tent, guarded by several Cordinen soldiers, that looked exactly like the tent that had housed the optoglean during his trials. The three other Patronese halted their horses just outside the tent and dismounted, with Morganuke following suit. The four then entered the tent to reveal the optoglean, its blue eye etched on each side. Morganuke shuddered at the sight of it, remembering the events from his trial and imagining what was to come.

The four of them did as before, each going to a corner of the optoglean and lifting it in unison, carrying it out of the tent and towards the front line. Morganuke could see a tall tower rising from a wall surrounding the city a little way in the distance. The four Patronese made their way slowly towards the tower, and a line of Cordinen soldiers in front of them advanced towards the tower at the same pace. Immediately beneath the tower, Morganuke now made out large wooden reinforced gates in the city walls.

Suddenly a volley of arrows hailed down on them, shot from the tower and walls. The leading Cordinen soldiers raised shields above their heads, and the Patronese fell in behind. As the arrows struck the thick wooden shields, a chorus of swacks sounded, and some cries of pain when several arrows found their mark. About two hundred paces from the tower, the advancing Cordinens and Patronese stopped, shields still raised.

"Focus your attention on the tower," said Karorkin to the other three. Morganuke followed the orders and applied all his focus on the tower in front of him. A warm flow started to run through his body, and he felt energy coming from the optoglean. He remembered what had happened during his trial, and for a moment his focus waned. The other three Patronese looked at him intently as they felt his focus slip away. Then Morganuke remembered his friends and the danger that they were in, held by the Cordinens as hostages, and immediately his focus returned all the stronger, energy now rushing through him in a hot streaming gush. The handles of the artefact glowed red-hot, causing the other three Patronese to release their grip with cries of pain. The flash of intense light that came soon after was blinding to all around, Cordinen and Epleon alike, and the following blast of wind was even stronger than it had been during the trial. Once the dust had cleared, nobody, not even Morganuke, was left standing. The wind sucking everybody towards the vacuum that had been left at the centre of the point that Morganuke's had been focusing on.

Morganuke's five friends clung to the sides of the covered wagon as it raced across the countryside. They had no clue as to why they had suddenly been taken from their tent. Morganuke had left them to look for something, and soon afterwards Cordinen guards had ordered them from their tent and into the wagon.

"Where are they taking us?" Melinor wondered as she held her little sister Alorie in one arm whilst using the other to hold on to one of the wagon's cover poles.

"I don't know," Lengrond replied. "Maybe Morganuke has gone on before us, and they're trying to catch up."

"I hate being at the whim of these disgusting people," Calarel moaned. "Why doesn't Morganuke tell us what is going on?"

"We can only wait and see where our journey takes us," Chanterly said more prudently. "Morganuke may not be aware of the Cordinen plans for us, either. Let's not jump to any conclusions."

The party remained silent as the wagon trundled on its way at speed, leaving a dusty trail behind it. Chanterly peered out between a small gap at the bottom the wagon cover and could see several Cordinen soldiers riding alongside. She quickly closed the gap in the cover when a soldier glared at her.

After travelling for the rest of the day, they finally came to an abrupt stop, sending the friends flying to the front of the wagon. The back of the wagon cover was thrown open, and a mean-looking Cordinen soldier with no teeth peered in.

"Quickly, out of the wagon," the toothless soldier spluttered, sending spittle in all directions. Bruised and battered from the journey, the friends climbed clumsily out of the wagon and followed the soldier to a holding cage set among several tents. Inside the cage they were shackled to posts that had been driven deep into the ground.

The light was growing dim, and early evening stars began to appear in the clear sky. They could hear the clatter of many soldiers moving through the camp and the occasional neighing horse in the background.

"Do you think that we have been brought to the front?" Calarel asked, looking through the bars of the holding cage to see what was going on. "Morganuke did say that we would be taken to the camp, but where is he? I just want to get out of this place and be free. We need to find a way to escape so we are ready when the opportunity arises."

"We are tied to posts and locked in a metal cage in the middle of a Cordinen stronghold," Lengrond added grimly. "How are we expected to escape?"

"Morganuke said he would create a distraction, but we need to be able to free ourselves from these bonds when that happens," Chanterly pointed out, tugging at the chain binding her to the post.

"And we need keys to get out of this pen," added Lengrond.

"I can help with that," Calarel said, taking everyone by surprise. "I can pick a lock with my pin." Calarel held up a thin metal pin about as long as her little finger. "Let me try one of the locks on our chains."

Calarel held the lock on her chain and inserted the metal pin in the keyhole. She carefully moved the pin in different directions until there was a click and the clamp around her ankle opened. The others gasped open mouthed, surprised at Calarel's resourcefulness.

"Where did you learn that little trick?" Lengrond asked, staring at Calarel.

"My father makes locks in his smithy, and I used to study them. Very useful for getting into places that I was not allowed to go."

"You're full of surprises, Miss Calarel," Lengrond replied.

"Quick, a guard is coming," whispered Chanterly. "Cover up the open lock." Calarel quickly threw her cloak over it as she sat back against the bars of the holding cage.

The guard peered into the pen, holding up a flaming torch. He sneered at the occupants and then moved on.

"That was close," Calarel said. "We need to be careful. If they find out that we have been fiddling with the locks, then we're done for."

"We can wait till morning or when Morganuke returns before we undo the locks," Chanterly suggested. "Once the main attack starts, then hopefully the Cordinens' attention will be on that and not us." She looked across at Melinor, who was holding her sister close to her, trying to keep her warm, their chain tethers stretched to the limit. "How are you and your sister?" she asked. "This must all be quite an ordeal for you both."

"It's all right, really," Melinor answered. "We have got used to hard times and discomfort. We have survived long enough as slaves in the Cordinen camps. My sister does find it hard at times. I comfort her as best I can, but this is all very different from our lives in Vesnick."

"You come from Vesnick," Chanterly acknowledged. "That is a beautiful part of the world, and the people are so friendly. How did you come into the Cordinen hands?"

"We were captured by a Cordinen raiding party last year whilst we were swimming in the sea. We haven't seen our parents since then, and they must think that we are dead now. I miss my home and family so much and hope that one day I will return."

"Well, if we have anything to do with it, we'll make sure you do," Chanterly said firmly, smiling at the two girls.

"I miss Mamma and Pappa," Alorie said, looking back at Chanterly through teary eyes. "But I am glad that my sister is with me."

It was getting late, and they were feeling very tired after their uncomfortable journey. The cage was big enough for them to lie down. Soon all were asleep.

They were awoken the next morning with a rattling on the bars of their cage. "Wake up, you lazy maggots!" came a shout from the toothless Cordinen as he shoved bowls of unrecognisable food into the cage. "Breakfast is here!"

Calarel picked up one of the bowls and sniffed the brown sludge in it. She gagged and started to throw the bowl to the ground, some of its contents splashing Lengrond.

"Don't waste it!" he snapped, catching her by the wrist. "It may be the only food we get today. I'm starving and could eat anything." He took the bowl and sniffed it himself, trying to hide his disgust. "It smells like sh—"

"Let's just eat, shall we," Chanterly interjected as she tucked into the contents of her bowl without sniffing it first.

"So it's agreed then?" Calarel said as she sat down with her bowl trying not to look at the contents. "I pick the locks to our shackles and the door to this pen, and we wait for the battle to start before escaping."

"Then where do we go?" Lengrond asked.

"Anywhere but here," came Calarel's curt reply.

"We'll head north and cross into Epleon-held territory away from the front line," Chanterly answered, still tucking into her bowl of brown sludge.

"What about Morganuke?" Lengrond asked. "Do we wait for him?"

"Morganuke said to head for Protor, and so that's what we'll do, with or without him," concluded Chanterly finishing her breakfast and throwing the bowl to the ground. "Nothing like a nice, tasty breakfast to start the day off."

In the distance, a Cordinen officer shouted an order, followed by the sound of a thousand feet trampling undergrowth.

"Look!" Calarel shouted, pointing in the direction of the trampling sound. "Isn't that Morganuke? Carrying that box thing with three others that look like him."

The others crowded on that side of the pen to look, pulling at their tethers. They could clearly see Morganuke and the other Patronese carrying the optoglean and following a line of Cordinen soldiers. They watched them moving forward toward the front line until they were obscured by the undergrowth and trees. The trampling sound stopped, followed by a moment of silence. Then there was a bright flash, quickly followed by a howling blast that sent everything, including the party of friends, flying towards the flash.

When they came to, the five of them had been thrown against the bars of the holding cage. They slowly got to their feet and looked around at the devastation. Tents, horses, and men were strewn everywhere. Some of the men lying on the ground began to groan as they slowly revived.

"Quick!" whispered Chanterly. "Unlock the chains and the door before they recover." Calarel did as she was bid, quickly unlocking the shackles one by one and then the door to the cage.

"Crawl close to the ground," Chanterly whispered as they exited the holding cage. "Make for that mound of grass just beyond the clearing." The five friends carefully crawled in the direction Chanterly had pointed out. There was now more movement from the recovering Cordinen soldiers with the odd shouted instruction. The group carried on carefully, desperate not to be detected before they were safely away. At last, they reached the mound of grass. They paused to plot their next move, then continued through a grove of trees and hedges lining the road leading into the camp. They cut across the road and through the hedgerow and then headed into the woods.

They were almost beyond the tree line when a shout went out from one of the Cordinen officers who had found his feet. "The prisoners! The prisoners have escaped! Find them!"

"Quickly! Run!" Chanterly shouted. They had all reached the shelter of the trees and started running as fast as they could, not daring to look back. They could hear the soldiers looking for them, their voices growing closer. Alorie fell to the ground, tripping on the undergrowth, but Lengrond at once lifted her in the air and then carried her over his shoulder.

Suddenly there was another flash of light followed by a blasting wind. The five friends were pulled backwards onto their backs as the blast enveloped them, though with less force this time. Moments later, they were on their feet again and running from the carnage left behind them.

CHAPTER 20

The Chase

Morganuke lay on the ground, darkness and dust all around. He still couldn't see clearly after the flash of light, and his body ached from being thrown to the ground by the blast of wind. Gradually he got to his feet, looking around to see the once proud lines of Cordinen soldiers lying on the ground, groaning, recovering from the blast. The three other Patronese were still unconscious on the ground, but the optoglean they surrounded stood intact.

With the Cordinen soldiers slowly coming to, Morganuke realised he had to move quickly if he was to return to the Cordinen camp several hundred paces away and find his captive friends. He passed wreckage and men lying everywhere until he came to the outskirts of the camp. He made his way through the derelict campsite as more Cordinens were struggling to their feet, towards the centre he came upon an empty holding cage with its door left open.

Just then Morganuke heard one of the officers calling out about escaped prisoners and realised that the holding pen must have been where they had held his friends. He saw a detachment of Cordinen soldiers leaving the camp and heading towards a grove of trees just beyond. *I can't let the Cordinens find them now,* Morganuke thought, *they will surely kill them.* His desperation and anger brought the familiar warm glow inside. Not sure what else to do, he began following the soldiers, keeping a distance so as not to be detected, and as he focused his attention on them and what they might do to his friends, the feeling got stronger and stronger, until the flash of light came, followed by the withering blast of wind. Morganuke was knocked forward off his feet. He lay on the ground for a few seconds and then got to his feet again. Looking around, he couldn't see or hear any of the soldiers and proceeded stealthily in the direction that they had been going, stepping over unconscious men as he did so.

Morganuke followed the path for about an hour. Eventually it took him close to the riverbank. Hoping that his friends would be heading towards Protor as he had suggested, he needed to cross the river at some point and start heading south, but at this point the river was impossible to cross. The level was high, and the water was gushing at speed. Although he was a good swimmer, he knew that he couldn't swim against such a strong current.

For another hour Morganuke continued along the path running parallel to the river. He finally spotted a bridge ahead, but as he got closer, he saw a large contingent of Cordinen soldiers on it. He hid in the undergrowth and watched, hoping the soldiers were on patrol and would move on. After another hour of waiting, it became clear that the soldiers had been stationed there to guard the bridge.

Do I to try and cross here at the risk of being detected, or move further upriver to cross? Morganuke didn't know what to do. The river was still flowing in rapids, with torrents of water sending spray in the air as it thundered over the rocks, making it impossible to swim across.

The chilly air was made damp by the fast-flowing water. Morganuke huddled down in the undergrowth, wrapping his cloak around him, trying to keep warm. He wondered about his friends, whether they had been captured or managed to make their escape across the river. If they had crossed, it would be almost impossible to catch up with them before Protor. *That is where I need to head for now,* he thought. *I'll take the safer long way around if needs be.* With that decided, Morganuke again began to move further up the river to find another place to cross.

The rest of the day passed as Morganuke made his way further and further upriver. He knew that if he continued in that direction, it would eventually take him to Castle Stanver, another stronghold held by the Cordinens. He had to find a way to cross the river soon and head south towards Protor. He had given up any hope of catching his friends before Protor, but that was over one thousand stances away and at least four weeks travel on foot. Anything could happen in that time.

As the light began to fade, Morganuke looked for a sheltered place to camp for the night. It was cold, and a light wind bit into his skin like icy daggers. He hadn't eaten all day and felt faint with hunger and fatigue. He made his way over a hill lined with small trees and bushes. Just beyond this, there was a rocky dip at the base of the hill that Morganuke thought could be worked into a temporary shelter. He gathered branches from the trees roundabout and piled fallen leaves, twigs, and thin turf cut with his sword placed over the top to provide some shelter from the wind. Once he had gathered enough dry wood and kindling, Morganuke set about lighting a fire, remembering what his father had taught him.

After several attempts, the fire was lit and blazing nicely. He crouched as close to the flames as he dared, thankful for the warmth it gave him. Now he was warm, hunger struck him like a dagger. He needed to find food if he was to have the strength to continue his long journey. He had his sword and a knife, but these on their own would be no good for hunting. Something that Tomlin had taught him was making a spear from a knife, a long stick, and binding, so he set about making one from a long stick and ivy he had found nearby.

With his makeshift spear in hand, Morganuke ventured from his camp to hunt any small game he could find. He made his way upwind so that his scent was carried away from the direction he was going. The moon gave just enough light to see ahead. At a bramble patch amongst a clump of trees, Morganuke stopped and crouched in the undergrowth. He listened to the breeze which blew the leaves in small gusts every now and then, with stillness in between. Then he heard a faint rustling ahead.

With his legs beginning to ache from his crouching position, he kept as still as he could, listening for the rustle and watching the direction it was coming from. Just then, a rabbit popped out from the brambles and hopped along the edge of the patch. Morganuke lifted his spear carefully and aimed, following the rabbit's path as it continued to hop. Then it stopped, turning its head towards Morganuke just as his spear found its target. With a high-pitched squeak, the rabbit lurched into the air and convulsed on the ground.

Back at his camp, Morganuke was feeling very pleased with himself as he gutted and skinned the rabbit, and then roasted it over his blazing campfire. After eating every morsel and drinking the water he had collected earlier in his water skin, he felt very full and relaxed. He settled down on a pile of leaves he used as a makeshift bed for the night, hoping that he would not be disturbed by dreams.

The next morning Morganuke woke feeling very cold. The fire was out, and his teeth chattered uncontrollably. Stiff and aching, he got himself up from his makeshift bed the best he could. His mind was fuddled with the cold, but he had to think carefully about what to do next. Should he try to cross the river here and risk being drowned, or travel further north and risk being detected by Cordinen patrols? He made his way to the riverbank and to his dismay saw that the river was still fast-flowing, and impossible to cross. Convincing himself that travelling further north was the only option, Morganuke continued his journey.

Morganuke followed the path of the river for the rest of the morning, occasionally checking for any way to cross. Sunlight shone through the sparsely leafed trees, the branches swaying in the cold gusts of wind that blew around Morganuke's body. His feet ached, but he could not stop to rest, desperate to find a crossing and the relative safety of Epleon-held lands.

Morganuke came to a small clearing in the trees, where he caught sight of two figures approaching. He dived into the undergrowth, flat on the ground, determined not to be seen. He waited there for several moments until he could hear the voices of the two figures he'd seen earlier. *Wait, I recognise that voice.* He slowly lifted his head up from the undergrowth, and to his boundless joy saw a familiar face.

"Lengrond!" he called, rising.

Lengrond stopped abruptly in surprise. He was with a man

Morganuke did not recognise, who carried a large bow. He swiftly brought it up, nocking an arrow he drew from his quiver. Lengrond almost dropped the clutch of rabbit carcasses he held as he called "Morganuke!" The two hurried towards each other and embraced. "We thought you were dead."

"Where are the others?"

"The others are at Fenlop's hideout," Lengrond replied, nodding toward his companion by way of introduction. "He is giving us refuge from the Cordinen patrols whilst we recover our strength for the journey ahead."

Fenlop still had his arrow aimed steadily at Morganuke's chest. "I take it you know this man," Fenlop said, not taking his eyes from the Patronese looking man in front of him.

"It's all right, he's a good friend," Lengrond answered, gesturing for Fenlop to relax and lower his bow.

"I thought you would have crossed the river by now," Morganuke said. "I gave up hope of catching up with you."

"Fenlop suggested that we wait and cross further upriver once we have recovered our strength," Lengrond explained. "The water flow is less severe, and the river shallow enough to cross. We need to be careful of the Cordinen patrols, however."

Fenlop gestured for Lengrond and Morganuke to follow. He led the way through the trees and thick undergrowth for about an hour, when they came to a wooded hill, a few paces from the riverbank. The sound of the water cascading over rocks from the nearby river and the wind gusting through the branches of the trees filled the air. Fenlop led them up a slope to the top of the wooded hill and beyond, where the path dipped towards some rocks.

As they got closer to the rocks, Morganuke spotted a cave entrance hidden behind some carefully placed vegetation. They continued through the entrance of the cave, where they were met by another man holding a bow.

"Welcome back, Fenlop," the man holding the bow said. "I see you've found another stray, and an unusual one at that. He looks like a Cordinen spy."

"This man is with the others, Drenden," Fenlop answered. "Don't worry, he's not a Cordinen spy."

"I thought all the Patronese were with the Cordinens," Drenden said, looking Morganuke up and down.

"Well, this one isn't," Fenlop insisted. "As I said, he's with the others."

Fenlop continued to lead them deeper into the cave. A pitch torch wedged between two rocks lit the way ahead, showing a passageway just wide enough for a man to pass, which eventually opened out to an area large enough to serve as a room. Several people sat with their backs against the rock walls, around a large fire blazing in the centre. Smoke rose through a natural opening at the top of the cave, which let in some natural light. Morganuke appreciated the comforting light and warmth from the fire.

Fenlop took the clutch of rabbits from Lengrond and held them up for all to see. "We bring food," he announced to the group. Two women, clothed in animal skins, came forward to take the rabbits eagerly and went to prepare them for the evening meal.

Morganuke's eyes were still adjusting to the dim light when he heard his name called.

"Morg!" exclaimed Calarel with a big grin. "It's so good to see you." She jumped up and instinctively wrapped her arms around him, but quickly let go as she realised what she had done. What have you been doing, you big fool?"

Morganuke was taken back by Calarel's response but was quietly pleased. He was about to reply but another pair of arms grasped him tightly around the waist. It was Melinor, burying her face on his chest. He lifted her face, which showed tears and a smile. He gently kissed her on the forehead, and she sat down with her sister again.

"So what happened at the Cordinen camp?" enquired Chanterly from her place at the fire. "We saw you with some of the others who looked like you, carrying a large box."

"We were going to destroy the Epleon defences with that artefact thing they call an optoglean," Morganuke said. "I got so angry at the Cordinens and focused all my power on them instead. Then there was a flash and a great blast of wind, which sent me and everyone else around flying about."

"Yes, we saw and felt that," Chanterly said. "That's what allowed us to escape our holding cage. We were running into the woods when there was another flash and blast of wind, which allowed us to get away."

"Yes, that was me too," Morganuke said. "I saw that some of the Cordinens had recovered and so needed to do something quickly."

"Where do all these powers come from?" Calarel asked.

"Don't know," Morganuke answered. "Something to do with my origins, is what I've been told."

Voices were raised from the entrance of the cave. Morganuke looked around to see Almen stride through the passageway towards him, followed closely by Albrin. The last time he had seen Almen was at Castle Medogor under very different circumstances.

"Why didn't you destroy the artefact?" Almen shouted at Morganuke as he drew near.

Morganuke said nothing and stared angrily into Almen's eyes.

"You had a golden opportunity to destroy the artefact outside Stacklin," Almen continued. "Now that opportunity has gone."

Morganuke looked at Almen, keeping his composure. "And how do you think the opportunity was created?" Morganuke asked rhetorically. "It was my actions that caused the Cordinens' disorganization. I was on my own and could not carry the optoglean nor destroy it. It's a miracle that I'm here at all. I barely had time to escape and have been looking out for my friends. Don't you dare accuse me of not doing what I should have."

Almen kept quiet for a moment, before stepping back to regain his usual calm demeanour. "All right, it's done now. But we must replan and take advantage of any remaining disorder in the Cordinen ranks."

Chanterly approached the two men. "I am Chanterly Bowderlong of the women's island militia," Chanterly announced to Almen. "And who might you be?"

"I am Almen Pratage of the island insurgent group."

"He is one of the Militia forward contacts," Morganuke said.

"I along with three others in my team," Almen said, "have been sent behind Cordinen lines to aid the Epleons and the island militia where necessary."

"I see," answered Chanterly. "I heard you mention destroying the Patronese artefact. Of what importance would this be in the war?"

"It could turn the odds in the Epleons' favour," Almen said. "Since their use of the artefact with the help of the Patronese, the Cordinens have made significant gains in the war. They are now close to breaking through the Epleon defences, which would be catastrophic for us all. It's crucial that we stop them before they have a chance to take Stacklin."

"As I see it, we can give thanks to Morganuke here that the Cordinens were not able to break through this time," Chanterly said, putting her hand on Morganuke's shoulder. "It was his actions that allowed us to escape."

Almen closed his eyes and raised his head up, taking deep breaths before responding. "Then we need to take advantage of the Cordinen confusion while it lasts and destroy the artefact."

"And how do you plan to do that?" Morganuke asked. "Our numbers are few, and the Cordinens still have many active soldiers."

"We need a distraction. We have a means to contact the Epleon forces remotely and can signal them to counterattack," Almen answered. "Then we sneak into the Cordinen camp while their attention is drawn away and destroy the artefact."

"We can help as well," Fenlop added. "My group is small but willing and able to help where we can."

Almen nodded in appreciation to Fenlop, and then turned to Morganuke and Chanterly awaiting their response. They looked at each other for a moment, and then turned to Fenlop to nod their acceptance of his plan.

CHAPTER 21

Retracing Steps

The *Aurora* sailed into Stacklin harbour, battle-scarred from the encounters with the Cordinen warships. The dockside was busy with Epleon soldiers moving supplies offloaded from other ships recently arrived. Fraytar noticed an urgency in their movements, as if some event had recently shaken them, but saw no evidence of an attack.

As the *Aurora* pulled alongside, Fraytar observed several Epleon officers standing on the docks, looking surprised at the ship's condition. Once the gangplanks had been placed, Fraytar immediately made his way down to talk to the officers. The Epleon soldiers disembarked too, some struggling to walk through injury and others carried on stretchers. The officers looked on glumly as the trail of wounded men left the ship. Among them Fraytar recognised Commander Besnit, who had sent them off on this misbegotten mission.

"Welcome back, Captain Fraytar," he said as Fraytar approached. "Your mission was successful, then, but where are the other two ships?"

"Successful?" Fraytar answered. "It was a complete disaster. We were set upon by four Cordinen warships before we reached our destination, and the *Aurora* only just managed to escape. The other two ships were lost, I'm sorry to say."

The officers looked at Fraytar with their mouths open. "But what about the flashes of light and the blasting winds that sent the Cordinen attack flying?" Besnit asked. "We had assumed that was caused by our forces you took behind the enemy lines."

"I know nothing of that," Fraytar replied flatly. "As I said, we were set upon and did not make it to our destination. You can see for yourself the resulting damage to my ship."

"Then who thwarted the Cordinen attack?" Commander Besnit asked. "At least two thousand Cordinens were advancing on our defences until a great flash of light came from who knows where and sent their soldiers in all directions. We surely would have been overrun had it not been for those bangs and flashes. We are trying to build up more forces here as fast as we can to take advantage of the situation and counterattack."

Fraytar thought carefully before speaking. "A flash of light, you say? And then a blast of wind? It must have been Morganuke. I've heard of his powers, and this has the signs of his intervention."

"Morganuke?" Besnit responded. "If it was him, then he is indeed a powerful individual."

Fraytar noticed the concern on the officer's face as the words left his mouth. "Let me try to contact the insurgents and see what is going on," Fraytar offered, before realising that he needed to keep the talking boxes secret from the Epleons. He remembered what Commander Tradish had told him about the Casdredon priests and that they would not take kindly to him possessing "magic" boxes. "There may be some insurgents still nearby I can locate," he quickly added. "I need to repair my ship before venturing out to sea again, Commander. Please would you help me to find the supplies to do this?"

"Yes, of course, Captain," Commander Besnit answered. "Give me a list of what you need, and I'll arrange to have it delivered to you. I do hope that you can continue to help us." Fraytar gave his thanks, relieved that Besnit did not press him about how he was going to contact the insurgents. He asked a few questions about their plan of attack and felt reasonably assured.

Fraytar waited until nightfall before attempting to use the talking box. He followed the usual procedure to initiate the talking box, knowing that it had been exposed to plenty of daylight on the journey to Stacklin. From the information Almen had given him, he selected a contact point closest to the front line. The box came to life with the usual crackles, but there was no answer, even after several attempts. He was just about to give up when he heard Almen's tinny voice come from the box. "Fraytar, is that you?"

"Yes, it's me, Fraytar."

"Thank thunder we made contact," came Almen's relieved response. "We need the Epleon forces to create a distraction whilst we destroy the Patronese artefact."

"That's well timed," Fraytar replied. "The Epleon forces are preparing for just such an event." He sketched out what Commander Besnit had told him.

"Excellent. We'll await your signal and then make our move. The surviving Cordinen soldiers are still reorganizing themselves after Morganuke's demonstration of force. I doubt that the Epleons will be able to overcome them. To avoid too many losses, a limited counterattack should be sufficient as a distraction."

"Morganuke is with you?" Fraytar asked excitedly. "We thought he might be behind the flashes and bangs."

"Yes, he's here. Along with his friends who escaped from Cordinen capture."

"Is Calarel there too?"

"Yes, she's here."

"That's good news. Her father will be glad to hear it. I'll inform the Epleon forces in Stacklin about all the information you've shared. Look out for any signs of the counterattack."

"We'll look out for any signs of a counterattack from the Epleons before we make our move. Message out." There were a few crackles from the box as Fraytar deactivated it. He was overjoyed at learning that Morganuke and Calarel were still alive and safe and couldn't wait to tell Tomlin.

Later that night, Fraytar met with Commander Besnit to report in greater detail what had happened to them with the Cordinen ships and how they had failed to reach their destination. He then went on to propose the plan to destroy the Patronese artefact with the help of a diversion from a limited Epleon counterattack from this side of the front.

"Limited counterattack, you say?" the commander said doubtfully. "Surely, we have the Cordinens at a disadvantage and should press for an all-out attack."

"Commander, my contact strongly advised that the attack should be a limited one," Fraytar replied. "The Cordinen forces are still very strong, and there is no hope of overwhelming them with the limited forces you have."

"How does your contact know so many details about the enemy?" Besnit asked suspiciously.

"I can't tell you that," Fraytar said. "Nor do I know more about their plan. The important thing is to cause a diversion, to allow the forces behind enemy lines to destroy the artefact. The Cordinens will surely break through your lines if they manage to use that in their attack."

"I have heard from the surviving Epleon soldiers who sailed with you how bravely you commanded your ship and the soldiers in taking out two of the Cordinen warships. I do not doubt your resolve. I am, however, wary of the accuracy of the information that you have been given. Once we attack, any element of surprise will be gone, making it more important to press home our advantage. Tomorrow we will attack and break the Cordinen lines." The commander raised his hand in dismissal, and Fraytar felt he could add nothing further to convince him.

When Fraytar returned to the *Aurora*, he was greeted by Tomlin, still smiling at the news that Calarel was alive. "Why be he so glum, Fraytar?" Tomlin asked joyfully. "'Tis a time to be happy at the news of Calarel and Morg."

Fraytar nodded and kept his frustration to himself, but his thoughts remained with what he knew was to come, wondering whether any of them would survive what was about to be unleashed.

In Fenlop's cave hideaway, Almen stood in front of the campfire, explaining his plans for destroying the Patronesc artefact. The flames lit up his weathered face and sent shadows dancing across the ground as he articulated the plan with his hands.

"We have been keeping watch on the Cordinens as they recover from the recent upheaval," Almen explained. "They keep the artefact some way back from the front line, in a small tent guarded by several guards. The Patronese who control the artefact are in a separate tent a little way away." Almen picked up a stick and drew marks in the sand on the cave floor as he spoke. "There is plenty of vegetation that we can use as cover a little way behind the artefact tent. We can hold there undetected until the Epleons attack starts. The attack will be a limited diversionary one, and so we shall have limited time to get to the tent, take out the guards, and destroy the artefact."

"What about escape?" Fenlop asked. "We shall also need time to make our escape."

"Of course," Almen said. "The Epleon distraction should still allow time for that."

"What about the Patronese?" Chanterly asked. "Do we take them out too?"

"I don't see a need for that," Almen responded. "Without the artefact, the Patronese won't be able to do much."

"But I could," Morganuke interjected. "I am still able to project my power without the box. It was made easier with it, but I could do a fair bit of damage without it."

"You are truly exceptional, even for Patronese standards," Lengrond replied, standing up to be noticed.

"Why don't we just send Morganuke in, and he can take out the whole Cordinen army single-handed?" Calarel jokingly added with a chuckle.

"It doesn't work like that," Morganuke replied despondently. "I can only do it sometimes, mostly when I'm angry at something, or in a tricky situation."

"I've got a few ideas to make you angry," she quipped.

"We do this together or not at all," Chanterly intervened, looking sternly at Calarel.

"Agreed," Almen said. "We must all be in this together and support each other. It won't work otherwise. Margins will be so tight; we must work as one. As soon as the Epleon attack begins, we all advance on the artefact tent together and take out the guards. I'll have plenty of pitch to destroy the artefact. Then we can escape the way we came as quickly as possible. Are we all agreed?" The group murmured their agreement.

"So, what next?" Chanterly asked, pulling Calarel back as she looked as though she was about to say something.

"We make for the cover behind the artefact tent tonight," Almen added. "We need to be there for daybreak. So we will have to move quickly but quietly to avoid detection."

"That's impossible!" Lengrond exclaimed. "It must be a good day's run from here."

"Not if we use the river to take us most of the way," Almen said. "There are boats we can use a little way upriver. The current is strong and takes us in the direction of Stacklin. We should remain undetected from any Cordinen patrols under cover of darkness and can disembark upriver from the front line. From there we can make our way behind the Cordinen lines and to our waiting point."

"You really do have this all worked out, don't you?" Chanterly concluded.

"As I said before, we have been keeping a good watch on the area." Almen scrubbed out the markings he'd made on the floor with his foot and hastened everybody to get prepared.

As Morganuke was about to leave with the others, Melinor came up to him and hugged him tightly. "Don't leave me, my love," she whispered softly in his ear.

"You stay and look after your sister," Morganuke replied, kissing Melinor gently on the lips. "I promise I'll come back. I'll not let anything happen to you or your sister." Morganuke followed the others out of the cave, feeling the eyes of Melinor and Alorie on him.

The group found the three canoes moored a short way upstream, as Almen had said. It was a little tricky getting down the riverbank, which was steep and slippery, but everyone managed it. The group of twelve entered the three boats, four in each canoe, sat in line with a paddle. They began to make their way downriver, manoeuvring the canoes with their paddles.

The river current was fast and strong. The occupants of each canoe had to work frantically to avoid crashing into the bank or the occasional rock that appeared ominously in the starlight above the torrents of water. Water crashed over the sides of the little boats as they were tossed about like corks in the raging river. Occasionally the paddles were laid down inside the boat to allow water to be bailed out using the water skins everyone carried.

What is Almen leading us into? Morganuke wondered as he paddled desperately with his paddle, first one side and then quickly swapping to the other side, as the boat lurched the other way. He caught sight of Calarel, who was paddling just behind him. Her hair was soaking and lay flat against her wet face, framing her perfectly formed features.

Just then there was a loud crack as the boat lurched over a rock that all four paddlers had missed. It seemed like an age until the boat crashed back down in the water, sending everyone tumbling towards the front. Calarel gave out a short scream as she was sent sideways, letting go of her paddle and heading headfirst for the water. Morganuke managed to catch her round the waist before she fell overboard.

They had only a moment to look at each other before resuming their composure, Calarel giving a shy smile. As her paddle had been flung overboard, the three remaining paddles had to work all the harder to keep the boat on course, and she focussed on bailing.

The crashing and bumping progress downriver carried on for another two hours, before the river widened and the current slowed. By that time everyone was exhausted almost to the point of collapsing. They lay back against the sides of the canoes, gladly letting the modest current carry them along. It was dark, with no moon and only starlight, which was ideal for them to remain undetected by any Cordinen patrols. Morganuke could just about make out Almen's boat just ahead.

They continued downriver for another hour, letting the current take them. Occasionally the river bent tightly, requiring some paddling, but the lurching and crashing had stopped. It was a manageable pace, almost pleasurable, had they not been on such a dangerous mission.

They approached a point where the river narrowed again, and Morganuke feared that they would have to repeat the nightmare progress from before. However, whilst the pace quickened, there were fewer rocks and twists to contend with, making progress far more manageable.

Ahead, Morganuke could see Almen's silhouette, frantically waving and pointing to the side of the river. Almen steered his boat carefully towards the right bank of the river, and Morganuke told the others in his boat to follow as well as signalling to the canoe behind. Tree branches and bushes overhung the water's edge on that side, and the three canoes made their way under these for cover. They were perilously close to the riverbank and had to be careful not to ground or entangle the canoes.

Morganuke looked across the river and now saw what Almen had been pointing at. It was a Cordinen patrol slowly coming towards them along the riverbank. The three canoes continued downriver as silently as they could, the concealing branches brushing over their heads. Calarel gave a sharp intake of breath, just managing to suppress a yelp, as one of the branches scratched her cheek, leaving a red bloody mark.

The canoes were now directly opposite the Cordinen patrol, and the overhanging growth was quickly thinning as they continued downriver. Everyone in the canoes kept as still as they could, with the occasional careful movement of the paddles to keep the canoes as close to the opposite bank as possible. Morganuke watched as Fenlop handed his paddle to Calarel and then notched an arrow ready on his bow. They wouldn't stand a chance if the Cordinens saw them and Morganuke knew their chances were slim, but they would at least go down fighting. As the branch cover was thinning even more, they soon would be completely exposed, but with only the starlight for visibility, they might still be difficult to see at a distance. Morganuke just hoped that the Cordinens' eyesight was no better than theirs.

At last, there was a slight right-hand bend in the river. Manoeuvring past it entailed some subtle paddle work, but once the canoes were past the bend, they were out of sight of the Cordinens and could resume their course in the centre. The current continued at a modest speed for the next couple of hours.

Morganuke saw Almen ahead pointing to the left bank and feared that another Cordinen patrol was approaching. He was relieved when Almen steered his boat into a small inlet, the water was much calmer. They easily beached the boats and disembarked.

"We take the land route for the rest of the way," Almen said. "Take a rest while I scout inland for Cordinen patrols."

They were all very wet and cold by now, but they had only a brief rest before Almen returned and told them to follow.

"It's crucial to reach the holding point behind the Cordinen lines before the Epleon attack starts," he prodded them on, despite their moans and groans.

The twelve continued making their way through the undergrowth, urged on by Almen for three more hours. The sun was beginning to rise, to everyone's relief, as it signalled that temperatures would soon rise a little. However, it also indicated how short of time they were before the Epleon attack would begin. Exhaustion and cold was slowing their progress, and Almen's desperation showed. *Have we come all this way for nothing?* Morganuke wondered as his teeth chattered uncontrollably with the cold.

He was just about to collapse in a heap on the ground, resigned to the thought that they had run out of time and energy, when he heard voices and the slow clop, clop, clop of hooves coming from behind a hedge they were following. He looked over at Almen and saw he had heard it too. Signalling for the others to wait, the two men cautiously made their way through a gap in the hedge and onto a bank overlooking the track below.

Crouching down low, they could see just below them two Cordinen horses and carts, each driven by a single Cordinen soldier with a single outrider alongside each cart. Almen and Morganuke looked at each other.

"You go for the outrider in the rear, and I'll go for the other one," Almen whispered.

There was a muffled yell from the Cordinen outriders as Morganuke and Almen fell on them, taking them off their horses and onto the dusty ground of the track. They quickly buried their knives into the outriders' necks. The two Cordinen carts began to race off as soon as their drivers realised what was happening. Morganuke and Almen mounted the two riderless Cordinen horses and raced after the carts. As they were pulling up alongside, there was a whoosh through the air, and two arrows struck home. Looking up, Morganuke saw two of Fenlop's archers, Drenden and Escolar, at the top of the bank above the carts, each with a bow in hand. The Cordinen drivers were dead. Morganuke was pleased with the way it had panned out and how they had worked together. It seemed to him that it had been an impressive series of coordinated actions by the four of them, even though they were exhausted and had had no time to plan. *This is a good omen for what we'll no doubt face later, that is if we managed to reach the artefact before the Epleon attack*, Morganuke thought.

With the help of the Cordinen horses and carts, the twelve could now make faster time towards their destination without tiring themselves out. Almen and Albrin donned the Cordinen outrider uniforms and weapons, riding alongside the horse and carts, now driven by Fenlop and one of his followers. The other eight rode in the two carts, making out that they were prisoners. They would still try to avoid Cordinen patrols, but at least now they had a disguise and a backup story.

"Luck has been on our side so far," Almen said spiritedly. Cheered with their success, Morganuke took on new energy as they continued their journey, ready to finish what they set out to do.

CHAPTER 22

The Optoglean

As the new day dawned, Morganuke and the group continued their journey towards the Cordinen front line outside Stacklin. As the sunlight began to appear over the horizon the group was made more aware that time was running out. Morganuke, Lengrond, Chanterly, and Calarel travelled in the leading cart that Fenlop was driving hard over the rough tracks, followed closely by the other cart.

"How much further is it?" Calarel complained as she was thrown from side to side in the cart. "Travelling is becoming a habit, and my back and sides are aching."

"Hush!" Chanterly snapped hoarsely. "We need to keep quieter so as not to alert any Cordinen patrols. It will take as long as it takes. Remember you're supposed to be acting as a prisoner."

Fenlop turned his head to speak back to them. "Sounds like a Cordinen patrol up ahead." Just around the next bend, they were confronted by a Cordinen patrol of six well-armed men on horseback. Morganuke quickly ducked covered his head with a blanket so as not to be recognised.

"Halt there and state your business," demanded a surly-looking Cordinen leading the patrol.

"We're transporting prisoners to the front line," Almen responded in a confident voice, riding his horse up close to the Cordinen soldier.

"Prisoners?" enquired the surly Cordinen. "Let me see these prisoners." He rode up beside the leading cart and looked down into it and saw Morganuke lying on his side with the blanket pulled up around his ears. "What's wrong with this one? He looks sick."

"He's come down with a fever. Be careful, he may be contagious," Almen responded.

The Cordinen soldier immediately moved away from the wagon. "All right, on your way. And watch out! There are enemies loose on this side of the river."

Thank goodness for quick thinking Almen, Fenlop thought.

The group continued for a few more stances. There was still no sign of the Epleon attack, and Fenlop hoped that they still had time to reach the holding point.

Fenlop brought the group to a halt after they entered a heavily wooded area. "We need to abandon the carts and continue on foot from here," he announced. "We can go round the Cordinen forces off the track and avoid encountering any more patrols. It shouldn't take us long to reach the holding point."

"Ah, good, time for a nice leisurely stroll in the woods," Calarel said, causing one of two to chuckle.

Once they had hidden the horses and carts in the trees, the group continued on foot. Occasionally they would hear a group of Cordinen soldiers nearby and moved very quietly on their way so as not to be detected. The going seemed painfully slow, and Fenlop expected the Epleon attack to start at any time, thus ruining their chances of destroying the artefact. He and his band has been hiding from the Cordinens for longer than he could remember. Now it was his opportunity to do them some real harm. He really hoped this operation would be a success.

"That's the hiding place I mentioned," Almen said as he pointed out the thicket to the others. Fenlop looked to where Almen was pointing and saw a clump of thick vegetation and small trees just ahead.

The twelve of them made their way into the vegetation and spread out amongst the bushes and lay flat, waiting for the Epleon attack to start. They stayed still for a good hour before a mighty roar erupted from the Epleon lines.

Once the Cordinen forces engaged in meeting the Epleon attack, Fenlop and the others followed Almen towards the sound of fighting.

They were still under cover when Almen alerted everyone. "That's not good," Almen remarked quietly. "They outnumber us two to one. There are too many for us to attack head on."

Fenlop looked for himself and could see at least twenty well-armed muscular Cordinens positioned ahead of them. He immediately thought of Morganuke. "What about the Patron, can't he help with the odds?" Fenlop whispered.

"Morganuke!" Almen hissed.

Morganuke crawled up to Almen and Fenlop. "What is it?" He asked.

"We need you to do something about those Cordinen's standing between us and the artifact. Can you use your powers on them?" Almen asked.

Fenlop looked at Morganuke as he lay there looking intently ahead. *Could it really be true*, Fenlop thought as Morganuke continued to look silently ahead. *Can this man really possess that power without one of the Patronese artifacts?* He had thought to himself of splitting the group and attacking the Cordinens from both sides at once and was just about to suggest that, when Morganuke got up on his knees.

"Get down, you fool, what are you doing? They'll see you," Almen hissed at Morganuke. But Morganuke remained kneeling.

Fenlop beckoned to his men to ready themselves and readied his own sword to meet the Cordinen attack that he was sure was about to come. Morganuke remained kneeling and started to shake. Fenlop crawled closer to Morganuke ready to pull him to the ground. He looked up into Morganuke's face and was startled to see it horribly contorted as though he was straining against something, his eyes bulged and looked redder than before, like fire. His face no longer pale but crimson with purple veins protruding on his forehead. His silver hair stood on end alarmingly. Then suddenly Morganuke slumped forward. "It's no good," Morganuke groaned. "I can't do it."

Fenlop pulled Morganuke to the ground, just as one of the Cordinens looked over in their direction. They lay there still for moments. Fenlop dare not move to look up to see if the Cordinens had seen them but forced himself to do so, lifting his head. Four Cordinens were now walking in their direction.

Without warning, Morganuke stood up pushing Fenlop away and unsheathed his sword. Fenlop watched on, thinking that Morganuke had gone mad. Morganuke started to run towards the oncoming Cordinens, holding his sword out in front of him. Other Cordinens had now noticed Morganuke and had also started to move in his direction, drawing their own weapons. As the four leading Cordinens were about to slice into Morganuke, his sword gave out a bright ring of light that flashed ahead of him fanning out as it did so. As the light hit the Cordinens, they were thrown backwards with incredible force. Half the Cordinens were taken out with this burst of light from Morganuke's sword. Morganuke seemed to weaken and sunk to his knees again, leaning on his sword.

Fenlop couldn't believe what he was seeing but didn't wait to think about it. He ordered his men to attack, ignoring any objection from Almen. Fenlop and his five men ran towards the remaining Cordinens, two with bows and others with swords, shouting as loud as they could. Almen and Albrin now began to run towards the enemy as well, waving their swords in the air, closely followed by Chanterly, Calarel and Lengrond.

It was not as Fenlop had imagined it or wanted it to be, but he had no choice now. It was do or die, and he had no intention of dying that day. He ran past Morganuke who was still kneeling on the ground sloped against his sword. He ran past the strewn bodies of the ten Cordinens struck down by Morganuke's strange sword of light. He ran on until he met the first Cordinen waiting with a double headed axe in his hands, ready to bring it down on Fenlop. As the Cordinen's axe came crashing down, Fenlop deftly side stepped its path and sliced his sword upwards into the Cordinens stomach. Guts and blood poured out of the first stricken Cordinen as Fenlop twisted his sword forward into another Cordinen's mouth, sending teeth and blood everywhere. Fenlop's caught sight of his men joining in the battle as the second Cordinen slump to the ground, the top of his head now missing.

As the battle raged on, Fenlop slipped into the artefact tent. He took out several pitch balls from his side pack and placed them under the device. The size of a large man's fist and infused with sockulen powder, they were lethal when set alight. He lay a short trail of pitch from these to the tent entrance. As Fenlop set the pitch trail alight, he was set upon by two Cordinens. He desperately defended himself, but the Cordinens were strong, and their axes were large. Fenlop continued to duck and dart away from the deadly axe blows. Without warning Almen's sword blade suddenly appeared from one of the Cordinen's mouth. At that moment, Fenlop sent his own sword into the other Cordinen's throat. Almen stood over the Cordinen he had slain and nodded to Fenlop.

When the flames reached the pitch balls beneath the artefact seconds later, there was a bright flash of ignition, quickly followed by a deep thud. Flames engulfed the artefact and the tent. Fenlop looked around to see that all the Cordinens guarding the artifact had been killed, but two of his swordmen were also dead on the ground.

Fenlop spotted the three Patronese running up to the burning artefact tent. They were accompanied by eight Cordinen soldiers brandishing longswords. The Patronese dashed into the burning tent and dragged out the artefact, still intact and untouched by the flames, and started to run away with it. Fenlop attention was shifted to the other Cordinens that had now reached him and the others.

Morganuke was still kneeling but felt his strength slowly returning. He had felt so drained after using the sword. He knew not why he had done what he had. It was a desperate measure and felt drawn to the sword as he approached the Cordinens. Then it was almost as he was in a dream, one long forgotten as he raised his sword at the on coming Cordinens. Then an overwhelming pulse of energy rippled through his body just before that strange light was emitted from the point of his sword. He couldn't remember any more and found himself kneeling on the ground propped up by his sword.

He watched as his friends battled the Cordinens in front of him. He tried to stand but was still too weak. Several other Cordinens had now joined the fight. He watched as Calarel, Chanterly and Lengrond fought as a team against the ruthless Cordinen swordsmen. Back-to-back they stood slashing desperately at the foe as they attacked. Then he saw them; the three Patronese dragging the artifact from the burning tent. Morganuke tried to stand again and this time his legs held. He stood up and started to follow the Patronese as they dragged the unblemished optoglean across the ground. He got stronger with every step he took, dragging his sword on the ground behind him. The Patronese were now to one side of the ongoing battle between his friends and the Cordinen swordsmen. The main battle continued in the background, showing no signs of abating. On Morganuke went, now feeling his strength return. He had one aim in mind.

For a moment, Morganuke felt a sense of guilt prick his conscience. These were Patronese, his supposed fellow people from the land of his birth, wherever that may be. His guilt was soon replaced with rage, a rage that he wished he had felt when he first faced the Cordinens on this field of death. He felt rage about what the Cordinens had done to his family and the futile effort towards destroying the optoglean. His focus now on the optoglean, and his anger grew to a level he had not experienced before. The optoglean began to melt in the hands of the Patronese. Then, with a bright flash, the optoglean and the Patronese were no more.

Fenlop hacked off the head of the last Cordinen swordsman. The others stood exhausted around him. The main battle between the Cordinens and the Epleons continued in the background. *That doesn't sound like a limited distraction*, Fenlop thought. He looked over at Morganuke, who was standing over a scorched piece of land just ahead of him. He ran over to Morganuke and grabbed him by the shoulder.

"Morganuke, we must leave this place of death," Fenlop implored. Morganuke looked at him blankly.

"The optoglean is no more," Morganuke said slowly.

"What is no more?" Fenlop asked, thinking that Morganuke was still touched with the madness he had demonstrated earlier.

"The artifact has been destroyed," Morganuke said, pointing at the scorched piece of ground.

"But how can that be? I saw the Patronese drag it out of the tent unharmed. The pitch ball had not touched it."

"I caught up with them and melted it before sending it to oblivion along with the Patronese. I don't know how I did, but I did. There was no crater or blast of wind, they just vanished in a flash."

"Come, we must leave," Fenlop said pulling Morganuke towards him.

Their mission now seemingly completed, if Fenlop was to believe what Morganuke had said, he led the group of now ten towards their starting point. They kept going until exhaustion had nearly overcome them. They were well clear of the Cordinens, and Fenlop told them to take a rest. Almen seemed happy for Fenlop to take command. The group gladly took cover in a thicket of bushes, well hidden from the outside war and huddling together to keep warm.

"Is it finally done?" Lengrond gasped, lying on his back looking up at the thick bushes above him. "Let's hope that destroying the artefact helps end this wretched war."

"It won't end the war, but it may help to even the balance of power," Almen answered numbly. "There is still a lot to do before this war ends."

"And what then?" Calarel asked, her face covered in blood. "Our lives have been turned upside down. Things can never be as they were. Although I will fight to keep my freedom from those vile Cordinens."

"Things may not be as they were," said Chanterly, "but we can at least make things better by bringing peace and the people together. My life now revolves around the war, I had never realised how privileged a life I had. I firmly believe that there is a better future for us all if we persist. Life is tough, and more so now, but I'm sure we will come through this."

Lengrond had been sitting quietly but spoke up again. "My life also revolves around the war. I joined the army and followed my good friend Seedon to fight. I have lost my good friend in this war but fight on I must. I know not what I will do if it ever ends. Nevertheless, I fight for that end. Morganuke, you have lost much in this war. What say you?"

Morganuke looked drained and lethargic and kept silent for a few moments before answering Lengrond. "My life has been completely turned upside down," Morganuke eventually said. "It's true I've lost so much but I'm learning new things as well. Destroying the optoglean does not end things, it only signals the start of our struggles. I am now even more determined to find out more about where I came from. Only there will I find the secrets that we seek to stop this madness."

"How will you find out about your origins?" Calarel asked. "Surely you don't plan to have any more to do with those terrible Patronese people who are working with the Cordinens."

"Well, I am one of those terrible people," Morganuke said abruptly. "There are others I can find out from."

"Others?" Calarel asked with a grimace. "Don't say there are even more of those people."

"Melinor told me about a small group of Patronese that lived where she comes from. They keep themselves to themselves and have nothing to do with the Cordinens."

"You believe her?" Calarel snapped.

"Of course, I believe her," Morganuke replied combatively.

"Will you two be quiet?" Almen intervened with a raised hand. "Remember we are still in enemy territory and must keep quiet."

Fenlop, moved closer to Almen and whispered, "I think we should stay hidden until nightfall to avoid being detected." Almen nodded and shared the intent with the rest of the group.

Time went by very slowly as the group of friends remained hidden in the thick bushes, waiting for darkness to come. They huddled together as best they could to keep warm as the day drew on. When night finally came, Fenlop crept out first to make sure all was clear, and then the others all emerged and followed.

It was not possible to row the boats upstream against the strong currents and so the group had a long march ahead of them. They were cold and tired, and their limbs ached from being still for so long. They made slow progress all through the night, until Fenlop in the lead began to recognise some familiar landmarks. The group staggered on, exhausted, hungry, and cold, and fell to the ground at the entrance to the cave hideout at last.

"I hope your cooks have a good stew on," Lengrond said to Fenlop as they lay panting on the ground.

Fenlop gave no answer but sat up to look around pensively. "Where are the guards? My people should have met us before now, and someone should be guarding the cave entrance." His instincts warning him that something was not right, he pressed his finger to his lips and beckoned everyone away from the cave entrance.

Fenlop kept watch as he guided the others away to a new hiding place, then told them to stay put as he went back to the cave. Searching around the cave entrance, Fenlop found signs of a struggle. There was blood smeared just inside the cave entrance and a discarded shoe. He carefully made his way inside, stopping for a moment to allow his eyes to adjust to the dim light coming from the entrance. He listened, but there was no sound other than the water dripping from the cave wall. He ventured further in, feeling his way with his hands. He stumbled on something, falling forward on his hands. Something soft touched his hand and made him jump. He drew his sword, and groping around with his other hand, he felt the outline of a body on the floor in front of him.

The cave must have been attacked by the Cordinens, Fenlop thought. He forgot his measure of caution and rushed to retrieve an oil torch from a wall mount close by, which he quickly lit with his flint. Grasping the torch, he saw that the body at his feet was one of his men, left behind to guard the cave. He went further until he reached the chamber area, and found two more of his men dead, but nobody else was there. Fenlop sank to his knees when he fully realised what had happened and put his head in his hands. Eventually he got to his feet and went to find the others.

Fenlop met Morganuke as he left the cave. "What's happened?" Morganuke demanded.

"The Cordinens attacked whilst we were away, killing three of my men and taking the rest prisoner."

"Where is Melinor and Alorie?" Morganuke asked frantically.

"Gone," Fenlop answered in a daze. "The Cordinens must have taken them too."

"Then I shall go after them," Morganuke asserted. "I promised Melinor and her sister that I would look after them and I will not give up on that now. I will die before I do."

"You can't go on your own, you big silly fool," Calarel said, emerging from the undergrowth behind them. "I'll come with you."

"We should all go," Chanterly added as the others came forward and gathered around with murmurs of approval. "Let's all stand together as one to get the girls and Fenlop's people back."

Fenlop though devastated by what he'd discovered in the cave was determined to find the rest of his people and take revenge for those that had died. He led the group with renewed vigour to track down the Cordinen captives.

CHAPTER 23

The Aftermath

From the upper deck of the *Aurora*, Fraytar looked across Stacklin harbour towards the walls of the city. It had been several hours since the Epleon attack had started, and the noise of battle had subsided. Looking through his spyglass, through gaps between the roofs of the town buildings, he could see a few Epleon soldiers on the walls looking out.

"What do he see?" Tomlin asked, screwing up his eyes trying to see at the distance. "Have them Cordinens been beaten yet? Be me daughter safe?"

"I can't make out what is going on," Fraytar answered as he continued to look through his spyglass. "I can't see past the city walls. I just hope all those soldiers that we saw leave the city haven't been killed by the Cordinens, or we're done for. The ship still isn't seaworthy yet, and if the Cordinen attack comes, we shall be in the middle of it. I need to see how the carpenter is getting on with the repairs."

Fraytar made his way to the lower decks. Crewmen were busying themselves tidying up the ship from the clutter left by the battle with the Cordinen ships. Fraytar squeezed his way past the working crew, offering words of encouragement.

"When will we be setting sail again, Captain?" one asked,

bare-chested and sweating with exertion. "Be we ever goin' to sail again? The ship 'tis right messed up."

"It's a good ship and we shall be sailing as soon as the repairs are complete," Fraytar replied over his shoulder as he continued below deck.

When Fraytar eventually reached the front of the ship, his heart sank. The damage was worse than he had thought, and water had started to seep through the ship's planking again. He looked at the carpenter as he and his men tried to do what they could to stop the leaks by replacing damaged planking and applying tar.

"How goes it, Carp?" Fraytar asked the ship's carpenter in as jolly a sounding voice as he could. "I see you've got the lads working well down here."

"We can just about keep abreast of the leaks, Captain," answered the ship's carpenter as he worked on the planking. "Unless we get better quality wood, more tar and nails soon, I fear she'll sink."

"I'll go and chase up the supplies that the Epleon commander promised us," replied Fraytar, unable to hide his frustration. "Just do your best and keep my ship afloat."

Fraytar made his way to the dock to get the needed supplies for the ship's repair. *I need to find Commander Besnit,* Fraytar thought as he walked along the harbour's edge, accompanied by two armed crewmen. He looked around to see if he could see any Epleon soldiers nearby. Most had gone with the attack force, but there were still a few dotted about. Those who remained looked lost, no doubt wondering what had become of the attack force and whether a Cordinen counterattack would come soon.

As Fraytar started to make his way towards the nearest detachment of soldiers, he spotted a young woman leading a small child along the street. Most of the locals had left the city for safer locations, once Stacklin came under attack by the Cordinens, but a few remained. The woman's face was gaunt and expressionless, almost as though she were in a trance. Every now and then she turned to the child and beckoned her to follow closely. The child did as she was bid but kept looking behind her at the city walls.

These people look as though they have lost all hope, Fraytar thought as the woman passed him, still encouraging the child to follow. The city seemed dark and ominous, and Fraytar felt a little sick in the stomach. Rubbish from recent battles littered the streets, which was very uncharacteristic for an Epleon city.

"Can you tell me where Commander Besnit is?" Fraytar asked as he approached some Epleon soldiers. One of the soldiers pointed to a nearby building and Fraytar acknowledged the soldier's directions and thanked him.

At the building the soldier directed him to, a single guard slouched against the wall outside the main door. There was litter everywhere, and from the outside the house looked abandoned.

"I need to see the commander," Fraytar announced to the guard as he approached the door. The guard just gave a brief nod and remained slouched. Fraytar entered the building without comment.

Inside, the hallway was littered with rubbish and dust, looking like it had not been cleaned for weeks. Fraytar thought it was unlike the Epleons to keep a building of some importance in such a state; they were usually very fastidious in the appearance of themselves and of their buildings. On a door immediately opposite hung a hastily written sign indicating that was the commander's office. Fraytar knocked and waited.

"Enter!" came a loud but surprisingly jolly voice from inside. Fraytar opened the door and entered the cluttered office, to be met with a sight he did not expect. Behind a large desk, stacked with papers, sat the Epleon commander—quite young for a commander, and wearing a scruffy uniform. His hair was long and dark, coming past his shoulders, and his face was unshaven. But after the gloomy outlook that Fraytar had perceived throughout the city, what most surprised him was the commander's demeanour. He looked very jolly, possibly from drinking too much, and had a broad, almost welcoming smile on his face.

"Welcome, Captain Fraytar. Welcome indeed," the commander greeted him without even extending his hand. "Commander Sebastian Goodforelong. What can I do for you?"

Fraytar paused to recover his composure before answering. "Forgive the intrusion, Commander, but I have come to find out what the situation is. Commander Besnit promised supplies to repair my ship, but we have heard nothing more about this since before the attack began. We fear that the ship will be lost if we do not set sail before any counterattack by the Cordinens."

Goodforelong gave out a loud raucous laugh. "There's no fear of that, Captain. The Cordinens retreated with their tails in their hands. There is no longer any sign of the Patronese artifact, and it is presume destroyed by the undercover agents. Without the artifact, the Cordinens will fear to proceed any further into Epleon."

"Why is the city in such a state?" Fraytar asked. "It looks like it has been subject to Cordinen attacks."

"It was early in the battle," Goodforelong explained. "A detachment of Cordinens got past our attacking forces in the field and pushed forward to the city walls. We just about managed to hold on and repel them, but it cost us many lives."

Fraytar now understood why soldiers in the city looked so dazed. "Have you not told your soldiers about the main Cordinen force retreating?"

"They will be informed as soon as we have received news of the Cordinens' main force location. The bulk of our forces are trailing them now to ensure that they don't double back. As far as your supplies, you will find plenty on the other side of the city walls. I take it you particularly need tar, wood and nails, and fortunately, in their haste to leave, the Cordinens have left plenty of that behind from the siege weapons they were constructing."

"Where is Commander Besnit?" Fraytar asked. "I was expecting him to be here."

"He is with the Epleon forces in the field chasing after the Cordinens," Goodforelong replied. "He has left me in charge of the city in his stead. I'm expecting the overall commander of the army to arrive soon. Commander General Yaloop. Have you met him?"

"No, I haven't had that privilege yet," Fraytar replied. *I wander what he will think about the state of the city, whilst its stand-in commander gets idly drunk*, Fraytar thought.

Fraytar was relieved that there would be no imminent attack from the Cordinens and that supplies were available to repair the ship. He thanked the commander and made his way back to the ship. Excepting the gloomy looks from the Epleon soldiers, the city did not look so dark to Fraytar now as he strode happily back to the *Aurora*, where he was met by Crouch.

"Well, Captain, how bad is it?" Crouch asked with a worried look.

"It seems that we have been given a second chance. There won't be a Cordinen attack any time soon. Gather some of the crew. We have supplies to collect."

Melinor was cold and uncomfortable, but relieved that she and her sister were still alive. Several hours after Morganuke and the others had left the cave to go after the artefact, the Cordinens had found the hideout. Melinor and Alorie had watched as their protectors were mercilessly hacked to death by the Cordinen soldiers. Only one man and two women among Fenlop's people had been kept alive, and the five of them were bundled up and carried off to a nearby Cordinen camp.

For a day and a night, Melinor and Alorie had been held in a small, caged wagon, where the passing soldiers sneered and spat at them. Melinor didn't know what had happened to the other three.

Melinor held her sister close to her, keeping her warm as best she could. Mercifully, Alorie had managed to fall asleep in exhaustion. It was not quite so easy for Melinor, however, and she lay there wide awake. She tried to think of happier times when the two of them went swimming together and played on the sandy beaches near their home.

She also had very fond memories of when her father used to train her in the practice of stokado, an ancient form of stick fighting originating from her homeland. Each competitor held a long cane in both hands. The object was to retrieve ribbons attached to your opponent's body with the stokado cane without losing your own ribbons. Melinor and her father would practice for many hours at a time. Melinor, with her natural athleticism and speed, became quite good at the sport. She remembered how she would train by herself in grace, flexibility and speed, executing complex combinations of gymnastic moves. It was almost like dancing to her. She would replay moves in her mind over and over again. All those memories seemed so long ago now.

Melinor's thoughts were brought back to the present when she heard voices coming closer. She feared that more soldiers were arriving to beat them again. Two of them stopped just close enough for Melinor to overhear.

"We've been hearing that the army is pulling back," one of the soldiers said. "We are to follow and assemble with the main force at the base camp."

"Why is that?" the other Cordinen asked. "We have been winning easily up to now."

"Something about a counterattack at Stacklin and losing the optoglean," the first Cordinen replied.

Melinor's heartbeat quickened when she heard this, and she thought of Morganuke. He had done it then—managed to do what he set out to do. She thought fondly of his touch and wished that he could be here with them.

"What do we do with the dog females and the man?" the second Cordinen asked as the two walked away.

"We'll kill 'em before we leave," Melinor heard the first voice say to her horror. "We can cook 'em and eat 'em with some nice onions I found."

"But that be forbidden by the higher grades,"

"Who's going to know."

Whether the soldiers really intended to eat them or were just trying to scare them, Melinor did not know. They had moved out of earshot, and she had no intention of staying to find out. She had noticed that the soldiers who had captured them were ill disciplined and of a lowly sort—slow, dim-witted, and not of the same standard as the soldiers she had been used to at the military complex. Maybe there was a way of fooling them?

She looked around the cramped cage for a means of escaping. *What about the cage bars? Maybe one is loose*, she thought in desperation. She tested the bars, grabbing each one in turn and shaking it hard, but they were as rigid as could be. *What if I lie down and pretend I'm dead, then run out of the cage when they come to see?* But she knew her sister would not be as quick as she was, and they would surely catch her.

Melinor slumped down beside Alorie and started to sob quietly with her head in her hands. Her sister stirred in her sleep, and so she forced herself to stop. *Get a hold of yourself, Mel*, she thought. She had to be strong for Alorie. There had to be a way to escape.

"What you doin', dog woman?" One of the soldiers had come back to the wagon.

Melinor jumped back, startled, and let out a yelp. She looked desperately around the cage again.

"Time for dinner, and you'll be the main course," the Cordinen sneered, showing his blackened teeth. "Come to me, you little wretch. I'll strangle you with me bare hands then boil you up into a nice juicy stew."

The Cordinen took keys from his stained britches pocket and slowly unlocked the cage door, his fingers fumbling with the keys. Melinor backed away as the cage door opened with a graunching squeak.

As the drooling Cordinen entered the cage, Melinor's only thought was escape. Without thinking, she leaped towards the startled soldier, then rolled head over heels past him as she snatched his dagger from his belt. In an instant and in one continuous move, she rebounded behind him and buried the dagger deep into his neck. The clumsy Cordinen had no idea what was going on as he fell forward into the wagon with blood spurting from his throat and his legs still planted on the ground.

Melinor looked around at what she had done, stunned by how quickly it had all happened.

"Grumold!" the other soldier called out as he approached, too distracted by hauling his huge sack of onions to notice what had happened. "I got me onions, so we can have a nice feast before we leave."

Melinor knew she had no time to come up with a plan. She ducked for cover on the other side of the wagon She looked across at her sister who started to stir. Alorie opened her eyes and caught sight of Melinor, who raised a finger to silence her.

When the other soldier got no answer, he paused for a moment, puzzled at how intent Grumold seemed on the cargo inside the wagon. "What you doin' over there? Don't you go eatin' those dog females before I get some." He shoved Grumold with one hand and momentarily froze when his body slid to the ground, covered in blood. The next thing he saw was Melinor leaping out of the darkness with her face spattered in blood. She buried the dagger deep into the Cordinen's eye. He gave a muffled groan as he sank to the ground, falling dead onto his companion and releasing his bag of onions to roll bloodied across the ground.

Melinor quickly climbed into the wagon to embrace her sister. "We have to move," she said quietly but urgently. "Now, before the others come!" Alorie's eyes were full of sheer terror as she looked at Melinor's blooded face and then, as they climbed out of the wagon, at the two Cordinens lying on the ground in a pool of blood.

But now that they were free, Melinor did not know what to do next. She had no idea where Morganuke and the group that had set out for Stacklin could be. *They will probably look for us*, she thought, *and find the Cordinen campsite before following the Cordinen's trail. I must leave a clue to show them which way we went, but what?* She looked at the ring she wore on her thumb. It was precious to her as it reminded her of her homeland. Morganuke had often commented on it and thought how dainty it looked. Reluctantly she took the ring off and threaded it on a branch at eye level before proceeding south with her sister.

For several hours the girls kept moving away from the Cordinen camp, until Melinor felt far enough away to rest in the safety of a thickly wooded hill. They both were exhausted after the distressing events of the day, and the hill offered good cover to hide in so they could get some rest.

Alorie snuggled up to Melinor and looked up at her intently. "Why are you covered in blood? Did those men hurt you?"

"Don't worry about those men," Melinor answered quietly but firmly. "Those brutes can't hurt either of us now."

"But what happened?" Alorie asked, looking very worried.

"Never you mind what happened, little sis. We're safe now. In the morning, we will look for Morg. You go to sleep now, and I'll keep watch."

Still looking concerned but overcome with tiredness, Alorie was soon fast asleep. Melinor was very tired too and desperately wanted to sleep as well, but she knew that she could not. She willed herself to stay awake. She needed time to think clearly about where they should go next.

In the quiet, Melinor became aware of the sounds of a river nearby, which reminded her that they had followed the river for a time before reaching the cave. Then she remembered that Stacklin was someway downriver from the cave. The Cordinens had said they were retreating to their base camp away from Stacklin, and Morganuke would surely be there after destroying the artefact. Melinor decided that at daybreak they should head for Stacklin by way of the river.

After discovering that the Cordinens had taken Melinor and her sister from Fenlop's hideout, Morganuke and the group of friends had been following the Cordinen tracks for several hours, when Fenlop held up his hand. Everyone stopped behind him and waited.

"I see signs of an abandoned camp up ahead," Fenlop announced. "Almen, come with me and we'll look. You others stay here until we signal."

A few minutes later, Fenlop signalled for the others to come closer.

"What's happened here, I wonder?" Morganuke said as he approached. "Dead Cordinens, but there's no sign of anyone else. Very strange." He bent over to inspect the two dead Cordinens closely. "One has been stabbed in the neck and the other in the eye. Must have been a mighty warrior to kill these two like this. Do you know of any friendly forces close by, Fenlop?"

Fenlop shook his head and came to look at the bodies himself. "These wounds look to be inflicted from a Cordinen dagger. Look at those marks around the stabbed area. Only Cordinen weapons do that, caused from its outward jagged edge."

"Killed by their own, do you think?" Morganuke asked.

Fenlop shrugged. "It's all very odd."

"Do you think there's any chance that they will return to this camp?" Morganuke asked.

"Unlikely. They would have posted guards if they planned to return," Fenlop answered.

"There are tracks leading north just up there that look to have been made by the bulk of the Cordinen force," Almen reported as he returned to where the two men were standing over the Cordinen bodies. "There are other much lighter tracks leading south. Made by small folk, I would say. Grass is still trampled down south facing, and so they cannot have been made that long ago."

"Seems strange that the Cordinens are heading north," Fenlop reckoned. "South is where the fighting is. We should follow the Cordinen trail and not be diverted."

Morganuke didn't answer. The tracks leading south played on his mind. "Almen, can you show me the tracks leading south?"

"Follow me," Almen responded, leading Morganuke to the other side of the camp, where he pointed to some flattened grass tracks. The two men followed the tracks into the dense woods. Morganuke had to look closely and was amazed that Almen had noticed them. He stopped to get his bearings amidst the woods and noticed something in the branches glinting in the morning sunlight. He went to inspect it more closely and immediately recognised it as Melinor's ring by the inscriptions.

"This is Mel's," Morganuke declared as he carefully took the ring from the branch. "She must have gone this way."

"How could the girls have escaped on their own?"

"I tell you, this is Mel's ring, and she would not have dropped it without cause," replied Morganuke with agitation.

"Let's speak to the others and decide what to do," Almen said.

They made their way back to the campsite and found Fenlop looking agitated. "Where have you been?" he demanded. "We are wasting time. We must catch up with the Cordinen patrol before they rejoin their main group. I want to get my revenge for what the Cordinens did to my people."

"We were checking the tracks to the south," Almen replied. "It seems that it could be the girls—"

"That's not where we want to go," snapped Fenlop, interrupting Almen before he could finish. "We must follow the Cordinen patrol *now*."

"But what of Melinor and Alorie?" Morganuke pleaded. "They've gone in the other direction and likely on their own."

"If they are on their own, then they are no longer in danger from the Cordinen patrol. We know where the Cordinens are heading, and so we go north."

"Morganuke, let's follow the Cordinens as Fenlop says," Chanterly intervened, seeing how worked up the two of them were. "Once we have rescued Fenlop's people, then we can come back for the girls. As Fenlop said, if the girls are out of the Cordinens' hands, then they are safer than Fenlop's people are."

"Then I'll go on my own," Morganuke snapped.

"You won't be able to follow them without a skilled tracker, my friend," Lengrond answered calmly. "We should all stay together. We shall need the numbers to ensure we overcome the cordinens when we find them. We cannot afford to split up."

Morganuke dropped his head and looked at the ground in front of him. He knew what the others were saying made sense, but he desperately wanted to find Melinor and make sure she was safe. However, he nodded his head reluctantly.

"So be it then," said Fenlop, gathering his things. "We continue north and find the Cordinens. Then we can go after the girls."

Everyone agreed and then made themselves ready for the continued hunt for the Cordinens.

"We shall need to move quickly if we are to catch up," Fenlop exhorted as the group moved out of the camp and into the woods heading north. Morganuke followed the rest with head bowed.

CHAPTER 24

The Divided Friends

Melinor hadn't slept all night so that she could keep a lookout whilst her sister slept. The ground was damp and cold against her back, and she ached. Alorie still lay against her, sleeping, as the first signs of daylight appeared through the trees. Reluctantly, Melinor woke her, as she wanted to keep moving. She estimated that there were still many stances to travel before they reached the outskirts of Stacklin.

"I'm hungry," Alorie complained. They hadn't eaten for a day, and their energy levels were getting very low. There was an abundance of fresh clean water nearby, but they needed food. It wasn't the season for fruit, and they had no way to catch game to eat, but Melinor thought she might be able to catch fish in the nearby water. She had some experience of tickling fish and decided to try.

The girls struggled to their feet, their muscles aching from the damp ground.

"I'm cold and hungry," Alorie continued to moan. "Can we get something to eat and light a fire?"

"I am going to find some fish to eat, and then we can light a fire," Melinor said, but she was wondering how she would do those things. "If we keep moving, it will warm us up."

Alorie screwed up her face but followed her sister towards the river. The girls clambered down the bank to the river's edge. The water looked cold and uninviting. Melinor dreaded the thought of putting her hand in the cold water, but knew she had to if they were to eat. Melinor looked up and down the river, but the water was flowing too fast, and she could see no sheltered spots.

"We'll need to go further down the river to find a likely spot," Melinor said.

"But I'm *cold* and *hungry*," Alorie whined.

"We'll soon warm up when we catch some fish and light a fire," Melinor said encouragingly. Further downriver, she found a good spot with shallow pools and overhanging rock edges. "This will do nicely," she said as cheerfully as she could. "See if you can spot some fish resting under the rocks. But stay away from the water's edge! The fish will be scared off if they see you."

Melinor slowly got down on her belly and slid along the riverbank edge to see if she could see any fish. Alorie did likewise—she even looked as if she might be enjoying her task. They crawled along for a few yards before Melinor spotted the fins of a fish under the rocks. She gently put her hand in the water, gasping at how cold it was on her fingers, then carefully moved her hand towards the fish and just brushed her fingers against its tail. Slowly but surely, Melinor moved her fingers to the fish's belly to start the tickling.

"Mel! I see a fish," Alorie cried, scaring Melinor's fish away.

Melinor gave a deep sigh as she took her freezing hand from the water. "Alorie, you must be quiet! I nearly had that fish." Melinor regretted her words as she saw her sister's eyes fill with tears. They were both very tired and in desperate need of food. She took her sister in her arms and soothed her the best she could.

"It's okay, Alorie," she said, stroking her head. "We can try again. You did well to spot the fish, but next time, please be as quiet as a mouse!"

"But mice aren't quiet," came Alorie's instant reply. "I heard them sometimes scratching at the walls when we were in the Cordinen camps." Melinor just laughed a little, not wanting to tell her that what she heard were probably rats, and big ones at that.

The girls continued to move downriver for another hour before

Melinor could try again. She spotted another fish hiding under the rocks a little way downriver. She repeated the process as before, and this time, thankfully, there was no calling out from Alorie. Melinor felt for the fish's belly through the cold and gently she started tickling. The fish stayed where it was. More tickling. Then, with a quick flick of her hand, which made Alorie squeak in surprise, Melinor flicked the fish out of the water and skilfully onto the bank. Melinor grabbed the fish as it began to jump and wriggle on the bank. She then smashed the fish's head against a rock and then gutted it with the cordinen dagger, once she had washed all the Cordinen blood off.

"You've done it, Mel!" her sister shouted in excitement and anticipation of a long-awaited meal. "You caught a fish."

"Yes, I did, didn't I?" Melinor replied with pride and relief. "Now let's go and make that fire."

Melinor knew how to make a fire with dry wood and tinder, but everything seemed so damp in this cold place. "Now we need some dry wood and kindling," Melinor said brightly to her sister. "Can you help me find some? Then we can light a fire and cook this lovely fish."

"Okay, I'm starving!" Alorie began looking around for what her sister had asked for, and soon the girls had collected the pile of dry wood and kindling they needed.

Alorie looked puzzled. "But how can we make fire with this stuff?"

"Just watch me," Melinor said. She crouched down to pick up a dry thin stick they had found, tapered at the end. She carved a flat edge on the larger piece of branch using the Cordinen dagger. She then piled up some of the fine dry twigs and lichen and proceeded to rub the small piece of stick against the larger flattened branch. It was hard and tiring work, and for several minutes there was no sign of anything happening. Eventually a little smoke started to rise, and then a small flame from the pile of twigs and lichen. Melinor gently blew the embryonic flames and had Alorie place more twigs on the pile. Soon the fire was well established, and she could add bigger and bigger pieces of wood as the fire continued to grow.

At last, they were ready to cook the fish. Melinor drove a thin stick through the middle of the gutted fish and held it over the fire. The smell of cooking fish made their mouths water as they eagerly waited.

"You're very clever, Mel," Alorie said, giving her sister a hug. "I wish I was as clever as you."

"You're clever too," Melinor said. "We make a good team."

The girls enjoyed their fish. They felt warm and content as they sat next to the fire. Melinor wished that they could stay there in the warmth a bit longer, but she knew that they needed to make progress towards Stacklin. She didn't know how many Cordinens might still be wandering the landscape. If they encountered a patrol, they would surely be taken captive again or eaten.

"We should move on now, Alorie," Melinor said.

"Oh no! Please, let's stay a bit longer," Alorie begged, screwing up her face.

Melinor noticed the dimples in her cheeks and thought how vulnerable she looked. "I'm sorry, Alorie, but we must move on." Melinor stood up reluctantly and encouraged her sister to follow.

The girls followed the river for the rest of that day. When the daylight started to fade, Melinor looked for a safe place to set up camp for the night so they wouldn't be detected by a cordinen patrol or attacked by wild animals. She had heard wolves howling some way away. The area was still sparsely wooded but flat, offering little cover. The sky had grown cloudy, and there would be no moonlight. Soon night would fall and leave them in complete darkness.

Melinor looked up at one of the trees nearby. It was climbable for her and, with a bit of help, her sister. However, they needed a fire to keep warm, so they continued to look around as the light faded. Melinor spotted a larger tree, looking half dead, with its roots jutting out of the ground and a large hollow in the centre. *This will have to do,* she thought.

Melinor cleared out the debris from the tree's hollow centre and laid their things on the ground inside. They found plenty of dry wood and kindling scattered close to the hollow tree, and Melinor set about lighting a fire a safe distance away from the tree's opening. Soon there were comforting flames to warm up the girls, but Melinor made sure she didn't make the fire so big that it would catch the hollow tree alight.

The exhausted girls lay curled up together next to the fire. They had found water to drink during the day but had not eaten since their breakfast of fish. Alorie complained of hunger, but Melinor insisted that they could not eat until the morning. That was assuming she could find something to eat. She had been quite fortunate in catching the fish that morning and was not convinced that she could do it again. The river's current had grown too strong for fish tickling as they had proceeded during the day.

Melinor wanted to stay awake again to look out for her sister, but exhaustion eventually overcame her, and she fell fast asleep.

When Melinor woke with a jump, the fire had died down to embers, and she was feeling the cold. Alorie was still fast asleep, softly snoring in her ear. Carefully, Melinor withdrew the arm that her sister had been lying on, then got to her feet to put more wood on the fire from the pile they had gathered. Soon the fire had built up again, and the flames gave out a comforting warm glow that cast dancing shadows across their little cozy campsite.

Melinor was about to settle down again when she heard a rustle come from the bushes nearby. She looked out from the hollow tree and glimpsed a dark shadow move across the clearing in front of the old tree. Then there was another, and another, followed by a low deep growl.

Wolves! She slowly reached over to pick up the piece of wood she had used to start the fire and squeezed some of the dry lichen on the end. She lit the lichened end in the campfire and picked up the Cordinen dagger before slowly moving back inside the tree. Two brightly lit eyes met her gaze, and beneath them, a snarling set of sharp teeth. The wolf was big, and she had brought her pack.

Melinor and the wolf looked at each other for moments, whilst the rest of the wolve pack began to move in. The only sounds with the snapping twigs in the fire and the low growls of the wolf. Suddenly

Melinor let out a scream, the loudest she could, and stepping forward waved the fiery stick frantically in front of her. Alorie woke, frightened by the screaming, and began screeching, "What's happening? Why are you screaming?"

To Melinor's amazement, the wolf ran off, followed by her pack.

"Hush now," she said calmly, going back to her sister. "It was wolves, but they have gone now."

"I'm frightened that the wolves will return," Alorie said, clinging tighter to her sister. "Will you tell me a story to help me sleep?"

"All right, little sister," Melinor replied, stroking her forehead. "I'll tell you about the times that I used to go hunting for rabbits with Papa."

Alorie settled down to listen.

"One day, when I was about your age, Papa said that he was going to take me out hunting in the woods with him. It was a bit like this, a dense wooded area with a large river running through it. We packed a lunch to eat out in the woods whilst we were hunting. Smoked cheese and taggle berry sandwiches."

"Yummy, I love taggle berries and smoked cheese," said Alorie with a faint smile, eyes half closing sleepily.

"We got up early on the day of the hunt and set off into the woods. It was a lovely sunny day, and masses of blue angel flowers lined the path. I can still smell their fragrance now. We walked for many stances, until we came to some hills rising in the middle of the forest. Trees covered the hills, which were steep to climb. Papa and I climbed to the top of one of the hills, where we found a small open area that had only a few trees, covered in bracken with patches of wildflowers in between. We settled down amongst the tall bracken, hiding ourselves to watch for any rabbits venturing nearby."

A gentle snore came from Alorie. *Oh, my story is that boring, is it?* Melinor smiled to herself and gently kissed her sister's forehead. She tried to make herself comfortable enough to rest but wasn't sure if she should sleep. She feared the shouts that had frightened the wolves away could have been heard by a Cordinen patrol.

Melinor gently lay her sister down and then reached out to put more wood on the fire, then lifted her sisters head onto her lap as she sat back against the roots of the old tree. Her sister stirred but remained asleep, quietly snoring again. Melinor stared at the flames dancing about and giving out a relaxing warmth. It seemed strange that something as destructive as fire could also be so comforting. She thought again about her hunting trips with her father. Many a night they had camped out beside a fire, just as she and her sister were doing now. The difference now, she thought grimly, is that now they were fugitives out in a wild land with no protection.

The rustling in the bushes returned, but blackness surrounded their camp past the glow of the flickering fire over the ground. Another rustle, and then a low growl.

Melinor gently nudged her sister awake. The wolves would not be so easily frightened away again. Alorie came to with sleepy eyes that at once turned worried. Melinor pointed up to the branches of the tree above them. Alorie looked up and shook her head, giving out a soft whimper. Melinor nudged her sister harder, pointing up and mouthing the word *climb*.

Alorie reluctantly got to her feet, and Melinor lifted her towards the lowest sturdy branch. Alorie was able to grasp it and heaved herself up onto it. Her sister followed.

The pack of wolves came into sight in the firelight, growling, noses turned up and baring their glinting teeth. The two girls scrabbled up another two branches, hoping that they would hold their weight. All they could do was sit there, clinging to the trunk and watching the wolves surrounding them below. *Would it be worse*, Melinor wondered grimly, *to be eaten by wolves or Cordinen soldiers?*

A high-pitched yelp came from one of the wolves and startled the girls. Then another yelp, and one more. Suddenly the wolves fled. Relief overcame Melinor, but not for long. As the wolves fled, they were replaced by a troop of mounted soldiers.

"How fare you?" one of the riders called up to them.

Melinor looked in disbelief. These were not Cordinens but troopers wearing the splendid armour of Epleon cavalrymen.

"You can come down now. The wolves have gone." The rider smiled up at them encouragingly. "I am Second Order Commander Craden

Brenadere of the Epleon Stacklin Defence Forces under Commander General Quatamire Yaloop. We mean you no harm."

Melinor was still a little wary after their ordeal, but Alorie was so eager to be rescued that she immediately began clambering down on her own. "I hope you have something to eat!" she exclaimed before slipping in her haste and falling directly onto one of the cavalrymen. As he caught her in his strong arms, she let out a sound that was half terrified scream, half hysterical laugh. Melinor jumped to the ground, disregarding her own safety, but Alorie just grinned as the Epleon held her safely.

"Little lady, you need a safer way to come down from a tree," the cavalryman said with a wink, adding, "But I have a daughter about your age who is just as bold."

Commander Brenadere dismounted and approached the girls. He was young for a commander, and Melinor thought his face was strikingly handsome. He was dressed in armour polished to a mirror-like sheen with a light helm with blue plumes, and a blue and gold surcoat emblazoned with a golden stag.

"Where are you girls from?" Brenadere asked. "These are dangerous lands, and young girls should not be straying alone in them. Especially ones who should still be schooled." With that he turned a lightly disapproving gaze to Alorie, still grinning shyly in the arms of her rescuer.

"We were captured by a Cordinen patrol and taken prisoner," Melinor said. "We became separated from our group when they went to Stacklin to destroy the Cordinen artefact."

"Destroy the artefact, you say?" Brenadere replied, looking surprised. "How many were in your group? It must have been a whole horde to attack the Cordinen forces at Stacklin."

"There were twelve that left for Stacklin," Melinor said, keeping an anxious eye on Alorie. "A few who stayed behind to guard us and their base, though we were overcome."

"Twelve!" the young commander exclaimed incredulously. "How could twelve hope to attack the main force at Stacklin? We had an army there and could only just hold our own."

"The Epleons were to create a diversion so that our twelve could raid the camp," she explained. "One in the group had special—" Melinor stopped. Given what the Patronese had done to the Epleons, she doubted that the commander would look favourably on Morganuke's special powers.

"Special what?" Brenadere pressed.

Melinor regretted her words and looked at him, steely mouthed.

"Tell me." The commander put on a stern but calm face and stepped forward to look her in the eye.

Melinor turned her face to the sky and gave a deep sigh. "Morganuke has some … *abilities* that he believed could allow them to destroy the artefact and so help the Epleon cause."

"I see," Brenadere said, though his furrowed forehead said otherwise. "So you don't know where this band of twelve are now?"

"I do not, My Lord," Melinor answered.

"I am not a lord," he said, smiling in a way that put her more at ease. He studied her a moment. "The Cordinen forces have withdrawn from Stacklin. It seems that your Morganuke achieved his goal. I would like to meet this fellow."

Melinor looked at him with astonished joy. She had almost given up hope that she would ever find Morganuke alive, let alone that he had triumphed so spectacularly.

"But for now," Brenadere said, extending his hand to her with a gallant gesture, "please allow us to offer you the safety of Stacklin, newly liberated from the Cordinen threat."

He gave a nod to the strong-armed cavalryman who had caught Alorie. Then he mounted and helped Melinor up to ride behind him, and with Alorie throwing her arms around her rescuer to hold on, the troop rode off in the direction of Stacklin.

CHAPTER 25

On the Trail

Fenlop led the others as they pursued the Cordinen soldiers north. He was determined to take his revenge and hopefully rescue the remainder of his people. He had noticed that Morganuke was looking very agitated and assumed this to be because they had not followed the girl's trail. They had covered several stances since leaving the abandoned Cordinen campsite, and now the sun was setting.

Fenlop fell back to walk alongside Morganuke. He could see how miserable he still was.

"I'm sure Melinor and her sister are well," Fenlop said, trying to cheer Morganuke up. Morganuke said nothing, and just carried on walking with a fixed expression on his face.

"What will you do when you find her?" Fenlop asked, not wanting to give up on exploring Morganuke's intensions. He knew that it was essential to have everyone focused and committed on what he believed needed to be done and so was determined to make Morganuke see it that way too. He didn't want Morganuke to think that he didn't care about his predicament.

"I haven't thought," Morganuke finally answered. "She will probably want to go back to her homeland with her family. I still want to find out about where I came from and what the powers that I have really mean."

"But won't that take you to Melinor's homeland? You said she told of some Patronese she knew there."

"It may. I really don't know. I feel that there are still things to discover from the Patronese about why they are helping the Cordinens and what it might have to do with me. It is too dangerous for Melinor to stay with me once we find her. She is better off going back to her home."

"You understand why I insisted on coming north first don't you, Morg?"

"Yes, I do. It doesn't make it any easier for me though. I desperately want to know that Melinor and her sister are safe."

"I promise you that I will help you find them once we've tracked down the Cordinens," Fenlop said, before leaving Morganuke to continue walking on his own.

"It's getting dark," Almen said to Fenlop as he joined him. "It will be difficult to follow the tracks in the dark. We should set up camp and rest for the night. The Cordinens will surely do the same." Fenlop frowned at the thought of stopping but begrudgingly agreed.

The group of ten quickly set up camp and got a fire going. Temperatures quickly dropped when the sun set. Fenlop was glad to get warm beside the fire with the others.

"What food have we left?" Chanterly asked. "We should eat something to keep our energy up. It would be useless if we finally catch up with the Cordinens and are too weak to fight."

"I still have some rabbits I caught this morning." Almen held up the carcasses with a smile.

"And I have some pigeons I shot," Albrin added. "They were masterful shots with my bow, even though I say so myself. I'll not tell you how many I missed however."

Fenlop helped prepare the game with the others and then cook it on the fire. The smell of the cooking made his mouth water. The cooked game was chopped up into pieces and distributed equally. Fenlop savoured every morsel, licking the bones until nothing was left on them.

The group took turns keeping watch overnight, three watching for two hours whilst the other six slept before changing over in shifts. Fenlop found it difficult to sleep and so kept watch with the others for most of the night. It wasn't until the early hours of the morning that he drifted off to sleep.

At first light, as the group prepared to leave camp. Fenlop still felt tired but was pleased to see that everyone else seemed reasonably fresh. Some of the food had been left over from the night before and this was distributed for breakfast.

They spent most of the morning following the Cordinen trail. The tracks of their wagon and numerous foot soldiers were easy to see during the daylight, and they followed them to another campsite.

Fenlop bent down to inspect the ashes in the extinguished campfires and found them still warm. "They can't be far ahead now," he observed. "They don't seem to be moving that quickly, and by the look of the dead Cordinens we saw at the last campsite, I would say that this group consists of some lowly soldiers. That should be to our advantage, regardless of how many there are."

"If we make haste," Almen added, "we should be able to catch up with them by nightfall."

Encouraged by the gains they were making, Fenlop felt less tired than he had, and he encouraged the group to pick up their pace. They made good progress, and as Almen had estimated, they caught up with the Cordinen patrol by nightfall.

From the hill he was on, Fenlop could see what looked like a disorganised rabble making camp a little way in the distance below. The men were flabby and dishevelled. There movement looked slow and clumsy. They certainly didn't look like the strong muscular specimens that they had encountered outside Stacklin.

"As I thought," Fenlop said. "This group is of poor physical health and lacks discipline. I see about fifteen or sixteen soldiers armed with only basic weapons and poor armour. This is our chance to seek revenge."

"And rescue your people," Almen said.

"Yes of course, rescue my people," Fenlop added. *Is this just about me getting my vengeance?* Fenlop thought, uncomfortably.

"How?" Chanterly asked. "They may be poorly trained soldiers, but they still outnumber us. We will need to take them by surprise."

"I agree," Fenlop replied. "Almen and I will scout ahead to survey their camp in more detail and locate my people. We can then plan our attack during the night whilst most of the soldiers are sleeping."

Fenlop and Almen made their way towards the Cordinen camp, whilst the others stayed behind and waited. As the two scouts got nearer to the Cordinen campsite, Fenlop pointed towards a hill lined with trees and bushes. "There, to the right of their camp—that would be a good place to observe from. I doubt that these fools would have posted sentries up there, as we have encountered none so far."

The two made their way to the hill, taking a wide arc around the camp to avoid being detected. On top of the hill, they had a good view of the campsite, which was lit up by several campfires and oil torches. Sentries had been posted at either end of the camp, with four tents in line. As Fenlop had thought, nothing had been posted on the high ground.

"I can't see any sign of my people. Can you?"

Almen looked carefully over the campsite but shook his head.

"Blast!" Fenlop exclaimed. "We'll have to get closer to make sure." He led the way down the hill. When they were close to the camp, the voices of two Cordinen soldiers just ahead stopped them short. Fenlop and Almen ducked down in the undergrowth to listen.

"Me feet aches," moaned one of the Cordinen soldiers. "I'm starving too."

"Yeah, me too. Seems ages since we last ate," said the other.

"That fat one was very tasty," the first Cordinen said.

"Yeah, but all the prisoners have gone now. We ate the last one this morning, and those two stinking girls escaped. The little one didn't 'ave much meat on her, but I bet they would 'ave been nice and tasty."

Fenlop couldn't believe what he was hearing. His people had been eaten by these creatures. He instinctively lunged, but Almen pulled him back and held him down.

"What's that?" one of the Cordinens said. "I heard a noise in the bushes over there."

"What noise? I can't see or hear anything." Said the first Cordinen

"Probably just an animal." Said the second Cordinen.

Fenlop stopped struggling, realising that it would only get them killed, or worse cooked and eaten, if he charged in now. Whilst the two

Cordinen soldiers continued exchanging their revolting culinary desires, the two men crept away to rejoin their friends.

They did not speak at first. Fenlop just flopped down on the ground and put his head in his hands.

Eventually, Chanterly broke the silence. "What did you find? Did you locate your people?"

"They've been eaten," Fenlop hissed, raising his head from his hands. His tear-filled eyes staring wildly. "I knew that these monsters were savages, but this goes beyond anyone's imagination." Fenlop leant over and vomited on the ground as soon as he had said the words.

"What do you mean, eaten?" asked Morganuke urgently. "Have they eaten Melinor and Alorie too?"

Fenlop shook his head before recovering his composure enough to explain. "The girls escaped the Cordinens, as you suspected. We overheard the soldiers saying as much."

Morganuke nodded in relief but said nothing.

Chanterly knelt beside Fenlop and put her hand on his shoulder. "My friend, I am sorry that your people died in such a horrible way, but we must be strong now," Chanterly said softly but with steely conviction. "We should not do anything in haste just to get revenge, but I think that we may have an opportunity here. In your opinion, can we take out these creatures easily and without too much risk to ourselves?"

Chanterly looked from Fenlop, who stared straight ahead and gave a single determined nod, and then to Almen, who closed his eyes for a second and then nodded.

"Then that is what we shall do," she said. "We must wait until most of the soldiers are sleeping. Then we'll bring all the might of Casdredon down on them," Chanterly vowed, looking intently at each member of the group as she spoke.

Later that night, the group of friends made their way up the hill to survey the Cordinen campsite. To ensure the greatest element of surprise, they would want most of the soldiers sleeping before they attacked.

"Do you have any of those pitch balls left?" Almen whispered to Fenlop.

"I have four in my pack," he replied.

"It would be best to give them out," suggested Almen. "Then on a signal, we can each lob one from a different direction. That should cause confusion and add to our advantage of surprise."

Fenlop nodded. "Do you know how to use them?" he asked, hauling them out of his backpack.

"Yes, I think so," Almen answered. "You light the fuse and then throw or place the pitch ball at the target."

"But wait until the pitch ball just starts to fizz," Fenlop cautioned, handing him two. "If you throw the ball too early, then the fuse is likely to be extinguished. Too late, and you end up as a ball of flames yourself."

"Hm, I'll try to remember that," Almen replied, frowning at the pitch ball in his hand.

Fenlop looked at Morganuke who had just joined them. "Can't you just summon up your powers and blow these Cordinens away?" Fenlop asked, only half jesting.

"You saw what happened the last time I tried that," Morganuke replied in annoyance,

Before it was time to attack, Fenlop gathered everybody together to agree a plan. "Morganuke, Almen, Albrin and I will go in pairs from each end of the camp. We'll take out the sentries stationed here and here." He pointed to a drawing he'd scratched in the ground with a stick as he went along. "We'll then lop ignited pitch balls against four of the tents. Drenden and Escolar will be stationed with their bows amongst the trees on either side of the camp to take out Cordinens as they come out of the tents. Chanterly, Calarel, and Lengrond will attack from the centre once the tents are ablaze. We'll charge in with our swords from each end. Everyone clear? Everyone agree?"

"Why doesn't Morganuke just—" Calarel started to ask.

"We have already discussed Morganuke's powers. Too unpredictable, and not an option," Fenlop said with finality.

Fenlop made sure that he got a nod from everyone, even Morganuke.

"Good. Then let's go and avenge my people."

The two pitch ball teams made their way into the camp from

each side. Fenlop gave the night bird signal, and all four sentries were dispatched man to man with timely precision.

Fenlop made his way behind one of the tents and made sure the other three did the same. He gave a quick whistle as he lit his pitch ball signalling to the others to light theirs at the same time. Once the ball had started to fizz, Fenlop lobbed it at the tent. He glanced either side to make sure that the others had done the same. Fenlop's tent caught fire before the others, waking their occupants. Morganuke and Fenlop quickly dispatched the occupants inside before they could alert the others.

Now the other three tents were ablaze, and with yells of panic, the Cordinens began to emerge, still confused by sleep. Fenlop prepared his sword as Cordinens started to emerge dazed from the blazing tents. He watched one and then another Cordinen fall as they were struck by Drenden's and Escolar's arrows. Fenlop charged at the nearest Cordinen and plunged his sword into his enemy's neck. Lengrond now charged in next to Fenlop and took the head off one particularly fat Cordinen struggling to exit his tent. He was closely followed by Chanterly who fended off a blow from another Cordinen about to cut her down before burying the tip of her sword in his chest. Calarel stood behind her facing the other way and fended off another Cordinen who was much too slow for her. Fenlop and the other three then worked as a team standing back to back easily outpacing several Cordinens that now surrounded them.

Fenlop and the others now had the advantage of numbers. More of Drenden's and Escolar's arrows struck their targets. The numbers of Cordinens dwindled in front of Fenlop. As Fenlop had expected, the Cordinens had proven to be slow and sloppy.

Once it was over, Fenlop still felt the rage that had built up inside him. It had all been too quick for the Cordinens. He wanted them to have suffered more, like his people had. He started kicking one of the dead Cordinens with all his might until Chanterly stopped him.

"It's over, Fenlop," Chanterly shouted. "It's done. Your people have been avenged."

Fenlop stopped, staring wide-eyed at nothing. He then turned and walked away from the group before sinking down on his knees, mourning the people he loved and had lost.

CHAPTER 26

Back at Stacklin

Work on the *Aurora* had progressed to Fraytar's satisfaction. But as he stood on the upper deck taking in what he hoped would be his last view of Stacklin for a while, he heard a commotion coming from the direction of the main city gates. He feared the worst. It had been two days since the Epleon counterattack, and while Goodforelong had insisted the Cordinens were now retreating, Fraytar was not convinced. Afterall he was only standing in for Commander Besnit temporarily.

"Break out the weapons!" Fraytar called out to Crouch. "I think the Cordinens have returned."

He was about to order the crew to ready the ship to sail when he heard sudden cheering mixed with the clack of horse's hooves on the cobbled stone. Turning back to look towards the city, he saw the people of Stacklin cheering as the Epleon cavalry streamed along the main street towards the docks at a trot.

"Belay that order," Fraytar shouted to Crouch. "The Epleon forces have returned. In triumph, by the look of it."

Fraytar and crew gathered to watch the Epleon cavalry ride up the street, adding their cheers to those rising through the city. As Fratar watched through his spyglass, he noticed that the youthful commander at the head of the column had a woman riding behind him, maybe sixteen to nineteen years old, very beautiful with long dark hair. He himself looked resplendent in his blue and gold uniform, the plumes on his crest bouncing with the horse's trot. Behind them an older cavalryman held a girl of about seven or eight, laughing with joy at the welcoming crowds.

The cavalry wheeled right and into the assembly square in front of the military command buildings.

"I'd like to give my regards to the returning heroes," Fraytar said to Crouch. "You have the ship."

Fraytar made his way down the gangplank and walked to the assembly area a few hundred paces away. A crowd of people had gathered on the edges of the assembly square and Fraytar made his way to the front. By now the array commander had dismounted, as had the two girls.

"Fraytar DeLance, captain of the ship *Aurora*," Fraytar said, offering his hand and forearm in a display of Epleon manly welcome. He had learnt quite a lot about the Epleon way during his time in Stacklin.

Array Commander Brenadere looked Fraytar up and down. "I've heard a lot about you, sir, and the help you and your ship have given to our people." He extended his hand, and they clasped each other's forearm in a single firm jolt. "I am Array Commander Brenadere of the Epleon Stacklin Defence Forces under Commander General Quatamire Yaloop. It's good to meet you."

"It's true then? The Cordinens have retreated?" Fraytar asked.

"Yes, it's true," Brenadere replied. "And if the information this young lady has given me is true, it may well be thanks to someone called Morganuke. Apparently, he possesses a strange power that destroyed the weapon that has plagued us for months. It seems that the Cordinen dogs are unable to fight a fair fight and must rely on these strange devices from the Patronese to fight their war for them."

Fraytar turned to Melinor, who had her arm wrapped protectively around her sister. "You know Morganuke?" he asked.

"Yes."

"Where is he now?" Fraytar asked.

"I don't know, Captain," Melinor answered. "When I last saw him, he was on his way to destroy the artefact. We stayed behind in a hideout but were discovered by a Cordinen patrol who killed the others."

"Then Commander Brenadere and his brave men saved you from the Cordinens," Fraytar said with a look of commendation at Brenadere.

"Not strictly true," Brenadere corrected him. "The girls had already escaped the Cordinens but were treed by wolves."

Fraytar's eyes widened. "Escaped the Cordinens, you say!" he exclaimed. "How did you manage that?" he asked Melinor.

Melinor looked down modestly, and her face flushed. "I had to kill two of the guards who were going to eat my sister and me."

Fraytar and Brenadere exchanged a look of utter surprise, then laughed.

"Beautiful and a sense of humour," Brenadere commented. "Now let's find accommodations for such a heroine and her sister." He nodded to two Epleon cavalrymen standing by who gestured courteously for the girls to come with them. "Good to meet you, Captain Fraytar," Brenadere said. "I hope we can count on your continued assistance. I must report to Commander Yaloop."

"Where is he?" Fraytar asked. "I had been told by Commander Goodforelong that he had not arrived yet.

"He arrived ahead of the main force yesterday, Captain." Brenadere answered. "I'm sure you'll get to meet him soon."

Leaving his horse in the care of a groom, Brenadere headed off, and Fraytar turned in the direction of the lovely young woman. "My Lady, I don't know your name," he called after her.

She stopped to look back at him with a smile. "Melinor."

"May I call on you, once you are settled in your accommodation? Fraytar asked, then at her look of uncertainty added, "I would like to hear more about Morganuke. He is a very good friend of mine, and I have been worried about him these past weeks."

"As have I. Please do call." She flashed another smile at him before letting the two cavalrymen lead her and Alorie to their new quarters.

Later that day, Fraytar and the *Aurora* crew joined the townspeople in welcoming the Epleon foot soldiers returned to Stacklin. A sense of relief was palpable in the city now that the threat of a Cordinen attack seemed to have passed, though nobody knew how long the peace might last.

"Commander General Yaloop has asked to see you, Captain," came a voice from behind Fraytar as he stood amongst the crowd. He turned to see two large Epleon guards. He sighed but nodded and allowed them to escort him through the streets to the headquarters where he had met the Commander Goodforelong before. The rubbish had been cleared from the surrounding streets, and the building was no longer full of debris inside. *That's more like the Epleons*, Fraytar thought as he was led into the commander's office.

Inside the office, Commander General Quatamire Yaloop sat at his desk. His uniform was pristine, and his desk was perfectly tidy. Commander Brenadere, resplendent as ever, stood beside him, and on the other side a man in religious robes.

"Captain DeLance," Commander Yaloop welcomed him. "I think you've met Commander Brenadere. I would also like to introduce you to High Priest Brendall Politon." They both responded with a bow of the head. "Please take a seat, Captain."

Fraytar sat in the chair in front of the three men.

"Captain, what do you know of the man called Morganuke Beldere?" Yaloop asked without further preliminaries.

"I've known him nearly all his life," Fraytar answered. Something about the atmosphere in the room and the tone of the questioning suddenly was making him feel wary. "I would say that I know him very well."

"We hear that he claims to possess *powers*," the priest said.

Yaloop held up his hand to continue. "Have you witnessed him exhibiting any of these … powers?" he asked Fraytar.

"Not exactly." Fraytar answered reluctantly. "Morganuke is a good man and has helped the cause on many occasions with his bravery."

"How does he achieve the things it is claimed he does?" the priest asked in an upbraiding, presumptuous voice.

"I'm not sure I understand what you mean" Fraytar answered. "What sort of things are you referring to?"

"I have been informed that Morganuke Beldere possess unexplained destructive powers and that he has been helping the Cordinens," the priest continued.

"I'm not aware of him having any special powers or that he has helped the Cordinens," Fraytar answered. "Indeed, he helped fight the Cordinens out of Stacklin."

"We have witnesses claiming that Morganuke has used unnatural powers," the priest insisted. "We cannot accept sorcery and witchcraft. Look at the others like him. Through their sorcery they have destroyed so many of our people, so much of our lands. Heretics cannot be allowed to defile our way of life so."

"It seems that you have already decided that Morganuke is your enemy, despite what he has done for you. The lad is like a son to me, and I know his heart is good. Now, if you have finished with your questions, I should like to leave."

"That is all for now, Captain," Yaloop said with a gesture of dismissal. "But we may have more questions later."

Fraytar quickly left the office and made his way back to the *Aurora*. "What did the commander want with you, Captain?" Crouch asked, upon seeing the anger on his face.

"We need to get the ship ready to sail as soon as the repairs are complete," Fraytar said. "The sooner we leave this place, the better." Fraytar headed to his cabin.

I must think of a way to protect Morganuke from these fanatics, Fratar thought, getting out his pipe.

Morganuke and the others had made good progress travelling towards Stacklin after they left the Cordinen camp. They had commandeered two horse and carts from the Cordinens making the going much quicker. They had stopped for the night and Morganuke sat with his friends in front of the campfire. He looked forward to eating some of the cooked wild boar that Albrin had succeeded in hunting earlier in the day to feed the group of ten. The smell of cooking over the open fire was a delight. Morganuke's mouth watered at the prospect of tucking intro the delicious smelling meat.

"The food is cooked," Almen announced. The group cheered and helped themselves to a portion.

"We should have a song," Calarel demanded suddenly. "Who has the best voice?"

"That's a great idea, Cal, but it may not be wise just now," Chanterly said sympathetically, "The enemy may be close by and so we should keep the noise down as much as possible."

Calarel pulled a face and looked upwards.

Although there was no singing, Morganuke chatted and laughed with the others as they ate. The food was as good as he'd imagined it to be and he felt full to bursting after the meal.

"How much further do you think it is to Stacklin?" Chanterly turned to ask Fenlop.

"With the two carts and horses we got from the Cordinen camp, it should be another full day's travel," Fenlop reckoned. "Are we set to do two-hour shifts in teams of three, as before?"

"I'll take the first shift," Morganuke volunteered.

"I'll join you." Lengrond got up to stretch his legs. Fenlop joined them for the first watch.

As Morganuke began his shift he thought about Melinor and her sister. *Where they were now, I wonder? Have they managed to get to safety? I do miss her so.*

In the last few months, he had done so much more and had met so many other people than he ever had in his whole life before. He was living a completely different life, and his views about himself had changed, now that he knew that his origins were linked to this mysterious race of people. He was desperate to find out whether the Patronese were all bad. He feared that might be so. He had been brought up on simple values defining good and bad but never in-between. Could someone be good if they sometimes did bad things? He visualised the Epleon prisoners that he'd had to execute and how they desperately pleaded for mercy of that wooden platform. Did this make him totally bad?

In the morning, Morganuke and the others ate some of the wild bore meat left from the previous night. Their spirits had lifted after a good night's sleep, ample food, and the thought of soon reaching Stacklin. Even Fenlop had started to laugh at some of Lengrond's stories over their breakfast.

Almen and Albrin drove the two wagons they had obtained from the Cordinen camp, whilst the others rode in the back. *Not long to go now*, thought Morganuke. *I wander what we'll find waiting for us in Stacklin. Will there be a welcoming party? Will Melinor be there? That would be so good if she is.*

The two carts followed the route of the river towards Stacklin. As the day dragged on, morning moved into afternoon, and afternoon into evening, with the occasional short comfort breaks. At last Stacklin came into view, and they hastened the pace.

As the group of ten approached the city walls, one of the guards shouted down from the rampart. "Stop and state your purpose!"

Fenlop stepped forward. "We are Epleon allies who have been fighting the Cordinen forces," he called back.

There was no reply. The group stood waiting. Fenlop was just about to call out again when the city gates started to open. Several Epleon cavalrymen, led by Commander Brenadere, rode out of the gates and surrounded the group of friends.

"Is the man Morganuke Beldere in your party?" Brenadere asked.

Morganuke stepped forward. "I am Morganuke."

"Morganuke Beldere, you are under arrest for heresy," Brenadere announced, then ordered, "Take all these people to the cells."

CHAPTER 27

Trial by Religion

Commander Yaloop sat at his desk studying the warrant issued on charges of heresy, Commander Brenadere at his side. "This puts us in an awkward position, Brenadere," Yaloop said. "Are all the accused contained?"

"Yes, Commander," Brenadere answered. "We have kept Morganuke Beldere in a separate cell, blindfolded and bound, so that he is unable to use his powers. The women, including the two girls I brought back from patrol, are locked up together. The men have been contained in a separate cell."

"This will not go down well with our new allies if they learn of it. But if we do nothing about the charges, we risk losing the support of the religious community." Yaloop sighed. "It is unfortunate that we rely so heavily on the Casdredon movement to fund this war. They are extremists who block any form of change or scientific progress if cannot be explained by the ancient holy book of Casdredon."

"But what else can we do if the high priests are demanding a trial? They will expect extreme punishment if the accused is found guilty."

"And you know as well as I that Banton and Cadmunese forces have agents posted all over the mainland. We won't be able to keep this from them. We can only hope that they understand that religion is part of our society."

"What I know is that the likely outcome of the trials will be death for the accused," Brenadere said heatedly. "Our allies would look very badly on that. It could threaten the whole alliance. The Cordinens may have retreated for now, but they will be back once they have replenished their confounded contraptions. We will need the continued support of our allies if we are to win this war."

Yaloop stayed silent, looking down at the papers in front of him. He had always resented the involvement of the religious sector in war strategy, and their insistence on following traditional ways was inhibitive. The Cordinens had taken advantage of unfamiliar technologies from another society and gained from it. The continued interference from the Casdredon religious movement stifled progress and prevented the Epleon military from making advancements in warfare.

Yaloop looked up, furrowing his forehead in thought. "Captain DeLance seemed very defensive during our last meeting. When he learns that we have taken his precious Morganuke prisoner and trussed up like a hog for slaughter, how do you think he will react?"

Brenadere thoughtfully stroked his chin. "You're saying there's another way."

"If Morganuke escapes, he can't be put on trial."

"That would be treason."

"I didn't say we would release him. But maybe we are less vigilant than we should be. The captain of the *Aurora* knows how to take a risk when given an opportunity." Yaloop shuffled the papers before him dismissively. "I expect you know how he gets his information. See to it."

Once Brenadere left, Yaloop considered his options. He was walking on a tight rope. He had had his suspicions about Brenadere being involved with the Banton Island spy network for some time but had overlooked it because it counteracted the Crasdredon's interference. But it was a dangerous game he was playing. However, if things did turn out badly, he could always shift the blame onto Brenadere. *Yes, I'll keep things as they are for now*, he thought. *Let's see how the young cavalry officer does.*

As Brenadere exited the command building, he thought about how he could get a message to Fraytar. With Almen and Albrin in the cells, they were no longer an option unless he could get them released. *I'll speak to Almen about contacting the Captain*, Brenadere thought.

At the holding cells, Brenadere approached the section leader of the prison guards.

"Bring the prisoner Almen Pratage to the interrogation cell, I need to speak to him," Brenadere ordered. Brenadere made his way to the cell whilst the guard went to fetch Almen.

When Almen was brought to Brenadere, they both sat opposite each other at a table in the cell. Brenadere dismissed the guard who had remained standing by the cell door. Once the guard had gone, Brenadere leant forward across the table after making sure that they were alone.

"I need you to get a message to Captain Delance," Brenadere said.

"How can I do that?" Almen asked. "As you can see, I'm not free to go anywhere, Commander?"

"I'll get you your freedom," Brenadere replied. "It's only Morganuke Beldere that the priests really want."

"What message is it that you want me to give the captain?" Alman asked

"I'm going to make Morganuke's escape easy, but it will rely on the captain's intervention to get him away from Lobos," Brenadere answered. "I don't have all the details yet but as soon as I do, I'll let you know."

"Very well, Commander. I'll help you with this, so long as you can arrange my freedom of course."

"Once you're free and I know the plans for Morganuke's trial, I'll get word to you through the usual network contacts," Brenadere said before calling the guard to take Almen back to his cell.

As Brenadere had promised, he was able to get the release of Almen and Morganuke's other friends, once he had demonstrated to the Casdredon priests that they had all been thoroughly interrogated. Now he had to come up with a plan for Morganuke's escape. The day for Morganuke's trial had been set for four days' time and so at least he knew when the escape should be.

He had sent a message to Almen requesting him to tell Fraytar to come back to Stacklin with his ship on the day of the trial and to ensure he brings enough support to aid Morganuke's escape. He laid out the framework of a plan in the message. Now he had to make preparations in the city to ensure that the plan succeeded.

Bound against the wall with straps on his wrists and ankles so that his hands could not move, and with his eyes blindfolded, Morganuke contemplated this latest situation and found it hard to believe that he was held captive yet again. The contempt he was shown by the islanders throughout his boyhood, being held captive by the Cordinens and forced to carry out their foul deeds, and now this utter humiliation, treated like a villain by a supposedly friendly regime—all he wanted was to use his powers and take his revenge. But to what avail? His friends would suffer the consequences.

Morganuke heard footsteps approaching, at least two sets by the sound of it, then jangling of keys and the unlocking of his cell door. He felt hands against his wrists and ankles releasing him from his bonds. It felt better to have his hands free. His blindfold remained in place. Then he heard one set of footsteps leaving.

"Hello, Morganuke," came a voice he recognised as that of Commander Brenadere. "I come to put a proposal to you. I hope you will listen to me. Your friends have been freed for now. Will you promise to listen to what I have to say and take no action, for the sake of your friends' continued freedom and safety?"

Morganuke just nodded. He felt hands at the back of his head, releasing the blindfold. When his eyes adjusted to the dim light in the cell, he saw Commander Brenadere standing alone before him.

"I am sorry that it has come to this. Commander Yaloop has found himself in a difficult situation. The Casdredon theocracy demands that all acts of heresy, as they define it, are investigated and brought to trial.

You must believe me when I say that many in the Epleon military do not want you condemned as a heretic. But we must appear to submit to their rule."

"You say that you have freed my friends? Where are they now?" Morganuke asked warily. He wasn't sure whether he should trust this man but would continue to listen to what he had to say.

"Your nine friends are safe in the city being watched." He hesitated. "We also had two girls you may know that have also been freed, Melinor and her sister Alorie."

"Melinor and Alorie are in the city?" Morganuke gasped with relief, unable to contain his excitement.

"Yes. They will remain safe so long as you listen and comply with my request. Believe me, this plan is to your benefit. I want to help you escape. But it is imperative that I am not implicated as that would weaken our position with the Casdredon theocracy. Your friend, Captain DeLance left with his ship soon after you were arrested. Maybe to devise something himself for your escape, I don't know. I have sent a message for him to return so that he is here on the day of your trial so that he can aid your escape from Lobos."

"What is it you want me to do?" Morganuke asked.

"If you were to escape with your friends and the captain," he continued, "no Epleon soldiers can be harmed. Do you understand me? And once you leave the Epleon land of Lobos, you can never return."

"You expect me to believe the Epleons would just let me go and then sail off?"

"Of course not. If we aided the accused to escape, then we could be charged with treason. But after our losses against the Cordinen navy, we have no ships close by at present to pursue the *Aurora*, should she sail away.

"Those are the terms. And we will have had no part in your escape. Whatever the outcome, we will deny it."

Morganuke was silent for a moment and then nodded.

Brenadere replaced Morganuke's blindfold and then called the guard to let him out and lock the cell again.

As Morganuke heard the keys lock the door his spirits were high. He was going to see Melinor again.

On the day of Morganuke's trial, four guards came to his cell to collect him. He was released from the straps that bound him to the cell wall, but his blindfold was left on and his hands were chained behind his back. Two guards supported him on each side as he was led along, their footsteps echoing through the cells. He felt the sun on his face and a bright glow of light breaking through his blindfold as he was led outside. He was then manhandled up by the guards onto what he perceived to be an open caged wagon. The platform lurched forward slightly as he was pushed up onto it and he felt metal bars against his skin as he rolled over, the sun still on his face.

Morganuke heard the clatter of several horses' hooves and ordered shouts. The wagon started to move with a jolt and his body bounced uncomfortably on the floor as they moved. Morganuke had travelled for about five minutes when the wagon suddenly came to a stop. There was the smell of smoke and a shouted command from ahead.

"Soldiers, lay down your weapons, and dismount," came a shout. "We wish you no harm and have come to retrieve the prisoner. I have ten expert archers hidden with their arrows aimed at you. Release the prisoner now or you all die."

There was a sound of swords falling to the ground, followed by horses neighing and the clattering of hooves.

Morganuke then heard a key in the lock of his cage and the door opening with a squeak. His blindfold was removed and as his eyes focused Morganuke saw Lengrond's face smiling at him, "come on old friend, let's get you out of here."

Morganuke and Lengrond jumped on two of the Epleon horses and made their way towards the docks with Fenlop and Drenden following some way behind on two more horses. As they raced onto the docks, Morganuke saw the *Aurora* by the dockside. The four jumped off their horses and ran up the gangplank.

"Raise the gangplank and cast off," shouted Crouch on the main deck.

Crewmen heaved on the ropes and the big ship slowly started to move. Morganuke looked across the docks as about twenty Epleon cavalry cantered towards them, led by Brenadere. But they were too late. With sails now raised, the *Aurora* made its way out to sea.

CHAPTER 28

The Reunion

Morganuke felt overjoyed when he saw Melinor running towards him on the main deck of the *Aurora*. She jumped into his arms, and they kissed. Finally, they were together again. Alorie stood a little way back looking a bit awkward, but Morganuke walked up to her and knelt in front of her. "Hello Alorie, it's good to see you." Morganuke said. Alorie flung her arms around him.

Chanterly, Calarel and Tomlin stood on the upper stern deck, where Morganuke joined them hugging them in turn. Fraytar stood behind the trio with the hint of a smile. Morganuke approached and grasped his shoulders with both hands.

"Thank you so much for rescuing us, Fraytar," Morganuke said emotionally.

"You are welcome," Fraytar replied. "I'm afraid accommodations are sparse, and so we you'll need to share the few cabins we have. I haven't decided where our next destination will be, and once you have settled in and been fed, that is something that we can discuss."

Once everyone had time to settle in, Morganuke went to see Melinor in her cabin she was sharing with her sister. He knocked on the cabin door and Melinor opened the door smiling sweetly at him. Although small, their cabin was cozy and clean. Two small beds were laid out on each side of the cabin. Alorie sat on her bed playing with some figurines. Morganuke and Melinor sat on the other bed.

"Those are nice figurines, Alorie," Morganuke said, leaning over to look more closely at them.

"Yes, Uncle Fraytar gave them to me," she answered continuing to play in her imaginary world.

"Uncle Fraytar," Morganuke said, grinning and now looking at Melinor.

"Fraytar's been very kind to us, even though we have only just joined the ship," Melinor said, taking Morganuke's hand into hers. "He said that anyone who is friends with Morganuke is his friend too. I think he's very fond of you Morg."

"You have blood on your clothes, Mel," Morganuke noted, looking concerned. "Where did that come from?"

"The blood? Oh yes, that came from two Cordinen guards I had to kill when we escaped their camp. If I had not, they would have eaten us."

"You are brave and courageous Mel," Morganuke said with surprised admiration. "I wish I had been there to protect you and Alorie."

"My purpose is not to fight unless I have to," Melinor said. "But I would do anything to protect my sister."

"I know, Mel, and you are a good sister to her. Where do you hope to go now? You must miss your home and parents."

"I want to be with you, Morg, but I do need to get my sister back home. She misses our parents and needs her schooling."

"Maybe an opportunity will come up for you to get back to your home. I would take you there if I could. I would also like to visit those Patronese people that you told me about and find out more about the land of my birth."

Later that day, Fraytar called everyone onto the main deck. He held a rolled-up map of Pagalan in his hands.

"Thank you all for coming to this meeting," Fraytar said. "I know some of you very well, and others I have only just met. You all have one thing in common, though. You are friends of Morganuke. I hope that makes you my friends too. Now we have left Lobos and the mainland behind us, it is important that we decide where our next heading should be. I have a destination I would like to propose, but wherever we decide, we need to take everyone's situation and needs into account. That does of course include the *Aurora* and its crew."

"So, what happens now?" Lengrond asked. "Where can we go if we can't go back to Lobos?"

"With only three of our partisan group left, it would be useless for us to go back there without additional support," Fenlop said. "I still can't believe that I lost all those people, and in such a horrible way."

"The Cordinens truly are savages," Albrin declared. "I wish we could go back and continue our fight with them."

"So, Captain," Chanterly said, "I think we should hear your proposed destination first?"

Fraytar leaned over the map he'd now unrolled and placed his finger at a precise point. "We are currently situated here," he said, "just off the coast of Lobos, heading away from Stacklin. With both the Cordinens and the Epleons our enemy we are in the middle of five thousand stances of hostile coastline: Lobos to the southwest and Ventor to the northeast. If we are to avoid detection by enemy ships, not to mention many months of sailing, some in unfamiliar waters, we must sail away from the mainland and directly onto Banton Island."

The group huddled close to study the map Fraytar held out, and there was some muttering as they took in Fraytar's proposal.

"What about the Cordinens?" Chanterly asked. "The last time we were on the island, the Cordinens had the upper hand. They had wiped out the island militia in the west."

"True," Fraytar admitted. "But that was not the case in the east when I left there a few weeks ago. In fact, the militia had built up their forces and were starting to push the Cordinens back. I'm proposing that we sail to Cradport on the east coast of Banton. For some of you, that was your point of origin before going to the mainland."

"What of us who came from the mainland?" Fenlop asked.

"We wait for an opportunity to get you back to the mainland on one of the other ships that sail between Banton and Lobos at some point. Banton is still an ally of the Epleons, even if I and my ship must now be regarded as a criminal. We also still have Almen's intelligence network on the mainland who can help support your remaining people, Fenlop."

The group asked a few more questions, but after some muttering, nobody was able to come up with an alternative.

"So, no objections to my proposal? Good," Fraytar concluded. "Then our next destination is Cradport on Banton Island."

"How long will it take to sail there?" Fenlop asked.

"The winds are generally southerly, and so it will take a little longer than if we were travelling from the island to the mainland. I estimate that we should arrive in Cradport in just under one month."

A collective sigh at the length of the voyage came from the group as they headed back to their accommodation or duties.

"Morganuke, can I speak to you for a moment?" Fraytar asked.

Morganuke waited to let the others pass him.

"You were very quiet in the meeting," Fraytar continued once the others had left the cabin. "I assumed you would want to go back to the island."

"I'm not sure I want to go back," Morganuke said, thinking about his conversation with Melinor earlier.

"Why not?" Fraytar asked, showing his surprise.

"Now that my parents are dead and the farm destroyed, I don't really have anything left on the island to go back to. I want to find out more about my people and where I come from. I want to know more about the strange powers I possess, and I can only do that by finding out more about the Patronese. Melinor told me that she knows of Patronese people that lived on her homeland. That's a good place to start."

"You are very fond of Melinor, aren't you?"

"Yes, I want to take her back to her homeland one day. It will also be a chance for me to find those Patronese."

"I understand now, lad," Fraytar answered, smiling at Morganuke. "Maybe one day you will get your chance to go there with Melinor."

The journey to Cradport took as long as Fraytar had said but went without incident. They did not see any Epleon or Cordinen ships on the way, and the weather was reasonably good over the four weeks of sailing. Morganuke had kept himself busy helping the crew and doing the occasional stint with the cook. It was good to see him again and hear the old stories he had to tell. Morganuke spent much of his free time with Melinor. He noticed how much more confident she seemed and with what she had told him about her time with the Cordinen's, she no longer seemed as fragile to him as he had first thought. Her strength had endeared her even more to him.

When the call went up from the lookout that land had been sighted at last, everyone congregated on the main deck. After so many days at sea, it was good to see land at last, Morganuke thought. Fraytar had the crew raise the militia flag.

As they sailed into the harbour, they saw ships flying flags of either the island militia or the Cadmunese. It became clear that Cradport still lay in friendly hands, and such a loud and joyful cheer went up on board, that it drew the attention of the Cradport residents. By the time the *Aurora* docked, a crowd had formed to greet them.

Morganuke joined Tomlin and Calarel as they looked over the docks from the *Aurora*.

"'Tis strange to think last time I wus 'ere I thought I'd lost you," Tomlin said to his daughter. Calarel looked at him and smiled. "Must make sure that I don't make a fool of me self this time."

Calarel frowned questioningly at her father. "You've been here before? How did you make a fool of yourself?"

"We came 'ere after we rescued the island refugees from Muskcove. I got drunk in the inn, and Fraytar had to carry me back to his ship. Twas 'cause I thought I lost he." Morganuke noticed that Tomlin had tears in his eyes.

"Well, no excuses for getting drunk this time!" Calarel said. "You've got me back now."

Standing between them Morganuke put his arms around Calarel and Tomlin. "Yes, we're all back together now."

Tomlin and Calarel both nodded and smiled.

Almen gave out a loud chuckle as he gave Morganuke a jovial swat on the back. "So, this is Cradport, the place where the great Morganuke made a name for himself as the local hero!"

Morganuke quickly moved away from Calarel and Tomlin, hoping they hadn't taken too much notice of Almen. He screwed his face up and went bright red. "How do you know about that?" Morganuke said feeling embarrassed. "I don't remember telling you."

"It was Lengrond that told me. He said you were the returning hero when you got back to your hometown on the other side of the island."

"Well, those days are long gone now," Morganuke answered, determined not to dampen the happy atmosphere.

When the *Aurora* was moored against the dock edge, Fraytar made his way to Morganuke. "I need to talk to the militia commander in Cradport before we do anything," Fraytar announced. "Please make sure all your friends stay on the ship for now until I return with instructions."

Fraytar watched the militia lining up for a few moments, then headed down the gangplank. The militia were smartly dressed in uniformed armour, with orange carcasses, and donning a curved metal helmet with an orange militia motif on each side. *If this is a typical example of the island militia, then the Banton defences have come a long way*, thought Fraytar as he continued to cross the docks towards the command building.

Fraytar reached the command building and was met by two militia guards outside the main entrance.

"My name is Captain Fraytar DeLance of the ship *Aurora*, and I have come to report to Commander Tradish," Fraytar announced.

"Yes, Captain," answered one of the guards, to Fraytar's relief. "The commander is expecting you."

Fraytar was surprised, they had not been in contact for months as he had been dealing directly with the local contacts. Maybe the excitement on the docks at the *Aurora*'s arrival had made its way up the chain of command. Fraytar was directed to the commander's office, where he knocked firmly on the door.

"Enter!" came a bellowing voice Fraytar immediately recognised as Commander Tradish's. He was greeted by the familiar sight of the commander behind his desk in his impressive black leather uniform.

"Captain Fraytar, it's good to see you return. Your work in Ventor and Lobos was successful, I hear." He gestured to one of the chairs opposite his desk. "However, I fear that was not the end of it."

"What do you mean," Fraytar asked.

Tradish looked more animated than Fraytar had ever seen him, fiddling anxiously with a piece of paper in his hands. "We've had certain … reports."

"I've been at sea for a month," Fraytar said. After the sporadic communications from the intelligence network, maybe all was not as well as it seemed at Cradport. "Reports of what?"

"That the Cordinens are regrouping for even bigger attacks than before."

"I feared as much," Fraytar said, but he sensed there was more. He decided to say nothing further, so that Tradish would feel compelled to speak.

Finally, Tradish heaved a sigh. "More Patronese have been sighted amongst the Cordinens," Tradish said, tapping the desk tensely, then leaning forward. "With several optogleans. Our scouts have seen their carts close to Smorsk, northwest of Ventor."

Fraytar was stunned, this time genuinely speechless.

"We need to know more about the Patronese and where they are coming from," Tradish said, staring at Fraytar so intently that he could only nod in response. "I'm told you have a Pale One on your ship. That would be Morganuke Beldere?"

Fraytar gave a noncommittal nod.

"How would you and Morganuke like to return to Lobos to work with the Epleons?" Tradish proposed.

No way, Fraytar thought, then composed himself. "There might be a few things you should know first." He recounted events at Stacklin, the charges of heresy and the escape, omitting Brenadere's role and saying only that as a result they were now fugitives from Epleon law.

"That is very unfortunate," Tradish said after hearing the full story. "At least the Epleon military are still our allies. We shall have to find a way to get around the high priests. We have to do something about the Patronese build up before they get a chance to deploy their devices against the Epleons."

"There are other Patronese," Fraytar offered. "A young woman we rescued from the Cordinens has spoken of a group of people living in her homeland of Trebos that she thought were Patronese. She's on the *Aurora*."

"Trebos, you say. That borders Lobos and so would be a useful location to work from, but it would take many months to reach there by sea as it's on the mainland's north coast. I would like to speak to this young woman myself, and Morganuke Beldere, whom I've heard so much about," Tradish proposed.

"I will ask them," replied Fraytar. "I will do my best to persuade them, but the decision must be theirs."

"Very well, Captain. But please do explain to them how desperate the situation is. If the Epleons fall to the cordinens, then our world will end up in chaos."

The next day, Fraytar returned to Commander Tradish's office with Morganuke and Melinor. They were happy to talk to the commander but, they had said, not ready to commit to more.

"It is good to meet you, Morganuke," the commander said. "I have heard a lot of good things about you."

"Thank you, Commander," Morganuke acknowledged.

"And you must be Melinor." Melinor instinctively curtseyed. "Please, sit."

They settled into the three comfortable chairs that had been readied for them.

"Oh—" Melinor exclaimed softly.

"Something wrong, miss?" Tradish asked.

"It's been so long since I sat in a proper chair."

He smiled. "I'm told you're from Trebos."

"Yes, My Lord," Melinor answered.

"So that is where you were born?"

"Yes."

"Do you still have family there?"

"My mother and father live there. I hope," she added wistfully. "I was captured with my younger sister and taken as a slave by the Cordinens two years ago."

"I am so sorry," he said. "How did they come to capture you?"

"A Cordinen raiding party captured us and then took us back to their ship."

Commander Tradish was silent for a moment, tapping his fingers on the desk. Melinor grew visibly nervous as she waited for him to speak.

"I'm told that you know of people who look like Morganuke living in your homeland."

"They lived in the hills near my home, just outside of Drobayer Town."

"Drobayer, you say?" Tradish said with a puzzled look. "I'm not familiar with that town. Where is it located?"

"East of Vesnick City in Trebos," Melinor replied, sounding very nervous.

"Did you ever see these Patronese you say are living in Trebos?"

Melinor, gathering her thoughts, didn't answer at first.

"Did you ever actually see these people?" Tradish pressed.

Melinor took a breath and met his gaze directly. "My Lord Commander, I do not lie, if that is what you are thinking. I did see them, but only once, when my father took me into the hills hunting."

The commander's expression softened. "You have spirit." He smiled reassuringly. "What can you tell me about them?"

"They were living in the remote hills, about twenty stances from my hometown. A small community of about ten families," Melinor answered steadily.

"And you're sure that they were Patronese?"

"They had the same colour of skin, hair, and eyes as the Patronese helping the Cordinens," she said with confidence. "Like Morganuke. That's what I can tell you." She paused, recalling. "Some of them also had a marking on their skin—a lidless blue eye."

Morganuke looked up, startled at the familiar symbol. The commander fell silent for a few moments, looking down at the papers on his desk with his chin in one hand. Finally, he looked back up and spoke. "Would you be willing to go back to Trebos and show somebody else where these people live?"

"Yes," Melinor said without any hesitation. "It is my home."

The commander turned to look at Morganuke. "Would you be willing to go with Melinor to speak to these people on our behalf?"

"Yes," Morganuke said immediately. He felt overjoyed at the prospect of meeting the Patronese. It was also an opportunity to take Melinor and her sister home.

"Thank you both for coming to speak to me," said the commander to Morganuke and Melinor.

Tradish then looked at Fraytar. "What would you say to a voyage to Trebos?" he asked Fraytar. "You would be well rewarded for it, and you would be helping the cause immensely."

"I would need to carefully plan a route that avoided Epleon waters, which would probably take us into uncharted areas," Fraytar replied. He paused for a few moments before continuing. "But I'm sure that would be possible. Yes, I can take my ship to Lobos."

CHAPTER 29

Preparations and Goodbyes

Fraytar pondered over sea charts in his cabin, making sure of the best route. He rummaged through the old books that Captain Amannar had kept in a chest, some so old that they were almost falling to bits. He found references to the Nebulee Sea, the Ridge and the Crackeldower Islands, all of which he would need to sail through or near on the eastern route around Ventor and then onto Trebos. For generations, the Nebulee had been an area that no ships had ventured into. He found many stories about monsters, haunted fogs, and ships disappearing in the old books, and no way to know whether these stories were fact or fantasy. He found similar references to the Crackeldower Islands, with more recent accounts of ships sailing to some of the islands and the crews later dying of strange diseases. The record of these journeys seemed more factual than the Nebulee stories. But they all confirmed that crews had reached and landed on the islands.

After studying the charts and the old books, Fraytar finally convinced himself that the eastern route was the best option. Now he had to persuade his crew. Tradish had agreed to a very generous bonus for each crewmember who joined the voyage, but Fraytar had a feeling that money wouldn't be enough to convince them. He gathered all the *Aurora* crew members, along with the civilians, on the main deck at midday. Fraytar stood on the upper deck, overlooking the gathering on the main deck, and steeled himself to give what was probably going to be the most important address he had ever given. Faces looked up at him in expectation, some a bit concerned.

Crouch stood on the upper deck beside him. Fraytar had explained the plan to him earlier. He needed to gain Crouch's support first, to help convince the crew. As Fraytar had expected of Crouch, who had always been his good and faithful first mate, he agreed without any complaints.

"Thank you all for gathering here today," Fraytar said, looking down at the sea of faces. "I want to tell you about the proposed route for our next sea voyage. This voyage has never been made in living history, and it comes with significant risks. However, our mission is of vital importance in the war against the Cordinens. We will be contributing to the cause of good against the evil Cordinen invaders"

Fraytar paused, taking in the expressions on the faces looking up at him. "The proposal is to take the eastern route to Lobos. To sail around the eastern tip of Ventor and then to go west onto Trebos, where are destination waits. This of course means sailing close to the Nebulee Sea, through the Ridge and then past the Crackeldower Islands."

Mutterings rose up, especially from the older crewmen, repeating the names of these darkly storied places.

"The Ridge?" one grizzled sailor shouted out. His name was Stellorgantis, but everybody called him Stell.

Fraytar had found several accounts in the old books about the Ridge, a known hazardous area where ships had foundered as they tried sailing off the coast of Ventor. "Some of us, like Stell here," he acknowledged him with a nod, "know the old stories about the Nebulee and the Ridge and Crackeldower, but after studying all the routes, I believe it to be less dangerous than sailing around Cape Logan. I know this crew can overcome any challenges presented."

There was more muttering, and Fraytar saw fear and concern on many faces. "This is a mission for volunteers, and any crewmember who decides to sail with me on this momentous voyage can expect a handsome reward."

"The nebulee be a terrible place," someone called out, followed by a chorus of mumbled acknowledgements.

"I heard that the Sproken isles make your toes fall off and your hair fall out," another called out.

I'm no sailor," Chanterly called out. "But I do know what it means to fight a war!"

Fenlop and Drenden, who had been in muttered conference, looked up. "I'm in," Fenlop shouted.

"Well worth the risk," Drenden added.

"Landlubbers," the veteran seaman scoffed.

"The captain's got us out of worse scrapes," Crouch shouted in support. "Is this not the same crew that fought off two Cordinen warships at once?"

"This be our chance to be famous," Drogar the third mate called out. "That route be never recorded before."

"I trust Fraytar and this crew to get us through this voyage," Morganuke chimed in.

"You mentioned a handsome reward, Captain. How handsome be that?" someone challenged from the back.

"Upon completion of the mission, each man receives a bonus of five hundred flants."

Five hundred Flants was a fortune to any crewmember and so, temporarily at least, seemed to remove some of the concern about the risks. The group assembled on the lower deck grew quiet again, and Fraytar noticed that the expressions on many faces had relaxed.

"Anyone who wants to sign on should see me in my cabin by the end of the day. This is your opportunity to make history, for us to sail to places that nobody in recorded history has been, to make the *Aurora* and its crew a formidable legend in our own right." The gathered crowd cheered at Fraytar's last words.

Fraytar left the upper deck and returned to his cabin with Crouch. He noticed a troubled look on his first mate's face. "Tell me honestly what you think."

"Many a time I be dreaming of making a voyage like this, but I'm not sure how many of the crew'll join the voyage, Captain," Crouch answered sombrely. "We'll be lucky to get half the men volunteering."

"We have a good ship and a good crew, and I trust that they will make the right decision." Fratar said.

"It do take many a year to gain total confidence in a captain, that be why Captain Amannar had that dedication, but the men do trust 'ee. I trust 'ee too, Captain," Crouch said sincerely.

"Let's see how many we get by the end of the day."

By that evening, almost three quarters of the crew had signed up for the voyage. It was more than Fraytar had hoped for. Although better than he and Crouch had expected, he was still short of crew and would have to approach Commander Tradish about getting more men. This journey demanded a full crew.

He was at his desk, updating the ship's log, when there was a knock on his cabin door.

"Come in," Fraytar said, putting his logbook away. To his surprise, in walked Chanterly, Calarel, Lengrond, Fenlop, Drenden, and Escolar. Fraytar sat open mouthed for a moment. He had thought they would be enjoying themselves on shore, after being cooped up onboard for the past four weeks.

"Er, what can I do for you all?" Fraytar asked.

"Captain Fraytar, we heard that you were short of crewmembers," Chanterly said, standing at the front. "We would all like to offer our services."

Fraytar wasn't sure what to say at first. "Well, I'm very grateful, but you don't have any sailing experience. Besides, you are needed here in the militia."

"With all due respect, Captain, we have sailed on your ship for several weeks," Chanterly answered. "During that time, we have applied ourselves to the ship's tasks. We can be an asset to your crew. You know we are excellent fighters and have worked together as an efficient team for some time now. The militia is well established, and adding our numbers to that force would not make that much difference. It would be much better to put our talents where they are most needed, accompanying you on the perilous journey."

Chanterly, as usual, had put the group's case very well. Fraytar couldn't fault the logic. It would help give him a full crew without having to bring in too many strangers. "Very well, I will sign you up."

For two days, the crew of the *Aurora* worked hard to prepare the ship for the voyage. Stores were loaded, rigging and sails renewed, and the hull beams and planking coated with protective sealing. On the third day, everything was ready, and they took their last shore leave before setting sail.

Morganuke and his friends were spending their last moments before leaving in the Jumping Fish inn. Tomlin was there as well. He would not be going on the voyage, as the best contribution a blacksmith could make to the war effort was making and repairing armaments. He had difficulty accepting that Calarel was leaving him behind again but had come to terms with it. "She be a woman now, so 'tis only right to let her go," he was mourning at the bar. He had remembered his promise to his daughter not to make a fool of himself and so was only a little tipsy.

The inn was packed with well-wishers and revellers who had been drinking and singing for most of the morning. Fraytar joined them after a last visit to Commander Tradish's office to finalise plans. Morganuke joined him at the bar, which was heaving with revellers. They looked at each other through the smoky atmosphere.

"I guess it'll be some time before we can relax and enjoy ourselves like this again, Fraytar," Morganuke said lifting his tumbler of ale.

"Yes, lad. Take it all in and savour it. These times are precious. But also think of the exciting adventures that await us."

Morganuke watched his friends singing happily at the table for a moment. He wanted to remember the happy sight before he set off on a voyage he was not sure to return from.

Eventually Fraytar informed everyone that the ship was ready to leave. Tomlin hugged his daughter, and the group of friends said their farewell to the crowd that had gathered to celebrate with them.

The mood grew more sombre as the group neared the *Aurora*. On board they took a last look around the docks, waving to the crowd who had gathered to see them leave, many having followed all the way from the inn to the docks.

After everyone else had gone to their accommodation to sleep it off, Morganuke stayed on the upper deck. He looked back at Cradport as it grew smaller into the distance. *I wonder if I'll ever see the island again*, he thought.

CHAPTER 30

Into the East

The *Aurora* had been sailing for a week after leaving Cradport. It would be three more weeks before they reached the first resupply point. Morganuke had followed their progress with interest and knew that the Sproken Isles would be their last opportunity to resupply before navigating around the eastern tip of the Ventor mainland. It would take them through the Ridge, renowned as hazardous, and then between the Ridge and the Sproken Isles was the infamous Nebulee Sea. What existed in that area was a complete mystery. Morganuke and Fraytar had been studying the stories of the Nebulee.

"I'm hoping that the accounts in these books are nothing but stories," Fraytar said, barely visible behind a pile of Captain Amannar's well-worn collection. "The stories must have meant something to Captain Amannar, else why would he have kept all these books?"

"What if they are true, and all these monsters and mysteries really are there?" Morganuke asked.

"Let's hope they're for entertainment! But we'll need to keep a sharp eye out and be ready for anything as we move through those waters," Fraytar answered.

Morganuke thumbed through one of the books. "This one says something about monstrous black obelisks rising from the sea," Morganuke pointed out. "These stories must be pure fantasy."

Morganuke moved onto one of the sea charts and rolled it out. "So, our next supply stop is the Sproken Isles," he noted. "Have you been there before?"

"A few times. They're not really on any normal sea route. Nothing sails beyond Ventros City, usually, but sometimes ships sailing between Ventor and Banton or the Cadmun lands get driven off course and shelter there in stormy weather. There's not much on those islands, but they do have plenty of fresh water. We will stop there mainly to replenish our freshwater."

Morganuke peered at the chart. "Then where is the next stopping point?"

Fraytar came over and looked at the chart over Morganuke's shoulder. "Asporania, north of the Ventor mainland." He pointed to an island about half the size of Banton.

"That's a long way," Morganuke answered, screwing his face up. "Will our supplies last that long?"

"The food should last, although the quality won't be good. The water is the biggest problem. By then our stocks of fresh water will have gone bad, and we'll need to rely on the ale stocks. That route hasn't been tried by anyone I know of. It will be difficult. I expect we'll need to ration supplies before we reach there."

"It'll be tricky then. With a risky unknown sea path and lack of supplies."

"Yes, I'm afraid so. You still glad to be on the trip?"

"Yes, of course I am," he answered with a smile.

"You've come a long way since your first voyage on the *Aurora*, Morg."

"Yes, that seems a long time ago now."

The two men went back to the old books and sat looking at them in silence for a while.

"How are you and Melinor getting on?" Fraytar eventually asked, breaking the silence. "You seem to be very protective of her. Are you two courting?"

Morganuke's face coloured, and he lowered his head towards the book he was holding. "Why are you asking?" Morganuke mumbled just loud enough for Fraytar to hear.

Fraytar smiled. "Are the sisters excited about returning to their homeland?"

"Yes, of course they are," Morganuke answered.

"Will you stay there with them? In Trebos, I mean."

"I don't know. It depends on what I find out about the Patronese. It's important for me to find out where I come from. You found me abandoned on a Banton beech, didn't you? If I originated from Trebos, then why was I abandoned so far away?"

"I can't answer that, Morganuke." He hesitated.

"It seems strange that someone should just leave me like that, and with that sword too."

"Yes, it's a shame you lost that sword, especially as you discovered that it had powers. It must have had some meaning."

"I didn't lose it. The Epleons took it from me."

"Well, maybe we can try and retrieve it at some time. Maybe with the help of Commander Brenadere."

"I don't hold out much hope of that. The existence of the sword makes it seems- all the stranger that I was just abandoned like that. Where was it you found me again?"

"I just found you in some form of sealed container in a small cove a little way north of Tannisport. There were no clues about who left you there or where you'd come from. It's only recently that we have seen people who look like you. That's why the islanders found it difficult to accept you as one of them. We thought you were some freak of nature."

"Freak?" Morganuke exclaimed. "That's unkind."

"Well, not a freak. But different in a way that the islanders didn't know how to understand."

Morganuke sighed, closing his book. "Maybe I am a freak, with these strange powers that I have. There is no doubt that I am Patronese. I do feel connected when I am with them. I just wish I knew all the answers, and how I can control those powers so I can be more help."

"Don't worry, Morg. We'll find the answers in the end. One thing I do know, and that is you are a good person."

Morganuke returned the book he had been looking at to the pile and cast an eye over the towering stack. "I'm not sure the answers are in these books."

Calarel sat against the wall of the women's cabin with her knees against her chest, her arms wrapped around them. "Oh my, nine months of this," she said.

"Look on the bright side—at least we're not in the hold this time," Chanterly pointed out. "You think things are bad now. Just wait until we've been at sea for months and the only things to eat and drink are worm-infested ship's biscuits and stale ale."

"Sounds like you've been at sea before our voyages," Calarel said, dropping her head to rest on her knees.

"Yes, I've been on long voyages before, mainly on my own trading ships. I admit that I had better accommodations than the crew, but I saw for myself the effect that long voyages can have on a person. Cramped conditions for the crew, the lack of freedom and private space, living with the same people in that space for months—it takes its toll."

"Thank you for that," Calarel said scathingly. "I feel so much better now."

"If you dislike this life so, Cal, why did you agree to come with us?" Chanterly asked, looking a little frustrated., "You have done nothing but moan the whole time. It does get a bit wearing after a while."

"I'm sorry," Calarel said, slumping her shoulders. "I can't help it sometimes. I get so worked up inside that I have to say mean things. I'll try and be a bit more positive. I do want to be on this journey, really."

"We should be thankful that we are here," Melinor spoke up, looking directly at Calarel. Alorie, who had been sitting next to her singing a song to herself, stopped in surprise. "We have a dry bed, warm clothes, and food provided to us. When you have lived as a slave, treated cruelly by your captors, and not knowing how much longer you will be allowed to live, this seems not so bad."

Chanterly and Calarel turned and looked at Melinor in surprise.

"Yes, that is true, and we should be thankful for what we have," Chanterly said. "I wonder, Melinor, whether you would like to train in the art of sword fighting?"

The tolling of the ship's bell interrupted them. "Oh, rats' droppings!" Calarel exclaimed. "It's time for my shift."

"Have the men been causing you any problems, Calarel?" Chanterly called after Calarel as she made her way out of the cabin. "Is that why you have been so irritable?"

"No. If they do, I'll slice them in half with this." Calarel turned, holding up her sword. Alorie gave a little chuckle, and Calarel smiled and winked at her, before closing the cabin door behind her.

Three weeks passed. The *Aurora* was approaching the Sproken Isles. Morganuke and Lengrond had just finished their four-hour shift and were more than ready for some sleep, when a shout went up from the lookout in the crow's nest. The islands had come into view. They strained their eyes at the horizon.

"So this is the last place of safety for some time," Morganuke observed when they finally made out the island they were nearing. "Nobody knows what lies beyond these islands."

Several of the crew were getting the rowing boats ready. The ship's cooper stood next to several large barrels stacked on the main deck for loading onto the boats. The barrels were mainly for collecting fresh water. How long the water lasted before it went bad would be up to how well the barrels were sealed, and so the cooper's presence was essential.

Morganuke desperately wanted to go ashore and see the islands. Fraytar had told him there wasn't a lot to see, but Morganuke volunteered for the advance party to locate the water source anyway. He joined the five other men, led by the grizzled Stellorgantis, rowing the boat into the shore. The waves were high at first, and the boat almost capsized more than once before the men adjusted.

At last the party made it to the beach. Morganuke had never seen such fine white sand. When he jumped out of the boat, he pulled off his boots to feel the soft sand under his feet, and he wriggled his toes deeper into it. The men hauled the boat onto the beach and pegged it down to prevent it floating away if the tide came in.

"Those tall hills yonder be the best place to look first," Stell said. He had given most of the orders as they rowed ashore.

The hills were richly vegetated, indicating the presence of water, but after searching for a while, the men still had found none. They reached the top of the highest hill, and still no source of running water. The six men stopped to rest for a moment. Morganuke turned and looked in the direction from which they had come. The waves washed the sandy beach, and the expanse of white sand seemed to stretch out for many stances. The rowboat they had come in on was just a small dot on the beach. The *Aurora* bobbed up and down with the waves off the coast.

Turning around to look inland, Morganuke saw lower hills sloping down with clumps of trees dotted here and there. As he surveyed the open land below them, he spotted a faint line leading up to the foothills. The trail outlined the rocky base of the next hill.

"It may be worth looking there," Morganuke said to Stell, pointing. "I see an animal track leading there, so it could be a possible place to find water."

The older crewmember looked to where Morganuke was pointing and shook his head. "I'm not so sure, lad," Stell said. "Further up yonder be another range of hills. We'll go there."

"It's ok I'll just go and check," Morganuke shouted as he started running down the hill.

"Silverhead, come back here, we need to stay together," the older man shouted after him.

Morganuke ignored Stell and carried on running. He reached the rocks the trail had led to, a little out of breath. He ducked behind a rock, breathing heavily to get his breath back. He didn't want the other men to know he was so winded. When he recovered, he began tracking the path through a rocky passage. Ahead he spotted a cave between two boulders, into which the path disappeared. He followed the path into the cave. It was dark inside, but he felt and smelt dampness in the air. The cave entrance barely gave enough light to see but he ventured further inside. He heard a faint dripping and stumbled his way towards it. He felt wet rock with his hands, and he made his way unsteadily crawling over the slippery cave floor.

The next thing Morganuke knew, he was sliding, slowly at first and then faster, more sharply downward and into darkness. He tried to grab hold of something to stop himself, but his hands only scraped over the slippery rocks until his fingers started to bleed. Then he felt no resistance at all for a moment and splashed into an icy pool of water.

When he came to the surface, gasping, Morganuke realised that he had found all the water they needed. He couldn't see, but it tasted crisp and clean on his lips. His moment of euphoria was short-lived. He had to get out of the cold water, and he couldn't see where to swim. He paddled in the direction he thought he had come from until he reached a rocky edge. He could get no better hold on the slick rocks than he had in falling. The ledge was too steep, and try as he might, he could not pull himself out.

Morganuke thought he heard something, maybe an animal. An animal whose eyes would be better adjusted for seeing in the dark than his. He heard sounds of movement. "Go away!" he shouted in a panic, whirling around blindly, trying to get his bearings.

"We could do that," he heard a voice behind him as light reflected on the water. He turned and looked up to see Stellorgantis leaning over the ledge with a lantern. "But then we wouldn't get our water."

"Stell!" Morganuke gasped.

"Course, if you think I'm drinking that water after it's had Silverhead in it, then you can think again," Stell said to laughs all round—including Morganuke, who extended an apologetic hand for a boost up.

Once Morganuke had been hauled out of the water, they made their way back to the beach. Just before they started to push the rowboat back towards the sea, Morganuke tapped the older man on the shoulder.

"Thank you for lookin' for me," he said sheepishly.

"Never leave a man behind. I'm sorry I doubted you ... Morg." Stell held out his hand.

It was not lost on Morganuke that Stell had not called him "Silverhead". The two men shook hands heartily.

They returned to the *Aurora*, and Morganuke watched from the upper deck as the rowing boats were lowered into the sea, each loaded with the barrels to hold the water. The ship's cooper went out with the first boat.

The excitement of the day and the cold had taken its toll. *I better get some rest before my next shift*; he thought as he made his way to his quarters. He hadn't quite got used to the smell in the main sleeping area. *There are too many sweaty bodies in too small a space*, he thought. But he found a bed and was soon fast asleep.

Morganuke looked around. The surroundings were unfamiliar—strange buildings made of a light grey material. He couldn't make out what it was. Wood or stone? It didn't look like either. He looked down and was surprised to realise that he was standing in water up to his knees. And all the time he could hear a strange low humming, like a beehive but deeper.

Then as he looked around, he felt himself rising out of the water. He thought that he might be flying, but when he looked down, he saw that he was standing on something that was slowly rising out of the water, and the deep humming got louder as it did so. The surface he was standing on was black and felt cold and hard.

Now he was about one eighty paces above the water, still standing on whatever it was, still rising out of the water. He turned and faced in the opposite direction, only to see that the object's surface he was standing was square with each side about fifty paces. He had never seen anything like it. The hum coming from the object grew louder, filling his head and making him nauseous.

Suddenly a pillar of bright light shot up just ahead of him from the object, and within the pillar of light a round door started to appear. The humming became even louder, and the light brighter. The round door opened, revealing the familiar lidless blue eye inscribed on the inner side, with symbols Morganuke could not recognise marked above the eye.

Morganuke tried to move away from the door, but he couldn't. He tried to move his legs, but he was paralyzed, helpless to do anything. Dizziness and nausea began to overcome him, and he felt himself falling towards the opening. There was nothing he could do. He was drawn slowly nearer to the opening and the eerie light that came from within.

"Morganuke!" Lengrond shouted. "You'll be late for your shift."

Morganuke sat up with a jolt, still feeling nauseous and dizzy from his dream. He sat on his bedding for several moments whilst he gradually regained his balance and his nausea subsided.

"That was a dream I shan't want again," Morganuke said quietly.

"What kind of dream?" Lengrond asked.

"It felt so real and strange," Morganuke said, still a bit groggy, "always with the Patronese symbol." He shook it off and forced himself to his feet. Legs unsteady, he made his way to the main deck for his four-hour shift. The sun was low in the sky, indicating that it was late afternoon. It would be dark in two or three hours, but the rowboats had not yet returned from the island with the fresh water.

Crouch called over to Morganuke, Lengrond, and another crewman. "You three wait here until the boats return." The three men leant against the railings of the main deck, watching for the returning rowing boats.

It was another two hours before Morganuke saw the boats returning, heavily weighed down with the barrels of water. When the first boat came alongside, one of the crew threw a rope up to a waiting crewmember on deck.

Morganuke and Lengrond then lowered ropes and a sling for hauling up the first barrel. Once the heavy barrel was secured in the harness it took Morganuke, Lengrond and four other crew members straining with all their might to heave the barrel aboard. Once the first barrel was on deck, the men sighed with relief.

"Phew," Lengrond exclaimed. "Only another nineteen to go."

By the time the last barrel had been lifted on board the *Aurora*, the daylight had gone, but it was another hour before the rowing boats and men were all aboard. The tired crew could finally relax and pat one another on the back at a job well done. Fraytar joined them with the cook carrying a hand barrel of Rum.

"Well done, crew," Fraytar said, as the cook handed out the tumblers of rum. "This water supply is essential for our next leg of the journey. We won't be stopping for another three months. We'll rest tonight and continue our journey at first light. Prepare yourselves, for we are about to sail close to the Nebulee, on a route that nobody has attempted in our lifetime."

CHAPTER 31

The Nebulee and the Ridge

The *Aurora* sailed past the Sproken Isles without any problems. The islands were far enough apart that the inlets between them were easily navigable. Morganuke watched as the *Aurora* moved further east, contemplating what would be waiting for them as they drew nearer to the Nebulee. He had been alarmed by the accounts he had read in Captain Amannar's old books but took solace in what Fraytar had said about them just being stories. However, there had been a marked increase in tension on board the *Aurora* since leaving the Sproken Isles.

Melinor joined Morganuke in watching the islands disappear. Melinor reached for Morganuke's hand and held it in hers.

"What will you do when you find your people?" Melinor asked. "Will you join them or go back to your home on Banton?"

"I don't feel that Banton is my home anymore," Morganuke replied, continuing to look out to sea. "My parents are dead, and the farm is gone. I feel more at home with you."

"What do you really want to do, Morg? Why did you really come on this voyage? I'm really interested to know."

"I want to be with you and take you home, Mel."

"What of the people that I told you about, the Patronese people I mean?"

"Yes, of course, I want to see them too. I'm hoping they will give me a clue about where I came from."

"Do you mean that you really want to go to the place where you were born and live with your people?"

"I do want to go to the place I came from to find the answers to lots of questions I have."

"What if the place you came from is not where I saw the Patronese village? It could be on the other side of the world."

Morganuke hesitated. "Then I would still try and get there. I feel that it is so important that I find answers to why I was abandoned as a baby with a special sword and why I have the powers that I do. Something tells me that my destiny lies with my people and the land I came from."

Morganuke and Melinor continued to watch the disappearing islands in silence.

On the evening of the sixth day since leaving the Sproken Isles, Fraytar had joined some of the crew as they were having their meal.

"Captain, what do he think was makin' those strange noises last night?" Snibbidge, one of the crew asked. He was a tall gangly man with greasy long hair tied in a ponytail and renowned for telling exaggerated stories.

"What strange noises?" I didn't hear anything strange." Fraytar answered.

"Well I 'erd it as clear as can be," Snibbidge insisted. "Creepy it were, like a deep moanin' it were. Gummy was on deck with me and he 'erd it too." Fraytar looked at the man they called Gummy, named such because he had no teeth. He eagerly nodded at Fraytar, his eyes wide open and his toothless mouth closed tight in a straight line.

"Don't worry lads," Fraytar reassured, "It was probably the sound of a storm some way off. Sound carries a long way over water."

"There be strange lights too," Gummy added, spraying some of the stew he was eating from his mouth as he spoke.

"Well, there you are. It must have been a distant storm then," Fraytar said.

The crew said no more about the strange sights and sounds and went back to eating their meal.

The last thing I need is for the crew to start rumours of seeing and hearing strange things just as we approach the Nebulee, Fraytar thought. *Everybody is already on edge about the Nebulee without adding to their worries.*

On the seventh evening, Morganuke was alerted by another one of the crew about seeing lights and hearing strange noises again. He went out on the deck to look for himself. He stood there for a few moments looking out to sea and listening. Then he heard it; like nothing he had heard before. It was like the sound of deep moaning coming from ahead of the *Aurora*. It sent a cold tingling through his body, and he felt the hairs on the back of his neck rise. Everyone who was on deck stopped and listened to it.

"Don't fret lads," Fraytar steeled himself to say. "It's just the wind." He wasn't convinced that the crew believed him, but they continued with their activities, nevertheless. *I've got to think of something to keep everyone's spirits up*, he thought. Fraytar knew that everyone was on edge, expecting some impending doom to befall them, and the stories of the Nebulee to be proven as fact.

On the eighth evening, as the *Aurora*'s bow sliced through the waves and the sails billowed out, the wind suddenly dropped, and the sea became calm and flat. It was as if someone had suddenly stopped blowing on a paper boat in a fishpond.

For the next day the *Aurora* remained almost motionless in the flat sea. No wind, no waves, and practically no sound. Tensions grew worse amongst the crew, and several fights broke out that required Fraytar and Crouch to intervene. Things came to a head later that evening whilst Fraytar was discussing the growing concern with Crouch. There was a loud shout from the main deck. Rushing out of his cabin Morganuke saw two men facing each other angrily, each with a knife in their hand. Jango, one of Fraytar seasoned older crew members had a deep cut down his cheek. The other man, Willy, was a more recent addition to the crew and known for his short temper. The two men looked as though they were ready to kill each other.

"You two men stand down now," Fraytar shouted to Jango and Willy. They hesitated for a moment, but then gradually lowered their knife hands. "Drop those knives now, before I have you both hanged." The two men did as they were ordered. "Crouch, have these two men escorted to the brig." Fraytar added, not taking his eyes off the two men, who were now looking up at Fraytar.

Once the men had been detained, Crouch rejoined Fraytar in his cabin. "Can I speak freely, Captain?" Crouch said to Fraytar. Fraytar curtly nodded. "We needs to make an example of these two, else things'll get worse."

Fraytar knew that Crouch was right but preferred the carrot to the stick. "They can stay in the brig for now. I'll think about what to do with them."

"Aye-aye, Captain. Whatever you say."

As the day went on, things started to settle down a little. Fraytar had an idea to put on a show for the crew but couldn't decide what to arrange. *Now who has talents?* He thought. *I've often heard the men mention Lengrond as a good storyteller. Stell has a good voice and can play the squeeze box well. But that won't be enough. The lovely Lady Chanterly must be well versed in the arts. I'll go and speak to her and see if she has any ideas.*

Chanterly and Calarel were standing outside talking when Fraytar approached their quarters.

"Hello, Captain," Chanterly greeted him warmly. "What can we do for you?"

Fraytar hesitated and looked down at his boots, his hands fidgeting behind his back. "Afternoon, Lady Chanterly and Calarel." He was silent for a few moments as the two women looked at him. "Eeerr ... I want to ask you something, Lady Chanterly."

"Captain DeLance, are you trying to ask Lady Chanterly here to court you?" Calarel blurted out, trying to keep her face looking serious.

Fraytar felt his face go bright red, and he didn't know what to say. "Ah ... umm ... no, of course not. Not that I wouldn't want to—aargh." Fraytar's face went a brighter shade of red. He gathered himself. "I would ask your advice on putting on a show for the crew to keep their spirits up."

The two women looked at each other and frowned. "What sort of show?" Chanterly asked doubtfully.

"Well, that's what I want to ask your advice about. As a lady, I thought that you might have been conversant in the arts, like the great playwright Willaby's plays or something like that. Just something to take the crew's mind off things."

"Captain DeLance, do you really think that your men will want to sit and watch a Willaby's dreary play or listen to chamber music?" Chanterly asked, with the hint of a smile.

"Lady Chanterly, my men may seem crude and base in your fine eyes, but I can assure you that they are good men. A bit of sophistication would be good for them," Fraytar answered, feeling a little indignant.

"Captain—," Chanterly started to say.

"Please, Lady Chanterly, you can call be Fraytar."

"Fraytar, I meant no offence to you or your crew. I know that they are a very fine crew. I would not have offered to sail with you had they not been. What I meant was, your men will want some fun and laughter to forget these troubling times for at least a short while. Did you have any other ideas yourself that were maybe more fitting with the men's sense of fun? —and please dispense with the Lady, I am just Chanterly to you."

"Well, Chanterly, I thought Stell could do a turn singing some chantey songs with his squeeze box and maybe Lengrond could give one of his humorous anecdotes. That's as far as I got, I'm afraid."

"You can leave it with me, Fraytar," Chanterly offered. "I have some ideas that could go well with your suggestions."

Fraytar smiled, feeling relieved at how the conversation with Chanterly had gone. "Excellent. Thank you, Chanterly. I'll leave it in your capable hands then."

The next evening, after another anxious day with no wind, Chanterly and her performing company were ready to entertain the crew. The crew sat around the main deck in good spirits. Fraytar watched from his viewpoint on the upper deck in eager anticipation too.

The first act on was Lengrond, who gave some excellent and humorous anecdotes about his life back on Cadmun. The audience showed their appreciation by cheering and clapping at the end of it.

Next up was Snibbidge with clacker sticks and upturned buckets., he clacked his sticks together in quick rhythm combined with matched rhythmic bashes on the buckets. He did this at the same time as moving his body in time. His dancing contortions with his gangly arms and legs in time with his improvised percussion was a marvellous spectacle and resulted in another resounding applause from the audience.

Now came Chanterly, Calarel, Drenden and Everland Croningthorp the ship's surgeon who put on a short comical play based on the famous folk tale 'Lord Wordingly's Haunted Woods', about two couples making their way through a haunted wood. In traditional style the men played the women characters, and the women played as men. It got many laughs from the audience. The backscene special affects provided by Morganuke and Gummy were also much appreciated.

The next act was a surprise. It featured Melinor and Alorie singing a traditional folk song from their homeland together. The two girls sung very sweetly and Fraytar spotted several of his crusty hardened crew with tears in their eyes during the endearing performance.

The final act was Stell and his squeeze box. Everybody joined in the well-known songs, even Fraytar sang along and had a little jig, until he caught Chanterly smiling up at him. Stell had to give two encores before the show was finally wrapped up.

From what Fraytar could judge, the evening's entertainment seemed to have been a resounding success. As the crew made their way back to what they were doing, Fraytar caught Chanterly's eye again and he mouthed the words 'thank you' to her. She responded by curtsying to him, but her smile looked genuine.

Early the next morning, Fraytar was alerted by the lookout of fog. When Fraytar exited his cabin, a thick fog had enveloped them. It was so thick it was almost suffocating, and the sense of foreboding amongst the crew returned. The strange lights and noises that had been occurring only when darkness fell and at some distance now were coming dimly through the fog. It seemed to surround them completely.

Fraytar watched as crewmembers nervously went about their activities on the ship. Those off shift remained out of sight, fearing to go out into the suffocating fog.

"What shall we do, Captain?" Crouch asked. "The crew be about to go mad. I already had to hold one crewman down before he be jumping overboard. They fear that we're so close to the Nebulee now and keep harpin' on about the old stories."

Fraytar thought for a few moments and then called out across the ship. "Raise anchor," he ordered. "If we start moving it should allay the crews' fears, hopefully."

"Launch all the rowing boats, Crouch, and man them with the maximum number of oarsmen for towing," Fraytar ordered. "We'll get this ship moving even if it's the last thing we do."

"Aye-aye, Captain." Crouch rushed off to organise the towing crew and boats.

Six rowing boats in all, eight men in each, were put into the water and tethered to the ship. The *Aurora* towered above them. The crew then started to row away. The fog was so dense that they didn't have to go far before the hull was shrouded from view behind them. The tethers grew taut, and the rowers felt the resistance increase as they pulled as hard as they could. Some of the men started to gasp for air in the stagnant fog soup.

Morganuke was assigned to the lead rowing boat. The fog made him feel claustrophobic, and he too had difficulty breathing. Closing his eyes helped a little, and for a while he rowed sightless. When he opened his eyes, through the fog he could just about see the next rowing boat and the men straining at the oars.

Morganuke noticed a thin layer of what appeared to be clear air a pace or two above the water line. He looked down into the murk of the sea and thought he saw a shadow in the depth. Between pulls of the oar in time with the man sat next to him, Morganuke kept casting his eyes into the depths. The shadow seemed to be getting bigger. Then he realised that it was a solid surface, rising up through the water and dimly glowing. Suddenly, Morganuke recognised in horror that the surface rising below them like some dark nemesis from the deep had been in his dream. It was the same square black shape with the faint outline of a round closed door in its centre. Morganuke froze.

The sound of shouts nearby snapped him back to attention as his rowing boat and the one beside it started to be lifted up, as if on the back of a monstrous black sea creature rising out of the water. Fraytar and the other men in the two rowing boats quickly jumped out and over the side of the still rising shape. It towered over the men, now swimming for their lives in the sea. Rising still further, the object now dwarfed the *Aurora*. It was like a giant black obelisk, five times as tall as it was wide, with a huge lidless eye marked on one side. The base of the obelisk still below the waves whilst the top towered over the boats and men below it. Morganuke began to feel a presence, something scratching inside his head, that low humming sound he had heard in his dream coming from the obelisk. The scratching in Morganuke's head persisted as he tried to swim towards the *Aurora*, making him dizzy. His arms pounded the sea as he continued to propel himself away from the thing. The feeling of a presence, the scratching in his head, like someone was inside scrambling his mind, got stronger. Then, it stopped.

Suddenly, the object started to sink into the water, and the presence scrambling Morganuke's mind disappeared with it. Soon it was completely submerged. Morganuke stopped swimming and just floated in the water on his back. Other men were in the water too, shouting and splashing. The fog was lifting, and as he looked around, Morganuke could see that four of the rowing boats were still afloat, though the men they carried were shouting to one another in terror. The other two that had been carried up on top of the obelisk were now upside down in the sea a little way behind, with the men who had been in them now swimming in the water. The fog diminished in seconds, and the blue sky was visible again. Morganuke felt a breeze against his face. He looked up at the *Aurora*, and the main mast flag was flapping in a brisk wind. The obelisk, the fog, the sounds, and the strange lights had all gone, as though they had never been there.

The men in the water swam back to their ship and climbed the nets aboard. The two overturned boats were retrieved by the other boats and hauled up onto the *Aurora*, and as soon as all the men were on board, Fraytar called out the order to raise the sail. "Let's leave this cursed place behind us."

"The stories are true," shouted Snibbidge. "Demons from the deep do exist in this place."

"Enough of that talk," Crouch said. "You'll be glad enough to see the wind in our sails."

"That's no demon or living thing from the deep," Morganuke said quietly as he stood beside Fraytar. "Whatever it is, that thing is manmade."

Fraytar looked at Morganuke. "What do you mean?" he said.

"I saw it in my dream."

"You've been having dreams again?"

Morganuke nodded. "Someone in that thing, or they, called out to me. It's manmade, I tell you."

"Well, it's gone now," Fraytar answered. "And we should be too. I hope we never have to return this way again."

Once he'd helped store the rowing boats, Morganuke went to the women's quarters to see whether Melinor and her sister were all right. Chanterly opened the door. Men were prohibited from entering the women's cabin, and he asked if Melinor would come out.

"Are you alright?" Morganuke asked when Melinor appeared, relieved to see her.

"Yes, but I was very worried about you. What was all that shouting and commotion out there?"

"Something huge came up out of the sea," Morganuke answered. "Snibbidge called it a demon from the deep, but I'm sure it was man made."

"What sort of thing was it and made by who, Morg?"

"I think it's something to do with the Patronese. I had a dream about it the night before. In my dream, the object had the Patronese symbol on it; the lidless eye."

"How can you dream of something that you have never seen before?"

"I don't know. It must be something to do with the powers I have. I keep thinking my dreams are telling me something. I also felt connected to the thing in some way. I'm so confused. It's driving me mad. The Cordinens think I'm someone important in the Patronese world. What does that mean, I wonder?"

"Hopefully when we find the Patronese in my homeland they will be able to tell you all you need to know," Melinor said softly, smiling at Morganuke and brushing some silver hair away from his eyes.

Calarel burst out of the cabin door at that moment, huffing as she slammed the door behind her. She looked at Morganuke and Melinor canoodling against the deck railing and huffed loudly again before stomping off across the deck.

"She's not taking the voyage well," Melinor commented. "She doesn't like being cooped up with us."

"I better go and talk to her," Morganuke said. "I've known Cal and her father for many years. We lived close to one another on the island and grew up together. She is my friend even if she can be a bit spiteful at times. I don't want to see her upset."

"Do you love her?" Melinor asked innocently.

Morganuke nearly choked. "No, of course I don't love her." He looked intently into Melinor's eyes. "I love you, Mel."

Melinor smiled and her eyes shone with sudden tenderness. "I love you too, Morg." She took his hand and pressed it against her cheek with a kiss before pushing it away in dismissal. "Now go talk to your friend."

Morganuke got up and walked over to where Calarel was leaning on the deck railings. "What's wrong, Cal?" Morganuke asked.

"What do you want?" Calarel snapped at him, turning her head only to give him a hostile look. "Better not leave your gushing girlfriend all alone."

"I'm worried about you, Cal. We're good friends, you and I. We have shared our lives in the same community. You have not been happy and have not been since we left Cradport."

"I think I made a mistake coming on this voyage," Calarel said, almost to herself. "That thing the men are saying came out of the sea back there. What in Crasdredon's name was that? How are we supposed to fight something like that? All those other things that have happened too. I try to be brave but inside I'm scared, and it annoys me that I'm scared."

"Cal, it's only natural to be scared. I'm scared too, I've nearly pooped myself so many times, I've lost count." Calarel sniggered, which made Morganuke feel a little easier about her.

"I don't have all the answers yet, Cal," Morganuke admitted, putting his hand on her shoulder. "That is why we're going to Trebos. To find out more."

"I thought we were going to Trebos to find the Patronese, so that we can stop them helping the Cordinens. What has that *thing* got to do with Trebos?"

"I believe what we saw back there, is connected to the Patronese somehow. Trust me, this is a worthy voyage."

Calarel looked at Morganuke and nodded her head thoughtfully. "You're a good man, Morg," She made her way back to the cabin and closed the door gently behind her.

The *Aurora* made steady progress for another week. The voyage had been straightforward, with no more fog, strange lights, noises, or objects rising from the sea, and relief of the crew was palpable. Fraytar had not had the heart to remind them that they still had the Ridge to negotiate. With its shallow inlets and rocky ridges, it would be a formidable line to cross, and they were drawing near to it. As he stood on the stern's upper deck, Morganuke approached.

"The crew are looking happy to be out of the Nebulee," Morganuke observed.

"Yes, they are." Fraytar surveyed the main deck below. "Now we have to get through the Ridge."

"Have you been through the Ridge before?" Morganuke asked.

"No. I have always taken the western route, through the Cragan Shipping Canal, when travelling to the northern hemisphere. That canal has saved many ships from danger and shortens the journey significantly. It's a real feat of engineering," Fraytar added with a glint in his eye.

"What is it like?" Morganuke asked.

"It's over five hundred stances long and can accommodate any ship. It's maintained and controlled by the Epleons, but nobody knows who originally built it. Had it not been for our recent run-in with the Epleons and the Casdredon priests, the canal would have been the obvious route to take."

"I'm surprised we've got this far," Morganuke noted. "When all those strange things have happened to us, I thought we were done for."

"The men told me that the obelisk you encountered just stopped and went back into the sea," Fraytar said. "It seems strange that it suddenly disappeared like that. What do you think happened?"

"I have my suspicions that they sensed me, as I sensed them," Morganuke answered, causing Fraytar to raise his eyebrows.

"What do you mean, sensed them?" Fraytar asked.

"I believe that the Patronese were operating that thing. I sensed it when I was close to the obelisk."

"Let's hope the Ridge goes more smoothly."

"Approaching the Ridge!" came a timely shout from the main mast lookout.

"Reduce sail and launch the sounding boat," Fraytar ordered.

Once the *Aurora*'s speed was reduced, they lowered one of the rowing boats into the sea. The four sailors manning it rowed ahead, taking regular depth readings whilst the *Aurora* inched its way forward. Rocks and small islets began to come into view all around them.

At the end of the first day in the Ridge, they anchored for the night. It was too dangerous to continue in the dark with so many hazardous rocks and sandbanks to contend with. The next day, progress was even slower.

"Steady as she goes," Fraytar shouted

They had come into a channel that seemed to be steadily narrowing. Soon the depth sounders in the rowing boat signalled the *Aurora* to stop.

"They be leadin' us down a dead end, Captain," Crouch reported.

"We'll have to warp the ship around using those islets as anchor points," Fraytar answered, frustrated. "See it done, Crouch."

"Aye-aye, Captain."

The Aurora was turned about by securing ropes at either end of the ship and then using anchorage points on nearby islets, crewmembers hauled the ship around, before making its way back out of the dead-end. The sounding boat took some time to find another way through, and by then night was drawing in. For a second night, the *Aurora* anchored to wait for the morning.

The way that had been found the day before proved to be successful, although very tricky to manoeuvre through. With skill and good signalling between boat and ship, the *Aurora* finally managed to get through the worst of the rocks making up the Ridge. The rocks and sandbanks grew sparser as they continued north, and finally they reached open sea. With full sail and a good following wind, the *Aurora* started making good progress.

"Glad to be through that tricky spot, Captain," Crouch said as he stood with Fraytar on the rear deck.

"Yes. The crew did well," Fraytar answered, puffing on his pipe. "How are the food and water supplies? It'll be another month's sailing until we reach our next resupply point at Asporania."

"Supplies be getting low, Captain," answered Crouch. "We only have hard tack and oats left, and the water stocks are down to four barrels, assuming that does not go bad. We could make it go further by making some grog, as there be plenty of rum."

"Tell cook to go down to half rations, and double the guard on the stores."

"Aye-aye, Captain."

The amount of food proved not to be their only problem.

"This is revolting!" Calarel squealed, poking the ship's biscuit on her plate, wriggling with worms.

"Don't look at it, girl," Fenlop advised. "Just wrap it up in a ball with some grog and shove it all in your mouth. Next time make sure you give the hard tack a good bang on the table to get those things out, or as many as you can." He demonstrated grimly.

Calarel broke up the biscuit and flicked as many of the weevil lava out onto the floor as she could. She then scooped up the crumbs in her fingers and put it in her mouth, swallowing immediately and then gagged.

"The captain says it'll be another four weeks before we can resupply, so you better get used to those biscuits, Cal," Chanterly said, whacking her biscuit on the side of the table then putting it in her mouth.

"I don't know what's worse, the thing from the deep back at the Nebulee or these creepie crawlies," Calarel said, gagging again.

"We're past the worst now that we've got through the Nebulee and the Ridge," Fenlop put in. "Hopefully it'll be plain sailing to Asporania."

CHAPTER 32

Into the West

It had been ten weeks since the *Aurora* had left Cradport, and the islanders and mainlanders were growing weary of life on board ship. They had begun to appreciate what long-distance sailors had to contend with. With their different shifts and crew assignments, there had been little opportunity for the group that had followed Fenlop on daring missions to get together, and they had gathered now on the upper stern deck in front of Fraytar's cabin.

"How many more weeks until we reach the next resupply point?" Calarel asked.

"Only another two weeks, I think," Fenlop said. "We have broken the back of this journey now."

"Thank the Casdredon Snarebits!" Calarel exclaim, looking up to the sky and putting her hands across her chest. "No more maggoty biscuits, dry oats, or foul grog. My stomach hasn't been right for days now, and I'm always feeling tired."

"That's assuming we can get the supplies we need on Asporania," added Drenden. "There's no guarantee of that. For all we know, the Cordinens may have taken that island already as a stopping point for their own ships."

"If we don't get supplies from Asporania, then the next stop will be

Crystalia Major, which is another five or six weeks further," Morganuke pointed out.

"Since when did you know all about where we are going and how long it takes?" Calarel needled him, smiling mischievously. "You spend too much time with the captain. You're the captain's pet, methinks."

"I'm just interested in where we are going so take time to look at the charts." Morganuke answered, taking Calarel's comment in good humour.

"You do, indeed," Fraytar said as he came out of his cabin to join the group. "We'll make a sailor of you yet, Morg."

"Do you think that we will be able to get supplies at Asporania, Captain?" Lengrond asked. "Some of us were wondering if the Cordinens had already taken that island."

"I hope we can." Fraytar took a seat among them. "It really depends on what they are intending for Crystalia. It would be a useful stopping point from the east of Ventor, if they are obtaining supplies there."

"So, Captain, what do we do if the Cordinens are there?" Chanterly asked.

"We'll just have to go on to Crystalia ourselves and resupply there for the last leg of the journey," Fraytar replied, lighting his pipe thoughtfully. He blew out a long thin line of smoke, which made Calarel cough. "Crystalia should be a neutral domain. We would be safe resupplying there. I hope."

"Oh no!" Calarel said and let out a big sigh. "I can't eat maggoty biscuits for another six weeks. The grog too—I just couldn't."

"I'll have a word with Cook and see if he can't recook the biscuits," Fraytar suggested. "That should kill off the weevils at least. It'll be like eating bits of wood but at least you won't have trouble with weevils, not live ones at least. As far as the grog—well, we haven't had much rain yet, but I'm sure we'll get plenty before we get to Crystalia."

"Talking of rain, looking at those clouds—it may not be too long before that happens," Drenden pointed out.

They looked up at the sky. Some very dark clouds were gathering a little way ahead, and the wind had started to pick up as well.

Fraytar puffed on his pipe, causing a big cloud of smoke to gather around him. "Hmm," he said. "Crouch, get some of the crew to secure water barrels on deck to collect rain. I think we may be able to replenish our freshwater stores after all."

The wind rapidly increased to the point where Fraytar ordered the ship's sails to be reduced. Waves began to crash against the hull, sending torrents of seawater onto the deck. The *Aurora* was being tossed about in the sea like a twig.

"So much for collecting rainwater," Fraytar commented. "Reef the sails!"

The most experienced crew quickly raised the reef sails. The men on deck worked frantically on the rigging, thrown about by the lurching ship. One man was washed across the deck and nearly went overboard, had it not been for the rope lashing him to the main mast.

For two hours the *Aurora* was battered by the storm, with waves crashing into the bow and sending seawater cascading over the deck. Inside the cabins and below deck, crew were thrown about like pebbles in a bottle. Ropes began to come loose on some of the cargo, sending it crashing across the hold.

Fraytar took up a position next to the helmsman Mordock as he wrestled with the ship's tiller. Mordock kept the ship steered into the waves. Several times the ship almost keeled over, but the skill of the helmsman prevented catastrophe.

The relentless wind and rain were making it difficult to see. Fraytar strained his eyes to watch for the next wave and saw a giant wall of water rising before him, looming above the *Aurora*. In all the years he had been to sea, he had never seen a wave that massive. He tapped Mordock on the shoulder and pointed. The helmsman with steely resolve adjusted the ship's tiller. On came the giant wave, blotting out the dark stormy sky as it closed in. The bow of the ship pitched upwards as it encountered the wall of water. The force was so great that Fraytar grabbed onto the tiller as well to help the helmsman hold steady. Up the *Aurora* climbed. Fraytar and the helmsman clung to the tiller with all their strength. Still climbing the giant wall, it seemed that they would never reach the top, and instead might slide backwards to their doom.

But the ship reached the top of the giant wave and lurched

downward as it started to descend the other side. Fraytar and Mordock were thrown forward against the railings as the ship dived downwards. Fraytar closed his eyes as the *Aurora* headed down to the bottom of the giant wave below. When the ship reached the base of the wave, water cascaded over them, as if they had been hit by a hundred hammers at once. The railing Fraytar was holding onto cracked and broke away, and he fell backwards. Then he felt a violent tug around his waist as his safety rope pulled him abruptly to a halt.

Fraytar lay on the flooded deck, composing himself. He struggled to his feet and before him saw the tiller waggling about, with no helmsman. He raced to take hold of the tiller again, looked ahead to find the next wave and adjusting the tiller to steer into it. Looking around again for Mordock, he saw only the snapped end of his tether.

Fraytar's heart sank. He had to think quickly. There was still a lot of sea to sail before they got to their destination, and it was essential to have a helmsman as experienced as Mordock.

The wind and rain began to die down. The worst of the storm was over. Fraytar was still holding onto the tiller, steering the ship into the oncoming waves, when Crouch approached.

"Captain, be you alright?" Crouch asked.

"Mordock has been washed overboard," Fraytar answered still focusing on the tiller. "Get Drogar, he's a good helmsman."

Grouch disappeared for a few moments and then came back with Drogar. "Drogar, you have the tiller," Fraytar ordered the third mate. "Keep us on a North-East heading to Asporania."

"Any other losses?" Fraytar asked Crouch.

Crouch answered. "We lost three of the crew, including Mordock. The others below deck and in cabins are shaken and battered but they be all right."

"Damage to the ship?" Fraytar asked.

"There be some damage to the main mast and rigging, but it's fixable," Crouch replied. "Biggest problem is the supplies. All but one barrel of grog has been destroyed or contaminated with seawater, and half the dry rations have been destroyed."

Fraytar sighed, "Then it seems we must take on supplies at Asporania,

Cordinens or no Cordinens," he declared. "Tell Cook to go down to quarter rations."

Morganuke, Fenlop and Lengrond were recovering on the fore deck. They had been violently thrown about in the storm. "I think my arm is broken," Lengrond groaned as he sat on the floor, holding his left arm.

"Let's look at it," Morganuke said. He scrambled across and lifted the misshapen arm. Lengrond yelped in pain. A small piece of bone protruded through the skin of the forearm. "The ship's surgeon will need to look at that."

Drenden and Escolar were bruised and bleeding, but seemed to be all right, without any serious injury. Morganuke's clothes were wet through, and he had a small cut on his forehead that was bleeding.

"Fenlop, can you take Lengrond to the surgeon. I must go to the women's cabin," he said. On the main deck, he saw pieces of wood, sails, and rigging strewn about. He continued to the upper deck at the stern, shocked to see all the damage. The supporting framework surrounding the ship's tiller was in pieces, but the tiller was still functional, manned now by Drogar.

The door to the women's cabin was open. Chanterly was propped against the deck railing with blood running down her face. She looked drowsy, as though she had difficulty keeping her head up. Calarel knelt beside her, mopping the blood from her face.

"Where's Melinor?" Morganuke asked.

Calarel wordlessly pointed to the open cabin door, and Morganuke feared for the worst. He ran in and was relieved to see Melinor holding her sister in her arms. Alorie was sobbing, but both were alive with minor cuts and bruises.

Morganuke rushed over and put both arms around the two. "Thank the stars you are alright!" he exclaimed. "I don't know what I'd do if anything happened to you."

The storm had subsided. The ship's surgeon set the bone in Lengrond's arm and put it in a splint. Morganuke was worried about

Chanterly, who had received a severe blow to the head. She lay on a bed made from any dry material that could be found, laid out on the floor in the women's cabin. Morganuke looked worriedly at her. She did not look well, and Calarel sat beside her, cradling her head in her lap. The *Aurora* dropped anchor to make repairs and clear wreckage.

Two weeks went by in relative calm, but the storm had taken its toll. Half the food and water supply, which was already low before, had been ruined. Morganuke had noticed that everyone he saw looked drawn and tired, as he did. His mood lifted when he saw Chanterly hobble onto the deck for the first time since the storm, with Calarel walking along beside her arm in arm to steady her.

"It's good to get some air," Chanterly said, catching her breath as she leant on the deck railing.

"It's good to see you up and about again, Chanterly," Morganuke said, nodding an acknowledgement to Calarel as well.

"Thank you, Morg. It feels good to be moving about again."

"We thought we lost you in that storm," Calarel said, leaning on the railings next to her.

"I thought I'd lost me too," Chanterly said with a smile. "My head still feels like it's been kicked by a bull, but I feel better than I did."

"Melinor and her sister have gone forward, I think," Calarel said to Morganuke.

"It's all right. I saw them on my way here," Morganuke said. "I really came to see how Chanterly is."

"Thank you for your concern, Morg."

Morganuke's stomach growled. He looked sheepish and tightened his belt buckle. "Fraytar says we need to stay on quarter rations until we can make port."

Chanterly and Calarel gave out a loud groan.

"Still, we should be past the worst of it now," Morganuke added. "A few more weeks and we'll reach Trebos."

"Thank you for those words of encouragement," Chanterly said with a wry smile. "I think I remember something like that was said just before the storm hit."

Fraytar had overheard the exchange between Morganuke and the two women with a solemn smile. His people had spirit, but he knew they needed a break soon. The *Aurora* had been making steady progress towards the island of Asporania, and it wasn't long before the lookout sighted their destination: Crale, a small harbour town. Fraytar looked through his spyglass but couldn't see any Cordinen ships. They would not be able to tell whether there was a Cordinen presence on the island until they got closer.

"What should we do, Captain?" asked Crouch. "Go directly into Crale, or wait offshore?"

"We need supplies, and I can't see any immediate signs of the Cordinens," Fraytar said. "Post a double watch, and let's go into the harbour and dock."

"Aye-aye, Captain."

The *Aurora* made its way into the harbour. It was small, with just a few small fishing boats moored, but deep enough for the carrack to dock. Once docked, Fraytar formed an ashore party for collecting the supplies they needed and had the gangplank lowered. He disembarked with Morganuke, Lengrond, and two other muscular crewmen. It had been some time since he was last in this area, and he wasn't sure what the reception would be.

Fraytar's concerns of hostility on the island were unfounded and the locals were friendly enough. Houses were arranged on the three inland sides of the docks. The narrow streets running between the houses and market stalls bustled with people. After scouring the town, Fraytar managed to get all the supplies he was looking for. Barrels full of salted cod, salted pork and tanglet fruit were loaded onto the *Aurora*, which resulted in a cheer from those left on board.

As soon as the supplies were loaded onto the ship, the *Aurora* set sail again for the penultimate leg of their voyage, northwest from Asporania. At least it was further from the mainland and Ventor than they had been, which meant less risk of encountering a Cordinen naval patrol.

CHAPTER 33

The Last Leg

Morganuke was relieved when they finally reached Dransorter. The five-week voyage from Asporania to Dransorter went without any major problems. They even had some good fortune on the way when the rains arrived, and the crew could collect enough fresh water to last until they reached Dransorter. It made a change, Morganuke thought, to arrive in a port not feeling exhausted and starving. Food and water had remained on full rations for the journey. Even so, Fraytar had said that they would rest up in Dransorter and allow the crew to prepare for the final leg of the journey. Besides, there was a lot to see and do in the city.

Dransorter was the main city of Crystalia Major, and the city and its harbour were much larger than the *Aurora* crew were used to. It took some piloting skills from Drogar to manoeuvre the ship into the busy docks, but he met the challenge well. Crystalia Major and Minor formed the northern trading federation, which had been made rich by numerous sea trading routes with the mainland and the western islands of Pinto and Quinn. The city of Dransorter showed the signs of that trading wealth. Large opulent buildings overlooked the harbour, some four stories high. The brightly painted, pristine buildings with streets packed with well-dressed folk going about their business made it look like a different world to Morganuke. Behind the houses lining the docks lay a metropolis where practically anything imagined could be purchased, if one had the money.

The crew of the *Aurora* were glad to find themselves on solid ground at last. They split up into small groups to explore the city, the biggest that most of them had ever seen. Morganuke stayed with Melinor and Alorie as they walked through the crowded streets. Alorie gazed wide-eyed at all the sights, the comings and goings of so many people, the magnificent houses and the many shops and market stalls. Morganuke wanted to buy Melinor a new dress, as the clothes she was wearing were very shabby and torn. The three of them looked destitute compared to the local people who wandered the street in their fine clothes, giving them strange looks and making sure to keep their distance.

Morganuke stopped outside a tailor's shop with many fine clothes in the large display window. His eye had been caught by a beautiful blue dress with ornate embroidery down the front, the sleeves and hem lined in delicate lace. "That dress would look lovely on you," he said to Melinor.

"Maybe, but it's too extravagant." Melinor started to move further down the street, but Morganuke grabbed her hand and Alorie's and pulled them back toward the shop entrance.

"Morg, what are you doing?" Melinor protested. Alorie just giggled.

Inside, the shopkeeper behind the counter looked the three up and down with a frown. "Peasants are not permitted in here," he said, gesturing for them to leave. Morganuke walked up to the counter and, looking directly at him, slapped down a money bag full of gold flants—the voyage enrolment money he'd received on leaving Cradport.

"I have money," Morganuke said. "That blue dress in the window, we want to see it."

The shopkeeper raised his eyebrows but went to the window to fetch the dress. "This one?" he asked, holding it up.

"Yes," Morganuke answered. "Mel, are you to try it on?"

Melinor's eyes widened. "I can't. It's too extravagant."

"No, that will not do," the shopkeeper said curtly. "You're filthy, and you stink."

Morganuke turned to the shopkeeper and gave him a scathing look.

He was just about to snatch the dress from the man but realised he was right. "Are there any bathing facilities close by?"

"What?" the shopkeeper asked. "Across the street a little way down."

Morganuke led the way to where the shopkeeper had directed them. The spar house looked very grand, like some ancient temple to Casdredon. Melinor was reluctant to go in at first, but eventually Morganuke persuaded her in. They were treated with as much disdain inside the bathhouse as they had been by the shopkeeper, but the sight of Morganuke's moneybag soon changed their mind.

Feeling refreshed and clean after their baths, the three returned to the clothes shop.

Melinor, Morganuke and Alorie tried on several different outfits, before choosing one each. Finally, the three left the shop looking every bit as good as the people milling around them. Melinor wore the blue dress, after the shopkeeper had made a few adjustments for Melinor's slim waist. Morganuke had always thought Melinor very beautiful but found her even more so when he saw her in the dress. He had chosen a fine slim-fitting red tunic with slashed sleeves and a blue surcoat, set off with a black leather belt with a large shiny buckle, and had not been able to resist a second stop at a cobblers to buy a pair of fine black knee-high boots, along with shoes for Melinor and Alorie. As they walked down the street, Alorie kept holding out the skirt of her new bright-blue embroidered dress, as if she could not stop admiring it.

The stop at Dransorter was a real boost for Morganuke. He felt good about being able to buy Melinor and her sister something nice and it had been wonderful to spend time with them off the ship. After two days, they all felt refreshed and ready for the final stage of the voyage. With the ship fully restocked, the *Aurora* set sail again on the third day.

The last five weeks of the voyage to Vesnick City went smoothly. The rations collected at Dransorter had lasted, and the crew arrived still in good spirits. Whilst not as grand and large as Dransorter, Vesnick City was still impressive, a busy working port with many cargo and fishing ships anchored there.

Morganuke, Melinor, and Alorie stood on the main deck as the *Aurora* entered the harbour. "At last we've arrived," Morganuke commented, holding Melinor in his arms. "Are you glad to be home at last, Mel?"

"Yes of course," Melinor answered with tears in her eyes. "I didn't think I'd ever see my homeland again. I'm so looking forward to seeing my parents."

"Where's Mamma and Pappa?" Alorie asked, looking eagerly at all the people on the dockside.

"Don't worry, we'll see them soon enough," Melinor said, putting her arm around her sister.

"I always wanted to go to sea, but after this journey, I'll be glad to stay away from ships for a while," Morganuke said with a smile.

The gangplanks were dropped, and the crew given shore leave filed off the *Aurora*. The three of them were soon walking through the streets of Vesnick City.

"So where is your home, Mel?" Morganuke asked.

"It's near the coast between Vesnick and Drobayer," she answered. "A ride of one or two days from here."

"Oh, I thought it would be closer," Morganuke replied with a frown. "We can't go there today, then. I shall need to arrange transport and find out what Fraytar wants us to do about finding the Patronese community."

"But why can't we see Mamma and Pappa today?" Alorie pleaded. "I have missed them so."

Melinor gave a nod to Morganuke and then knelt in front of Alorie to talk to her. "As I said, we'll see Mamma and Pappa soon. We must do what Morg says. It is too far for us to walk there." Alorie then started to sob and clung to her sister.

"We need to stay in the city tonight and leave in the morning," Morganuke said. "We shouldn't do anything without checking with the others first, though. Let's not forget our mission to find the patronese and get some answers from them."

Fraytar had watched from the upper deck as the happy crew disembarked.

Crouch joined Fraytar, accompanied by a man he did not recognise. He had the striking red hair and green eyes that were distinct Cadmunese characteristics.

"Captain Fraytar, it's good to meet you," the man said, holding out his hand. "My name is Voldinestor Blandistinor, and I am part of the northern surveillance group working for Commander Tradish as an intelligence officer."

Fraytar shook his hand. "It seems that Commander Tradish has his spies in every corner," he quipped. "What can I do for you?"

"I'm not a spy, Captain. I'm just an observer and contact point for the Island and Cadmunese joint forces in the north. We have restored communication relay points running all the way back to Banton and the Cadmun mainland. I have news for you about the whereabouts of Patronese agents assisting the Cordinen army."

"I see. But what does that have to do with me? My mission is to find the Patronese group living in Trebos. Their reluctance to accommodate outsiders is also why we have brought Morganuke Beldere to approach them."

"That may be, Captain, but we have had sightings of several Patronese agents with more of these weapons northwest of Ventor. It seems that they are accompanied by only a light Cordinen escort, which presents a good opportunity to ambush them before they rendezvous with the main Cordinen forces in the south."

"I must remind you that my ship and crew are not soldiers. We provide a transport service and do not fight unless we have to."

"That I understand, Captain, and we do not expect you to fight. There is a contingent of highly trained Epleon soldiers camped east of Stroyant, east of here in north Trebos. We need you and your ship to take them from there, as far up the river estuary as you can and drop them close to Smorsk, north of Ventor. We will also need Morganuke Beldere to go with you to deal with any Patronese threat. They will ambush the Patronese contingent outside Smorsk before rejoining your ship and escaping back to Trebos."

"That sounds like a suicide mission. My ship will likely be trapped in the estuary. There would be no escape if the Cordinen navy arrived."

"As when you smuggled agents to Cryantor, we will have the advantage of long-distance communication and observers posted in the area. They will warn of any approaching dangers. Besides, most of the Cordinen navy are in the south. If we fail to take this opportunity and allow the Cordinens to regroup with even more Patronese weapons than they had before, then the war will surely be lost."

"Where did you get those talking boxes?" Fraytar asked suspiciously. "If they are Patronese devices, then you must know where they came from. If we know that, then would it not indicate where the source of the Patronese helping the Cordinens are coming from. Surely that is where you need to strike to prevent any more help arriving"

Blandistinor kept quiet for a moment. "Very well," he finally said. "We have contacts in the Cordinen military—spies, if you like. They provided information that allowed us to capture several of the boxes, along with instructions on how to use them. You must tell nobody of this, Captain. As far as where they originated from, that we don't know. If we did, then of course it would be logical to do as you say."

"You do know that I'm wanted by the Epleons for helping Morganuke to escape the Casdredon priest, who were going to put him on trial for heresy?" Fraytar pointed out. "How then can we work with the Epleon troops."

"This request comes from the very top military command in Lobos," Blandistinor answered. "The situation with the Patronese artefacts is so desperate that the Epleon military are prepared to turn a blind eye to yours and Morganuke's involvement. The Casdredon priest need not know anything about this. You will also be well rewarded."

Leaning on the deck railings, Fraytar fell into silent thought. Had he and his crew not already done enough? They had sailed halfway across the world for the cause, which was understood to be to find the source of the Patronese help so that it could be stopped for good, and now this. It seemed to Fraytar that the Epleons were reacting too late to the events rather than trying to put a complete stop to the Patronese help from its source. Even if they managed to destroy this fresh batch of Patronese artifacts and handlers, there would surely be more that would follow later. But Fraytar knew what would happen if the Cordinens succeeded in getting the artifacts to the borders of Stacklin. The Cordinens would break through, and the war would be lost. Nowhere would be safe, and the world would change for the worst forever under Cordinen domination.

"I'll do what you ask," Fraytar said reluctantly. "Just give me two days to prepare my ship and crew." *Now I've got to convince Morganuke to come with me,* Fraytar thought. *That will not be easy.*

CHAPTER 34

The Chace

After being confined on the ship for weeks, the crew were all eager to explore the city, and Fraytar let them have their shore leave. They needed it, and it would give him time to think. When the time came for them to reboard, he called a meeting of the islanders and mainlanders who had joined up in Cradport, the remainders of Fenlop's band.

"The mission that you signed up for was to sail here so that Morganuke could speak to the Patronese villages located nearby," Fraytar stressed. "That mission, getting Morganuke here, has been achieved and you have all been well paid for it. It's now down to Morganuke and Melinor to locate the village so that Morganuke can get the information needed to find the source of the Patronese helping the Cordinens.

"I have recently received some additional information about a mission that is even more urgent than the original one." He paused, uncertain how this news might be received. "I have been informed that more Patronese, with several artefacts, have been sighted near Smorsk on the river Kanitor."

"Well, that's in Ventor itself," Fenlop pointed out. "We only agreed to come to Trebos."

"That is true, and while it is still vital to find the Patronese community described by Melinor, I have orders to take my ship to

Smorsk as soon as possible, with a contingent of Epleon soldiers to ambush the Patronese."

"That is madness," Morganuke interjected. "You and your crew are already fugitives from the Epleons, and it will be dangerous to go into Ventor itself. This is a trap."

"I have been assured that it is only the Casdredon priests who want our heads and that the Epleon military are ignoring their demands to track us down. We still have one of the talking boxes on board, it was undamaged by the storm. The allied spies will warn us of any Cordinen presence in advance."

"I agree with Morg, I'm afraid," Chanterly put in. "This sounds like an Epleon trap to capture you, or at best far too risky for you and your crew, Captain. We have fulfilled our part of the mission and can no longer be considered as part of your crew."

"Risky it may be, but I cannot believe it to be a trap, It was down to the Epleon military that Morganuke was able to leave Stacklin, although they would not dare admit to it. As for you no longer being part of the crew, well I am asking that you stay on as part of my crew for this extra essential mission. As I said, if we don't stop the Patronese advancing to Stacklin then the Epleon will very likely lose the war." Fraytar replied.

"But I will need help to get to the Patronese village," Morganuke said. "If you take everyone on this mission then Melinor and I will have to go alone."

"Forgive me, Morg, but you will be essential on this mission," Fratar replied. "Your trip to find the Patronese village will need to wait."

"But isn't the most important think to do is to find where the Patronese are coming from and stop them for good?" Morganuke asked, now looking very frustrated. "It had been my goal all the way through the voyage to get answers from the Patronese."

"Under normal circumstances that would be the thing to do, Morg," Fraytar responded. "But the Patronese artifacts that have been sighted are an immediate threat and must be dealt with first. They are already in the field."

No one said anything for a moment. Fraytar held his breath; he might finally have asked too much of them.

"I'll call out your name one by one for your decision; I do need your answer in this meeting so that I can make any necessary alternate arrangements for additional crew. But I really hope that you will all agree to come on this mission.

"Lady Chanterly —"

"Well, I've come this far. Yes, I'll come."

"Fenlop —"

"So that we can chop up some more Cordinens along with their Patronese friends. You don't even have to ask."

"Drenden —"

"Of course. I'll go wherever Fenlop goes."

"Escolar —"

"Yes, I'll go."

"Calarel—"

"I've hated every minute of this voyage. But what am I going to do stuck here on my own. Besides, Chanterly needs me. Count me in."

"Lengrond —"

"I'll go if Morganuke goes."

"Morganuke, your presence is essential to counter the Patronese threat. We will be relying on complete surprise, especially that far north of Ventor, but there is still a risk that the Patronese will have time to counterattack and the Epleon forces will be helpless against the long range Patronese artefact attacks." Fraytar asked calmly.

Morganuke closed his eyes and stayed silent for a moment. "If you promise that after this, I can seek out the Patronese village near Melinor's home then I'll come," he eventually replied.

Fraytar felt overjoyed at the responses, especially Morganuke's. He turned to Melinor, who was looking at Morganuke with tears in her eyes. "Melinor, I am not expecting you to come as you have your sister to look after. When we return, I promise that we will get you and your sister home."

On the *Aurora*, the final preparations were being made for the voyage to Stroyant. They could only take the essential stores as there needed to be enough room available for the Epleon soldiers.

There was a knock on his cabin door and Crouch entered, followed by Blandistinor. Fraytar rolled up the sea chart and sat back in his seat, waiting for what Blandistinor had to say.

"Good day, Captain," greeted Blandistinor. "I trust all goes well with the preparations."

"We'll be ready to leave first thing tomorrow," Fraytar said.

"Are you sure that you don't know where the Patronese help is coming from," Fraytar added, "What about your contacts that obtained the information about the talking boxes? Surely, they know something."

"Captain, as I told you before, I do not know where the patronese and the artefacts are coming from. The only information that I have been given, from our contacts in Ventor, is that the patronese and the artifacts are currently being held near Smorsk. This is our only opportunity to take them out before they can be used against the Epleon defences."

"Then our only hope of getting information about where the Patronese are based is to capture one of the Patronese alive or rely on the Patronese village the Melinor told us about," Fraytar concluded.

"Yes, it appears those are our only options," Blandistinor agreed.

As Fraytar had promised, the *Aurora* was ready to sail early the next morning. It was a bright clear day, and the sun shone warmly on Fraytar's face as he stood on the aft deck.

"Release the moorings and raise sails," shouted Fraytar to his crew. "Set an Easterly course for Stroyant, Drogar."

The *Aurora* followed the coast of Trebos, travelling eastwards. After the first week of sailing, they passed Drobayer. Fraytar remembered that was where Melinor said she came from and thought of the Patronese village close by, where Morganuke should have gone, and the missed opportunity to find out more about them.

Another week of smooth sailing went by. Eventually the outline of Stroyant appeared on the coast.

"Take us into port, Drogar," Fraytar ordered, looking carefully through his spyglass at the city and the surrounding coast. *I hope the epleon soldiers are there ready to board*, Fraytar thought. *I suppose I should check with the forward observers in Stroyant on the latest report about the patronese location. I just hope we are not too late.*

On reaching the outskirts of Stroyant Fraytar checked with the forward contacts using the talking box of the exact whereabout of the Epleon troops. To avoid drawing attention, it was suggested that the *Aurora* pick up the soldiers from a cove west of Stroyant.

As the *Aurora* approached the designated pick-up point, Fraytar scanned the coast with his spyglass. "Hurrah, at last, there they are," he announced as he spotted an Epleon soldier waving a signal flag on the coast. The fifty Epleon soldiers were brought onto the *Auroara* using the six rowing boats. An Epleon officer approached Fraytar, striking his chest with his fist in salute as he did so.

"Band Leader Progrius Yallimonder reporting Captain," the officer reported. He looked a typical Epleon proud officer in his mid-thirties.

"Welcome on board, Band Leader Yallimonder," Fraytar acknowledged. "We are behind schedule and so must press on."

They finally made their way towards the river estuary. Fraytar had been assured that the Patronese were still positioned near Smorsk by the forward contacts, using the communication device on board the *Aurora*. *Will all this be for nothing?* Fraytar asked himself. *The patronese could have left by the time we have sailed up the river estuary.*

As the *Aurora* closed in on the Kanitor river estuary, the forward lookout shouted a warning about sandbanks either side of the ship's path. Fraytar went forward to look for himself and was concerned to see how narrow the passageway was. Any slight detour from the only deep-water path leading to the estuary from the western approach would see them stranded on the sand banks. But Drogar had proved a worthy replacement for Mordock as the ship's helmsman. They made careful progress, just skimming one bank on one occasion.

The journey up the estuary continued to be no less frustrating. The wind dropped on two occasions as they sailed further in land, and they had to resort to using the rowing boats to keep the ship moving upriver until the wind picked up again.

At last, a week later than planned, the *Aurora* reached the furthest point inland that it could go. It was now up to Fenlop's team and the Epleon soldiers to find and destroy the patronese and their artifacts.

Fenlop's team of seven were in one of the first boats to go ashore. Morganuke was wary about the Epleon soldiers at first but his confidence in them grew the longer he spent with them. They were part of a special force specifically trained to work behind enemy lines. They seemed very dedicated fighters who cared nothing about the politics between the Casdredon priests and the military. Yallimonder came across as very approachable and friendly. Morganuke quickly warmed to him. He was glad to see that Fenlop also got on well with him, allaying any fears that Morganuke had had about any friction between the two leaders.

Once the attack team had been ferried ashore, now fifty-seven strong, led by Yallimonder, they moved inland to find the patronese handlers with their artifacts. Fenlop had been given the position of the last patronese sighting and they were to ambush the Patronese and cordinens outside Smorsk and conveyed this to Yallimonder. The Epleon officer had questioned how he knew so much about the enemy's position and Fenlop gave some story about runners conveying messages that he hoped would satisfy his curiosity.

A day later, Yallimonder's team located the Patronese with their Cordinen escort camped in a valley on the outskirts of Smorsk. Drenden and Escolar went ahead to scout the camp and assess the enemy's force. They returned two hours later to report that there were three optogleans with twelve Patronese handlers and a Cordinen escort of about sixty infantry men.

"Three optogleans!" Morganuke exclaimed. "I've only ever been up against one before now and that was a close-run thing. I don't have my sword this time and so am going to have to rely on being able to summon up my powers at the right time."

"We have the advantage of complete surprise this time and without any threat of the Cordinens bringing in reinforcements," Fenlop assured. "All the optogleans are located close together and so one attack from you, Morg, should take them all out at once."

Chanterly leaned across and put her hand on Morganuke's shoulder.

"You can do this, Morg, we have faith in you," Chanterly said calmly in Morganuke's ear. "Have belief in your own abilities."

"Just think that this is vengeance for your parents when you start your attack, Morg." Lengrond added.

Morganuke thought about his last attack on the Patronise optoglean and how he was unable to summon up his power on the first attempt. It was his sword that had saved him on that occasion, which he now didn't have. But he had eventually managed to destroy the optoglean when he had become angry. No, it was more than anger, it was absolute rage. Maybe Lengrond had a point. Although this time he didn't want to destroy all the Patronese. He wanted to capture at least one alive so that he could get information from them about where they came from. However, he remembered his conversations with the other Patronese he'd been with. Although they were supposedly on the same side, they were very reluctant to share any information about themselves. *What were they hiding?* Morganuke thought.

As Fenlop prepared their surprise attack on the Cordinen and Patronese camp, Fenlop took his team and flanked right to make their way towards the Patronese optogleans. This time Morganuke would attack the optogleans first and then Yallimonder was to follow up with the main attack force.

When he was in line with the patronese, Morganuke focused on a point just behind the centre of the three optogleans. He remembered what Lengrond had said and the rage he felt during the last attack, but he still struggled to maintain his focus. A mad thought suddenly entered his mind, and he took out his dagger and plunged it into his outer thigh. The pain was excruciating, and he stifled a yell, but he felt that familiar rage and refocused his attention on the optogleans. There was a flash, followed by a strong wind that pulled the patronese and some of the cordinens towards the point that Morganuke had been focusing on. Then came a roar to his left as Yallimonder's troops rushed down the valley hill and onto the still dazed Cordinens.

Morganuke and the others joined in the ensuing battle. Morganuke hadn't had chance to check the state of the Patronese or the optogleans after his attack. He knew from the flash of light and the resulting wind that something had happened but was not sure of the resulting damage. He was now consumed with the main battle, but he had to make sure that the Patronese and their optogleans had been disabled if he could. No matter how hard he tried to get closer to the position that the Patronese had been, a Cordinen attack would come and push him back or prevent him going around to get closer. The sword he'd been issued with felt cumbersome in his hands. He wished he still had the sword that Fraytar had given him. He slashed at the enemy in front of him, with his friends doing the same either side of him. The noise of clattering swords and shouts filled his ears. Chanterly and Calarel now fighting beside him on one side and Lengrond on the other.

At last, the sound of battle died down. Many lay dead on the field, mostly Cordinens but half the Epleons had been cut down too. Fenlop's team of seven had survived the ordeal. Morganuke now felt the pain in his leg and blood ran down his breeches from the self-inflicted wound. Then he remembered the optogleans and the Patronese handlers.

To Morganuke's dismay, the resulting charred crater that had been left was a lot closer to the Patronese position than he had calculated. Most of the patronese had disappeared, except for two bodies lying beside one of the artifacts. Yet again, Morganuke had failed to get information from the Patronese and where they had come from. The one remaining optoglean was picked up by four of the surviving Epleon soldiers as the attack group made their way back to the *Aurora*.

Fraytar looked pensively out across the riverbank, tapping his fingers on the railings of the upper deck. They had been waiting for two days and there was still no sign of Yallimonder's attack force.

Crouch stood beside him, looking just as pensive. "What be your orders, Captain. We have surely used all our luck. The Cordinens must discover us soon, exposed as we are."

"We shall wait until tomorrow and then leave, with or without Morg and the Epleons," Fraytar answered. "This looks as though it will be yet another failed mission. The patronese must have got to safety with those blowndering artifacts of theirs. We shall live to see our world torn apart as a result."

"Captain, over there, I can see soldiers carrying something. Looks like the Cordinens have found us," Crouch said, pointing towards the far riverbank.

"All hands-on deck!" Fraytar ordered. "Get ready to sail. We'll not go down without a fight." Then he peered through his spyglass at the soldiers emerging from the woods onto the riverbank. "Belay that! They're Epleons. The Epleon are back!" he shouted. "Launch the rowing boats."

The men put up a cheer and set to work, some launching the rowing boats and others readying the sails. As Fraytar kept his sights on the treeline for any sign of Cordinens, he saw that a team of four Epleons were carrying a box. Based on its resemblance to the smaller talking box, he assumed these were the Patronese weapons they were seeking. All the surviving attack team and the optoglean were soon safely on board.

Fraytar approached Yallimonder, who was standing in front of the optoglean that had been brought on board, "So few of your men have returned Band Leader, I'm sorry for that," Fraytar said, staring at the optoglean.

"It was a tough battle, and I lost half my men, but at least we achieved what we set out to do and retrieved one of the enemy's formidable weapons. All the enemy were destroyed, and we did not see any others on our way back here."

"So this is the mighty weapon," Fraytar said thoughtfully. "The cause of all our recent troubles." Fraytar went to touch the optoglean and then thought better of it. *Who knows what this thing will do if I touch it*, Fraytar thought.

"The surgeon will see to your injured men, and I'll get the cook to prepare a meal."

"Thank you, Captain."

Fraytar spotted Fenlop across the other side of the deck and approached him.

"How fares your team, Fenlop?" Fraytar asked.

"All survived, Captain," Fenlop answered. "Morganuke has a flesh wound in his leg, but nothing too serious."

"Really? Those Cordinen swords can tear at the flesh horribly."

"It was self-inflicted, Captain. I believe he did it to summon up his power. At one stage I thought it was going to be a repeat of the Stacklin battle, but he did well."

"Well, your all back on board now," Fraytar said, turning towards the aft deck. "We must make haste before we get penned in by the Cordinen navy."

Progress down river only took half the time going up, thanks to the ship moving with the current.

But as they approached the river mouth, the forward lookout shouted a warning. "Ships approaching ahead!"

Two Cordinen ships, each armed with giant ballista, were bearing down on the *Aurora*. The wind had barely picked up, and the Cordinens were gaining fast, threatening to trap the *Aurora* in the estuary.

"By the time we get out of the estuary, they'll be within ballista range" Crouch warned.

Fraytar looked up at the *Aurora* sails and willed them to fill with the wind. But it was still painstakingly slow going. The Cordinen ships were getting ever closer. The *Aurora* crept towards the open sea, still too slow.

At last, they left the estuary and entered the open sea. Fraytar smiled as the triangular sails began to fill with the wind. "Steer due West, Drogar," Fraytar ordered. "Let's see how they fair going through the sandbanks. Crouch, get double lookouts forward of the ship to guide us through. I'll wager that the Cordinens will be so focused on targeting us with those confounded ballista that they won't even notice the sandbanks."

Gradually the *Aurora* began to pick up speed as the wind filled the triangular sails. Two ballista bolts fell just short of the *Aurora* as the Cordinen ships fired their shots in desperation. They reached the sandbanks and carried on sailing at speed, Drogar making slight adjustments on the tiller from the directions given by the forward lookouts. Suddenly a loud graunching came from behind the *Aurora*, followed by yells. Fraytar looked to sea both Cordinen ships beached firmly in the sandbanks either side of the deep-water channel. Two more ballista bolts were fired from each of the ships but fell well short of the *Aurora*. A cheer went up from the crew as the *Aurora* continued, sailing out of the sandbank area. Westward they continued, now no longer pursued.

CHAPTER 35

The Wise One

The *Aurora* reached Vesnick City three weeks after leaving the Kanitor river estuary. Once they had docked and the Epleon soldiers disembarked, taking the captured artifact with them. Fraytar and Morganuke followed the Epleon soldiers ashore. Morganuke walked with a slight limp, his leg now bandaged but still a little sore from his self-inflicted wound.

"Where are you taking the optoglean?" Morganuke called to Yallimonder, who stopped and turned to Morganuke and Fraytar.

"We have been asked to keep the Patronese weapon here for the time being until it can be taken back to Lobos to be studied," Yallimonder replied.

"Isn't that a bit dangerous?" Fraytar questioned, frowning. "What if the Cordinen's recapture it? I thought the Epleons feared anything that they could not explain?"

"I only follow my orders, Captain," Yallimonder politely replied. "If you will excuse me, gentlemen, I have a lot to do," Yallimonder paused for a moment and then looked at Morganuke. "It has been an honour serving with you Morganuke Beldere. My countrymen owe you much and I do hope that they will come to recognise that eventually. Safe journey to you both." Yallimonder politely bowed his head and then left to join his men.

Morganuke continued to puzzle over why the Epleons would want to retrieve the optoglean. They had no way of using it and as Fraytar had pointed out, its existence risked it being retrieved by the Cordinens.

As they continued making their way through the busy harbour square, they met Voldinestor Blandistinor, who was on his way to see Fraytar.

"Hello, Captain," Blandistinor greeted. "I hear that you were successful in destroying the patronese party assisting the cordinens and that an artifact has been retrieved."

"Well, it was Morg here, along with the rest of Fenlop's team and the Epleons soldiers that did all of the work," Fraytar answered. "I just transported them there and back."

"But without your ship and crew they would not have succeeded. You have done a great service to the war effort. This should set the Cordinens back and prevent them from attacking Stacklin again. I hear too that the Cordinens have been driven from the island of Banton, which should allow the Island Militia and Cadmunese forces to assist the Epleons on the mainland. Alman and Albrin have reported from the field that things are getting back to normal in Stacklin too. They send their regards by the way. Maybe now the war will turn in our favour and allow us to finally defeat the cordinens."

"What ever became of the other two agents I help smuggle into Ventor, Jovish and Sebrin?" Fraytar asked.

"I believe that they are still operating close to Cryantor," Blandistinor answered.

"I'm glad," Fraytar responded. "It's comforting to know that we still have a presence behind the enemy lines. I don't believe that the Cordinens are ready to give up yet."

"We still need to find the source of the Patronese help," Morganuke added. "Only then can we stop their interference in this war. I was hoping to capture one of the Patronese during our ambush but failed; they all perished during the battle. Travelling to the Patronese village that Mel told us about now seems the only likely source of information."

"I agree," Blandistinor answered. "When do you and your party plan to leave for the village?"

"We'll need to prepare some transportation first," Morganuke answered. "I hope to leave tomorrow. We shall take Melinor and her sister back to their home first. It should be on the way to the village anyway."

"I can arrange horses and anything else you may need, Morganuke," Blandistinor offered. "This is now the most important mission. Maybe at last we can stop the source of Patronese help to the Cordinens for good." Morganuke savoured Blandistinor's words. At last, he now had the opportunity to get the answers he had been wanting to find for so long. The most important one being, to find out where he came from.

Morganuke met Melinor, Alorie and the rest of Fenlop's team on the dock early the next day.

"They look very fine horses," Morganuke commented, as he looked at the eight horses tied up on the edge of the dock next to his friends. "Blandistinor has done well for us."

Morganuke's party had a full day's ride to Melinor's home. It was getting dark by the time they neared their destination.

"My home is just beyond that hill," Melinor called to the others as they trotted along the dusty track. Alorie, who was riding behind Melinor, perked up excitedly.

Beyond the hill that Melinor had pointed out, a good-sized two-story farmhouse with fenced pastures set either side just about came into view in the fading light. Two large barns were set to one side of a spacious clearing in front the house.

"There it is," cried Melinor. "It looks just the same."

"Yippee, welcome to our home everyone," Alorie shouted in delight as they approached the house. Light shone out from the single window at the front, next to a wooden door.

Morganuke dismounted and then helped Alorie and Melinor from their horse. The two girls immediately rushed up to the door and opened it. The light from inside the house streamed out onto the stone path leading up to the door as it flew open.

"We're home, we're home," cried Alorie excitedly.

"It's so good to be back," Melinor added.

"My girls. My girls have returned," Came a woman's voice from inside.

"What? how can that be?" came a man's voice.

Morganuke and the others stayed back, tending to the horses to allow the girls some private time with their parents. The sounds of happy laughter and voices continued from the house, until Alorie came running out.

"Mama, Pappa, come and meet our friends," Alorie said over her shoulder into the house.

Morganuke watched from a little way back as he saw a beautiful woman step out of the door to join Alorie. Alorie looked up at the woman, who'd placed her hands lovingly on Alorie's shoulders.

"Mamma, these are our friends, and they have been so good to us," Alorie said smiling, her eyes glinting in the light from the house. Morganuke was surprised at Alorie's loquaciousness, he'd hardly heard her speak all the time he'd been with her.

"That is great to know, Alorie my sweet love," Alorie's mother said. "I hope you thanked all of them. Why don't you introduce Me and Pappa to them."

A tall lean man, also in his early forties then came through the door, his tall shadow from the house light spread across the ground towards Morganuke and the others. Melinor then followed. "Hi everyone," the man said in a soft confident voice. "My name is Tobias, Melinor and Alorie's father and this is Drayonette, their mother. You are all most welcome. I can't tell you how happy you've made us today."

Alorie bravely did as her mother had asked and introduced her and her father to Morganuke and the others. It was like she was a different little girl, full of confidence now that she was back home with her parents. It was like her spirit had been bottled up for a very long time and now was able to burst out into the open.

Both Tobias and Drayonette couldn't hide their curiosity at Morganuke's hair staring at it for a moment when Alorie introduced them to him. Morganuke said nothing, he was used to folk staring at him when they saw him for the first time.

Melinor's mother and father beckoned Morganuke and the others to come into the roomy house. Inside was a cozy homely scene. A fire burned brightly in a large fireplace on the other side of the room. A large table with chairs placed in the middle, with other comfortable looking chairs placed around the room. Against one of the walls stood a large bookcase stacked with books.

"I can't believe you are both back with us," Melinor's mother said with tears welling in her eyes. "I'm so happy. You must tell us everything that happened, Mel. We want to know more about your friends too."

Everyone found a seat and a brief moment of calming silence followed, as if to prepare for the continuous stream of questions and answers that was to follow. Morganuke looked on at the happy chatty scene feeling happier than he had done in a long while. Alorie's chatter had not disappeared, and she interlaced the discussions from others with stories of her own. Melinor told her parents everything that had happened to her and her sister since they had been captured over two years ago. When she had finished telling her story, her parents looked at the two girls in wonder, amazed that they had survived such ordeals. They then thanked each of the friends individually to show their gratitude.

Tobias and Drayonette prepared a meal for everyone. Morganuke thought it the best food he'd tasted in a very long time. After the meal the chatting went on for several more hours. A stifled yawn from Lengrond signalled that it was probably time to sleep. By then everyone showed signs of tiredness.

"You are all welcome to stay for the night," Tobias offered. "We have some room in the house and more in the barns. How long will you be staying?"

"Thank you, the barns will do nicely," Morganuke replied. "We are leaving in the morning to look for the community of patronese living in this area."

"The pat …, who did you say you are looking for?" asked Tobias.

"The patronese. The folk that look like me."

Melinor's father rubbed his stubbled chin and thought for a moment. "Ahaaaa, yes, the silver haired, red eyed folk living in the hills. They are very strange people. Forgive me young man, I meant no offence. They keep themselves to themselves and don't like strangers to go near."

"Have you seen much of them?" Fenlop asked. "Have you seen any Cordinen soldiers nearby."

"I've only seen the patro …, whatever you called them, from a distance a few times. I used to take Melinor up into the hills hunting and we saw them then. Once I tried to get closer to their village, but they became aggressive, throwing stones and shooing me away in that strange tongue of theirs. I can draw you a map to show you where we saw them."

"Papa, I will go with them," Melinor said, standing up in front of her father.

"You cannot go, my girl, it may be too dangerous," her father said, worry on his face.

"Papa, I must go with them. I have promised to show them the way. It is the least I can do after all they have done for me."

Melinor's father gritted his teeth and was just about to say more but held back.

"This is as we have taught her, Tobias," Melinor's mother said.

Looking around the room, welling up with tears, he slowly nodded his head.

"I will make sure no harm comes to her, sir," Morganuke added. "The Patronese should look sympathetically on me as I'm one of their own." Melinor's father put his hand on Morganuke's shoulder.

"If Mel trusts you, then I will too," Tobias said.

———◆———

The next morning Morganuke and his friends were up early preparing to leave Melinor's home. The horses had been saddled and supplies loaded into saddle bags. Melinor came out of the house followed by her parents and Alorie. They hugged each other and said their goodbyes.

Morganuke helped Melinor up into the saddle of her horse, before mounting his own horse.

"Bring our daughter back safety to us," Drayonette said. "Good fortune to you all. I hope you find what you are looking for."

The group rode off, kicking up dust from the path as they did so. Morganuke watched Melinor as she looked behind her. Looking behind he could see her parents and Alorie waving. He was touched with guilt as he caught Melinor wipe a tear from her eye and waved back. As they trotted over the hill, the farmhouse was soon out of sight.

Morganuke and the others had been climbing the hills south of Drobayer for two days and they had still not arrived at the patronese village.

"Are you sure this is the way, Mel?" Morganuke asked.

"Yes, I'm sure. I remember that distinctive cliff over there. It looks almost like a face. It isn't far now, maybe another half a day."

"How far did you and your father travel on your hunting trips?", Morganuke asked, shading his eyes as he looked at the cliff face that Melinor had pointed out.

"We used to go for days and travelled many stances."

They continued along the same path until the daylight started to fade. It had got colder the further up the hills they travelled and so were glad to stop for the night and light a fire. Fortunately, they still had plenty of rations and so ate well that night. They bedded down around the campfire, with two taking it in turns to keep watch and keep the fire going through the night.

The group made an early start the next day on what they hoped would be the last leg of their journey before finding the patronese village. The gradient up the hills had become steeper, making it difficult for the horses to keep their footing. A herd of deer ran across the hills above them, deftly leaping over low bushes and rocks.

"We may need to leave the horses and go on foot if it gets much steeper," Chanterly observed, holding on desperately to her horse and leaning forward in her saddle as she crossed the slope at an angle.

"I'm sure it's not far now," Melinor assured.

"What's that?" Lengrond asked, looking up. "A boulder! Quick, out of the way!"

The group quickly reined in their horses and either turned around or moved on across the slope as quickly as they dare. The boulder missed everyone and harmlessly continued to roll past them down the hill.

Morganuke looked up the hill towards the point from where the bolder had come from and caught sight of someone moving.

"It looks like there is someone up there," Morganuke said, squinting his eyes.

"Do you think they pushed the boulder deliberately?" Melinor asked.

"Maybe. If it's the Patronese trying to scare us away I best go up there myself," Morganuke suggested. "Hopefully they will trust me as one of them."

Morganuke began to climb the hill alone on foot. It got even steeper as he approached the point from where the boulder came from. When he arrived at the point he'd seen the figures, there was no sign of anyone there now and so he continued to climb further. Gradually the hill started to level out a bit, making his climb easier. He continued to walk until the ground levelled with two hills rising either side. The path continued between the two hills lined with fir trees. As he continued along the path, he saw two men standing before him. They had silver hair and red eyes like him. One older than the other.

"What doth thee wanteth in this lodging yond is not yours?", said the older man.

"I come as a friend," Morganuke answered.

"We doth not knoweth thee yet thee behold liketh us." Said the younger man.

"I'm looking for people that look like me," Morganuke answered. "I don't know where I come from and so am looking for some answers."

The two men looked at each other and whispered something amongst themselves. The older man then turned to him again. "The answ'rs yond thou art looking foir can beest did obtain from the wise one," the man said.

It was difficult for Morganuke to comprehend what they were saying with their strange dialect but clearly picked out the words Wise One. "Who is the Wise One and where is he?"

"The wise one dwells up on the hill there," The older man said, pointing to one of the hills beside the path. "Asketh the wise one bef're thee cometh to our home again." The two men then turned around and walked away, leaving Morganuke looking up at the steep hill that the older man had pointed to.

It was a difficult climb to the top of the hill, and Morganuke had to rest for a moment to catch his breath. He looked around but could see no signs of any dwellings. *Am I climbing the wrong hill?* he asked himself, dreading the thought of having to do any more climbing for a while. He sat down on a grassy hillock and looked around for any clues pointing the way to go. Just across from where he was sat, he noticed a small cave entrance set in the rocks. *I may as well look in there as I've climbed all this way*, he thought.

Peering through the cave entrance, Morganuke could see shadows of twigs and jagged rock dancing across the cave wall. The entrance was just big enough for him to climb through but the cave inside was very spacious, allowing him to stand up.

Is this it, he thought excitedly. *Am I really here? Will this cave lead me to the Patronese homeland?* Moving towards the source of light creating the shadows, he heard somebody humming. He felt a shiver up his spine daring to creep forward. Morganuke followed the light and the humming until he came to the source of both.

"I has't been expecting thee for neary ten and ten years," An old man said, sat huddled next to the fire.

Morganuke looked at the old man in silence for a few moments. He gathered his thoughts. There were so many questions he wanted to ask, but he could only think of one at that moment. "Are you the one they call the Wise One?" he asked.

"I am the Wise One. Welcometh, Mandrake Martilismore." The man looked at Morganuke, his grey straggly hair framing his deeply lined faced. He had piercing red eyes that looked right into Morganuke's. "Yond wast the nameth given to in Denesthear by thy house yond wast thy origins and f'refathers."

"What? Mandrake Martilismore is my real name you say, and I come from Denesthear," Morganuke clarified for himself.

The Wise One continued, "Others did fail to did rid the world of thee. Sitteth beside me so yond i can bid thee toyr destiny. Thee wilt learneth and proveth yourself worthy to returneth to the landeth of thy birth."

Morganuke sat beside the fire listening to what the Wise One had to say.

It had been over a week since Fraytar had arrived back in Vesnick City. He had expected Morganuke to return to the *Aurora* long before now and was worried about him. There was a knock on his cabin door. It was Lengrond, looking concerned.

"Sorry to disturb you, Captain, but I'm worried about Morg."

"Why what's he done? Where is he? I was expecting him to have returned to the Aurora before now."

"He's staying at the Cat and Mouse inn in the city. He's not been right since he returned from the Patronese village. He went up there on his own whilst we stayed back with the horses so as not to upset the villagers."

"So Morganuke managed to see the Patronese villagers."

"Yes, Captain. But he was acting strange when he returned and wouldn't talk to anyone, not even Melinor. I think he may……well.."

"You think he may have what?"

"…well..gone a bit mad, Captain."

"What? How can that be? Morganuke was very positive about the task when I last saw him. He must have some news about the Patronese homeland."

"As I said, Captain, Morganuke refuses to talk to anyone about what he discovered in the Patronese village."

Fraytar looked bemused and shook his head. "This just doesn't make sense. I shall speak to him. Come, take me to this Cat and Mouse inn now."

Fraytar went with Lengrond to the 'Cat and Mouse' inn. He kept asking himself why Morganuke would be behaving in such an odd way, it wasn't like him. Had the patronese turned his mind in some way? Had they used one of their infernal devices to scramble his mind?

Inside the inn, Fraytar spotted Chanterly and Calarel sitting at a table. He sat down beside them.

"What's this I hear about Morganuke losing his mind," Fraytar asked.

"He hasn't spoken a word since returning from the patronese community in the hills," answered Chanterly. She then went on to tell Fraytar the whole story; how Morganuke had gone on ahead to meet the patronese after they had rolled a boulder down the hill. "We saw nothing of the community ourselves," Chanterly added. "Morganuke was gone for some time. He insisted he go on his own to avoid upsetting the Patronese, who obviously did not want us there. When he returned, some hours later, he was very different, just saying that he had to return to Vesnick as soon as possible. We tried to get more information out of him afterwards, but he has refused to tell us anything of his encounter with the Patronese. He just looked straight ahead with his eyes wide open saying nothing."

"Let me talk to him," Fraytar suggested. "He may be willing to talk to me. Let me at least try. Until we know what he found out from the Patronese, we cannot know what our next move should be. Have we managed to put a complete stop to the Patronese interference or will this quest continue. Where is Melinor? They were very close."

"Melinor has returned to her home. She also tried to persuade Morganuke to tell us what happened, but he refused to talk to her as well. In the end she gave up and decided to go home."

"I'll take you to his room now, Captain," Lengrond offered.

Lengrond led Fraytar up the stairs to the boarding rooms on the first floor of the inn. They walked down the narrow corridor at the top of the steps until they came to a door with a sign hanging on the outside saying 'Do not disturb'. Fraytar knocked on the door and waited. There was no response and silence from within the room. Fraytar knocked again and this time announced that it was him. After a few moments the door unlocked and opened to reveal Morganuke standing in the doorway. He looked tired and dishevelled, with several days' growth of untidy beard. His red eyes looked dully at Fraytar as if he was in a trance.

Fraytar nodded to Lengrond who then left the two of them together.

"Hello Morganuke, my boy. Can I come in and talk to you?" Morganuke stood to one side to let Fraytar into the room. Clothes littered the floor and there was a smell of stale sweat in the air.

"Morg, you need to tell me what happened when you went to see the Patronese villagers. Please sit down and tell me everything. Have the Patronese that you met agreed to stop helping the cordinens? Do we even know where the Patronese helpers are coming from?"

Morganuke flopped down on the unmade bed, "No," he said to Fraytar, shaking his head slowly.

"Did you explain to them the importance of what we're trying to do and how evil the cordinens are?"

"No," said Morganuke, shaking his head again.

"Why not? You went all that way and didn't explain anything to them?"

"They are not the ones helping the cordinens", Morganuke said dispassionately.

"But how can that be? If you didn't explain to them about the Cordinens, how do you know that they are not helping them?"

Morganuke said nothing, just looking straight ahead as if in a daze.

Fraytar shook his arm to get his attention. "How do you know that the Patronese villagers are not the ones helping the cordinens?"

"The wise one explained it all," Morganuke said slowly. "He told me that I am from a high order house from Denesthear. That is where the patronese help is coming from. The patronese come from Denesthear. The same place that I come from. The wise one says it's my destiny to go back there and return balance to their world. But I must prove myself first."

"Morg, I don't understand. I've never heard of Denesthear. I've never seen that place on any chart."

"Yes, you have." Morganuke finally turned his head to look at his bewildered friend. "It's the Nebulee."

Fraytar drew back with a shudder. The Nebulee? Where the *Aurora* and all her crew had nearly perished?

"It's my destiny, the Wise One says, to go back there. To return balance to the world, I must return to the Nebulee." He fixed his red eyes on the sea captain. "And you are the one taking me."

The story continues in Book 2